| aftermath |

also by brian shawver

*The Cuban Prospect*

# aftermath

*A Novel*

brian shawver

nan a. talese / doubleday

*new york   london   toronto*
*sydney   auckland*

PUBLISHED BY NAN A. TALESE
AN IMPRINT OF DOUBLEDAY
a division of Random House, Inc.

DOUBLEDAY is a registered trademark of Random House, Inc.

*Book design by Jennifer Ann Daddio*

Library of Congress Cataloging-in-Publication Data

Shawver, Brian.
Aftermath : a novel / Brian Shawver. — 1st ed.
p. cm.
1. Teenage boys — Crimes against — Fiction.
2. Brain damage — Patients — Fiction.
3. Violence in adolescence — Fiction.   4. Children of the rich — Fiction.
5. Mothers and sons — Fiction.   6. Social classes — Fiction.
7. Scranton (Pa.) — Fiction.   8. Witnesses — Fiction.
I. Title.

PS3619.H395A69 2005
813'.6 — dc22            2005048612

ISBN 0-385-51481-6

PRINTED IN THE UNITED STATES OF AMERICA

February 2006

First Edition

1   3   5   7   9   10   8   6   4   2

TO THE BEAUTIFUL BABIES

lily, graham, and poppy

# acknowledgments

I am enormously grateful to many people who helped in the composition, editing, and publication of this book. First of all, thanks to Michelle Tessler, my dedicated and insightful agent, for her advice and confidence. Thanks also to Coates Bateman, who provided excellent editorial guidance as well as friendship, and to Nan Talese. Dr. Nick Evageliou of the Children's Hospital of Philadelphia supplied valuable information concerning medical procedures, and Ken Ebbitt offered extensive general advice throughout the writing process. I am also grateful to Nick Delo, Brian Fleming, and Jeremy Kryt, who are good friends and readers, and I will always be thankful for my association with the learning community of Fontbonne Academy. For their help in all aspects of my life, I would like to thank Patsy Shawver and Tom Shawver, my parents; and Erin Billingsley, my sister. And finally, I would like to express my gratitude to Pam August, who helps me in thousands of ways.

## PART ONE

# january

Hence it is evident that, simply and absolutely speaking,
transgression is a graver sin than omission, although a
particular omission may be graver than
a particular transgression.

—THOMAS AQUINAS, *SUMMA THEOLOGICA*

# one

*O'Ruddy's thrived* on Friday nights, under the steward-
ship of Casey Fielder. As the general manager he exercised absolute
power here, and he had to wield his power with composure and resolve, or his staff would be lost in the chaos, in the kinetic heat of bodies and track lighting and frying food, in the clamor of conversation
and complaint. On this particular Friday, as he watched and controlled the frenzy of the late dinner rush, it seemed to him that
O'Ruddy's was thriving as usual, and he approved.

Casey was not above sweating alongside his staff, and throughout
the dinner shift he bused as many tables, by his careful reckoning, as
Paulo did. Once or twice he threw together some house salads to help
out the harried sous-chef, and he ran meals to tables when the servers
asked. But mostly his job was to supervise: to judge, to correct, to encourage, and sometimes to condemn. He watched even as he wiped
down tables and mopped up spills, even as he talked with customers

and restocked the service stand, and tonight he was satisfied with the performance of his employees. The servers—all women, all sporting ponytails and pastel polo shirts, nametags bobbing on their breasts—wove gracefully through the maze of the dining floor, around the sluggish busboy. Casey approved of their pacing and their flirtations, of the way their singular pursuit of tips merged so neatly with the interests of the restaurant. When he crossed the threshold of the kitchen, that fluorescent, intense world, the usual racket struck him: a symphony of clattering plates, spurting water, the sizzling grill, the machine-gun Spanish of the cooks and dishwashers and the Latino radio station they listened to. In the kitchen, the workers moved with the frenetic purpose of ER doctors; sweat shook off the jerky limbs of the head cook like water off a Labrador. They were entirely unmoved by Casey's presence when he came to check on them, adjusting their behavior to his watchfulness not one bit. One of the prep cooks even had a cigarette hanging from his lips, and he did not apologize when Casey scolded him. But Casey granted the kitchen staff some leeway on Friday nights because of their stoic competence, and tonight they were meeting the challenges of the rush.

Casey was meeting the challenges as well, and most important, he exuded a sense of assurance and command. He had somehow kept his clothes pressed and his cowlick mastered, and the sweat stains did not show on his navy blue shirt, although he felt more disheveled than he looked. His feet hurt at the sides, and the grease-and-sweat stink of his undershirt had begun to overcome the Gold Bond powder he'd puffed into his armpits at the beginning of the shift. But no one at O'Ruddy's would ever suspect that the cares of management had worn him down tonight. He mitigated his tiredness with brisk, purposeful movement. He listened to the whining of his staff—*When can we switch to the unwrapped straws? Why does Julio put so much goddamn sour cream on everything?*—and he corrected their mistakes. Credit cards that had been overcharged, platters that had been ordered twice, a clogged toilet, an absent dishwasher. All the problems were laid at his feet, abandoned there, as if he could turn a magic wand on them and—*poof.*

There was something in Casey that loved this, or rather something that needed it in an elemental way, the way a plant needs sunlight. Something in him turned crisis into sustenance, made the restaurant—especially on Friday nights—a place where he felt more at home than anywhere else. Sometimes he did feel possessed of secrets and special powers, although it was really nothing more than experience, a personality suited for this kind of work, and the guidance of the manager's handbook, which he consulted several times a day.

Within these walls (where he could be found, on average, seventy-five hours a week), virtually every aspect of Casey's behavior had a foundation in the handbook. The expression on his face, for instance, was specifically calibrated according to the directive on page 18: *When interacting with guests about nonpecuniary matters, the manager's expression should be that of a dinner party host who is pleased to see all of his/her friends enjoying themselves.* Mindful of this advice, Casey held his eyes open wide against the scowl that often swelled inside. This gave him a look of perpetual expectation, as if he were always waiting for something to pounce on him.

His fidelity to the dress code was absolute, so much so that he found himself wearing his manager's uniform more or less continuously, regardless of the occasion. Page 32: *The manager's pants should be black and neatly pressed; the shirt and tie must be stately and of solid colors.* After eight years at O'Ruddy's, most of his wardrobe conformed to the dress code. Several months earlier, at the funeral for his Uncle Rich, he had looked down to find that he was not only wearing the requisite manager's outfit but had pinned his manager's nametag to the appropriate part of his shirt (on the left breast, one inch above the top of the pocket), though he wasn't going in to work that day.

Most of the handbook's admonitions had seeped their way into his habits during his tenure at O'Ruddy's. He had mastered the nuances and complexities of the place, and he considered Friday nights to be the reward for this mastery. On these nights he belonged among the happy, satiated crowd and the tip-giddy servers, because of the fact that he made it all happen, he provided for their comfort and fixed their problems. That they took him for granted was no matter, because he knew that without him it would all go away.

It had been his idea to focus their attention on Fridays, for example, by creating Friday prime rib specials and putting coupons in Thursday's *Beacon*. Though he never spoke of the strategy in a self-congratulatory way, he had come to see it as a marketing plan that was singularly appropriate for this particular township and restaurant. On Saturdays anyone seeking diversion drove the half hour to Scranton, where there was a cineplex and a mall. On Sundays the restaurants of the township were dominated by the senior citizens, enamored of half-sandwich specials and 6 percent tips. The location of the O'Ruddy's, south of Arthur Avenue on the cusp of East Breed's, was inconvenient for the white-collar workers who might have come in for business lunches or after-dinner drinks, and so the weekday receipts largely depended on East Breed's locals: the ironworkers, the unemployed. These people were suspicious of the restaurant—the forced festivity of its decor, the cost of its fried cheese appetizers— and usually favored the Dairy Bar, unless it was someone's birthday. There were lunch shifts, especially in the winter, when the cooks at O'Ruddy's didn't need to filter the oil in the fryer.

But all kinds of people came on Fridays, sometimes in droves, rambunctious from the cessation of work. Birthday celebrants, anxious first-daters, softball teams, lonely drunks eating fried jalapeños at the bar. The bartenders invented flamboyantly colored cocktails for the Friday drinkers, and Casey scheduled only his experienced servers for the dinner shift. On Friday afternoons the cooks would lay great slabs of poultry and beef on the back counter to thaw. The sous-chef would jam the chiller with as many premade house salads as he could fit. The Friday servers showed up early for side work, and the small platoon of pert young women would gossip and smoke as they each rolled fifty sets of silverware. By seven o'clock the hostess would be cautioning new arrivals of a forty-minute wait, and typically they waited. There weren't many restaurants of its kind in Breed's Township, and no one wanted to drive to Scranton on Friday night.

On these evenings O'Ruddy's was expected to total receipts of eight thousand dollars, in the course of serving around three hundred customers, including bar patrons. The restaurant was expected to accomplish this with a staff of six in the kitchen and six on the floor, plus the supervising manager. This, at least, was the benchmark set in previous years, and which had been surpassed every weekend this past fall, a season of bliss. The Breed's Township High football team had gone eight and one, and after each game a throng of giddy spectators trooped over from the nearby stadium to discuss what they had seen over Busch Lights and buffalo wings. The autumn weather had been mild and breezy, so people avoided the stuffy, windowless bars near the township center. O'Ruddy's had often reached the maximum capacity (112 persons, according to a brass plate in the entryway) and in Casey's memory that fiscal season was defined by a conviviality that he had not felt before, that gave him hope. The restaurant had churned out the happy atmosphere of fried food and celebration and alcohol and flirtation, and in the midst of this jovial mass Casey had acknowledged—with his own kind of joy—the real matter, the true success: the Breed's Township O'Ruddy's was flourishing under his command.

But it was January now, and things had changed, in spite of the sense of chaos and gluttony that surrounded him on this night, in spite of the frantic motion and the kitchen noise. Casey finally admitted to himself that the hectic activity of the restaurant belied another slow night. The sound and fury that reminded him of better times, and that had really lasted for only an hour or so, had been the result of a dearth of workers. In a time of hardship, which January was proving to be, Casey would schedule no more staff than was needed. This meant that there had been only four waitresses all night, and one busboy, and by eight o'clock the fifteen-minute wait (even as a half-dozen open tables, littered with used dishes, mocked the hostess) sent the later arrivals scattering to the Dairy Bar. The wait quickly shrank to ten minutes, then five, but by then it was too late, and at eight forty-five the hostess found herself facing a vacant foyer, chewing her thumbnail and waiting to be sent home. By ten Casey was sweatier and achier than he'd been during the busiest autumn Fridays, yet he knew it was because he had tried to summon that past glory through haste and micromanagement, and because he'd had to bus tables himself during the brief rush. The slump, which had begun in late November, had recently led to an exodus of the experienced girls, and those who remained were either too hard up or too lazy to find work elsewhere.

At ten-thirty Casey sent all but one of the waitresses to the break room to total up their receipts and roll more silverware. He told the bartender, who hadn't made a drink in forty-five minutes, to clean up and leave; if someone came in later, Casey would handle the bar. He retreated to his office, a square dark room next to the dry goods storage closet. Because of the stifling fires of the kitchen, they kept this back half of the restaurant minimally heated, and it was so cold in his office he put on his puffy brown coat and a scarf before he went in.

He printed out the preliminary returns from the computer and extrapolated the numbers to estimate how they would do, although he wouldn't know for sure until all the girls turned in their cash. He rounded up some of the numbers, and he gave generous estimations for the servers' cash receipts, in the hopes that this would push the final number into something short of extreme disappointment. It didn't help; they would be at least three thousand below average again, for the fifth Friday in a row.

It was not Casey's restaurant, not his investment that rode on these numbers. In fact the numbers would spell absolute disaster for no one. The octogenarian franchise owners, Mr. and Mrs. Ambrose Howard, were not going to allow themselves to fail this late in the game. There were indications (a house in Weston, Mrs. Howard's stockpile of minks, a new Skylark every other year) that the Howards' financial reserves were deep and diverse, though they were stingy enough when it came to running O'Ruddy's. Casey wasn't sure why they bothered with the place, unless it simply gave them something to do, and another way to prove their fiscal mettle. The Friday numbers were a disappointment, it was true, but they were only that—not a disaster, not a death sentence.

There was no comfort in this, however, unless it was to the Howards themselves, for there would still be blame, and this, like so much else at O'Ruddy's, would be laid at Casey's feet. Although there were many factors beyond his control to consider, the low numbers were a reflection on him in some way, or at least he knew they would be perceived as such. The blame is assigned to the general manager after five failing Fridays in a row, just as it is given to the coach when a team hits a losing streak, the president when the economy slumps. He knew he should be proactive in his defense.

He put aside the papers and began writing a memo on the computer. He addressed it to the Howards but sent a closed copy to the O'Ruddy's headquarters in Dallas. He restrained his language to avoid sounding accusatory of the headquarters, though in truth he directed much of his personal blame toward them. For one thing—and this is what he led the memo with—substantial losses could be explained by the "O'Ruddy's is on the clock!" campaign. A month earlier the marketing department had thrust this new promotion upon the franchise by shipping them a crate full of cheap fifteen-minute hourglasses and a video explaining the idea: once an order was taken, the server would turn over the hourglass, and if the food wasn't on the table by the time the sand ran out, the meal was complimentary. Casey's staff had proven themselves to be categorically unprepared for this challenge. *The end of the "O'Ruddy's is on the clock!" campaign,* Casey wrote to close the first paragraph, *is eagerly anticipated by the servers, cooks, and, I must confess, myself.*

He outlined other reasons, other justifications. The next one was the weather, which Casey admitted could not be blamed on the meddlers in Dallas. A vicious storm of freezing rain had struck in December, just before the deep freeze that came with Christmas, sheathing the township in ice for eight days. They were now more than two weeks into January, and each day of the new year had begun in the single digits. With the mean chill came heavy snow, although there were no snowmen, because even the children refused to stay outside long enough to make them. Headquarters and the Howards would have to adjust and be more understanding. He did not say it in these words, and in fact he euphemized the problem so much he wondered if they could even understand his desperation. He could not say what he wanted to say — that the weather was starving them of their guests.

He didn't want to mention the fight in the memo. Headquarters knew about it, and it would likely be the first thing they thought of when they saw the return address (they controlled forty-two O'Ruddy's franchises across the U.S., and probably remembered only the ones that had caused trouble). But still he could not write about it, even cursorily. Besides, he didn't really know if the fight had hurt business. It had been covered by the *Breed's Township Beacon*, much to the distress of the Howards, and for days afterward customers had asked him about it in serious, low tones, as if the brawlers might return and start beating on them during the Sunday buffet. But any press is good press, he had reminded the Howards. The media had made it clear that no one had been hurt or arrested, in spite of the fact that the fight had involved at least a dozen agitated teenagers. Casey didn't really think it would scare anyone away, and the coverage might remind people that the restaurant was there. He hoped very much that all of this was true.

And so he ended the letter with as obsequious a tone as he could muster after the end of a wearying shift, and folded it into an envelope. Then he heard Jenny, the remaining on-duty server, knock. He knew it was Jenny because she wore a large assembly of finger rings, and when she knocked it sounded like someone nailing something to the door.

She stuck her head in before he responded, the way they all did when they bothered him in his office. It infuriated him, not because he needed the privacy but because it seemed to him that in doing this, his employees were trying to catch him in the act of something illicit, and he did not know what they thought they would see. Did they hope to catch him skimming cash from the bank bags? Watering down the booze bottles? Masturbating?

But Jenny may have used the knock-and-enter technique as a simple extension of her personality. There was a kind of endearing impertinence to her. In some ways she showed deference to his role as her boss—refusing to use his first name, for example—yet she often used curse words when speaking to him, and he could never get her to stop chewing gum during shifts; she was never abashed when he lectured her about this touchstone of the server policy. She was young, the only server still in high school, and Casey liked her for the guilelessness that came with her youth. She had once told him, during her training, that she wasn't ready to be tested on the menu because she hadn't studied it. He had been moved by her stupid, naked honesty, though at the time he had sat her at table six and made her read the menu until she knew the thing by heart. Casey understood that honesty was hardly a common trait among teenagers, but in Jenny's case it seemed a function of her youth, something that would certainly dissipate as she grew older.

Jenny was also carelessly good-looking, with an eccentric sense of fashion that competed with her beauty. In addition to the mass of finger rings, she wore a huge assortment of hair clips and headbands, and her eyes were heavily shadowed. She often dyed her hair to match her polo shirt, and her earrings were conspicuous and dangling. But she was organically pretty, one of those girls who would have been more attractive naked and without makeup than at any other time, although Casey refrained from picturing her thus.

"Mr. Fielder," she said, still represented only by her head, encased in a mass of brunette hair streaked with bolts of scarlet. She was peeking through a small opening in the door, as if this stance were less of an intrusion. "You got to get out here, now." Panic, mitigated by her delicate voice but obvious nonetheless.

He clenched his muscles, sitting up straight and biting his teeth together. "What's going on?" he asked with a casual lilt, hoping for a mundane emergency. Jenny was the only server on the floor now, it being nearly eleven. Maybe there was a late rush after the Township High basketball game, or perhaps she had misentered a total for a credit card and the customer had turned hostile. She was a good server, personable and reliable, but she had her limits. It would be something of this nature, Casey told himself.

"They're back," Jenny said. "Those boys are back again."

# two

*He pretended* not to understand at first, which was ridiculous, and probably underscored his own panic. Upon realizing this, he stood and said, "How many of them?" in as even a voice as he could manage.

"I don't know. A bunch. More than last time, I think." She opened the door wider and started to back away, signaling that he should come with her.

When he stepped out of the office, he felt himself entering a world of eyes. It was as if Jenny had pressed the record button of a video camera that would be focused on him for the rest of the night. He felt himself being observed, not just by Jenny but by the world in general, by headquarters and the Howards, by whatever customers might remain on the floor, by the cooks and the handful of servers now in the break room, wrapping silverware in napkins. Though few people would actually see him, he knew that his actions would eventually come under scrutiny. He felt the pull of the handbook—how nice it would be to scamper back and thumb through its index. But he knew that nothing would be there; he had checked after the first incident. Nothing under "fights," "brawls," "conflicts," "teenagers." He would have no guidance tonight.

The boys that Jenny referred to were the same age as she, some of them her schoolmates and the others from St. Brendan's Academy. Exactly three weeks earlier, they had assembled in the O'Ruddy's parking lot to brawl. The shift manager that night, Chad Richardson, had called the police almost as soon as he had noticed them congregating. But the restaurant sat on the south side of Arthur Avenue, in East Breed's, where police response was sluggish. In this case, one ineffectual cruiser had arrived after fifteen minutes. In that span the twelve boys had punched themselves to exhaustion; some of them had fled by the time the cops arrived. The remaining boys had been lectured by a sergeant who was too cold to get out of the car and then had been sent on their way.

All in all, a minor affair. Minimal media coverage—mostly in the *Breed's Township Beacon*, which was perpetually cursed with slow news days—and no harm to person or property. Certainly nothing to make Casey panic now, nothing to make him think tonight would present him with something he could not handle.

But there had been a police report. This was the damage. The policeman had given Richardson a copy, and he had passed it on to Casey. Casey had followed protocol by sending copies to the Howards and to the headquarters in Dallas. Under the terms of the franchise contract and the insurance papers, this had to be done. The handbook was unambiguous—it was virtually the only directive in there about how to deal with police matters. But the Howards were displeased. The authority of the handbook was not absolute to them, they did not understand that their restaurant relied on its dogma.

Casey now walked briskly through the kitchen, taking off his coat and scarf as he moved, and Jenny followed. The cooks, distracted by the radio's salsa music and the elaborate process of shutting down the kitchen, paid no attention to him.

Out on the floor, once the swinging doors shut out the noise of the kitchen behind him, the world seemed silent and softly lit. He scanned the restaurant quickly, out of habit, and noted only one occupied table, where a short, curly-headed couple in their fifties hunched over coffee cups.

Tables five through nine, which lined the wall that overlooked the parking lot, had booth seating, and when Casey reached them he slid into the dark faux-leather booth of table eight, resting on his knees and holding himself erect as a prairie dog. This section had been closed down an hour earlier, the lights dimmed and the candles extinguished, so the tableau of the fluorescently lit parking lot presented itself clearly to those inside. The glass, a few inches in front of him, radiated cold, and he felt his chest absorb the frozen vapor. He thought about the exorbitant January heating bills, how he should have mentioned that in the memo.

Jenny slid into the same booth, resting on her knees on the seat opposite him, also facing the window. He gave her a quick, surprised look, slightly annoyed by her presence. She reminded him of the video camera, of the unseen eyes that would watch his performance in retrospect. He closed his gaping mouth and tried to adopt a purposeful frown. He noticed that she smelled like the kitchen—vegetable oil and lemon Fantastik. The front of her apron was smeared with mashed potatoes. Her nametag, askance, drifted on a breast that brushed against the window.

"Who are they, Jenny? The same kids?"

"More or less." She sounded unconvinced. "It's hard to say. They're all bundled up. Maybe if I saw their faces."

They both could tell which kids represented which schools. The St. Brendan's group held their position on the north side of the lot around a small number of SUVs, cars they had probably talked their parents into buying for safety's sake. The rich kids didn't drive Alfas anymore, the way they had when Casey had gone to Breed's Township High. The rich kids drove Yukons and Grand Cherokees, and the poor kids walked or rode in uninsured Ford hatchbacks.

The boys had not begun fighting, although they were well into their prelude: the nervous jabbering, the taunts and laughter. They reclined against their bumpers and hoods, as if lounging in this parking lot, in this cruel weather, might be something they would do regardless of the enemy presence. But this appearance was betrayed, more frequently as the minutes passed, by the shouting of insults and promises rising in calculated menace.

The shouts came through the glass clearly enough, drowning out the overhead Top 40 from the cassette tapes that headquarters sent to their franchises. Each boy's mouth expelled puffs of vapor as he threatened war. At first the fog dissipated, but then the frozen air began to congregate and jostle above them as the shouting heightened, and soon there would be nothing for the boys to do but run at each other and strike.

Casey counted about a dozen on each side. They had more numbers tonight than they'd had in December. He had not been there, but he had thought about it often, and the morning after the incident he'd called Chad Richardson in to narrate the scene for him. During the past few weeks, in moments of idleness, he had stared out the window and imagined the wrangling boys. He had wondered what he would have done in Chad's position, then abandoned the thought. Casey did not work well with theoretical scenarios.

The taunts increased, and the boys spread themselves out in a rough formation. The swearing had taken on a sinister feel, the shouts so foul that the frozen vapor that carried them seemed to be a very real kind of pollution. Casey broke from the spell of the spectacle and looked around him. Jenny was staring dumbly, hypnotized, as he had been. He looked toward the smoking section and saw that the couple who had come to drink coffee were transfixed by the scene as well, though they stayed in their distant booth. Chad Richardson had called the police before it had even come to this, he thought. But Chad Richardson had been wrong—wasn't that the consensus? Hadn't he called too early? Hadn't he shirked his responsibility?

"I think they're about to go at it," said Jenny.

He wondered what she meant by stating such an obvious thing. Was she trying to indicate that he was not playing his part?

"The Howards really scared me at that meeting," she said. "I mean, they sounded so serious. Oh my god, Mr. Fielder, I can't lose my job. Seriously, I can't."

Melodrama, thought Casey. If she thought she was the one who had been scared by the Howards' meeting, then she didn't know what scared was. But of course she didn't think much about him. She was simply laying another problem at his feet, formally passing on yet another crisis to the manager, who knew how to fix things. She didn't see it the way he did. The fight could not be allowed to happen, of course . . . but that meeting, the Howards' emphatic stance on the matter: no more police reports.

Outside the boys continued to yell, continued to inch toward collision. The screams overlapped, the voices competing, climbing on top of each other like rats escaping a swollen well. The bass was leaving them, the booming juvenile threats collapsing into a shrillness that indicated an inability to articulate, a need to shriek and rise, a need that would finally manifest itself in the beating of other boys.

The Howards had called the meeting upon receiving the memo, which had come via certified mail eight days after the December fight. Their understanding of the situation, Casey felt, was typical of them, typical of any couple who had made it into their eighties without ever living east of Keystone Avenue, who had sunk an afterthought of stock earnings into a chain restaurant where they had never eaten. They wanted this thing dealt with, they said. They ranted to Casey without acknowledging the reasonableness of his response, his deference to the handbook. There could be no more fights, they said, over and over again, so the employees were to do what they had to, whatever that meant.

Their strategy hadn't worked, evidently. As dangerous as this could be for him, Casey couldn't help but feel a small victory: the old couple who managed to control a thousand aspects of his life could not manage this handful of teenagers, they could not mandate them out of existence.

The message had been clear, at least from headquarters. The insurance would be revoked if there was another incident. End of story. They had heard about the news coverage, read the reports Casey had dutifully filed. It was an intractable situation, headquarters said. The margins were already too narrow, the premiums almost too high to sustain. With another fight, the insurance would go, and this would be the end of the Breed's Township O'Ruddy's.

A sandy-haired St. Brendan's boy, his muscular build evident despite his bulky black winter clothes, stepped forward, breaching a line that had been tacitly defined. Now the chaos of the screams accompanied action. A short, thin boy from Breed's Township High, wearing a ludicrous teal parka—Casey knew it was likely to be a Starter jacket for some expansion sports franchise—approached the one who had crossed the line. These two vanguards mirrored each other from a distance of five feet, spraying bad language and spittle so emphatically that the air between them soon became clouded.

Jenny spoke, and Casey's body jerked. "Oh shit," she said.

"What?" he said. "What? You know them, right? Do you know them?"

"A couple of them, yeah," she said.

"What's going to happen?" he said, but she didn't answer.

"Jenny, are these kids really going to hurt each other, or is this for show? Are they just showing off?"

She squinted at the glass, which her warm breath had fogged. She wiped the window with the hem of her apron. "Who would they be showing off for?"

"For each other? You know, a turf war kind of thing? To show who's in charge?"

She thought before answering. "They don't really care about that. The ones I know don't, anyway. Everyone usually just sticks to their own business. I don't really know what this is about, Mr. Fielder."

The window fogged again as she spoke. She pulled her face back like a snake about to strike, then touched her index finger to her blurred reflection. She absently traced her initials into the fog, then wiped the design away, sheepish.

"What are you going to do, Mr. Fielder?"

He didn't answer. The boys were still barking threats. The two at the middle had moved even closer together, both waiting for the tinder to catch.

"I can't lose my job."

"Goddammit, Jenny, neither can I," he said. "That's not what this is about, anyway." He bit his lower lip and squinted again at the parking lot.

Chad Richardson wasn't the kind of person who liked to handle crises. Chad Richardson seemed to manage the restaurant with the perpetual hope that nothing would go wrong, which was why he'd been stuck on the weekday shifts for two years now; on the night of the December fight, he'd been filling in because Casey had had strep throat. So while it was true, Casey thought, that Chad had called the police by this stage, the eyes that had watched Chad had not judged him kindly.

He had paused to tell himself this, to collect himself. He didn't like having said "goddammit" to an employee. There was something in the handbook about swearing, but he couldn't remember the exact wording.

"We've got to do something, though," he said to Jenny, in a much softer tone. They looked at each other now, and her face was honest and fearful. Seconds earlier, in her schoolgirl flightiness, she had written her initials in the fog of the glass, and the memory of this strange innocence, and the untouchable prettiness of the look she gave him, spurred him to make a bold claim. "We should call the police," he said.

She didn't respond for a few seconds, not until the boy in the teal jacket had knocked his coiled fist against the shoulder of the muscular boy from St. Brendan's. "Do it if you think you should," she said. "I'm just saying, I can't lose my job."

The St. Brendan's boy swiped wildly with an open hand at his opponent, knocking off the teal baseball hat that matched the Starter jacket. The Township boy had shaggy dark hair that bobbed as he ducked and struck back. His punch landed south of his enemy's face, striking him in the neck. A punch was returned, similarly off-mark. Once each had thrown a fist, the others raced toward the center, and the two lines of boys crashed together like cymbals. In this way the fight began and continued, the fists flying about with terrible randomness, punches landing everywhere and nowhere. Casey, never having witnessed such an event, watched with fascination. He had thought that a brawl might be more ordered, the brutality more expertly directed. He was now learning that rage is at its heart a graceless, inefficient thing. It seemed clear to him that the fight would continue in this way—chaotic, mismanaged—until the fighters fell from exhaustion and cold.

This was one hope the night offered. While it was true that the clashing fighters outside his window were intent on damaging each other, they were simply not very good at it. It was possible that in the end nothing would come of it, and eventually they would accept something less than total victory. He could imagine it happening because it would have happened before, he now was certain, if Chad Richardson had not been so eager to call the authorities.

Casey was not Chad. The Howards only put up with people like Chad, he thought, because they knew Casey was there to rein them in, fix their errors. What they had meant, when they said that it couldn't happen again, was that Casey could not let it happen again.

But what was *it*? Casey did not know whether they had meant that there could not be any more fights or simply any more police, and the ignorance seared him. He knew, or thought he knew, that there could be the fight without the police. This was the hope.

It was below zero, he thought, or close to it. Even with the exercise of fighting, their bodies could not hold out long. Hats were knocked off in the scuffling, and they had shed their gloves early on. In time the extremities would go numb and the fighters would be

made useless. Blows to exposed skin would sting like acid, and both
the puncher and the victim would suffer. The cold had also forced
them into these puffy outfits—they were swaddled in bulky parkas
and sweaters—so the arms they thrashed about were constricted, and
their punches often landed harmlessly on their enemies' bulk. The
bodies they threw at each other looked like those of upright weevils.

At this point they fought the way hockey players fight, hanging on
to each other for balance and leverage. A few had already fallen and
were wrestling on the ground; their only goal was to find the fulcrum
that might allow them to swing themselves on top of the other and
start flailing away. The muscular boy from St. Brendan's had his opponent in a headlock and drove repeated strikes into the exposed face.
The fighters kept to their zones and assignments, they fought in pods
and pairs.

"I really need to call the police," Casey said, but they were empty
words. He may have said them only because they were the last words
he had spoken, a full minute before, the only words still in his brain.
He did not really acknowledge what it might mean to call the police,
what physical action this might entail. The ugly ballet outside the window held him rapt, and the eyes, the absent observers, were forgotten
now. He had become the spectator, and there was no room left in his
trance for whoever was watching him, whoever would watch him.

He did not notice when Jenny scooted out of the booth. He registered her absence only when she spoke. Her voice came from several
feet behind him, but his mind did not process what she said. He
swiveled his head to look at her and saw that she was at the server
stand, with the phone receiver pressed to her ear. She repeated herself.

"The phone's out again, Mr. Fielder. We can't call the cops."

He turned back to the window and heard Jenny set down the receiver and return to her position in the booth. She settled herself there
carefully, as if trying not to wake him.

Outside the restaurant, only a few of the boys remained standing,
circling each other and thus marking geometric shapes on the thin

layer of snow that had fallen in the morning. They would have looked like weary boxers but for the fact that they could not keep their arms up, and so instead they looked like drunks searching for a place to pass out. The parking lot was speckled with coupled figures—one boy prone and protective, his counterpart thrashing above him, lost in a dream of fury. One of these fighters, a stout, black-haired boy, rose with a grimace and deliberate slowness, like an old man with a bad back. His victim rolled over and spit bloody goop onto the snow. The wide boy summoned two other boys from his crowd. These friends made their way toward him, huddled together, and then the three of them walked toward a light blue sedan.

*This is how it should end*, Casey thought, snapping out of his haze. One of the victors, afraid of getting caught or simply wasted by the cold, would have to leave. There would be no shame in it for him, since he had been winning, consistently and obviously. The other boy, the beaten one, could not be the first to run off. In Breed's Township, a reputation for cowardice circulated too quickly and stuck too permanently.

With something like glee, Casey watched this boy, together with his staggering friends, climb into the sedan and drive out of the parking lot. He had to weave around fallen, wriggling pairs of bodies, and someone shot a snowball at his windshield, but in five seconds he was gone, and Casey watched the taillights fade away down Arthur Avenue.

Soon others left. Using the diversion of the fleeing sedan, two St. Brendan's kids sought refuge in a Pathfinder. They escaped notice until the engine started and all the St. Brendan's boys, recognizing the highly tuned motor of one of their own, turned their heads and saw the abandonment. One of the boys scuttled in front of the Pathfinder as it drove toward the exit, patted the hood, then hopped into the backseat.

Now that the precedent had been established, there were more defections, although they did not happen at once. Though depleted of the energy that had made it spectacular, the fight continued, and

Casey continued to watch it from his perch. It seemed that he, rather than any of the teenagers, had won the day. After two haggard Township boys finally managed to start the engine of a brown Pontiac, twelve boys remained in the lot, only a handful of them still engaged. One pair of boys fought by falling into each other, like trees crashing together in the wind. If he called the cops now, they would laugh at him. He was handling it, he was letting it play out. It was the sort of advice the handbook might have given. The eyes would approve, he thought.

It didn't occur to Casey, as it later would, that he could have shooed them off. It would be obvious to those who judged him in hindsight, the retrospective eyes, but it just never entered his mind. There may have been subconscious reasoning behind it, he told himself later. For one thing, it probably wouldn't have done any good. He had no confidence in his ability to scare teenagers, or even to talk to them; they seemed like deer who had long gotten over their instinctive fear of humans. But in truth he just never thought about going out to speak to them. He was an observer tonight, a fascinated spectator of a remarkable pageant, a show that he'd never seen before. The idea that he might participate in this scene, play his own role in it, had become ludicrous even before he went through the motions of telling Jenny he would call the police.

One Township boy, who had spent most of the fight pinned to the cold ground by a fat St. Brendan's kid, finally freed himself and stood, shaking off the chill and the wounds. He seemed to notice for the first time that the numbers had dwindled, and upon realizing this he raced for his car, pausing only long enough to open the door for a comrade. Within twenty seconds another car left, this one a RAV4 holding two boys from St. Brendan's.

After the flight of this last SUV, only four boys remained in the lot. In the span of two minutes most of the combatants had fled in shame and pain. Casey waited for the simple problem of four boys to resolve itself.

But something had changed in the scene outside the window. The

boys were not fighting. They all looked the same to Casey, all of them
hatless now, their hair tousled and powdered with snow, their faces
red, swelling, trickling blood. Frozen vapor now came from their bodies as well as their mouths, though they weren't speaking. Jenny
pressed her face to the glass and cupped her hands around her eyes to
see better.

It had just struck Casey that of the four boys, three of them were
from Breed's Township High School—one of them even had a letter
jacket on—and only one was from St. Brendan's. He had been left behind.

It was the boy from the beginning, the muscular, handsome boy
with short sandy hair and expensive black clothes. He held his hands
at his sides and stood tall, but he moved backward as the three approached, trying to steer himself in the direction of a Jeep that sat
alone at the south end of the lot.

"He's all by himself," said Jenny.

Casey moved away from the window, his eyes still focused on the
parking lot. Like the boy from St. Brendan's, he backed away slowly,
as if walking in the dark. "I need to call the police," he said.

And he would have found a way to do this, he believed he would
have, but at that moment one of the three sprang at the tall St. Brendan's boy, driving a fist into his crotch, and the boy fell onto his side.
Jenny had her hands over her face, looking through her fingers as if
she were watching a horror movie.

Now the three from Township High stood like points of a triangle
above the fallen boy, and they spoke to each other, gray breath dart-
ing from their mouths. One boy, wearing a puffy yellow jacket, jogged
to a car.

*They're going,* Casey thought. *Just one last cheap shot at their rival, and
now he's starting the car. They will leave.* The cops could do nothing now
except necessitate a report. Get the restaurant closed down. Cost him
his job.

But instead of leaving, one of the remaining attackers got behind the sandy-haired boy and pulled him to his feet. He kept his captive's arms pinned behind his back and accepted his weight.

"That's it," said Casey. He had now retreated to the server stand and put his hand on the phone receiver. But then he froze where he stood, afraid that any movement would disturb his view, and he had to watch. He saw a figure dart from the black car, sprint across the parking lot to the others. The figure held a gray rod in his hand. The boy who held the captive's arms ducked, and the attacker swung the rod laterally, like a side-armed pitcher, and struck the sandy-haired boy in the jaw.

Unconscious, the boy slumped to his right, but he was kept off the ground by the one who held him from behind. A sticky string of red dropped from his mouth onto his coat. The boy in the yellow jacket calculated his next strike based on the new angle of the victim's face, held the rod with both hands, and swung from the left, up and to the right, smashing the side of the head. The boy crumpled now, in spite of the efforts of the one holding him, and lay on the ground. The three from Township ran toward the black sedan, and the car jolted out of the lot, running over the curb and hedges directly onto Arthur Avenue, at about the same time Casey and Jenny broke from their stupor.

"Jesus!" Jenny gasped, in a voice already debilitated by an onslaught of tears. "Bleeding!"

Casey ran. "Call 911!" he shouted on his way out, once to Jenny and once to the stupefied couple who still sat with their hands around their coffee cups. He jerked open the two sets of doors that led outside, slipped on a patch of ice, then sprinted toward the fallen boy, whose head had leaked a dark puddle on the snow.

# three

*Lea Chase's son* Colin had left home in the early evening, as he did most Fridays, nodding in uninterested agreement when she said, "I guess I'll just cook for two." Her tone fell somewhere between self-pity and earnest regret. It typically worked with her husband, but Colin was immune; sometimes she wondered if he simply didn't know how to feel guilt. Tonight, as always, he said he had to go meet some people, then took money from her purse so that he could get something to eat with his friends.

They sat down to dinner late, as they usually did. Geoffrey Chase would soon enter the phase of his career as an internist when four or five hours at the office would suffice—would, in fact, indicate his status—but he was not there yet. He'd left before she even woke up that morning, and he returned shortly after eight.

He thanked her for the food and commented on the candles and the music. He had never been one of those husbands who take such things for granted, even though she cooked as her share of the division of labor. She believed she needed to be thanked for it no more than he did for working, but she was glad of his consideration. Many of her friends had stopped complaining of their husbands' ingratitude. Some had even stopped complaining of their husbands' affairs. She knew she was lucky, in her way.

"Colin's out with friends?" he asked.

"I believe so."

He nodded at this and took a bite of fish. He wasn't going to comment anymore, and she understood that he had known the answer and had asked from a sense of obligation, the same way he had commented on the table setting and thanked her for the food.

"I don't know what they plan on doing, though." She waited, listening to him swallow. "He didn't say who he was with, either."

"The usuals, I imagine. The guys from the team."

"I suppose," she said. The vague notion of "the guys from the team" comforted her husband more than it did her. There was a heartiness to the phrase, insistent heterosexuality, grit and mettle. The autumn warriors out on the town in January, after a strong showing in the December regionals. Geoffrey had not played football in high school himself, and so this particular activity of his son's and his son's friends' had taken on large dimensions.

"I worry about them," she said. "They seem reckless sometimes."

She said this not because Colin had seemed different today. She was working on no specific knowledge. She said it because it was January, and it was becoming clear to her that she and her husband had decided to wait out the problems that Colin presented until he had left for college. They were killing the clock on their son, having recognized that there wasn't time enough to change him. Maybe they were relieved; she didn't know what she would have done with him if he weren't going away soon. But she at least felt a responsibility to acknowledge this.

Geoffrey stopped eating, again as a sign of concession and responsibility. "Do you have something to tell me?"

"What do you mean?"

"What is this about recklessness? Did you find something in his room?" She shook her head. "Did Brother Carl call again?"

"It's nothing specific," she said.

They had never been good at talking about him. This was strange, because they spoke easily enough about everything else. They still had much in common. They both appreciated subtle, subversive humor, though she didn't consider either of them to be particularly funny (Geoffrey tried more than she did). Often they were able, without being obnoxious, to finish each other's sentences, and they had always been this way, even in their courtship. They made love twice a week, and they were well matched in tennis and racquetball, and though they now differed on a few points in their Republicanism (thanks to Geoffrey's run-ins with HMOs), they still managed to discuss politics in a respectful way. Many of her friends did not know how to speak with their husbands about anything but the children, and she wondered if fear of this, of learning in middle age that all they had shared was their offspring, had made her and Geoffrey shy away from the subject of their boy. In recent years—in the period that began with his matriculation at St. Brendan's—when they spoke of him at all, it tended to be out of obligation and guilt, as it was now. Maybe they hadn't talked about him enough, she thought, although she had always been smug about this when discussing marriage with her friends, about how she didn't need the boy to connect her to the man.

Colin was not degenerate, not sociopathic. He did not shame them, exactly, he did not provoke pity in other parents. What was wrong with him was difficult for her to explain to herself, and for a long time she wondered if nothing was wrong at all, since her husband assured her he was a normal boy. Whatever that meant.

"I wouldn't worry," Geoffrey said now, and returned to his fish. "They're kids, Lea. We've talked about this before."

"That doesn't always explain everything. Yes, they're kids. Kids can be reckless, that's the whole problem."

"Well, I don't see what you're saying. What do you want me to say? What do you want me to do?"

The problem was inexpressible. The problem, and the reason it would continue, unresolved, festering, was that Colin, in her opinion, was an extremely difficult boy to love. The problem was that she thought maybe she didn't love him. It was not something to bring up at the dinner table, not over broiled orange roughy.

Geoffrey's love was so simple and literal that she envied him nearly every day. He loved that the boy was a starting linebacker for St. Brendan's. He loved that Colin not only had attractive, athletic friends but that he was the leader of them, the one they deferred to. Geoffrey loved that Colin sometimes showed up at the breakfast table with hickeys, that every year an increasing number of girls from St. Theresa's called to invite him to their dances. Lea hadn't known Geoffrey in high school, but she knew that he hadn't been like this, not in any way. He'd gone to Breed's Township High School, for one thing, which meant that he had been poor. His yearbook photo told her what she could have assumed: he'd always been skinny, his ears had always flapped out to the sides. He had debated and run cross-country and won two academic scholarships. He must very nearly have been the opposite of Colin, and Lea knew that this was the spring that his love for the boy flowed from.

It was not that he needed to live vicariously through his son, for Geoffrey was a successful man by any standard. He had finally, in early middle age, become handsome, and he had a wife who had always been pretty, and a four-bedroom colonial-style house in Weston and a partnership in a medical practice that prospered in part because Geoffrey was a very good internist, and trustworthy. He did not have to wait for his son to earn him dignity on Friday nights. Geoffrey loved Colin out of gratitude, he loved him for being all that a man could ask his boy to be, the Platonic ideal of an American son. Kindness, Geoffrey would have said (if he ever put his love into thoughts and his thoughts into words), was something that Colin could eventually grow into. Kindness was not the province of boys.

But Lea needed it. She needed to feel that there was something in Colin that responded to love before she could give it, and she needed to feel that he could love her back, and sometimes she looked into his eyes for so long and so aggressively that it made Colin uncomfortable, almost furious, and she saw nothing of that in them. She hadn't seen him cry since he was eleven. She was not allowed to hug him anymore, even when his friends weren't around.

The last time she had hugged him he had been in the ninth grade. She had taken him to St. Brendan's, his new school, and hugged him quickly before he slid out of the car to enter this new life. He was different from the first day, eight hours later, when she picked him up and he insisted on sitting in the backseat on the way home. He had loosened his tie and untucked his shirt, and he casually said to her that the brothers had already given him his first detention.

St. Brendan's was a harsh place, Jesuit and severe, a place that created boys who looked very good on paper. All through that first day a part of her had hoped that it would not work out for him, that he would not succeed with those austere priests and the cold, attractive boys. St. Brendan's was a place where even the wealthiest and most Catholic parents would not send their son if he had asthma or if he threw like a girl. For a meek child at St. Brendan's, the fine line between character building and lifetime emotional scarring could be easily crossed. In looking at parents who had shielded their children from this—they usually commuted the kids out to the Episcopal school near Scranton—Lea had noticed a kind of bond that Colin would never have considered establishing with her, the kind of love that comes from being protected, and from protecting. On that first St. Brendan's day, a part of her had hoped that when she went to get him, he would dash weeping into the car and beg her to drive off, beg her not to make him go back. She would not have made him, she would have faced down Geoffrey on that occasion.

But Colin had succeeded at St. Brendan's, in a sense, quickly becoming the kind of boy that the parents of awkward boys distrust, the kind of boy that awkward boys fear. Before his mother's eyes, his dirty-blond hair and wide white smile had become sinister. Within his first two years football had turned his body sinewy and confident beneath the school blazer and khakis. The moment he noticed his looks, he began to use them to please himself. Lea was sure that he was having regular sex, and had been for some time, but thankfully she didn't know any details. She had never met one of his girls, and he had forbidden questions about such matters early in his tenth-grade year, during an edict in which he also announced they were no longer to address him by any childhood nicknames. But girls had called the house shamelessly for three years, often with undisguised hopefulness in their voices. She assumed that it was an easy matter for him, that credulous girls offered themselves in the master bedrooms of his friends' absent parents.

"Six months from now," Geoffrey said, rather unexpectedly, "he will be completely on his own. His own person in every sense. In just six months."

Geoffrey seemed to think he had made a point, but Lea could not discern it. She squinted at him over the square expanse of their teak dinner table.

"What I mean is, it's pretty much out of our hands. When he goes away, he'll be able to do whatever he wants, with whoever he wants, and we'll just have to trust the fact that he knows what he's doing. So we may as well start offering him that trust now."

"He already does whatever he wants, with whomever he wants."

"So what's the problem? That's just what I'm saying—let him have that freedom now. Let him exercise his own judgment while he's still living with us. How else do you get them ready to be on their own?"

She shrugged. "But Geoffrey . . ." She considered what she wanted to say, aware of the danger of telling him too much. "What if I don't trust his judgment? What if I don't believe he knows what he's doing at all? And what if I don't think you should trust him either?"

She knew this had killed their conversation. He became defensive about Colin quite easily, and this was too sensitive a nerve for her to have struck so openly. She didn't let him respond—she was certain he wouldn't have any substantial response anyway—and instead she waved the words out of the air and said, "Wait. I'm sorry. I don't know what I'm saying. Let it drop." Before he could agree to this, she was out of her chair and pushing through the swinging door of the kitchen to dish out fruit salad.

They spent the late evening in the living room, where Geoffrey made a fire. He then sat in a leather chair reading a medical journal. She lay awkwardly across a rattan loveseat, finishing in her head the conversation she had nearly had with him.

The phone rang and she jumped up, as if woken from a dream. Geoffrey placed his hands on the armrests and began to push himself up, indicating that he would have answered the phone if she hadn't gotten up so fast. This gesture annoyed her. A manifest politeness, a sense that he wanted to make things easier on others, governed nearly everything Geoffrey did. She motioned for him to sit back down.

The person on the line was already speaking, but not to her. She heard several voices, all of them scratchy and distant. She could tell from the buzzing static that the call came from a cell phone. She said hello twice before a thick, slow voice began speaking to her.

"Is this a Missus . . ." Here he paused and said something to someone near him. "Is this a Missus Chase?"

"Yes," she said, understanding in an instant what this was all about. She knew it was a policeman, knew something had happened with or to Colin. In her overwhelming fear, her imagination didn't get specific about the scenario that had engendered the call, although the slow-speaking, distracted policeman certainly gave it a chance to. Instead she stood still and waited, and understood that she was about to be told something that would change her life.

He exhaled over the next few seconds, betraying his dashed hope that he would reach an answering machine, or at least the man of the house. "This is a damn difficult thing to say, Mrs. Chase. I hate to be the one to have to tell you this."

# | four |

*Chula Vista,* she told herself. *Remember that time at Chula Vista, when we went to visit Geoffrey's sister and Colin — he was six — chased the squirrel up into the tree, and before he realized it he was thirty feet high and bawling for help. After we'd extracted him, he slapped his hands together and giggled and said, "Mommy, I want to do it again!"* That was what she should be remembering. The past. What she had loved about him, when she had loved him.

But she couldn't. She tried to focus, saying things to herself like *Chula Vista, remember Chula Vista,* or *Think about his fourth birthday, when he ignored the Lincoln Logs and the ice cream cake and instead became fascinated by the roll of wrapping paper you left in the kitchen,* but she could not set her mind onto such paths. It was like trying to conjure someone else's dream; it just couldn't be done.

Instead she thought about the future, and after a while this made sense. It was, after all, a time of loss, and therefore logical to think about what had been taken away. She saw images, clearer to her than the memories she had vainly tried to recall, in which Colin graduated from high school, returned at Thanksgiving from college so that she could do his laundry, came back for Christmas break with a girl whom he did not yet know he was going to marry. She imagined him as a middle-aged man, coming to her with secrets about a failed marriage. As an older man, trying to talk her into moving into a nursing home, delivering the eulogy at her funeral. *This is what has been lost,* she told herself. *It is okay to think about this.*

Geoffrey moved from room to room, consulting with people whom Lea had previously seen only at dinner parties and fundraisers. He spoke to them in the language of their shared profession, and she let the gracefully imposing words cascade over her like rose petals. Subdural hematoma, parietal lobe, diffuse arterial pressure. The words were soothing to her, because she did not know what they meant.

The police came, and Geoffrey dealt with them. Lea sat on a brown plastic chair that was curved like the bucket seats of a muscle car, and she thought about the future that Colin might not have anymore. The work of an instant. She watched Geoffrey talk with a policeman who wore a crisp blue uniform, and she wondered if this was the man who had called her. She saw in his body language the same hesitant quality that she had heard in his voice. He wouldn't have wanted to deal with this sort of thing tonight. He would have gone into his shift expecting perhaps to nab some East Breed's kids for vandalism, or maybe break up a house party in Weston. As he questioned Geoffrey, he grimaced and shook his head, just as he must have when he called her and said that Colin Chase had been taken to Mercy Hospital because he had suffered a massive trauma to the head. He didn't know much more than that, he had said, except that they were still looking for whoever had done it.

The policeman closed his notepad, and then he and Geoffrey shook hands. Lea looked back at the television and waited for her husband to join her in the row of plastic seats, which he did shortly, sliding beside her and kissing her on the forehead. He cried then, for the first time, and he explained without looking at her. A fight, an enormous brawl somewhere on Arthur Avenue. Three against one in the end, three against their boy. A metal rod. Twice to the head. Her husband then wept into his hands. Lea wept quietly and understood that Geoffrey cried now because it was suddenly nonmedical. It was not intracranial pressure or neural edema, it was their boy alone, facing other boys who for some reason wanted to knock the brains from his head.

After fifteen minutes Geoffrey retreated into the white hallways of the hospital ward. He saw patients here sometimes, and so he was not challenged. From time to time he came out to the waiting room and leaned toward her, looking straight into her eyes, the way doctors, not husbands, approach the bereaved. *We don't know much*, was the gist of his first report. And then, *He's still in trouble*. And then something else, and something else, and finally, at two in the morning, something about the swelling of the brain, an image that was so startling to her she almost blacked out. She focused her eyes on a distant television as he explained it.

The brain was expanding, but of course it was still encased in the unforgiving prison of the skull. The expansion would have nowhere to go. She did not ask Geoffrey questions, though she had a thousand of them. *And when the brain keeps swelling and the skull keeps resisting, what happens then? Does it explode, like a balloon in a vise?*

There was an operation they could perform, a way to relieve the pressure. "I should hope so," Lea said, the first words she had given Geoffrey in a long while, and he smiled more at their sound than at their content.

They stayed in the waiting room. Lea watched the television throughout the night. It received only five channels, the horizontal hold was sporadic, and yet it was chained to the wall. *Who would want to steal that TV?* she thought.

Geoffrey managed to sleep in patches. When awake, he found himself some sort of mission, either scuttling through the corridors for updates or hunting and gathering from the vending machines. Lea's sister, Megan, showed up before two, along with her husband, Shane, who responded to the tragedy by speaking no more than ten words all night; this was so far out of character for him that Lea imagined her sister had instituted a gag rule so he wouldn't say something inappropriate. At four in the morning Geoffrey's father came, straight from a shift on the highway, where he operated Caterpillars. Lea had never gotten much out of the man, and suspected no one had. The elder Mr. Chase was clearly uncomfortable when Geoffrey cried openly in the lobby, but still she saw an enormous sympathy in the old man, for the first time in the two decades she'd known him. She was touched that he had come straight from work, smelly and worn, and that he stayed, saying virtually nothing to anyone, until Geoffrey commanded him to leave for the fourth time.

At nine in the morning a nurse came to whisper to Geoffrey. He turned to his wife, and she shooed him away, mumbling, "Go find out."

He came back within ten minutes, knelt beside Lea, but spoke loudly enough for his sister-in-law to hear. "He's stable, thank God. But they think there's been some damage. We won't know for a while."

Lea did not know how to react, and she felt her sister and Shane and Geoffrey watching her intently, perhaps in search of a model for their own expressions. He was stable. Is that what she was meant to react to? Or the brain damage? She kept her face inert, numb.

Geoffrey looked down. "At some point we're going to have to go home. They don't want us here. There's nothing we can do. Frankly, I think I'm beginning to get on their nerves." He flashed a sheepish smile. Megan gave him a reassuring pat on the shoulder and contradicted him—*Oh, Geoff, I'm sure that's not true*. But Lea knew that it must be very true. If Geoffrey had picked up on the fact that he was bothering the staff, then their annoyance must have been severe. But mothers don't leave. Not with words like *brain damage* in the air. A mother does not go home at such times, especially a mother such as

Lea, who understood too well that she did, in fact, want to go home and sleep in her own bed.

"I don't think so, Geoffrey. You guys should leave, though. Shane, you've got work. You were sweet to come down. I'll be fine here."

"A half hour, then," said Geoffrey, unusually forceful. She wondered if the chief of surgery had given him an order, threatened him in some way. He must have made quite a nuisance of himself in there, she thought. "The thing is, Lea, he just got out of brain surgery. He's not waking up anytime soon. Probably not for ten hours, and even then he won't really be conscious of anything. We can't do anything here. So another half hour, and then I'm taking you home."

There was not much she could say to him when he wielded his expertise. She found it insufferable even in small doses, and especially now. Though she was relieved that he had given her permission to abandon the vigil, she wanted him to go away.

"Another half hour," he said again.

And so they waited, and then left, and returned at seven in the evening. Nothing had changed, except that the word *coma* was used for the first time.

# | five |

*Casey was interrogated* in his office by a policeman named Janda. The cop was dressed in corduroy pants and a downy sweater, the kind of outfit one might wear to Thanksgiving dinner. Casey couldn't tell exactly how old he was, though all his physical distinctions were the products of age: wispy hair, bad posture, a belly like a mother kangaroo's. The other policemen called him Pat, but he had introduced himself to Casey as Sergeant Janda.

"I got to tell you, young man, I can't for the life of me figure out why you didn't just call us."

Casey's instinct was to say something about the Fifth Amendment, but he thought this might be out of place. He knew that it was his right not to say anything at all, though perhaps this might not apply to him, since he wasn't a suspect. Perhaps he did not have the right to avoid incriminating himself if there was no way to incriminate himself. He thought about that word, *incriminate*, and it sounded strange in his head. He knew it meant "to charge with a crime," but as he considered it, it sounded as though it would mean "to become a criminal," to commit an act that transformed a normal person into one who does criminal things. To jump into crime with both feet: *to incriminate*.

The boy had been breathing when he got to him, but the blood had been spilling eagerly, even when Casey had pressed his handkerchief to the wound. The ambulance had arrived quickly, and its crew had shoved him away and loaded up the boy in a blur of motion and left him and Jenny standing alone. The paramedics had left as suddenly as the attackers had, and they had been just as forceful, and as oblivious of Casey's presence.

There was a span of silence, and Janda looked at Casey the entire time, until he finally said, "For shit's sake, son, do you have an answer, or don't you? Why the hell didn't you just call the police?"

"It happened very, very fast," he said. He knew this was the right thing to say, although it was nothing like the truth. The fight, in fact, had seemed to progress very slowly. Twenty minutes, more or less, he had since pieced together. But it had taken up the entire evening in Casey's mind, it had been an epic of sorts, so that the previous happenings of the day and night at the restaurant seemed to have occurred in another life. It hadn't been fast at all, it had been terribly slow. But Casey had been slow as well, made slow by the fight itself. It had seemed, throughout the twenty minutes, that he had been encased in a thick atmosphere.

"Well, you must have seen the fight brewing. We've heard witnesses say they were out there for ten minutes before they even threw a punch. So what were you doing for that whole time?"

"What witnesses?" Casey asked. Then, seeing a violent annoyance in Janda's face, he waved away the question. "Okay, okay. First of all, I wasn't there the whole time. I was in my office when Jenny came to get me. And those twenty minutes went by awful fast, if that's really how long it was. It seemed like a blink of an eye." He wanted to keep talking but cut himself off.

"Are you saying you meant to call the police? That you were going to, but it just happened too fast?"

"Is that what I said?" Casey asked, again causing Janda to pinch between his eyes and grimace. It was like talking to a woman, Casey thought, the way they get mad and you don't even understand what you did.

The policeman cursed again, exactly as before. "For shit's sake," he said. Then he wrote something on his notepad.

Casey seized the silence and Janda's distractedness to ask again, "What witnesses, sir?"

Janda mumbled his response. "A couple that was in the restaurant. That little waitress of yours." But no kids. They hadn't caught any of the kids.

"Are you looking for the ones I told you about?"

"You didn't help us out much with the description of the car," he said. "Neither did any of the other witnesses." He looked down at a notepad in front of him. "Three white kids, medium height. Black four-door sedan. Yeah, we're looking." Janda shut his notebook and started tapping his pen on the arm of his chair. "I wouldn't worry about that right now. Right now I'm interested in you."

Casey could feel the interrogation, like everything else that night, spinning wildly out of control. He recognized the need to have this man on his side, and saw in his dress and aspect something kindly, something that might respond to his natural inclination to please authority figures. Yet he felt himself coming off as smarmy and sarcastic. Now they were watching him for real; now he was under observation in the most literal sense.

"Like I said, the fight apparently lasted about twenty minutes. That's a long time to let kids rumble. Unless you got a reason for it. Do you see what I'm getting at?"

"I can't say that I do, frankly."

"I wonder if you didn't call the police because you thought it would be your ass. Especially after that incident a few weeks ago. That must have entered your mind."

"Well, that's an interesting thing you're getting at, sir," he said. His voice sounded raspy. Every word he spoke, even the articles and prepositions, resounded with weight, felt heavy coming off his tongue. He might spend a good part of the rest of his life thinking about these words, about how much they weighed and cost. So he spoke different ones, lighter ones.

"It really just happened so fast. There was no time for that kind of thinking."

The detective smirked in disappointment and, possibly as a form of punishment, made Casey go through the story of the brawl again. Casey recited it as accurately as he could, remembering the color of two of the cars, the make of an SUV. He remembered a puffy yellow jacket, and he remembered that the baggy pants of one of the assailants had something written on the side of the leg and that all of the boys wore heavy black boots.

Something occurred to the policeman, and he flipped ahead in his notebook to start a fresh page. "Do you ever hire any kids from the high schools?"

"Sometimes. Always from Township. I can't imagine many St. Brendan's kids work after-school jobs. Jenny's the only one we have now."

The policeman turned to look at the door, and though it was closed, he looked at it for a long time. "She's a good-looking girl. Don't you think?"

Casey had been prepared for this. Jenny's attractiveness was indisputable, and a certain kind of man always gave Casey a lecherous wink and nudge when he saw her. "I don't see what that has to do with anything. I have a girlfriend, by the way, and she's in her thirties."

He shouldn't have mentioned Rachel, and he surely shouldn't have said she was in her thirties. He could practically feel her swatting him on the shoulder in recrimination. The policeman didn't really care about her, but it annoyed Casey to be thinking of her at this moment. Rachel was someone who required a good deal of thinking about.

"I guess I've gotten all I'm going to get out of you," Janda said, but he leaned back in his chair and made no sign of ending the interview. "You know, you could be liable for this."

"What does that mean?"

Janda shrugged and tugged the rising hem of his sweater over his belly.

"I know what the word means, but what are you saying? You mean someone's going to sue me?"

The policeman shrugged again, clearly delighting in Casey's discomfort. "They could, sure. Maybe the parents of the kids. Maybe the restaurant. You know them better than I do. They could get sued by the parents and then take some of it out on you. But I also mean that there could be a criminal complaint."

There was the word again, or at least a derivative of it. *Criminal. Incriminate.* Had he incriminated himself? Had he shown himself to be a criminal, had he *become* a criminal?

"What?" he said, trying to sound outraged.

"Gross negligence. You should have called the police. That's a pretty obvious fact."

"It's easy for you to say that. It's easy for anyone to say that now," Casey said. "But it happened really, really fast."

The policeman was finished with him. He dismissed Casey, who felt a physical pain at being told to leave the office, which was, after all, his. But Janda didn't leave it open for discussion. Casey loped out of the office, through the blackness and stink of the empty kitchen, into the somber lighting of the main floor.

The policemen had shoved tables two and three together to set up an impromptu headquarters, with three uniformed officers sitting around a mass of clipboards and forms in triplicate. Jenny sat at the head of table three, ignoring the activity around her. She still wore her uniform and nametag, and she still had pencils stuck behind each ear.

The police had dismissed the kitchen staff, who hadn't seen anything, as well as the two customers—Janda mentioned they hadn't seen much—so besides the cops and Jenny, the only ones in O'Ruddy's were the Howards, who had appeared during Casey's interrogation. The Howards sat at a booth in nonsmoking, table fifteen, both speaking at the same time. Casey imagined that this was the first time in decades they had been awake simultaneously at two in the morning.

Mr. Howard summoned him by banging his coffee cup on the table and pointing at him. Casey glanced at Jenny as he passed her table, but she was counting her tips.

It would have taken Casey a lifetime to decide which of the Howards to sit next to, so he pulled up a chair and sat at the end of the table. He decided to speak first.

"Mr. and Mrs. Howard, I don't know what happened here. I was trying to do what was best for the restaurant. I think you probably know that."

Casey had first met the Howards eight years ago. Mr. Howard hadn't seemed to grow any older in those years, because he had looked so ancient to begin with that there really hadn't been any way for him to get any more decrepit. He was one of those old people who had shrunk with age, and the gray hair that was left on the fringes of his head was wispy and patchy, like the hair of a chemo patient, and very much like the hair growing out of his ears. His enormous glasses enlarged his milky eyes and the liver spots on his face. For some reason he wore a mustache.

"Don't tell me that," said Mr. Howard. "Don't you say a damn thing until I'm finished." He pulled himself into a straighter posture and adjusted his tie. Like most of his physical efforts, it took a long time and brought a grimace to his face. Over the years Casey had learned that though the Howards rarely left their house, Mr. Howard wore creased pants and a sweater vest and a coat and tie every day. Casey admired this effort.

"You're fired. There, I'm finished."

Casey looked at Mrs. Howard, not so much for help as to see if she was as surprised as he was. She returned his stare squarely, her face expressionless beneath a huge lacquer of makeup that made her look like a corpse in an open casket. She was not the type to allow her husband to make any kind of decision on his own; Casey suspected she was the one who made him dress up every day. Their marriage had obviously involved sixty or so years of jockeying for position.

On the point of Casey's dismissal, however, there seemed to be accord. He hadn't really expected to be fired, even after the policeman pronounced him liable. He didn't think he felt liable. He didn't think he had incriminated himself. He wanted someone to explain exactly what he had done wrong.

"I've got to tell you, Mr. Howard," Casey said, staring straight ahead at a wall that was decorated with fake memorabilia—a tin Bull Durham sign, a mounted harmonica. "I don't know what you would have had me do. I thought you made it clear that we couldn't have any more trouble with the police."

Mrs. Howard ducked her head low and spoke in a kind of whisper. "What in God's name do you call this? We didn't mean you were supposed to let those thugs kill a child! That could have been our grandson!"

She now sat up straight and spoke in a more composed tone. She accented random words, like a character in a Victorian novel. She always did this when she spoke about important matters. "Your job was to prevent them from fighting here in the first place. To prevent them from gathering at all." *Job, fighting, first, gathering.* "We did not expect you to stand by and watch them attack each other. That's simply reprehensible." *Not, stand, attack, reprehensible.*

And so here it was. They were incriminating him, explaining to him his error, his crime. He knew that it was their way of getting out of it. He knew that on the ride over, Mrs. Howard having pried the basic story of the evening from whatever policeman had called them, they would have fretted over liability. Strangely enough, of course, liability—that favorite word of O'Ruddy's insurance carriers—had begun it all in the first place. They would be liable, the Howards had told Casey in December, if the kids fought again on their property. Liable to the parents, to the community, to the children themselves. But most of all (and Casey could tell this had been the salient fact), they would be liable to headquarters in Dallas. The restaurant could be shut down, just like that.

"How was I supposed to prevent them from gathering, Mrs. Howard?" said Casey. "You never explained that. The handbook doesn't say anything about that. How do you stop those kids from coming to the restaurant unless you call the cops? And you made it clear that there couldn't be cops."

Mr. Howard interjected, "These questions should have been asked long ago."

With that they reached an impasse. He wondered if their motives weren't as clear as he had imagined. Maybe they had told themselves that this was the truth, that they hadn't really meant that Casey should let anyone get hurt. But he didn't really think they would have minded so much about the boy if the cops hadn't come at all. If Casey had called them at two in the morning to say that a kid had been pummeled outside the restaurant, that the boy was bleeding but the cops had not been called, he honestly believed that they would have been relieved, and at some point they would have thanked him for his discretion. The Howards had owned the restaurant for twelve years, and for eight of them Casey had witnessed the lengths to which their avarice would carry them. He had known them to purchase bulk orders of cheese that was past the expiration date, to encourage the recycling of fries that had not been eaten, to pay the illegal dishwashers three dollars an hour. He could not guess where their protection of O'Ruddy's would end, and so he assumed that to the Howards, the survival of the restaurant was certainly worth a beaten boy or two.

He rose and put his chair back. He removed two keys from his keychain and placed them on the table in front of the Howards. It was something of an act, since the other dozen keys to the multiple

O'Ruddy's locks were on a large ring that he kept zipped in a side pocket of his brown coat. But he felt the gesture was appropriate for the moment, the equivalent of a soldier's being stripped of his stripes.

Casey wanted to leave, but he knew he would regret it later if he didn't ask the question now. "What about terms? Severance?"

Mr. Howard turned red, scrunching his already wrinkled face into a mass of raging furrows, and pointed at him. Casey thought he might begin swearing, but Mrs. Howard, her face equally contorted by a sudden sense of injustice, spoke first, and her husband deferred.

"Listen to me. You don't deserve anything from us," she said. "In fact, we retain the right to sue you if we think it might be worth it." She took a sip of coffee for effect, and in this pause her husband took over.

"Yesterday was payday. You'll get one more check, in two weeks. It'll get mailed to your house. That's all you're getting from us, and you can count yourself damn lucky."

Casey walked to the policemen's table. What exactly could he be sued for? he wondered helplessly. The term *negligence* floated around his thoughts now, the way *incriminate* had before. *Negligence* seemed even less concrete to him than *incriminate* had. It was just like him, he thought—the one time in his life he may be charged with a crime, it was for something that he did not do.

Janda was out of the office now, standing over a seated policeman and chuckling about something. Casey sauntered up to them like a shy child hoping to be let in on the conversation.

"Mr. Janda," he said, "I wondered if you'd heard anything further about the boy."

"Yeah," he said, pronouncing the word with two syllables. "Still out. Unconscious. Not much else to tell just yet."

The second question Casey did not phrase as a question at all, terrified that it might be contradicted. "I assume I'm free to leave."

Janda looked at him with a slightly open mouth, as if surprised that Casey would make such a large assumption. "Just a second," he said, and went over to where another policeman was filling out another form.

Casey and Jenny looked at each other. She waved an open hand, slowly, twice, like a windshield wiper, and she kept her mouth slack and her eyes wide. It was a kind gesture, but she refused to hide her sadness, or her disappointment, whichever it was.

"You're not being charged with anything right now," Janda said, "which means you can go. Just don't leave the county, and hope the kid gets better. I guess you lost your job."

Casey nodded. It was time to recalibrate the scope of things. The detective had assumed, as a matter of course, that he would get fired for this, while Casey had been enormously surprised when it had happened. "Yeah, I lost my job."

"So." The policeman held out his hand and began counting on his fingers. "You might have killed a teenage boy because you didn't call us, you might get charged with criminal negligence, and you're out of work. I'd say those are your problems in order of seriousness. There's not much you can do about any of them now. So go home and wait."

There were other problems in Casey's life, of course, but the policeman was right; these three had shot to the top of the list. It was upsetting, however, to realize that as soon as he left the restaurant, the other problems would materialize again. He thought about Rachel, and somehow this made him ask if Jenny was free to leave also.

"Hell, yes," said Janda. "We've been telling her she can go for a while, but she seems happy to just sit around. Go ahead and take her."

Casey asked Jenny if he could give her a ride, and she nodded and began pulling on her coat right away, as if she had been waiting for him to ask. "Okay," she said. "Let's get out of this place."

| six |

*As soon as* Jenny got into Casey's Honda Accord she began to change the radio station. "Do you mind?" she asked. When he shook his head, she turned the volume up, even though the station she'd settled on was broadcasting a commercial.

He didn't know where she lived, and rather than give him a specific address, she provided the information on a need-to-know basis. "Down Arthur Ave. that way," she said, pointing east. "You'll be turning left after a while. I'll tell you when."

She kept her body clenched and narrow against the cold, sitting on the edge of the vinyl seat. Soon the heater kicked in and the radio commercials gave way to a song, but she continued to sit this way, as if enduring chronic pain.

She abruptly began speaking about one of the policemen, asking if Casey had noticed the way the cop spoke. "He sounded just like

Elmer Fudd. Seriously. Just like him. I thought he might have been kidding at first."

"What did they ask you? The cops?" Casey said.

Jenny raised her eyebrows and let the corners of her mouth droop—a facial shrug. "Probably the same things they asked you. Did I see what happened? How fast did it happen? Why didn't we do anything about it?"

"What'd you say?"

"I don't know. What did you say?"

Casey didn't answer, but took his eyes off the road to scowl at her.

Jenny acquiesced. "I said I didn't know why we didn't call the cops. Is that what you said?"

"I said it happened pretty fast," said Casey.

"Yeah. Wait—it didn't, though. It took a while, actually. But that's the same thing I said. I wonder why that is?"

She told him to turn left onto a street that was residential and dark. He knew they would be at her home soon, and he could feel her desire to leave his car. He could feel something like fear coming from her. He wondered if she now hated him for what he had done tonight. She seemed to him like a hitchhiker who has suddenly understood her error in accepting a ride from a stranger.

"You knew that boy, didn't you, Jenny?"

"What?"

"You knew the boy who got hurt. I could tell."

She turned to look at him now, tilting her head, tucking her legs under her. In other circumstances the gesture would have been coquettish, but now it confused him.

"Yeah, you're right. I knew him pretty well."

"How, then? He wasn't from Township, was he?"

In response she told him to take a sharp left, and then another left into what in a more affluent part of town would have been called a cul-de-sac.

"I just knew him. From parties, I guess. From friends. It's the one with the big black mailbox in front."

This was not the salient feature of the house, and he found it piti-ful that she chose to identify her home by the plain black mailbox that stood at the curb, and not by the other details that made it stand out. The most obvious was that it was the smallest, and set back farther than the others. Its size seemed at first to be a trick of perspective, but as he parked in front of the mailbox he saw that it was in fact half as big as its neighbors, which were all one-storied, boxy things with alu-minum siding and stocky driveways. Jenny's house had no driveway at all. He assumed that it must have been something other than a res-idence at some point—a storage facility, maybe even a garage. It was painted egg-yolk yellow, but even in the dark, even from a distance, Casey could tell that the paint job was poorly done. He wondered if Jenny had done it herself, in a moment of fiat, the way she dyed her hair.

"But if you knew him, Jenny . . ."

"If I knew him, what?"

"Couldn't we have done something about it?"

She looked at him harshly. "Couldn't we have done something about it? Jesus. *Yes*. Of *course*." Then she got out of the car and shuf-fled across the snow-laden lawn, making tracks like dark arteries toward the boxy house.

He knew this neighborhood, having grown up a half-mile away, and so he took a back route through this easternmost part of Breed's Township to his own apartment, which was near the center of town. Nearly all the homes were one-story, few of them more than four rooms, and many of them looked like trailer homes that had become settled permanently into the ground. They were coated in the lead-based paint that could be had at a discount. Most had screened-in side porches filled to brimming with the kind of junk, Casey noticed, that his own mother had held on to with the idea that it might someday re-claim its value: console televisions, exercise bicycles, obsolescent air conditioners—items saved as a genuflection to value, to the price that had once been attached to them.

The homes had all been built in the fifties, except for a few stone bungalows that had originally been hunting lodges. The builders had leveled trees and landscaped the ground to make way for this subdivision, the half-dozen square miles now known generally as East Breed's. The bordering forest to the northeast was dense and hilly, blending into a woodland that did not yield until it reached New York State. Unlike some of the dirt-faced villages to the north, Breed's Township had become large enough to create barriers between itself and the wild, a place civilized in the sense that its residents were not likely to worry about their dogs being attacked by badgers, civilized enough so that everyone in town now had access to cable television. But here on the outskirts, in the neighborhoods of the working poor, the lines could become blurred. The trees behind the houses that Casey now drove past were not the uniform oaks that lined most of Arthur and Keystone Avenues. The trees he saw in the darkness, hovering over the short houses, seemed feral and confrontational, the vanguard troops of a forest that wanted to infiltrate the township.

Some of these trees had launched a kind of first strike in December, during the ice storm. The storm had wrought havoc for a week, canceling school, murdering business at the restaurant. The streets had been vacant, the township as barren and still as it would be after a nuclear holocaust. Ice had turned Breed's Township into a fairy-tale city, a shining and treacherous and opulent place. The evenly spaced trees along Arthur Avenue had looked like gargantuan chandeliers, and the sunlight glistened on the rooftops during the daytime. The sky was green with the phosphorus emitted from broken power lines. At night people had stood on their porches and listened to the vicious cracking of tree limbs, sounds like shotgun blasts. The blackness of the nighttime had made them feel primitive; it was a blackness that had rarely been seen in their century. After the first day bemused deer had wandered into the township from the forest, assuming that the time of humans had come to an end.

They could expect to live with the damage, they had been told, well into the spring. Electrical power had returned to Weston and Leawood within two days of the last ice and to East Breed's within a week. But the phone system had been less resilient. Some homes, Casey knew, still didn't have phone service at all. Most of the people in East Breed's, in fact, had gotten cell phones; enterprising local dealers had offered storm-victim discounts. People who had not done this were the kind who held on to their disgruntlement as evidence of their mistreatment and their suffering.

Casey now stared southward at a great telephone pole that had refused to tumble in spite of the concentrated efforts of three large trees. One tree had been jolted out of the forest by the ice, and in its fall it had swiped at an oak in the side yard of a house at the corner of Newbury and Ridge, jostling that fat oak from its foundation. The oak had then tilted against a taller, narrower elm, and this elm had crashed into the telephone pole that stood at the intersection of streets. It did not seem possible to Casey that the pole could still stand, but there it was, bending near the top as if it were made of rubber. The branches of the dead elm were caught in its wire and metal, and so the tree slanted diagonally. The trunk of the oak touched the elm near the base, throwing its indirect weight into the job of pulling down the telephone pole. But the pole, festooned with the tangled mess of its wires, stood resolute among the branches. Workers had cut some tree limbs in preparation for the elm's removal, but it still leaned up against the stout pole like a drunk sleeping against a stranger on a bus. Because of this odd and, the phone company insisted, intractable arrangement, the phone service in the entire grid, including the phone service at O'Ruddy's, was sporadic.

Casey had been here before. After the storm, the phones had not worked at O'Ruddy's for five days, and Casey, in frustration and despair, had driven out to inspect the hobgoblin himself. He had accepted the phone company's excuses with a new patience once he'd seen it. He considered it a small miracle when, after a week, some kind of service was achieved, though the connections were indeed sporadic, and continued to be so. The phones had worked all day Wednesday, he recalled, and all morning Thursday, but they had been out for a block of several hours during that evening's dinner shift. Friday morning the service had come and gone, sometimes in the course of a single failed conversation. He'd been cut off from a supplier, he remembered, then reconnected, then cut off again. During the lunch cleanup a server who had finished her station early argued with her boyfriend on the phone at the server station. In the midst of his eavesdropping he had suddenly realized that the phone was working again, and he was glad for it, since sometimes people called for Friday night reservations.

This remembrance led to a revelation that made Casey stop his car at the intersection, step out into the night in spite of the brutal cold, and look intently at the tangled mess of the phone lines. With his eyes he followed the maze of wires, trying to find a split in them, a place where the rubber had cracked and exposed the magical guts that allowed people to talk to each other, but the casing seemed intact. He did not know the mechanics and could not really guess at them in a reasonable way. For whatever reason, the phone service to O'Ruddy's was sporadic because of the grotesque juxtaposition of the phone pole and the wild, dying trees. Because of this configuration, the service had been intermittent in the morning but functioning in the afternoon. And because he remembered this, he remembered also that Jenny, in the course of the brawl that in time sent a damaged boy to the hospital, had told him something of great significance.

It had been during his catatonic reverie, when he had been staring at the angry bodies and drifting on the stream of his consciousness, that he had become aware of Jenny speaking to him but had been unsure of what she said. He had told her immediately before that they needed to call the police. And he now remembered—lucidly, radiantly—that in response to this she had left her post at the window, walked over to the service station, picked up the receiver, and said to him in a stern and fearful voice, "Mr. Fielder, the phone's out again. We can't call the cops."

A wind kicked up, and even the weight of this memory—this ex-

culpation?—was not proof against it. He left off his staring and retreated into the car. But before he got in, he saw again the mass of
black and brown destruction from the corner of his eye, and the col-
lusion of wire and tree branches and telephone pole and snow looked
to him exactly like an enormous dead beast.

## seven

*Rachel did not like* to be woken up. Nor did she like to listen to Casey justify himself, nor did she like to fake sympathy. Casey understood, as he dropped the brass knocker of his girlfriend's house, that he was about to require her to do many things she did not like.

There was a chance that his story was significant enough for her to forgive the intrusion, but he didn't think it was likely. Waking her at two-fifteen in the morning might be the act she considered the most grievous of his evening's offenses. Shortly after their relationship had turned sexual, ten weeks ago, Rachel had established that Casey was not to come to her house after a Friday night shift, and tonight he had gotten away from the restaurant hours later than usual.

He was surprised that he wanted to see her so badly. Rachel would not offer him comfort; she never did. She would be disappointed in him, even ashamed of him, and she would not bother to hide it. But Casey needed to see her to gauge the value of what he had just remembered about Jenny and the phone line. If this was something important, something, as he suspected, that would clear him of a large measure of blame, then surely Rachel would know, and surely Rachel would tell him.

She was already awake. Having heard his footsteps, she opened the door before he had stopped knocking, and she waved him into the living room. "Come on," she said. "Come on, it's goddamn cold."

Rachel lived in the house she had grown up in, and though her parents had been dead for almost a decade, she had not changed it at all. It seemed very much the house of an upper-middle-class Breed's Township couple with one child and no mortgage. The two corpulent couches in the living room were beige and clean and complemented the carpet. The television hid discreetly inside a walnut cabinet; impressive hardback books lined the built-in shelves. There was a distinct feeling of disuse about the place, as if it were the house of some notable person that had been turned into a museum. When her parents' car had tumbled off a cliffside in Nova Scotia, Rachel had been at NYU, and she had stayed in the city for the next several years, returning to Breed's Township and her childhood home only the previous spring. She had been quick to tell him that her preservation of the house was not macabre. She simply hadn't had time to redecorate, but she planned to.

Since she was awake, he reasoned that she must know about the fight. Rachel valued sleep more than anyone he'd ever met, and if she was awake this late, it meant that someone had woken her up.

"Kim," she said. "Kim told me." Kim was a guidance counselor at Breed's Township High, where Rachel taught history. Kim was Rachel's best friend, although "best friend," as with everything regarding Rachel, was highly relative. Because of a previous career in marketing, Kim had been designated as the faculty member in charge of public relations for the school. Casey understood.

"The cops told her about it?"

"Yeah. She didn't know much, though. She didn't go down there. I guess you know that."

Rachel was dressed in sweatpants and a plaid work shirt, not the kind of clothes she usually wore to bed. He noticed a cup of tea on the coffee table, next to an open box of pretzels. He took this to mean that she had been up for a long time, talking on the phone to Kim about what her boyfriend had done, evaluating what this meant about their future. He was disappointed that he had not been able to wake her up. He wondered if he had come over just to do this, to show her that her rules were not absolute, that he could override them if he experienced something monumental enough.

"So, Casey," she said, sitting in a corner of the couch and gesturing for him to sit at the opposite end, "what happened?"

Rachel had secured her hair in a hasty ponytail, and the plaid shirt was large on her. She looked at him now with an overt expression of anticipation, as if he had promised to share a secret.

"It was a dark and stormy night," he said.

She frowned. "Are you going to tell me what happened?"

"I thought you already knew what happened. I'm sure Kim told you as much as I can."

"That can't be true. Kim didn't know anything. She said some of our kids fought some of the St. Brendan's kids at O'Ruddy's. She was actually calling to get more information—she thought I must have talked to you by now."

There was an accusation in this last part, though she said it in the same tone. A quiet voice, but never faltering. It was confident, purposeful, measured. It was severe. Casey often pitied her students.

"They just let me go a few minutes ago. I've been at the restaurant the whole time."

"You didn't even call me, though. I would have come to pick you up."

"No, you wouldn't have."

It was true enough, and they both knew it, but their relationship did not yet allow for this kind of honesty.

Rachel looked at him with rounded eyes, lips pursed.

"I wouldn't have?"

He didn't apologize, because now he felt like one of her students, and he knew that an apology would confirm this role. He would mumble it, avoid her stabbing eyes. She had that effect on him in these moments, the same quality that gave her authority with adolescents. So instead he sucked in air at the back of his mouth to indicate regret, the noise you make when you stub your toe.

"I don't think you know enough to say that kind of thing about me."

They had not been in a crisis together, so he did not know how she would respond, although he believed he had made an educated guess. He nodded his head to indicate shame and said, "Yeah, I know. Long day."

"It was a terrible fight, Kim said. She said a boy had been taken to the hospital."

Casey nodded. "He was the only one hurt. It looked like the thing was over. But it came down to just him and three other kids, and they held him up and one of them bashed him over the head with a rod. Like they were trying to kill him." He didn't see the scene during this brief narration. He saw only Rachel's drawn face, the pale inverted triangle of skin above where the flannel shirt parted, rising to her shoulders. He heard his words, felt the weight of them, but they projected no image into his mind. He was very much in the present.

"And the police weren't there yet?"

"No. They hadn't come yet."

"Jesus. You'd think, after last time . . ."

"They hadn't been called yet."

"What? What do you mean?"

Casey didn't answer.

"Why not? Why hadn't you called the cops?" There was an eagerness to her now—her feet were on the floor, her elbows on her knees, her hands clasped together. This pose, this greedy hunger, confirmed what Casey had suspected from the start: that she had known all along that he had not called the police. Kim had told her that much, at least. Rachel just wanted to hear him say it, she wanted to hear him justify himself.

He took a pretzel from the box on the coffee table and began crunching on it, certain that his mouth should be doing something.

"Why didn't you call them?" Her clinical voice, not accusatory, not even really curious, just robotic, absolute, the tone used by the clerk at the DMV who tells you that you have to go wait in a different line.

*Because the phones were dead. Jenny told me so.* Was this a lie? No, it had happened, he was certain of it—or at least the second part was true. Jenny had said this. As to whether this was the reason he hadn't called . . . he hoped that wasn't relevant.

"Rachel. I've spent the last hour and a half answering questions. And I lost my job. I know you're curious, but it's just been such a long night. I really don't want to be questioned anymore." He was laying it on thick, but he didn't think she could refuse him this small mercy. He wondered if she now regretted her decision to wear an old lover's flannel, if she suddenly saw these small experiments of hers as petty.

"Tell me why you lost your job and I'll leave you alone. I really don't think you should keep all this to yourself. Just tell me why the Howards fired you."

"Because I didn't call the cops, I think. Actually, I don't really know." He sat up from his slump. He didn't understand it, now that he'd put it into words. They hadn't really needed to fire him, since presumably the whole staff would lose their jobs as a matter of course. "The restaurant's closing. The insurance company won't carry us now that we've had two incidents, and especially since this one was . . ."

"What?"

"Tragic? Is that the word?"

Rachel raised an eyebrow, willing him to avoid digression.

"Is that accurate? Tragic? The kid's not dead. Does he have to die for it to be a tragedy?"

"Yes."

"I don't think that's right."

"You're getting distracted."

"Since this one was so serious, headquarters will shut the restaurant down. The margin of profitability was too narrow. They always told us that. One bad season, a scandal, a major health code violation—it's easier for them to punt."

She nodded and took her own pretzel, but kept her eyes on him to let him know that he wasn't finished.

"So I don't know why they fired me. Maybe they were just mad that I'd let it happen. Maybe they were trying to remove themselves from it. But it was over anyway. If I'd called the cops earlier, we would have had to file an incident report with headquarters, and that would have ended it. I couldn't really have done anything right, I don't think."

Now Rachel looked puzzled, and it wasn't an artificial expression. Her mouth hung open; her head was tilted back. "Huh," she said.

When he was with Rachel, Casey often felt like the subject in a psychology experiment, or like some Pygmy warrior under the observation of an anthropologist. She never hid the fact that she was studying him, that she carefully processed the minutiae he offered her, and she never, ever told him what she made of it. She might as well have been wearing a lab coat.

But she had shared secrets too. He remembered this now, as he sometimes did when he felt the least charitable toward her. He would remember what she had told him, how she had made herself vulnerable before him. If this confession of hers had been some kind of prepayment for the right to analyze him, the *quid* that she offered for his *quo*, then at least it had been an honest gesture, worth a measure of respect.

"All right, there's more. Something none of them know." He took hold of her hand and held on to it with both of his. She looked down at this gesture and scowled.

"Rachel, they all thought it was my fault. The main cop in particular. Everyone looked at me like I'd hit the kid myself." He wouldn't cry in front of her; this was a given. But his voice cracked, and she knew enough to nod along and lift her eyes in a comforting way, in imitation of someone who wanted him to feel better. She couldn't last long in this vein, however.

"Well, I've got to say I agree with them," she said. "You don't even see their point a little bit? That you had the power to stop this from happening and you didn't?"

"I'm getting to that, Rachel." He let go of her hand. "I watched it start. Jenny told me the kids were out there, and I went and watched them, and after a while they threw the first punches. And yes, I wanted it just to be over with. I guess I was hoping that they'd just rough each other up and get on their way. It was negative three degrees tonight, for God's sake! How could they stand it?"

"If they'd left, things would have been okay, is that what you're saying? No cops, no trouble with the insurance, you keep your job, yes?"

"Well, yes. Of course."

"So that's the mitigating evidence, that you were just trying to save your ass?"

"Let me finish. Okay. After it started for real, with all the kids going at it . . ." He didn't know how to approach this, and for the third time his words felt heavy. He didn't know which of the statements that followed would be true, and what he knew about Rachel—this, in fact, was what he feared most about Rachel—was that she could detect a lie from a thousand yards. He stopped with the setup and just said it. "At a certain point, I said I thought I should call the cops. Jenny went over to the phone, picked up the receiver, and told me the phone was out." This elicited no response, so he continued. "No service. Because of the ice storm. I've told you about that. The tree that crashed into a telephone pole. Sporadic phone service."

Still she did not respond, and he slouched lower on the couch, resting his hands on his middle. Finally she said, "So you couldn't have called the police, is that what you're saying?"

"Yes."

"And therefore you can't be to blame for it. Since you wouldn't have been able to get the cops even if you'd tried?"

"Yes."

"Hmm. Would you have called them if the phone had worked?" Before he could answer, she stood up and carried the box of pretzels into the kitchen.

He could not stand the coldness of her judgment now. She had shrugged off the mitigating evidence of the phone, pretending that to return the pretzels to the pantry was of more immediate concern, and with the rhetorical tone of the question she had implied that she knew the answer well enough. This was what it would be like when she eventually broke up with him, he thought: she would simply turn her back, express nothing but the fact that he no longer held her attention.

Perhaps the moment had come, he thought, to throw it back in her face. He had not judged her, after all, for her great crime, whereas she judged him more or less constantly. He hadn't even begun the process, hadn't even decided to what extent he disapproved of what she had done in New York. His response then and now had been a sort of admiration for the largeness of the deed, the chutzpah, along with gratitude for having been let in on the secret.

When Rachel had come back to Breed's Township, her hometown, in early May of the previous year, eating had become a problem. She hated fast food, and she hated to cook. She hated chain restaurants as well, but this seemed the least of the three evils, so she became a regular at O'Ruddy's that summer. She ate alone, at the bar, always reading. Casey got to know her because she went to him to complain about the food at least once a week. She would complain about the consistency of the au jus sauce, the breading on the onion rings, the density of the Gooey Guiltalicious Gateaux, and he responded the same way every time: *We make it according to specs from headquarters, miss, and that's not going to change.* And every time, a look of unutterable anxiety would appear on her face, a face that exceeded in loveliness that of any woman he'd been with (not that there had been many), so much so that he almost considered taking her into the kitchen and cooking for her himself, though the handbook of course forbade this kind of thing. Finally, more because he was at the end of his rope than with any romantic intent, he told her that the food wasn't going to change at O'Ruddy's and so maybe he should take her to a restaurant he knew about in Scranton that might satisfy her.

That she agreed had always puzzled him, almost as much as the fact that he'd asked her out in the first place. During their first dates, it did not seem to him that they'd hit it off in any obvious way, but she eventually developed the objective interest in him—in his goals, in his past, in his outlook—that he now recognized as their true bond. She had clearly never dated anyone like him before. For one thing, he was not blatantly attractive like she was. He could admit this. Not hideous, perhaps, but certainly not in Rachel's class. He had a high, wide forehead, which was rapidly annexing territory from his hairline. When he looked in a mirror, his skin seemed pasty, and his cheeks and eyes drooped. He was tall and thin, his body created by overwork and genetics, whereas hers was firm and lean from the classes she took at the gym. When meeting new people in the presence of Rachel, Casey was often given the benefit of the doubt; for a man who looked like that to get a girl like Rachel, everyone assumed, he must have a hell of a personality. Casey was aware that he frequently disappointed the expectations of these people.

But there was more that separated them, more that fascinated her. He was the manager of a chain restaurant, had gone to Breed's Township High, had grown up in East Breed's, wore clothes he bought at Marshall's. These things would have been out of her ken during her adolescence in the northwest section of the township, and had certainly become more foreign to her during her sojourn in New York. He was the kind of person she might have described to New York City friends when they asked her what the guys were like in northeastern Pennsylvania, and to actually date such a specimen must have seemed like a strange, brave experiment. *Why not?* she must have thought at first. It would have been part of the larger experiment that was her return to Breed's Township, a chapter in her life that she approached with quiet, amused caution, as if she were doing it on a dare.

Casey accepted this, all of this, even if he tried not to think about it much. She was a woman you did not give up, this much he knew. She had Mediterranean skin, thick black hair that he loved to smell and sift his hands through, and breasts that the boys in her classes could stare at for entire class periods without losing interest. She was bold, and sometimes she made him laugh, though her humor was usually caustic. The terms of their relationship were clear, and while this was unromantic, he appreciated the order of it. Rachel came with a sort of handbook of her own. He was not to wake her up. They were not to discuss her parents. He was not allowed to ask questions about her time in New York. After sex he was to return to his own apartment no later than eight the next morning. He was to take her out to a restaurant in Scranton at least once every two weeks. He was not to bore her with details from his job; he was not to ask any probing questions about hers. It was understood that any violation of the statutes could result in dismissal. The rules ensured that the relationship was entirely in her control, but Casey was fine with that. She so outclassed him in terms of attractiveness and sophistication, it would have been this way in any case. A man like him, he had decided early on, did not let go of a woman like Rachel.

To her credit, at times Rachel understood the necessity of tenderness, even if it didn't come very naturally to her. She knew that her appearance, and her New York City exoticism, and the prospect of regular sex, would not suffice indefinitely, and she might even have recognized that she owed him more. Toward this end, at irregular intervals, Rachel would become remarkably open with him. At times this meant violating one of her own rules and delivering a poignant monologue late into the night, perhaps over a shared bottle of merlot or a tub of Edy's, about the death of her parents, or her childhood. At times it meant sex in strange places, at unusual hours, or gifts given spontaneously. And one time it meant a secret, an opening of the vault of her past. He was not under any circumstances to repeat it to any-one, and he was to understand the trust in him that the sharing im-plied. Along with these spoken caveats came a tacit directive: Casey was not allowed to judge her for it.

Upon receiving her master's from NYU, Rachel had landed a job at James Ferguson High School in Manhattan. Being a first-year teacher, she was given a heavy load of lower-level classes: five sections of ninth-grade world history. She thus began her career.

She soon met with the frustrations of most beginning teachers: poor funding, inadequate disciplinary mechanisms, uninterested youth. The extent of this last problem astounded her. She had never, she confessed, given much thought to the fact that the students might not be very interested in what she had to say. At St. Theresa's, from which she graduated two years after Casey left Township, this hadn't been an issue for teachers, she said. Interest had somehow been com-pulsory. At Ferguson High, some of the kids had to be told to turn off their Walkmans as she lectured.

After two years the frustration became too much for her, and she developed a system of revenge, aimed not just at the students but also at the administration, which continued to stick her with the five stan-dard freshman sections. If she had to spend another year teaching fourteen-year-old idiots about the Ur Valley, she told Casey, she was going to melt. And so she began a program of misinformation.

It turned out to be quite a project, she told him. Lying is a difficult thing, and systematic, repeated lying is the most difficult kind. Not only did she have to draw up all new lesson plans, she had to keep careful notes in class, to make sure she didn't contradict herself in a future lecture. She had to develop a course packet rather than work from a textbook. And she had to make sure, in the thrill of it, that she didn't go overboard; they would catch on if history began to seem too exciting.

Casey hadn't really believed her at first, and when he asked for ev-idence, she had sat him on the couch and stood in front of the wall and delivered a typical lesson. Her performance had startled him. She proved to have a latent flair for drama, and he could not, in the end, doubt that what she showed him was very much what she'd performed for her students. She told him, earnestly and engagingly, about how the ancient Mesopotamians developed the assembly line. She explained that the pharaoh Clovis built the pyramids as a tribute to his favorite camel. She told the story of the invention of the sundial, which she credited to Alexander the Great, who was the son of Marco Polo and Cleopatra. Casey was intrigued by the overwhelming audacity of the plan, and by her confidence in the face of the danger. In his entire life he had never transgressed to this extent, and he had felt a kind of danger then, born of being in the presence of a woman who would even think of doing such a thing just to make a point.

"You've got to be kidding," he had said, and her shrug told him this was a pedestrian response, one she was used to.

"Nope. During our unit on classical civilizations, I switched everything about the Greeks and the Romans. Told them the great Greek playwrights were Augustus and Tiberius and that the Golden Age emperors were Sophocles and Aeschylus. I said that Greece invaded Gaul and Britain and that Rome fought against Troy."

"Some of them must have caught on."

"It's not that they couldn't have figured it out, it's that most of them weren't listening. So I could say whatever I wanted."

"What happened, then? How did it end?"

She became grave, and she could not hide a sense of pride. She was like a mad scientist revealing a plot to flood the world. "It ended because I got tired of it. I think I'd proved my point. It didn't matter what I was telling the kids. I could get up there and talk nonsense, tell them that the Hundred Years' War only lasted a week, or I could tell them the truth. In the end, the truth was easier, since the lesson plans and quizzes could come right from the teacher's edition."

Only toward the end of the story had Casey realized that she was not necessarily showing off, not telling an interesting anecdote but explaining the reason she had come back to Breed's Township.

"Finally I got caught," she said. "One of my former students, this brat named Lisa Lipton, went off to Tufts and took a freshman seminar in western civilization, and apparently the professor laughed at her when she said that Charlemagne discovered Greenland. She visited the principal during her next trip home. They started an investigation, and in the end I had to explain myself. Pretty ugly times."

"How the hell did you get a job at Township?"

She smiled, almost sweetly, the way she might have smiled at her credulous students. "Don't kid yourself about Township, Casey. What kind of teachers did you have when you were there?" The smile broke. "Actually, that's misleading. They would have hired me anyway, I think, but they didn't know. It was part of the deal with Ferguson. They were pretty embarrassed, and of course there could have been lawsuits, so they somehow managed to shut up Lisa Lipton, claimed I was overmedicated, I think, and told me they wouldn't mention it in my reference letters as long as I never taught in New York State again. So hello again, Breed's Township."

Perhaps they belonged together then, Casey thought, now that they had both played a part in damaging youths. He wondered what she would have said to this connection, if she would have thought he was missing the point. As she had taken pains to explain, she had committed her crime as an experiment, and she seemed to think this justified much. She had wanted to see what would happen. This was nowhere near the excuse Casey could provide. The one he'd made for himself, the exculpation offered by the mangled phone line and Jenny's emphatic words, didn't really explain anything, did it? This was what she would have said, so when she came back from stashing the pretzels he stood up to leave.

"You're going?"

"It's two-thirty. I could stay, I guess, but . . ." He didn't know why it seemed reasonable to leave. He'd slept over a number of times (fourteen so far—yes, he was counting) and the roads were icy. But he finished putting on his coat.

"Okay, you can go," she said. "But I want to hear more about this. I'm having lunch with Kim tomorrow, but I think she's told me most of what she knows."

He walked to the door, and she followed. She kissed him quickly on the lips. "Are they going to arrest you?"

"Why would you say that?"

"Jesus, Casey. Snap out of it. Seriously."

He shook his head at her response and opened the door. She flinched against the cold burst. "No, Rachel. Tell me. Why would you ask me that? Why would you think they would arrest me?"

She squinted at him and tilted her head, like a sheepdog that has heard a strange noise. "Because you're guilty," she said.

# PART TWO

# february

If any man is able to convince me and show me that I do not think or act right, I will gladly change; for I seek the truth by which no man was ever injured. But he is injured who abides in his error and his ignorance.

—MARCUS AURELIUS, *MEDITATIONS, BOOK VI*

# eight

*Every schoolday* since Colin's injury, prayers for his recovery had been read over the St. Brendan's PA system, along with the morning announcements and the Our Father. The school had not yet held a formal ceremony to recognize Colin's debilitation, but Lea knew the brothers were getting antsy. It was not their habit to let momentous events pass unnoticed. In the past week, Brother Carl had left four messages on the answering machine, and finally, on the Friday that marked the two-week anniversary of the fight at O'Ruddy's, he caught her at home.

"I don't mean—that is, it's not my intention, Mrs. Chase, to ask questions that should not be asked," he said. "That is, I don't mean to pry into your personal business."

"Uh-huh," said Lea. She knew she had to give Brother Carl room to ramble and prevaricate; eventually he would come out with it.

"Well. Well. Frankly, I have heard any number of rumors in the halls. And if I'm hearing them, you can be sure the boys are hearing them. I quash these rumors when I can, but I must admit I'm at a loss to answer the boys when they ask me about Colin directly. I am at a loss as to what your poor son is going through. What you and Mr. Chase must be suffering. 'And hope does not disappoint us,' says Paul. Indeed. And yet Paul may be talking about a different kind of hope from the one we would like. He may be talking about a better kind of hope, difficult as that can be to hear. Do you see what I mean?"

"Are you asking if Colin's going to die?"

When he spoke again, after a few moments, his voice had deepened. "Mrs. Chase. You've always been frank with me, and I can see now what a great gift God has given you in that. It is akin to the gift of fortitude, since the most difficult things to wrestle with are often our words."

"Uh-huh. Thank you, Brother Carl."

"We simply want to know what to do. We would like to hold a service in which we petition the Lord for Colin's recovery. It has been brought up here, though, by those who have also heard rumors, maybe more rumors than I've heard, that . . . How should I put this? I seem to be having trouble speaking today, Mrs. Chase. I apologize."

"Just take your time, Brother Carl. What are you asking?"

"I suppose I'm asking, of what nature should our petitions to the Lord be?"

"Of the nature that I don't know if he's going to die or not."

Brother Carl breathed into the phone. She spoke again before he could. "Geoffrey says that Colin's stable. He thinks he'll stay that way. But he's having another surgery soon, and there's always a risk. According to Geoffrey and the doctors. I've talked to a lot of doctors."

"Praise God that there is reason to be optimistic."

"Yes, praise God." Brother Carl's religiosity didn't bother her, but it didn't comfort her either. It was just another tic of his, like his circuitous way of talking. "I think a service would be fine, brother."

"You mentioned a surgery. Would it be all right, then, for us to wait until the day before the surgery? It would seem an appropriate time to ask for blessings."

"Yes, Brother Carl. He'll certainly need blessings right about then."

The preparations were baroque. The brothers actually asked Lea and Geoffrey to come in for a rehearsal the day before the service, as they were to light the first candles in a specific way and to sit in a re-served spot in the front pew. They complied, victims of a sort of numbness that Lea hoped would break once Colin left the hospital. She had surprised herself by agreeing to the service in the first place; she had never liked attention, let alone pity, and at St. Brendan's she was certain to become a lightning rod for condolence. She had granted her agreement because Brother Carl, with backup from God and Saint Paul, was too formidable to resist.

They held the service the following Wednesday, in the main chapel, a gray Gothic thing that clashed with the rest of the St. Bren-dan's campus (most of the alums had made their money, and their do-nations, during the postmodernist period). It would be an open service; the school had even published a notice in the *Beacon*. Brother Carl had encouraged Lea to invite her family and friends. Geoffrey had told people at his practice, or someone had spread the word for him.

As they walked through the parking lot to the chapel, Lea clutched at Geoffrey and he clutched at her. They kept their heads down because they did not want to talk to anyone yet. When they reached the great iron-hinged door of the chapel, Lea looked back to the parking lot and saw two young nurses from Geoffrey's office shuf-fling to keep purchase on the ice. The black hems of their dresses flapped beneath heavy coats. Lea realized that she too was wearing black, and that Geoffrey wore a suit of midnight blue. She then un-derstood what was so familiar about this scene, and why she had clutched at Geoffrey so meekly, and why it was an open service, when usually St. Brendan's was so wary of outsiders as to appear paranoid: in spite of Brother Carl's talk of hoping and petitioning, in spite of the confident prognoses of the doctors, this was a funeral, Colin's funeral, and everyone seemed to know it.

They performed the candle lighting competently enough, and Brother Carl smiled down at them proudly. A range of boys—representing, according to the program, the diversity of the St. Brendan's community—read petitions to the Lord. One boy read in Spanish, a black student said the Hail Mary, a teammate of Colin's read St. Sebastian's prayer for athletes. There were more than a dozen readings in all. Two of the boys were scholarship students, probably from East Breed's Township.

The service, she was surprised to learn, moved her, almost as much as it did Geoffrey. He had always been more susceptible to religious comfort than she, though as a family they had abandoned mass shortly after Colin's first communion. Throughout the petitions Geoffrey cried quietly, his hands cupping his mouth and nose. Lea's arms were wrapped across her chest, and she connected herself to him by rubbing the fabric of his sleeve between her fingers.

She had not planned to take comfort in any of this, but the music, the darkened hall, the sight of the mourning brothers—so austere, so competent at grieving—affected her while she wasn't noticing. By the end of the third petition she was crying too, exactly as Geoffrey was, in dignified placidity. It was not a mass but a prayer service, and so the momentum was not broken by the bothersome mechanics of distributing wafers. They all just prayed and listened, and she felt a warmth, the kind she remembered descending upon her during her first throes of religious belief in a Scranton Sunday school, where faith was associated with doughnuts and pink dresses.

By the end of the service, however, she had noted a conspicuous ambiguity in Brother Carl's speech. He had not said anything about Colin's soul, the way he might have if the boy had died, and Paul's words of hope were not invoked. Brother Carl spoke more about the people in the room, about the necessity for everyone to carry on— words that at a real funeral would have been bookends for memories of the deceased. Here at Colin's service, there was little talk of his life.

Perhaps they couldn't think of anything nice to say about what he'd been like, Lea thought at first. But then she realized that they avoided eulogizing his life because it was not technically over, that this homily had been more difficult for Brother Carl than a funeral mass would have been. The only comfort available when a boy is lost—that his soul is in a better place—could not be offered, not in any theology. The body remained, and so whatever Colin had been, whatever part of him Lea had loved, was gone forever. Even Brother Carl could not tell her otherwise. She realized this during the benediction, and then it was time to mingle in the foyer.

"You dear thing." Lea would hear this said innumerable times before the event was finished, but this one startled her. She didn't think she had signaled her readiness to be approached yet. It came from Margot Miller, the mother of the football co-captain. She and Lea had organized last year's team banquet. Margot's husband pulled Geoffrey away with a handshake and a shoulder squeeze. Throughout the evening, Lea would notice how instinctively those offering condolences segregated themselves by gender.

"Graceful, always graceful. Look at you. I'd be such a wreck."

"I feel like a wreck. Really, I do."

"But you're *handling* it. Anyone can see that. You're just so strong. Tell me, though, Lea—what can I do? Just give me something to do."

Lea knew that Margot meant it, that she wanted to show her sympathy through action; she probably felt as keenly as Lea did how inadequate *You dear thing* had been. In December, Margot had done most of the work for the football banquet, and Lea suspected she was responsible for the table of cheese squares and crudités that were now in the center of the foyer. She might have farmed out the coffee to the brothers, but Margot wouldn't have let them do the food.

"I'm not sure what there is to be done, Margot."

Margot scanned for eavesdroppers, then leaned forward. "What did you think about what he said up there?"

When Lea didn't say anything, Margot continued, scanning the room more thoroughly and leaning in even closer. "I tell you, after four years, I'm just about up to here listening to speeches about social justice. It's all fine and good, to an extent, of course. I know those service hours at the clinic did a world of good for Nolan." Now her voice dropped another level in volume, and another octave. "But after something like that happens to one of our boys?" She stressed the word *our* and squinted as she did it, as if Lea might contradict her taking such ownership of Colin. Margot shook her head with deliberation. "That's where my compassion for the wretched refuse stops."

They were joined by two more mothers, and so Lea did not have to worry about fashioning a response. It had taken her some time to understand Margot's reference to the service, and only gradually did she remember that Brother Carl had spent a large part of the homily dwelling on his traditional themes of compassion for the less fortunate, justice for the oppressed. At the time she hadn't thought much of it, but she could understand Margot's interpretation: she thought Brother Carl had been warning them against taking the incident as a chance to vilify East Breed's. It certainly might have been his motive. Though the brothers seemed to encourage their charges to be as hard on themselves as possible, they also drilled into the boys the importance of compassion and charity, and now the oppressed had turned on them with violence. The homily might have been damage control, and as Margot implied, to counsel mercy and forgiveness for the children of Breed's Township High School might have been inappropriate under the circumstances.

Lea didn't entirely believe Margot's vitriol, though. They'd known each other since the boys played Pop Warner, and Margot had never before said anything that smacked of elitism. She had, in fact, always seemed squeamish about her wealth, and Colin had once grumbled that Nolan's parents were making him do extra service hours at an East Breed's clinic for the good of his character (the implication had been clear: it wasn't going to fly if the Chases tried it with him). Lea decided that Margot had just been making an awkward gesture of sympathy. As a clumsy way to express her grief, Margot had spewed anger. It was almost thoughtful of her.

Another hour passed before Lea encountered this theme again. The St. Brendan's community danced around the issue with practiced facility. Many of the Breed's Township wealthy had earned their money, as Geoffrey had, via student loans and graduate school, and viewed the East Breed's unfortunates with a kind of there-but-for-the-grace-of-God sympathy. Leawood and Weston voted Republican, but their motives in doing so were financial. Polls showed that West Breed's Township considered itself socially liberal, and Nolan's parents were not the only ones who dropped their boys off in East Breed's to pad their service hours. The fight at O'Ruddy's threatened the balance they had achieved between respecting the poor of the township and not having to deal with them much. No one wanted to think about what might have happened if Colin's assailants had been black.

The most common questions at the postservice gathering were medical. For the first hour Geoffrey held a kind of open lecture by the coffee table, surrounded by a mass of husbands, and quietly explained the specifics of the brain injury. If anyone asked about the diagnosis, Lea motioned toward his cluster and said, "The doctor is in—go ask Geoff." With Lea people discussed the loveliness of the service, asked if they could leave casseroles on her porch. But an hour into the gathering, one of the husbands returned to the subject Margot had obliquely broached, and an awkward moment threatened.

The husband was Steve Deane, who had been a great athlete at Breed's Township High back when East Breed's hadn't been quite as poor as it was now, or at least when the poverty had been associated with the dignity of hard work, because the mines were still open. Since he had been something of a celebrity, and since he had risen above his economic class (he owned a car dealership) on some occasions he granted himself the prerogative of waxing intolerant. He was stationed beside the buffet table, facing Lea, and his voice was rich enough to allow, even invite, the eavesdropping of a half-dozen others.

"I don't know how you can stand it. Good God, this would tip me over the edge. If some white-trash punks decided to have a go at my boy . . . For what? Because he dresses nice? They hate us, Lea. That's all there is to it. They hate us 'cause we have what they want. Don't shush me." He turned to his wife, who had not made a sound but who was indeed trying to shush him with her expression. "You feel the same way I do about it. They all do, I bet." He waved his orange juice around to indicate the crowd, and almost elbowed an eavesdropper as he did so. "But no one wants to say it. We're afraid of these people, Lea." He dipped his meaty head lower so she wouldn't have to look up at him. He seemed composed, persuasive. Lea understood why people bought cars from him. "Been afraid of them since the day we stopped being like them. Your husband knows what I'm talking about. And now we're afraid of their kids. Maybe we've got a right to be, after what happened. But no one wants to say it. And these people"—he waved his drink around again, like a drunk at a wedding—"these sallies, they keep equating anger with bigotry . . ." He trailed off, uncertain where his sentence was going. "They tell the cops to take it easy on the Township kids, because they don't want anyone stripped of their rights just because of where they live. They worry that if anyone says anything harsh about the people who broke your son's head, then we'll all look like oppressors. Quite a way to think. The result will be, next time some Township punks don't like the clothes my boy wears or the car he drives, well, maybe they'll beat the crap out of him. 'Cause what are his parents going to do? Throw together some committee on East Breed's awareness, that's what."

Lea hadn't thought of it in those terms, though she supposed it was natural for other parents to do so. It required selfish thinking to view Colin's injury and their community's response to it as something that poor, violent kids might take a lesson from, as if this were just a test case, a crime perpetrated so that they might gauge the reaction of the rich folks.

Steve hadn't exactly caused a scene. The others knew what to expect from him, and while some shot Lea a rolled-eyed glance of vicarious embarrassment (his monologue had attracted almost as large a crowd as Geoffrey's), no one chided him. The subject was changed, and then he grew silent, pouting. He escaped censure because of the very crisis in courage that he railed against. The others wouldn't rebuke Steve for his prejudice only because he was from East Breed's. To criticize his small-mindedness might imply a general criticism of that community as a whole and imply that he should have stayed with his kind, that his ignorance and provincialism were not welcome at St. Brendan's. Ever since he had broken his knee and lost his scholarship at Penn State, Steve had benefited from playing up his working-class small-mindedness, which was interpreted by his new social class as something genuine. When Steve sold someone a car, he might try to break the ice by telling a racist joke, but at least this was genuine East Breed's racism, Herrenvolk democracy bred into him by a black-lunged daddy.

Lea was interested more in the specifics of his speech than in the tone. She wanted to hear more about the police being told to take it easy on the Township kids, more about the general pose of weakness that Steve accused the community of adopting. She had read the editorials, one in the *Beacon*, one in the *Scranton Times*, both of which viewed the fight as symbolic, even archetypal, and used the opportunity to warn readers against class anger. Similar viewpoints were expressed in the follow-up letters to the editor and on a radio news program out of Scranton. She had begun to wonder if the argument weren't something of a straw man: everyone in the media, everyone at St. Brendan's, pleaded for understanding, tolerance, dialogue, social justice. Who exactly were they arguing against? Who but Steve Deane seemed angry at East Breed's for doing this to Colin? Lea and Geoffrey weren't screaming for the heads of the Township boys. And the police, whether they had in fact been asked to exercise caution, had told her that at this point capturing the assailants was unlikely.

The detectives seemed much better at keeping her apprised of their progress than at actually making any. She had achieved a first-name basis with Pat Janda, the primary investigator in the case; during the first week he had called her almost daily to say they had not turned up any leads. On the Monday after the fight, he and his support team had gone to Breed's Township High and interrogated over two dozen kids, hauling in any student with so much as a scratch on his face. The principal of the school, who must have been as anxious about the implications of the fight as Brother Carl was, had sworn justice for Colin Chase. During the first week he had conducted an investigation of his own, based on hunches and experience and his power to hand out suspensions, until he punished a boy who had gotten a black eye while building a fence with his father. After the father threatened legal action in a letter to the superintendent, the principal summarily ended his prosecution of justice. Pat Janda had not called in several days, and the reporters had not called since Lea told them her boy would live.

The Jesuit brothers of St. Brendan's had taken a different approach. Though they too had interviewed the walking wounded on the Monday after the fight, and though three of the most obviously battered boys were handed over to Pat Janda for further questioning, they learned nothing of significance and didn't seem to expect to. In the morning announcements, in the conferences with parents, in the bimonthly newsletter, the brothers said nothing about retribution, punishment, or culpability but instead insisted that they would use the terrible crime as an opportunity to reach out. This position had been neatly codified in Brother Carl's homily, though Lea had not realized it until speaking with Margot.

The first initiative had been the ad hoc committee on East Breed's awareness, which Steve had scoffed at toward the end of his screed. The committee was put together by Brother Nick, the campus youth minister and the only St. Brendan's brother under forty, and a woman named Janet Gross. A week after the fight, they invited Lea to join the committee as a founding member, and when she declined they sent her a copy of the minutes of their first meeting, at which they developed a mission statement. Every sentence in it, she now remembered, would have thrown Steve Deane into another tizzy of upper-middle-class frustration. In fact, she remembered being a bit exasperated by the thing herself, though much of it was clearly designed to placate what they imagined must be her intense hatred of the East Breed's community. The mission statement, she remembered, had reveled in mixing its metaphors—there had been something to do with bridging the gaps between the two parts of the township, and in the same sentence a reference to the fact that Arthur Avenue acted as a wall between two communities. She thought of this now, remembered the phrasing accurately, because Brother Nick was approaching.

Well, she thought, was it a gap or a wall? It had been a composition mistake, she knew, but the question began to appeal to her, even to take on some profundity. *Is there something separating us,* she wondered, *or is it just that there's nothing between us?* It didn't seem to matter much in the end. Gap or wall began to fade in her thoughts when she thought about Colin's injury, as did the entire notion of the violent posse of East Breed's teenagers. She supposed that Colin had done something to bring it on himself, and so she had never achieved the hatred of East Breed's that the brothers must have presumed her to have, that Steve was nudging her toward.

Brother Nick had waited to approach her until the crowd had thinned, until those who remained judged themselves important enough either to the Chases or to St. Brendan's to engage in the silent battle, often waged between these mothers, over who would be the one to exhibit the most compassion by staying the longest. Brother Nick told Lea that Geoffrey had apprised him of Colin's status and that he was pleased to hear hopeful news. His eyebrows, always arched, were bushy and black, and his cheeks were spotted with moles. His body was lumpy, and he was about the same height as Lea. It was easy, if ungenerous, to assume that he had taken the vow of celibacy with a sort of shrug of the shoulders. "I'll pray for him tonight, of course, and tomorrow," he said to Lea. "Colin was always a strong boy, and I'm sure the Lord won't take that gift from him now."

"We do appreciate it, brother," said Geoffrey, who sidled up to them suddenly. He had abandoned his post by the coffee, having been energized by the conversation and the caffeine. Lea wondered if he didn't trust her to speak to priests by herself today.

Brother Nick turned to Lea formally, shifting his entire body. For a moment it seemed he might bow. "We understand your not wishing to join the committee, Mrs. Chase. Really we do. I only hope . . . I only hope that you can see we want to do God's work."

"That's your business, brother. I'm fine with it, really. I'd just rather not be involved."

Geoffrey was embarrassed. He grasped her arm behind the elbow. "If something good comes out of this, brother, then of course we'll be thrilled. It's just that we're so tired, and really, I think neither of us can get involved in committees and such."

Brother Nick closed his eyes and nodded his head once, apparently to indicate the wisdom of Geoffrey's words. "We'll keep you abreast of our activities, if you don't mind. We've been planning a few events that might get groups together from both the high schools, though the logistics are difficult. We can't assume the boys from Breed's Township High School will have transportation, and the school's funds are stretched as it is."

For an awful moment Lea wondered if Brother Nick was hitting them up for a donation, and even Geoffrey assumed the startled look that came upon him whenever he sensed someone was about to ask him for money. Fortunately, they had misread his words, or Brother Nick had gotten the hint.

"We will find a way, of course. It's too important a cause. The boys need to meet with their counterparts in other communities—they must come to see them as peers, not as adversaries. I sometimes wonder"—here he leaned forward—"if we do our boys a disservice by sending them to East Breed's only for volunteer work, never for play or sport. I fear they come to see it as a place they should pity, and those whom we pity we often view as our inferiors."

"Well, that's true enough. I've learned that the hard way," said Lea, though she soon regretted it, for Geoffrey's sake. Brother Nick raised his bushy eyebrows even higher and opened his mouth. He would have begun to apologize, Lea knew. He would probably have explained the difference between pitying the poor and expressing condolence to the grieving, but Geoffrey, overcaffeinated, sensitive to Lea's capacity for embarrassing him, and naturally deferential to priests, began to babble.

"You know, I come from East Breed's myself, as it happens, brother, and I think you hit it, absolutely. Those boys should get together more with our boys, there's no question about that, I think . . ." Lea walked away, spurring Geoffrey into even more discomfited rambling, and she hurried her pace to get out of earshot.

On the drive home they held hands, but they did not speak. They would not go to the hospital tonight, because they would be there all day tomorrow, while Colin was operated on, and all night as they watched him sleep. His head would be swaddled in white bandages. His tongue would loll in his mouth. Lea and Geoffrey would slouch in the stiff chairs of his private room, drink lots of coffee, eat very little, make quiet phone calls to relatives and friends.

| nine |

*Casey had not* been unemployed for this long since he was thirteen years old. During his last free summer, in 1982, he had spent the time riding his bike on the dirt mounds that remained from a defunct construction project behind the middle school. Every morning he rode over the mounds with Chris Craig and another boy, whom Casey remembered only by the synecdoche of his bike, a yellow Huffy with blue tires. Every once in a while a janitor from the middle school would come and chase them off. Chris somehow had access to fireworks, and in the afternoons they would crouch behind one of the mounds, like soldiers waiting in ambush, and toss lit M-80s at the crows on the telephone wires. It passed the time. The next summer Casey got a job at LuLu's Ice Cream House, and his longest vacation since then had begun when he left the township to begin his freshman year at Penn State and had ended six days later, when he saw that Red Lobster was hiring waiters.

It had been four weeks now. Before this had happened, Casey would not have thought that he could last so long. He would have assumed that four weeks of this boredom and despair would certainly drive him to some kind of psychosis. But he was holding up. During the first week, after shaking off the stupefaction and gritting his teeth through the withdrawals (he had been at O'Ruddy's for eight years; it was nothing if not an addiction), he had decided to make rules. On a sheet of legal paper that he taped to his desk, he codified his behavior during unemployment. No sleeping past eight-thirty, no matter how late he'd been up. No television before seven o'clock at night. No tangible acts of self-pity. No purchases of more than twenty dollars on the credit card. No talking to Rachel more than once a day. He had not forgotten the verdict she'd given him that Friday night, or the casual, indifferent way she'd delivered it. Talking to a person who was so certain of his culpability would not be helpful during this time, no matter what she looked like. He didn't want her out of his life, but neither did he want her too actively involved in it. She didn't seem to mind, or to notice.

The last rule was an injunction against rereading the articles. The papers had called early that Saturday—the *Township Beacon*, the *Scranton Times*, even the *Philadelphia Inquirer* (although it ended up not running the story). He had given generic comments, mostly along the lines of "It happened very fast." Casey had told only one of the reporters about the downed phone line, and he spoke about it cautiously, almost as a postscript, and the article mentioned nothing about the phone. The fight was the lead story of the Sunday *Beacon*, of course, and reached the front of the metro section of the *Times*. Casey had saved these papers, and the three or four follow-up articles, almost without thinking. The articles had his name in them, and he had some instinct to keep them.

But he told himself not to read them again. The journalists had not been there. They had taken their story primarily from the police report. Jenny had apparently been incommunicado, and the curly-haired couple was not mentioned at all. The articles were for the most part factual, almost boring after the shocking promise of the leads. What followed were times, precedents, hedged promises from the police to apprehend the violators, speculations from locals. The papers quickly and lazily grabbed on to the rich-versus-poor theme. It may have saved Casey, to some extent, and at first he read this hungrily, grateful that the large drama of class warfare had supplanted the less grandiose story of a neglectful manager. Because no one seemed to know who had called 911, the final two paragraphs used the passive verb: "Paramedics were summoned at approximately eleven-twenty, and Chase was taken to Mercy Hospital." Nothing about the delay, nothing about what might have been done to prevent it.

Those came later, after the furious presentation of the facts on Sunday. Monday morning, the *Beacon* ran a short article below the fold on the front page that began to explore the matter of liability. *Fingers pointed at manager for O'Ruddy's rumble.* The article quoted a source inside the police department, certainly Janda: "It might not have turned out the way it did if the manager of the restaurant had called us sooner." Casey was identified as the manager on shift. It was revealed that the eventual call came from an unnamed couple, the only remaining customers. Again Jenny had not been available for comment.

On Tuesday an editor at the *Times* used the O'Ruddy's incident as a springboard for a polemic in the opinion section about the general indifference of bystanders in today's society. He referred to a certain clause in the Good Samaritan law in Minnesota, which went beyond the usual Good Samaritan statutes and declared that spectators who did not act in an ethical manner could be held liable for the crime itself. The editor defended the law and implied that it might be applicable to someone like Casey. The headline was "Standing Idly By."

Casey surprised himself by feeling a twinge of hope when he read the editorial. He recognized that he had been entirely blamed, held up as an exemplar of moral failure. He even thought that the writer's logic seemed in place, that his argument was basically the one Rachel seemed to endorse; and yet there was hope in it. The writer referred to the Minnesota statute as if it were some new thing Pennsylvania should think about enacting. This meant that the state didn't have anything like this yet, that Janda's threats about criminal negligence may have been hollow. Casey didn't live in Minnesota. The police still hadn't contacted him, and it was Tuesday.

He could not help but think this way, though he knew that it would have been interpreted by anyone with access to his thoughts as the cold-heartedness and the cowardice that had got him into the mess in the first place. But he thought the way he thought, and he could not apologize for it. He did not rethink that evening; he did not look deeply into himself to ask what he should have done differently. There were no answers there, no answers anywhere. The way to run the restaurant was spelled out in the handbook, and a crisis that was not addressed by the headquarters could not be put on his shoulders. He closed his eyes to the harsh reasoning, the castigation of the newspapers. They didn't understand, it was as simple as that, and beside all this, beside all the sanctimony and Ethics 101 questions and pop psychology, was the largest fact of them all: they didn't know about the phone line. They didn't know that he couldn't have called the police even if he had meant to.

He waited them out. He did not answer any more questions from newspapers, and by Friday, the one-week anniversary of the fight, the matter had mostly dissipated in the press. The *Township Beacon* brought up the matter only once more, two weeks after the fight, when it announced that an open prayer service for Colin Chase would be held at St. Brendan's Chapel and that Colin had suffered severe brain damage.

Casey read that article. He wished it had not happened to the boy. That was as far as he would allow his thoughts to investigate the matter, and he did not need to include this injunction on the yellow sheet taped to his desk.

After this, the first order of business was clear. He needed to find a job.

During the second week he had begun mailing out résumés. There were, by the phone book's reckoning, twelve restaurants in Breed's Township (not counting O'Ruddy's), but three of these were Chinese, six fast food, and one was of the sort that he thought of simply as "fancy," the place where high school kids went on prom night. Only two were chain restaurants, his particular niche, and so these were the only local places to which he applied.

The other résumés he sent to Scranton and Wilkes-Barre, which had more chain restaurants than he knew about. He didn't want to make that commute, but he knew that if he had nothing after a few weeks, he'd be happy to get an interview in Trenton. At one point during his search he wondered how he had become so overspecialized, for he literally did not consider applying to any restaurant that was not a franchise of a chain. He assumed he had the skills needed to manage a fast food restaurant, but he dismissed the idea out of hand.

Casey had determined long ago that he would pass his career working in restaurants of a specific genre. He had already worked in a few of them, though he'd spent the last eight years at O'Ruddy's. The others had similarly jaunty names that had been invented in boardrooms: J. D. Krutzenwaller's, the Purple Pickle, Frank P. Dott's. It was the prefabrication, the calculation of these places that gave Casey comfort. He liked the fact that they were all alike. It had struck him on his first visit to a different O'Ruddy's, the one in Baltimore, how entirely the conglomerate believed in the value of conformity. Virtually everything in the restaurant he visited was the same as in the one back home, including the wall decor, which was meant to have a haphazard, everything-but-the-kitchen-sink look to it (in fact, as a tongue-in-cheek reference to the cliché, there actually was a kitchen sink attached to the wall, high above table sixteen). In Baltimore he had found the same ersatz paraphernalia, which was designed to look like some folksy restaurateur had ransacked his attic to decorate the place, although most of the objects were produced in a Hackensack factory. The Baltimore O'Ruddy's had the yellowed map of County Cork, the mangled trombone, the taxidermied brown trout, the photograph of Michael Collins, all identical to the ones he had left in Pennsylvania, and all were similarly arranged. He knew it sometimes disappointed people to learn this, but he thought it was a brilliant thing, and it spoke to everything that he loved about working for the corporation. It indicated to Casey that headquarters believed in a rigidly literal adherence to the rules, the same insistence on conformity that he found in the management handbook, in the guidelines for employee conduct, in the food preparation manuals. It meant he did not have to improvise and did not have to tolerate improvisation among the cooks and servers. If he was supposed to do it, it would be in the handbook.

He granted now that his faith in this system may have been absurd, given what had happened. But he knew there had been a reason for his devotion to it, that it had come from necessity. A restaurant, he had come to learn, was something that needed to be tamed, mastered. Arbitrary rules and implementation, even regarding the trivial, would give the restaurant space for mutiny. What had happened to him had been caused by this, by the intervention of the Howards, who didn't really care what headquarters had to say and who had never even read the handbook. They trusted their instincts too much. This is what happened, Casey believed, when you had to improvise, when you were asked to act without guidance. His task now was to find another place to take him in, to offer him this shelter.

Nothing came of his first round of résumés. He spent another week in silence, adhering to the set of rules taped to the desk. The yellow paper, the firmness of the dictates, provided makeshift comfort. Often at six-thirty he would sit at the desk and alternate between glaring at the desk clock and glaring at the rules. When the second hand swept past seven o'clock, he would turn on the television, not because he wanted to see anything but because it reinforced his adherence to the code he had laid out.

As dictated by the rules, he talked to Rachel once a day, sometimes not that often. Unlike the newspapers, Rachel had been unwilling to let the matter of Friday night drop. Also unlike the newspapers, she kept her opinions to herself, as if she recognized the inappropriateness of her early judgment. He knew that she hadn't revised her opinion of what he had or had not done, but she didn't speak of Friday night in those terms anymore.

Instead she kept him abreast of the investigation, which she was particularly close to, given the effect it had had on the school. The administration of Breed's Township High had reacted strongly. On the Monday after the fight, any male student who showed up with a facial bruise or cut had been suspended indefinitely. The punishment was applied to five students, until the parents of a falsely accused boy threatened a lawsuit. Sergeant Janda had spent many hours at the school but apparently wasn't getting very far. The word around the teachers' lounge was that the investigation was losing steam, mostly because not one of the battered kids had admitted to anything, in spite of threats of expulsion and criminal charges. "It's not like they have anything to lose," Rachel had said. "These aren't the kind of kids who will get much out of a high school diploma anyway, and loyalty is an important thing to them." She was clearly impressed by their distorted sense of integrity. Self-sacrifice had likely been in short supply at the school on the Upper West Side.

After four weeks, on a sleeting day when the sun seemed to have set by noon, he ripped the yellow sheet off his desk. The very simplicity of the list, the six unforgiving commandments, had become an unbearable check on his behavior. On some days it was impossible not to watch television before seven, and on others it was strangely impossible not to call Rachel two or three times a night. On most days it was impossible for him not to return to the articles, to examine every word for any kind of subtext that might have lessened his culpability. This was often how he spent his mornings.

As the Howards had promised, his last check had arrived about two weeks after his firing. After the third week the problem of money had begun to appear as a distant cloud, and he found that he approached the problem theoretically; he could not anticipate how the impending poverty would affect his life. Or, more to the point, he could not remember. He and his mother had been poor enough to qualify for food stamps every other year or so, but that had been long ago. As soon as he had been able to work legally, he had. As long as Casey had been in control of where his money came from and how much of it he earned, he had not thought again about poverty. By the age of fourteen he'd been buying his own school supplies, his own birthday presents.

Money, in the end, had been why he'd dropped out of Penn State. He felt too keenly the idleness of the lifestyle. Since his first stint at LuLu's, he had reckoned his time in terms of dollars. If he could spend his hours making money, he might as well do it. In high school, a Sunday spent watching the Eagles game equaled a net loss of about thirteen dollars, his wages for three hours after taxes at LuLu's. In college, he could only consider five hours spent studying the Holy Roman Empire as an exercise in fiscal irresponsibility: if he hadn't needed to pass the Western Civ test, he could have turned that time into thirty-five dollars at the Red Lobster. The decision to drop out had been easy to make, since the numbers were quite clear.

For Casey, impending bankruptcy was a failure in a more immediate, practical sense than the kind the editorials were rambling about. He had never done anything as dramatic as vowing to himself never to be poor again, but the promise had been implicit in his way of life. He had never questioned his stinginess, had never seen it as a flaw or a virtue. It simply was ingrained in him, because he had grown up with the awful lack—and therefore the awful love—of money, and there was nothing he could do about it. The upside was that he'd put away considerable savings over the span of his working life. His account with the First Bank of Pennsylvania was eighteen years old and had been founded with a paycheck of thirty-three dollars. Though he had never stopped fretting about money, he had always known that he was prepared for the worst.

This time of his life certainly qualified as such, and so it was especially painful to dwell on the timing, to remember that if his mother had chosen to stick it out in East Breed's for one more year or so, he would have been able to tell her honestly that he needed the money for himself. Instead she had decided in August, shortly after her thirty-fifth anniversary at Fontaine's Dry Cleaners, that she had enough of the weather, enough of the work, enough of the township.

She had needed a loan to go in with her sister on a condominium in Oklahoma City. He had not even asked her what had become of her savings, knowing that there had never been any, but she was still defensive, because he had hesitated. She reminded him of the expenses of raising a son alone on the pittance the Fontaines gave her. She said she deserved a rest, she deserved not to shovel the driveway, to wear shorts every once in a while. He could not argue with this, although he always shoveled for her, and although he knew her money had mostly gone to bingo tickets and cigarettes. He could not argue with her because at sixty-two she looked more tired than anyone he'd ever seen, and because she was killing herself with smoking and would not be around long anyway and she just wanted to finish strong, just a couple last years with a clean house and dependable weather. Social security would see to her expenses, she said, she just needed a lump sum to send to her sister's agent. After the agent cashed Casey's check, a thousand dollars was left.

He became even more careful after that. Throughout the fall, he begrudged any expense that did not directly account for the sustenance of life and health, though he had to make some exceptions for Rachel's sake. By the time his mother finally moved into the new place, he had pushed the account above two grand. Around this time, which coincided with the record-setting autumn at O'Ruddy's, he recognized that it was his rare attitude toward money, his belief that it could be made to represent virtually everything (time, energy, sugar packets, an extra ounce topping a glass of Diet Coke), that made him a superlative restaurant manager. His job, in many ways, was to pinch pennies, an action that came naturally to him, and since he did it under the aegis of the franchise owners and headquarters, it was not a personal flaw. He did not have to think of himself as a miser, because it was not his cash.

Keeping track of his own finances, and keeping track of the mechanics of his life in general, had apparently gone hand in hand with the job. During the first week of unemployment, with no books to balance or cleanliness inspections to make, no food to check on, no bathrooms to stock, he had removed these responsibilities from his personal life as well. He didn't cook at home anymore. The job of going to the store, making an omelet, doing dishes afterward, was suddenly too onerous. He didn't clean the bathroom during his month of unemployment. Twice he forgot to take out the garbage on trash day. And he didn't touch his checkbook, didn't keep a single receipt, at the one time in his life when he should have been most attentive to such things. Rachel cautioned him against falling into lassitude; she said he could easily slip into depression. But Casey knew it wasn't that. He wasn't giving up, really. It was that the habits that governed his life had been broken by his removal from O'Ruddy's, and this had shut down everything.

He knew the money was slipping away. He was probably spending more now than he ever had. Since O'Ruddy's had so utterly consumed his previous life, there hadn't been much of a chance to spend his checks. Unemployment was expensive. To stave off cabin fever, he lounged around the bookstore by the mall, drinking coffee in the café out of loiterer's guilt. He went on rambling drives through the wooded hills to the north, burning up gas at $1.70 a gallon. Before he finally abandoned his restriction on television, he bought a new magazine nearly every day. And Rachel still had her requirements. They still went to movies and to the Italian place in Scranton. When he resisted, she said it would do him good, a phrase that seemed meaningless to him now. By the fourth week it didn't seem possible that good could be done to him anymore. He knew that someday soon he would check the ATM receipt and find that all the money was gone, and he didn't know what would happen after that. It seemed brutally fantastic. At thirty-three, he had logged more hours working than many people would in their entire lives, and the dollars with which he had kept track of all those hours, which he had always sought to protect, would soon disappear entirely.

He had passed the four weeks in a whirl of loneliness and fear and simple, desperate boredom. But the police had not called, not once.

# | ten |

*They brought Colin* into the house with grunts and sweat and thuds, as if they were movers bringing in a new couch. He sat in a wheelchair, unable to propel it himself, and Geoffrey and Shane maneuvered the boy and his chair up the porch stairs and through the narrow front hallway and into the living room. They did all this gracelessly, hunching their backs, taking short rapid steps, knocking over things that weren't even in their way. *The thing is on wheels, for God's sake,* Lea thought. *How hard could it be?* She leaned against the wall in the living room.

"Maybe we should move some of the stuff around," said Geoffrey.

"Or maybe we should try not to steer his chair into the furniture," said Lea, with a distracted voice that made them pause for a second before they understood she had insulted them. Megan went to the linen closet to get another blanket for Colin's lap.

"Why is that, I wonder," said Shane when Megan came back with an afghan and tucked it around the boy's legs. Colin stared at her face with animal-like curiosity as she did it. It looked to Lea as if he might bite Megan on the nose.

"Why is what, honey?" said Megan.

"Why do people in wheelchairs always have blankets in their laps? Why are their legs so cold? I mean, people who walk don't wrap blankets around their legs."

Shane was an appliance salesman and a community college dropout, and because of this and because the question was vaguely medical, Geoffrey leaped to answer. "The muscles of the legs—or any part of the body, really—generate heat as they move. If your legs can't move, they won't generate heat, so they'll feel much colder than the rest of the body."

"Oh, I see," said Shane. "Makes sense in a way." Then, squatting beside the wheelchair, he bellowed, "You warm enough, buddy?"

Colin looked squarely at his uncle, and though it did not seem that the question had registered with him, he understood enough to nod his head.

Shane stood up, satisfied, and folded his arms. "Maybe you could get him some special pants or something," he said to Geoffrey. "They should make special pants for people in wheelchairs. With thicker fabric around the legs. You know what I mean, pants with insulated legs. For cripples."

"Shane," said Geoffrey, "Colin's not paralyzed. They don't want him to walk for a little while because of the medication, but physically he'll be the same as he always was. In a week or so we'll send back the wheelchair." Geoffrey spoke slowly, exaggerating his patience. They would laugh about Shane once they were alone, or at least they would have before any of this, if he had said something like that in a different context. Whether or not Lea would still laugh about her idiot brother-in-law would indicate to Geoffrey how much had changed.

"Honey, you knew that," said Megan. She was sitting on the sofa, leaning forward and clasping her hands.

"Oh, yeah, yeah. Yeah, I knew that. I just meant in a general way, maybe someone should start making pants like that for people who are in wheelchairs all the time."

"Hmm," said Geoffrey. "Yes, there may be something to that idea, Shane." Again, a mocking tone that he knew Shane would not pick up on, although Megan probably did. Lea knew that her sister disliked Geoffrey for this very reason, for the fact that he so often fired insults below Shane's radar.

"Physically, though, everything is okay?" Megan asked Geoffrey.

The question pulled Lea into the room. "Tell them about his condition, Geoffrey," she said as she took a place on the sofa near her sister. Megan reached out and held her hand. She had spent almost as much time at the hospital as Lea but had kept a strict deference while there, never asking questions for fear of asking the wrong one. Lea was surprised to realize now that Megan honestly didn't know what the doctor had told them, though she must have assumed it was not good.

During the four weeks since the accident, much had been unclear. The doctors had felt confident, a full day after the accident and the first surgery, that Colin would not die. A day after receiving this information, however, Lea was told that they could not guarantee he would come out of the coma he'd slipped into. Four days later, he was alert and even mumbling words, but no one would say what this implied about his future. Two weeks after that, and one day after the service at St. Brendan's, the surgeons performed what they called a successful operation, but they elaborately qualified what they meant by the phrase. She liked it best when they told her they suspected the news was not good, because then at least she knew they were not lying to her.

A few days after the surgery, Dr. Hammond had sat Lea and Geoffrey down with charts and textbook photographs and X-rays and support group phone numbers and explained what he thought the rest of Colin's life might be like. *There is always hope*, he had said, but his tone had been careful to avoid meaning, careful to avoid, in fact, any trace of hope; it had been as if he had said, *There is always weather*. Since that day, Geoffrey had been straightforward in explaining what Colin had gone through, what he would go through still. He used clear, unequivocal language, which was remarkable considering the jargon he typically wielded when speaking about all things medical. Lea felt a very specific kind of love for him when he spoke this way about their son; it had become an emotional turn-on for her.

"You're right, Megan, that we think he's okay physically. Meaning, I suppose, that everything below the neck will be the same as it always was. His balance is a little off, and may be for some time. We'll have to watch for signs of epilepsy and motor-function loss, though we've seen some positive signs there. And there will be some loss of muscle tone, since he won't be working out as much as he used to."

"And no more football," said Shane.

"No," Lea said. "That's done with." Megan squeezed Lea's hand tighter.

Geoffrey went on. "Parts of his parietal and frontal lobes were injured. He's kept many motor functions, but his language skills have deteriorated. He seems to have little memory. No advanced cognitive ability. Basically, there was brain damage." With this harsh phrase, some tears scurried down Geoffrey's face and his voice cracked, but he kept speaking. "There's so much that we don't know about the brain. So much can change. There really is hope. There really is. But the doctors have warned us, and we have to be realistic. The way they're saying it, the way they said to think about it, is that his brain is on the level of a four-year-old's."

This was a phrase that had been tossed around in the hospital so much that Lea had become immune to its implications for her life. She couldn't imagine that it was at all helpful in describing Colin. What did it mean, that he had a four-year-old mind, as if some mad scientist had replaced the brain of her son with that of a child? What kind of four-year-old? The kind that ate glue and cried when the air conditioner was too loud, or the kind that took Suzuki lessons and already knew the times tables? Did it mean he would begin wearing Kermit the Frog pajamas, sleep with a stuffed animal? Would he once again watch *Sesame Street*, give her a bowl of cornflakes for her birthday? Every question she came up with was too ridiculous to ask.

The phrase also was misleading. When Colin had been four, there had always been the hope of five, of ten, of twenty-one, thirty-five, fifty. "Four years old" implied a set place in the continuum of a life, a signpost of childhood, a marker to be reached, experienced, and passed in the course of a year. But Colin would be "four" forever; they had taken pains to assure her of this probability. Therefore, given the implication of a chronological label, it meant that he wasn't four at all. He was nowhere, and yet he was everywhere that he would ever be.

Megan and Shane ran out of things to say in the span of the next twenty minutes, and it made Shane fidgety. He was the kind of man who took silence as failure. Finally Megan stood and kissed Colin on the head, and she and Shane walked out, muttering sober goodbyes.

They wheeled Colin into his bedroom. He was now slack and weak from medication, and each of his 182 pounds sought its way toward the earth, but Geoffrey and Lea managed to maneuver him — upper torso, rear end, legs — into the thing that was called the AdjustaRest and that had cost them three thousand dollars. They laid the boy down on top of the covers, and then they both stood without speaking, basking in the fact that Colin was at least home, and that he would probably not die. They stared at him stupidly, much as a new couple stares at a baby they have just brought home, although their faces were placid, joyless.

Then, in an unexpected division of labor, Geoffrey went into the kitchen to thaw something a neighbor had brought them while Lea stayed in the room. Geoffrey did not offer to help tuck him in, and she understood that this was because it would happen so many times from now on. They would each put him to bed alone a thousand times, and a thousand times after that. No need to inaugurate the chore.

They had bought two new overstuffed chairs, one for either side of the bed, and a humidifier, which sat in the corner and hummed. The room would have to be redone, a therapist had told them. They had described it to her, and she had said that there were too many stimuli, as was typical in a case such as this. The belongings of a teenager, the therapist had said, were no longer appropriate to him, and might be confusing. The posters of rock stars and supermodels, the trophies and the postcards, would have to come down. The walls would be repainted, the dark wood dresser and desk replaced with furnishings less stark, with a bedstand and a table painted in primary colors. This, after all, was no room for a four-year-old.

It still was a hostile place to Lea. Over the past few years, the only visits she'd made to the room had been spent looking for contraband. She had last searched it in November. One Thursday night Colin had come home late from football practice with rosy eyes, smelling of pot and Right Guard. The next morning, indignant and insulted, she had begun rifling through his drawers minutes after he had left for school, but soon she plopped on his bed, suddenly very cold and lonely, as if it were not her house she sat in but instead a desolate hotel room in some foreign country. She had been overwhelmed not by the sense that she was invading Colin's privacy but by something very different, nearly opposite. She had felt burdened by the lack of invasion she practiced, the fact that she did not know what sort of substances she was looking for among his possessions, nor where he might keep them. She was also struck by her insistent need not to know these things, the intensity of her desire to have Colin leave the house, go to college and take his vices with him, so that she and Geoffrey could exercise a more practicable form of denial.

Now there was nothing for Colin to hide, nor was there anything for them to fear discovering. It was not Colin anymore. If she found a bag of marijuana, a package of condoms, a pint of Scotch, they would belong to someone who was not with them. The new Colin, the only Colin, lay on his back on the AdjustaRest, his eyes half closed. He would be asleep soon. He would awake as he was now, groggy and vacant and unsuspecting. She could search the room in front of his curious stare, and no sense of invasion or betrayal would register with him. And because of this, it seemed pointless to do it. There would be no one to castigate for whatever remnants she found of the reckless son she had once had. She might as well burn his things, preserving her ignorance of his former life, an ignorance that was not quite bliss but something equally in need of protecting.

Colin suddenly frowned and shifted in the bed. He still wore his clothes, and she stood up and began unlacing his tennis shoes and telling him that it was time for him to be tucked in. She wondered if she should promise him a bedtime story, or if this was one aspect of his new reality that did not conform to the four-year-old model.

She untied the string at the waist of his sweatpants and slid them off. He offered no help and no resistance, instead keeping his eyes trained on the strange project going on before him. There was a slight dampness around his loins that could have been sweat or urine. Her hand jerked back when she discovered it. It meant that she would have to bathe him now, the way the nurses had taught her.

With the control panel she adjusted the bed to lean him up, and then she pushed his torso forward to slide a rubber mat underneath him. Then she lay the bed down flat and lifted up his legs to spread the mat on the bottom end. She got the bathing supplies—a bucket and sponge and towels and some liquid soap, as if she were planning to wash the car—and returned to take the rest of his clothes off.

Colin remembered how to take off his shirt, and he offered her help in the form of raising his arms, very much the way (she hated to admit it) he had when he was four years old. He lay back down, naked but for his damp underpants. She knew she would have to re- move them, but she wondered if she should go have a drink of some- thing before she did it. Geoffrey, she thought, was taking his time with the casserole.

In this pose the boy's body seemed to his mother not very differ- ent from certain statues she had seen in Europe, or like the young men on music videos who barked lyrics at the camera while ripping off their shirts. It was a body he had worked at with diligence, and yet since the source of this diligence could have been only a vast well of self-regard, she could not admire whatever the old Colin had done to achieve it. But the body itself could be admired for the simple thing it was. No boys had looked like this when she had been in high school. The muscles of his stomach and his chest pressed out against the skin. Colin saw her staring at him, and he stared back, unaware of the elegant body that he was sovereign of, and unaware of the previous owner whose vanity had crafted it.

She turned her head to the side and grasped the waistband of his underpants and pulled them down his legs. It was repulsive not because of the smell but because it was a maneuver that had up to this point in her life been a completely sexual one. This act, every single time she had performed it for a man, had always preceded intercourse. She felt bile rise in her throat.

Now her son was naked before her, and she began sponging his feet. Colin spurted out a giggle and his legs kicked reflexively.

"Does that tickle, baby?" she asked him.

In response he closed his eyes. He had gone through this procedure many times in the hospital. It would be one of the experiences in his new life that was familiar to him, and he was settling into this comfort.

She rolled him over onto his side to clean his back and discovered his tattoo. It was stark and ugly, and she shuddered, as if she had found a spider in his bed. The tattoo was about the size of a fist, drawn in the space between his jutting shoulder blades. It portrayed a smiling death's head encased in a football helmet, with blood dripping down its skeletal teeth. She sponged over it, with the vague hope that it might come off with the gentle rubbing, but also because it was his skin, and it needed to be washed like the rest of him. She rubbed this black and green skin leisurely, examining the design and reminding herself that he had not done it, that the boy she touched now was not the one responsible for the body.

Underneath the right arm she found a long red scar, the remains of a wound that would have needed medical attention and that she was ignorant of. It ran from just below his underarm hair down toward his nipple in a perfectly straight red line. It must have been a terrific gash at one point. She stared at it for some time as she washed it, thinking again that it might come off if she scrubbed. Despite her curiosity, she found that she could not call in Geoffrey to inspect it with his physician's eye. Perhaps she would try to explain it to him later. At the moment—she learned as she tried to say Colin's name, to tell him that they were just about finished—she could not speak.

After she cleaned his chest, she resoaked and wrung out the sponge, then stood at the side of the AdjustaRest and robotically moved the sponge over his privates. Colin squirmed and squeaked. Lea stared at his face, then at his feet, then at a candle on the bed stand, but none of these benign sights offered any measure of relief from her distress. Lea had now become entirely aware of how humiliated the first Colin would have been by this experience, how enraged and vitriolic it would make him, even now, wherever he was, to learn that his mother had taken this prerogative. She could see him in this rage, his lips curling with indignation, sweat beading on his forehead. She could hear the words, tightly enunciated, violent. *A hell of a mother you are*, he would say. *I've had that tattoo for three years, and you didn't even know. You didn't even know I got stabbed.* She could sense his judgment and his hatred of her, and she knew that the old son needed to be exorcised.

She was certain that Colin had brought his injury on himself; the damage he had incurred must have been a retribution. She had known this immediately, the moment Geoffrey described to her the beating he'd taken in that parking lot.

She looked at her son and said, "Colin, what did you do? What did you do to make them hurt you?"

He didn't answer, but only pulled his arms tight to his chest, an indication that he was cold. She began to towel him off, helped him into his pajamas, and then maneuvered him under the covers and kissed him on the forehead. Throughout this she could still feel scorn coming from somewhere, from the son she had lost and whose only remaining life consisted of the ghostly presence of his judgment, the scarring and musculature of his body, and the artifacts of his bedroom.

*Yes*, she thought, *I will have to reckon with this. I will have to find out.*

| eleven |

*On Monday* of the fifth week, the general manager of the Tacqueria de Paco called. They were looking to replace the night shift manager, he said. He announced a time for Casey to meet him the next day, then hung up.

Tacqueria de Paco was a Mexican chain restaurant in Scranton, a bit of a drive but close to the highway. Casey spent much of that night ironing. He decided to wear a dark blue shirt, which he thought would contrast well with the soft yellow lighting typically found in Mexican chain restaurants. He ironed the pleats of his Dockers with a thoroughness that was pathetic; he knew that only a desperate man spent more than twenty minutes ironing pants. And yet, he thought, if the shoe fits . . .

He met with the general manager, a man named Jake, at ten in the morning on Tuesday. The lunch servers showed up about the same time Casey did, to roll extra silverware and divide up the table assignments. He held the door for a pair of teenage waitresses who ignored him entirely. Jake took Casey to a booth in the back.

The lighting was indeed yellow, and the walls had been treated to look vaguely adobe-like, and here and there Casey noticed murals involving a cactus with arms and a cowboy hat, which seemed to be the logo of Taqueria de Paco. Jake's nametag was shaped like this cactus, as were the menus. The muted sounds of a mariachi CD drifted through the place, and the listless servers clumped around the bar to wait for the first customers.

Jake belonged to a subclass of restaurant manager that Casey knew well, a type that he thought of as "the hearty managers." He was under six feet, with thick arms from which hair sprouted like black alfalfa. He was moderately heavy, and his handshake testified to his body's power and advertised his heartiness. Casey knew that Jake would be the kind to encourage nicknames in the workplace, to flirt and joke and talk about sports. He would use outdated slang, and the teenage waitresses would certainly deride him in private for his forced chumminess, but they would use their coquettish powers on him like sorceresses. The hearty manager violated Casey's belief that managers can't seem to like their staff very much, let alone be friends with them. The O'Ruddy's handbook had concurred. Page 4: *Your servers don't need a friend. They have friends. They need a leader.* Casey couldn't act hearty if he tried, although this did not, at the moment, stop him from trying.

He pumped Jake's hand with vigor and even shot him a wink, and prepared himself to chortle and to drop the pitch of his voice, but when they sat in the table Casey noticed that Jake had become subdued.

"I got to tell you, Case," he said. "If it's cool that I call you that?" Casey nodded.

"I got to tell you, I didn't know about your . . . I didn't know about that thing that happened at O'Ruddy's, not until this morning."

Casey wondered if he should walk out, if this was how it would be from now on, at every place that called him in without realizing until it was too late that he was *that* guy, the guy who had let *that* happen at O'Ruddy's. Perhaps he could take a real estate course, perhaps he could learn to fix small engines.

Jake continued, brightening for an instant. "I went snowmobiling with my girlfriend about a month ago, that weekend all that happened." Casey imagined the thick-chested man zipping across white valleys, hollering and whooping in the stillness. "It was a hell of a time. Went to Lackawanna. You ever been? Oh shit, you got to go. Anyway, I was swamped when I got back. *Swamped.*" He raised his eyebrows, nodded gravely. "So I guess I just missed it. Didn't read the papers or anything, didn't hear any news." He bobbed his head, looking distressed.

"So." Casey let it stay there, through the silence, adding nothing until Jake found his own way back to the original point.

"Right. So I didn't know about that O'Ruddy's shit until this morning. Your name came up, and someone recognized it. Kind of makes sense now why you applied here. I guess you're all out of work now."

"Right."

"Anyway." Jake was completely somber again. "It makes it difficult—you understand that, I guess."

"It makes it difficult for me, that's for damn sure." Casey was getting the sense that he should occasionally curse around Jake, so that he didn't seem disapproving.

Jake nodded. "I bet. You're back on the horse pretty quickly, though. I got to admire that. The thing is, that night's going to be a problem. The franchise owners are in Philly, and they don't come up much, but I still can't hold out something like this on them. They'll want to know your story, and I'll have to give it to them."

"I'm sorry, Jake, I don't think I get it. What is my story?"

Jake laughed, quick and short, more of a chortle. "You know better than I do, I think. I don't know, man, help me out here. The full story, why it wasn't handled as soon as the kids showed up, that kind of thing."

Casey felt an odd comfort, knowing that the job was lost. The lighting and the prefabricated southwestern motif seemed soothing in the midmorning cold, the snow-born brightness angling in through the faux mesquite shutters. He felt relaxed and playful. "Do you think you know the full story, Jake?"

Jake sat back, all smiles gone. He spoke more slowly now. "I've heard the details. Is there something I'm missing?"

Casey shrugged. He looked to his left, frowning at the intentionally peeling paint of the adobelike wall.

"I tell you what, Case," Jake said, in the tone hearty managers use to make their employees think that an enormous favor is being granted. "Why don't you tell me your version of it? To tell you the truth"—he looked around and lowered his voice, another hearty-manager trick—"I've been given instructions not to interview you at all. Once I talked to the franchise owners about you this morning, they told me not even to meet with you. But I want to hear your story. Give me your side of it, and if you got screwed, maybe I can talk to the owners." Jake gave a kind of aborted wink. "They listen to me about most things."

And so Casey began the story again. He almost sighed, almost protested at having to tell it yet again, but he saw the necessity of it, even if he weren't going to get this job. He actually hadn't told it all that much—three times to the police, once to Rachel, once (in a highly abridged version) to his mother. It was only to himself, he realized, that he had innumerably repeated it over the past four weeks, and he had done so with equal parts of delusion and truth.

He began with the parking lot, the gradual accumulation of teenage rancor. He told of the voices, the ridiculous outfits, and the even more ridiculous anger. "What do kids that age have to be so angry about, anyway?" he said. Jake nodded and gave an ain't-it-the-truth look of sympathy.

Casey talked about Jenny, and he found himself talking about her more than he had to Rachel or his mother or the police. He told how she had rapped on his door when the boys first came and said that he needed to do something. He was layering the story to prepare Jake to hear the salient matter, that it may have been she who precluded his calling the police, by that simple phrase that he could still hear, in profound clarity, spoken in the light timbre of her voice: "Mr. Fielder, the phone's out again. We can't call the cops."

He let out, in measured, objective sentences, the fact that Jenny had retreated to the server stand at a certain point in the violence. As he spoke, Casey stared out the restaurant's window, as he had done on that Friday. But this was no re-creation; he did not will himself to see the boys all over again in the snow-packed Tacqueria de Paco lot. Instead he stared intently at the glass of the window, at the wisps of reflected light in it, and he was aware of nothing but the narrative, the impotent words, staggering from his mouth.

"Right about when we saw the first blood, or about when I did anyway, she went to the phone. I didn't remember that for a while afterwards. I didn't even tell that to the police. It was a few minutes into the fight. The fight was going slowly, all those kids all wrapped up in their coats and gloves and their big baggy pants. Those goddamn baggy pants. There was a lot of just wrestling around. It kind of reminded me of those promotions where people dress up in sumo wrestler suits and try to knock each other over. But one kid got a punch in, and it dropped the other kid to his knees, and all of a sudden his face was all red, like he'd been hit with a tomato. That was when Jenny went to the phone." Again he didn't see it, not as he wanted to, either in his mind's eye or in the lot outside. But he spoke and heard the words somberly, knew by his very tone that he spoke the truth, and a second later he confirmed this in his memory. This was when she had gone to the phone, this was why she had picked it up, this was the source of the tremor in her voice as she informed him that there was no dial tone. The wicked punch, the smattering of gore—this had not been enough to prod Casey to action, but Jenny had backed from the window as if it had shattered.

Jake had retreated into himself, uninterested in the story now that it seemed to be more introspective than gratuitous, now that Casey had betrayed himself. But Jake did not cut him off, and Casey took this chance to look away from the window, back at his interviewer, and show him a thin smile.

"A few months ago my alternator broke," Casey said. "So I took the bus to work for a week or so. Jenny takes the bus, so a couple times we sat together on the way to the restaurant. One time a retarded man got on—he was going to one of those jobs they set up for retarded people. He had his lunchbox, he was wearing a tie. He was all excited to go to work. He sat down next to two kids, teenagers, Township kids. They started in on him right away, messing with his tie, going through his lunchbox. I sat there and fretted about what to do, like everyone else. Jenny let it go on for about five seconds, then she got up and spit a huge gob in one of the kids' faces. There was dead silence for a second, then she rang the stop cord and told them to get off the bus, and they did it. They just got up and left."

Jake scowled and nodded. "Whoa," he said. "Tough girl."

Casey understood that Jake must sympathize with the teenage boys in his anecdote. Jake had begun hearing the tale with a smile, perhaps ready to laugh at a comic story regarding a retarded man on a bus. It exonerated Jake, Casey thought, much more than if he had sympathized instead with the grown men who sat on the bus with Jenny, trying to avoid the demands of conscience.

"But that's not what I mean," said Casey, aware of the vanity of explaining it to Jake, again committing the narration and its exegesis as an exercise, or a salve. "Her reaction was immediate, instinctive. As soon as she understood what they were doing, she got up. The rest of us were just sitting there, thinking about what to do. But Jenny didn't think or plan or worry. She has that—it's a precious thing. That instinctive reaction to cruelty. The way some people know in their guts when something shouldn't happen, and they do something—again, *without thinking*—to make it stop."

Jake chewed on a pen. "So you're saying you wish you'd have had that on that Friday night. I guess you wish you were like her, huh? That you'd have just acted right away without thinking so much."

*Well, of course,* thought Casey, *of course that's what I wish.* But he had not meant for Jake to take this from what he had said. He shrugged. "Maybe. What I mean is, Jenny has that instinct. I don't know about me. I don't think many of us have it. Most of us have to think things through. I don't see what's so wrong with that. You can't train yourself to react automatically, to understand automatically what's right and wrong in a split second. But Jenny can—that's my point. That's why she went to the phone, is what I'm saying."

It satisfied Jake, because it put an end to things. And it satisfied Casey more thoroughly. He felt he could walk away from this meeting now, still unemployed but having somehow reckoned with something. It was true that he saw in Jenny a kind of visceral goodness, an integrity in her behavior that made her flaws immaterial. Jenny had what Janda had implied Casey lacked: an innate sense of right and wrong. She did not suffer injustice or cruelty, she did not give prerogative to fear or even foresight. It was the sum of Jenny's character. She acted rightly, and she worried about the consequences later. And on that Friday night, Casey had done no more and no less than what Jenny had done. Innocence by association.

He was only bothered by the fact that he seemed to have forgotten that incident on the bus entirely until now. It had not been so long ago, and now that it had returned to him, he saw that scene vividly. He remembered the chill that had grown in him when the boys began taunting the retarded man, the icy awkwardness among the other passengers. And then Jenny just stood up and spit on them. How could he have forgotten something like that?

"Wait a second," said Jake. "Waitwaitwait." He tilted his head to the left, brought his hand to his face as if it were a telephone receiver. "What about a cell phone? Why didn't you call the cops on your cell phone?"

"I don't have a cell phone," said Casey.

This fact seemed to affect Jake more than anything Casey had heretofore told him. He registered it with a look of utter bemusement.

"Oh," he said, clearly unsure how to respond, or perhaps feeling that he should no longer be talking to such a person at all. "Weird. And the girl?"

"No, she didn't have one either. I know it's weird, but she didn't."

"Then how did you call the cops in the end?"

He didn't, that was the short answer. He never called the cops, never once performed the one physical act that might have exculpated him. He had dashed out of the restaurant, and the cold had met him with aggression, thrusting into him like an invisible train. He ran through it and slipped on the ice but quickly righted, his boots crushing pieces of the rock salt he had sprinkled on the walk before the dinner shift. The boy lay on his back with his legs crossed and contorted. His head had turned to the side, and the bloody drool had begun to freeze on his collar.

"The couple," Casey said. "There was a couple, middle-aged, short curly black hair. They were one of those couples that look alike. I guess they had a cell phone." His voice had begun to fade, and he cleared his throat. "Jenny ran out soon after I did. I imagine she asked them if they had a phone, maybe filled them in on the address and so forth. She was outside twenty, thirty seconds after me."

Jake nodded and flagged down a passing waitress. While Casey looked into the opaque reflection of the yellow bulbs on the deep red table, Jake corrected his employee on some imperfections in her uniform. He called her "A-Train," and she smirked when he said it, and as she walked away Casey could tell, from the shift in her arm and the reaction of one of her colleagues, that she had brought her hand up to her chest and retroactively given her boss the finger.

"She was still just wearing her polo shirt, but she didn't seem to notice how cold it was," Casey said. "She was crying. Like you wouldn't believe."

"Must have been upsetting for the kid. Look, Casey, I don't know what else to tell you. I realize you're in a tight spot, but—"

"No, it was more than just being upset. She was really out of control. When the paramedics came, we had to drag her off him." It was true, and again the truth revealed itself first through the act of speaking and was seconded by his memory.

The blood from the boy's head hadn't bothered her. She let it stain her arms, her hair, as she bent her head to his chest, listening for a heartbeat. She didn't acknowledge Casey, who was squatting beside the boy and keeping some distance, like a policeman analyzing a piece of evidence. Tears spread the dark mascara across her cheeks. She moaned, low-pitched and wavering.

"Oh my God, you know what I think?" Casey sat upright, focused on Jake's face again. "I think she had something with that boy. That must be it. She knew that boy, she admitted that. But I think there was more to it. Jenny and that boy had something going on, a relationship."

The hint of salaciousness roused Jake's attention again, if only for a moment. "Yeah?"

"Jenny knew some of the guys from St. Brendan's, she said. She didn't say who she knew, but there's no other explanation. She wouldn't have carried on like that for just any guy. She was stroking him, whispering to him. She wasn't disgusted by the way his head leaked. She would have been if she hadn't known him. That's a fact."

Jake had tuned out again. He stood up. "Okay then, I hope this helped you work some things out, Case, but obviously I can't hire you."

"Oh yeah, I know that."

"Good luck to you."

Casey didn't really hear him, and he didn't even shake his hand, or notice that it had been offered. He did not feel the usual burn that rose when he left a place where he had embarrassed himself. He thought about his words, the truth of them. He made himself draw the image. The pictures came to him if he squeezed his eyes shut.

The body, limp on the pavement. The girl, prudently afraid to cradle the head for fear of spinal damage but otherwise unintelligent, animal-like in panic and grief. The shower of snot and tears, steam rising from the broken head and from Jenny's open mouth. She stared into the boy's inert face and soon her howl turned into a whimper. The flowing blood made small crunching sounds as it melted the snow.

They were lovers, Casey thought. Certainly, most certainly, they were lovers.

| twelve |

*They discussed legal action.* The corporate headquarters of the restaurant would make the most likely target. It was located in Dallas, Geoffrey told her, and his tone implied that he associated this city with the phrase "large settlement payout."

He had been back at work for a week now, where his colleagues must have stoked the notion of a lawsuit. With certain men of his generation and social class, Geoffrey felt comfortable exposing his natural pragmatism. He had probably explained the prognosis frankly to them and solicited their opinions. For Geoffrey, the question in the beginning, of who was to blame for this, had fluidly transformed into the more digestible one of who should pay for this. He was glad to turn it into a project, a crusade. He had not done well speaking of his boy to the women in his life—his aunt and Lea's mother, his sister in California—because they cried with him and commiserated but really offered no practical solution. With the men, he must have felt like he was getting somewhere.

"There was negligence," he told Lea. They sat at the kitchen table, where they had eaten from a casserole dish. This was the meal table in times of crisis or exhaustion, at times when the artifice of matching napkins and separate salad forks could be jettisoned from the routine. Lea doubted they would ever return to the dining room.

"Negligence?"

"The police report came to my office last week. I spoke to Phil Lucas and faxed him a copy."

Invoking the name of Phil Lucas, a fraternity brother from Penn State who was now a lawyer in Weston, irreversibly tainted the crusade her husband had made this out to be. He hurried past the name and its associations.

"There was negligence on the part of the manager of the restaurant. He watched the entire fight and didn't do a thing about it. You remember that article in the paper. From the report, it's pretty obvious the cops think he should have called them earlier, as soon as the fight began. He didn't even go out there, not until Colin got hurt, and even then he wasn't the one who called 911. It was some customer."

But it was the boy, Lea thought. There was a boy out there who had picked up a metal rod and staved in the head of their son. Nameless, anonymous in the memory of everyone involved because of his bland winter wear. How could this be a crime of negligence?

"He probably doesn't make more than forty grand a year, though, so he's not a feasible target. But he represented the company, so they're responsible for his behavior, in a legal sense."

She suddenly liked his mercenary approach. She liked that Geoffrey had already surmised, had probably researched, the annual salary of the restaurant manager. She understood why Geoffrey had given himself the eminently approachable task of discovering liability rather than blame.

The question of blame was problematic. For one thing, there was Colin himself. His demeanor on the surface had seemed mild, stolid.

His apathy, worn like a badge, had probably been an attraction for his girls and his friends. But there was a rage contained in this quietness, and sometimes football was not enough to release it. In November, outside a strip mall, Colin and one of his friends had scuffled with the entire starting secondary of St. Viator's and had had to be handcuffed by security guards. Spring semester junior year, Brother Carl had requested that the boy enroll in anger management counseling. She thought of the litany of offenses she had listened to at parent-teacher conferences. A troubled, angry boy, yearning to fight and therefore skilled at enraging others, skilled at inspiring wrath. Where was his blame in this?

Or the parents. It always came back to them. They had been home on that Friday, responsible and sedate, but they had not really expected to see their son again that night, would not have waited up to chide him for breaking curfew or for smelling of beer. They would have turned in early, in fact, hoping to avoid him, because he would not have said five words to them anyway, and his stench of alcohol would have mocked their cowardice. What had they done, so far away from it all, to bring about the tragedy? Lea's brain almost shut down at the thought of this question. She was glad for Geoffrey's insight, so happy for the way he had thrown out the ancient, agonizing question of blame and had instead, with a simple call to Phil Lucas, alchemized it into a matter of liability.

"I'm not saying that money will make up for it, Lea. That's not what I'm trying to do here. But it will make things more comfortable for him if we don't have to worry. Whatever he needs, we're going to get for him. There are people who have to take responsibility for it."

She couldn't understand this righteous justification until she realized that she had not yet responded to anything he'd said, and he had taken this as condemnation. "I know, Geoff. I just don't like thinking about it."

It was what he wanted her to say. They were assuming their roles; Geoffrey was hoping she would grant him the reins to this new project. He would go and sort out the messy business of liability, culpability. He would do the research and send the faxes, and in the end it would be easy for him to tell, based on settlement checks and assurances from Phil Lucas, whether or not he had won. By default, and by her tiny admission — *I just don't like thinking about it* — she had released herself from this consideration. It had always seemed like one of their strengths as a couple, this tacit and sensible way in which they divided their labor.

"I'm going to go sit with him," she said.

"I thought he was sleeping."

"Yeah," she said, and walked out of the kitchen without clearing the plates.

In his bedroom Colin was indeed sleeping, lying on his back, breathing noisily. She looked at him once, then turned away and switched on a small lamp that didn't seem to bother him. She began to work on her own project.

Lea had decided to excavate her son's room. Let Geoffrey manage the lawyers, let him conspire to identify the restaurant manager and the besuited drones in Dallas as the perpetrators. She almost pitied him, his crusade seemed so useless. The blame was here, in this house, in this room. It was true that another boy had performed the terrible physical act, and she hated this anonymous boy and hoped he would be found and punished. But more to the point, and much more taxing to Lea's mind, was her certainty that Colin had somehow done it to himself. That the damage inflicted on him was the whirlwind he had reaped from an adolescence of sowing anger and violation and crimes she had never speculated about. Lea would excavate the depths of her old son's depravity. She would begin in this room.

The first phase of the project was to go through his clothes. The room was unkempt, but she had discovered a sort of order in the chaos. Colin had kept his pants piled on a folding chair, separate from the pile of jeans, which was shoved under the desk. She instituted a system as she went through his pockets, folding each garment and stacking it on top of the easy chair once she had searched it. She did not analyze the contents yet. Every item she found, whatever its nature, she placed on a large plastic serving tray they had bought during their recent shopping spree at the hospital supply store. When she finished his pants and jackets she went through his winter coat, then his sports jackets, then any shirt that had a front pocket. She was rewarded by Colin's forgetfulness; in almost half the garments he had left something, some bit of evidence.

She sat on the floor with the tray in her lap and examined the materials. Many of the thin bits of white paper she'd found turned out to be detention slips from St. Brendan's, certainly nothing too unexpected, although Lea was startled by the volume of them, and by the array of offenses that were detailed in the lines where the teachers described what he had done wrong. Colin's detentions, it seemed, usually required elaboration.

On January 8, from a Spanish teacher: *Student arrived in class with a box of doughnuts and refused to stop eating them.*

On November 19, from the assistant headmaster: *Detention was received because the student made a lewd suggestion regarding the sexual orientation of a faculty member.*

On November 14, from the custodian, who Lea didn't think even had the authority to issue detentions: *He broke a tape measure in my office.*

On December 20, from the school secretary: *This young man needs a talking to.*

On December 11, from a history teacher: *The student received a detention because of his flagrant and distracting refusal to sit up straight in his chair.*

On November 4, from the gym teacher: *The student received a detention because he shaved off a classmate's eyebrows.*

This one she knew about. The detention for this offense, when brought to the notice of Brother Carl, became an in-school suspension. Brother Carl had called to tell her that Colin would be spending the day under supervision in the library. His behavior was becoming intolerable, the headmaster had said, but then he assured her that the brothers were handling the matter. Lea deferred to them, she said, and felt responsible for doing so. The stern Jesuits certainly would deal with him more efficiently than she could. He was her only boy, her only child. She had never known how to make him stop doing anything he wanted to do. Appeals to his better nature, to his reason, to his fear, had been entirely ineffectual, especially after he entered St. Brendan's. She had nothing, it would seem, with which to threaten Colin. He was shaving the eyebrows off other boys in his gym class—the idea was so foreign to her, so strange. Why would this be something that appealed to him, why would it even have occurred to him? The notion that she or Geoffrey might understand how to make him stop was ludicrous.

The other items on the tray mostly proved indecipherable or irrelevant. A few scraps of paper with phone numbers; several beer bottle caps; a few blank, folded worksheets from trigonometry class; the profane lyrics of a song he had printed from the Internet. She threw away most of them, even the detention slips. Only one of the discoveries seemed to be a real clue, an artifact of significance: a folded sheet of notebook paper that had begun life as a homework assignment (the heading read "Colin Chase, American Government 00.43") but had become a mass of doodles and, eventually, a sort of budget.

Coming In
    $20 from Kurt—booze for J. party
    $15 from P.—gas from road trip (MAKE HIM PAY IT)
    $150 from parents
    $100 from Alex, last night

Going Out
    $30 to P.—lost bet
    $300 to Dashner, for the goods

Below this he had totaled up the numbers and circled the figure –45 twice, and then had written "SHIT" and underlined it. Below this he had made a rudimentary to-do list:

Call Dash (new cell # 513-2938) to postpone buy

Get advance from parents

Call Jenny

Go to practice.

Lea didn't know a girl named Jenny, but this meant nothing. She didn't know any of the girls. She had heard of Dashner, though, she knew she had, but she could not recall where. A friend, she supposed, but this felt wrong, and she strained to remember but came up with nothing. Dashner. She knew there was a Dashner in his life, but she didn't remember how. He had been Colin's drug connection, evidently, if she jumped to a pretty safe conclusion, but that told her nothing. Colin wouldn't have told her the name of the man who sold him pot. She must have heard of Dashner from somewhere else. It didn't come to her.

She had finished with the clothes, and she now expanded the search into the large closet. She began looking on the upper shelves, where he kept his sweaters in short stacks, and soon she came upon a shoebox—finally, something he had bothered to hide. She took the box back to her place on the floor, at the foot of Colin's bed. She shook the contents onto the plastic serving tray and began sorting through them.

The box held a mass of messages on notebook paper, written in the looping handwriting and purple ink of teenage girls, folded into the squarish origami of high school notes. Colin had opened them all and had tried to refold them, but not with the care and technique that the girls had used in crafting them.

The notes were from girls who seemed to like Colin intensely, though not all of them confessed as much. There were clues indicating that most of the writers were from St. Theresa's, the St. Brendan's counterpart. They were the girls that the boys in Colin's social set courted, the ones the boys knew from church or the country club or family connections. The St. Theresa's girls were generally from Weston and Leawood and were therefore reliable. They would have spending money for beer and pot. They would be attractive with the accoutrements of wealth—perpetual tans and Ralph Lauren outfits and bodies toned from tennis courts. They could be counted on, if it came to it, to terminate a pregnancy.

The notes had been written in school, of course, perhaps out of boredom, perhaps to indicate to Colin that the girls had been thinking about him all day. They would have passed the notes to him after school, maybe through an intermediary who lived near the Chases, or maybe they would drop them through the slots in his locker when they went to St. Brendan's at night for CCD class. Lea was amused by the melodrama, the despairing refrain of frustration at being locked away in a girls' school. The girls were hardly sequestered— Lea saw them at the football games, she smelled them on her son's clothing—but they clearly enjoyed the romance of this kind of com- munication. They would write him notes as if they were courtly lovers or fifth-graders, and then on weekend nights they would have sex with him.

She could literally feel her heartbeat speeding up as she read the letters. Her apprehension was soon justified. There were things in the notes that she certainly did not want to know, but she had chosen to know and refused to abandon this decision. She felt a kind of courage building inside her, and she understood it was a wonderful thing that she didn't throw them away along with the detentions. She could have put them in a trash can and set them on fire. It would have been much, much easier that way.

None of the notes were dated, but after several readings she was able to guess their chronological arrangement, and she placed the notes in seven different columns on the rug in front of her, with the most recent ones at the bottom of the column. She felt confident about her guesswork, and she was impressed with herself.

She sat still for a few minutes and listened to Colin breathe. He was still asleep. She could no longer see the stripe of light under the bedroom door, which meant that Geoffrey had retreated to his study. She waited another minute, then read the notes in their columns, from top to bottom, this time as a history of a small patch of her son's private life, told by his friends and lovers.

COLIN

Hey hot stuff! I'm soooooooooo bored. SPANISH SUX!! I wish there were guys here. UGH! Why do I have to go to a girls school?

I meant what I said about Jess. She can be a real bitch when she gets really into a guy. I just meant that you should watch out. That's all. I know she's my friend and everything, but so are you and I don't want you to get into it without knowing the full deal.

That sucks that your parents took away your phone. Your mom sounds like a bitch. So's mine, but she never took my phone away. Thats okay though, it just means I get to write you notes!

You were totally wrong about me and Chris by the way. I thought things were cool but then I called his cell three times last week and he never called back. HE'S SUCH A PRICK! I'm never doing that for a guy again in my life.

Gotta bounce!
LUVYA
Michelle

The mention of the cell phone placed it sometime in early October, when Geoffrey and Lea had suspended Colin's phone privileges for forging their names on a progress report. In the other note in that column, Lea learned that Michelle had spent a Saturday night succumbing to the charms of Chris again and therefore had not spoken to Colin much at the party they went to, but she had heard that he "got it on with Jess in Tommy's parents room." The second note ended with a reference to St. Brendan's game against Clarendon and therefore must have been written toward the end of October.

The next writer had sent four notes, none of them significantly different in tone or matter from Michelle's. The girl seemed to be a private school Samuel Pepys, recording in obscene detail the ins and outs of their particular clique's social escapades, but she recorded nothing that told Lea anything of value, as the writer (who signed her name "G," followed by a star) ignored Colin's activities, perhaps out of some sense of decorum. From these notes Lea understood that Colin went to a lot of parties and drank a lot of booze, and that he and his friends experimented voraciously with sex, but she had, of course, always known this.

The third writer was the Jess that Michelle had referred to. Her notes were short, written in small handwriting, without the pictures and doodlings that decorated the others. She made no specific references to events, but Lea had no trouble placing them in chronological order.

Colin:

I'm so glad we got together finally. It seems like things between us have been kind of heating up since we met last summer, and I'm relieved that you admitted how you felt. You know that I feel the same way now, right? I think I showed you that, anyway.

I'm not sure when you get your cell phone back, but you can always call me from home if you want.

Jess

The signature was written differently from the rest, in large, swooping letters, as conspicuous as John Hancock's. Lea decided that the girl had done this to cover up the white space that surrounded it, the notable lack of "Love" before the signature. She must have agonized over the decision, Lea realized. She must have sat in some class in St. Theresa's absolutely consumed with whether she should write "Love" or "Luv ya" or "Talk to you soon" or even "Sincerely." In the end she had left it blank, covering her indecision with an enormous signature.

The next one:

Hi Colin:

That was really nice on Saturday. It was a lot better than the first time. I don't mean the first time was bad, I just mean that I was nervous cause I didn't really know you all that well, and it was nice that this time we had a bed. I could tell that you liked what I did for you. I like doing it for you.

You should call me soon, and we can talk about meeting up at the dance. They're not letting seniors in, but there's a door in back of the art room that has a busted lock, so I could wait out there and get you in and no one would notice. It would be really cool, I think. We could be together again just like Saturday, I don't know where, but we could find a place.

Love Jess

She had gone ahead with it this time, Lea noted. After two nights of sex she felt confident enough with Colin to sign her note "Love Jess," although she took care to write the words next to each other, not separated by the intimacy-inducing comma.

Lea hesitated, aware of an impending failure of nerve. She knew what the next note said, having read it several times to ascertain its place in the column, but she had not taken in its meanings or its implications until now, and she did not want to be reminded of them. She did not want to see how this story ended. She sat alone in the near-darkness, the bulb of the lamp seeming dimmer and yellower. Colin shifted his feet in bed but stayed asleep.

Colin:

What is wrong with you? Why didn't you show up to Katie's party? I TOLD Katie to throw the party so that you would come! I can't believe you didn't even call me. Michelle says you called her the other day. I bet you guys talked about me. Michelle says she's my best friend but she talks about me all the time. Holy shit. Are you fucking Michelle? Oh my God, that would not surprise me at all. I hate you both so much.

I can't believe you did that to me. I guess I knew that you would, but after the things you said I thought maybe you really cared about me. And you didn't even try anything for so long. We were friends for like two months before you even kissed me. Why would you do this to me? Do you think I fuck a lot of guys? You were the first guy, you fucking prick. I don't want to fuck another guy ever again, I really don't.

I hope you die.

Jess

Lea wondered if the girl remembered what she had written and felt guilty about it now. He hadn't died, of course, but it would have been the same thing to the teenagers who knew Colin. She thought about this faceless girl and her wasted virginity, about the hate that she expressed so suddenly and, Lea assumed, so uncharacteristically. Her boy was capable of bringing out such things in people. He had been a reckless boy.

She wanted to write to the girl and explain, but she did not know how she would. She did not know if there was an explanation for it. The further she read in the notes, the more Lea understood that her mission had perhaps been ill-conceived, that it would not satisfy her. She had sought to learn what kind of boy Colin had been, what he had done that she did not know about, but now she was understanding that none of this would explain why he had been this way. She might never understand why her son had played with these girls like a malicious god, why he had thought it right and good that he should shave the eyebrows off another boy. All she knew was that the more she looked into his life, the more she would begin to understand that Colin had most likely received exactly what he had had coming to him, and that the people who had known him in his brief life—the girls, the Jesuit brothers, the teachers—would, if pressed, agree with this assessment.

The remaining columns of notes illuminated a similar pattern in Colin's behavior, although these girls seemed to have understood what they were getting into. The last note in the last column betrayed the writer as vaguely wounded, but hardly as vitriolic as Jess. Colin had apparently tired of her in late November. "I heard you're taking that Township bitch Jenny to the Christmas Dance. Have fun with that skank. She must suck dick like it's her job, cause she's a fucking loser," wrote the last author, a girl named Kara. Another epistle, written by a different author at some point near Thanksgiving Break, made reference to Jenny from Breed's Township High as well, but Jenny herself did not seem to have written to Colin.

The girls, Lea came to understand, saddened her as much as anything about Colin, as much as his handicap, his amorality, her own failures that his character spoke to. They would still be out there, not absolved of their sinfulness by the grace of brain damage. They would be out tonight, Lea thought, right now, at the home of someone's absent parents, yielding to the desires of their drunken, muscular lovers, telling themselves lies about the nature of love so the boys wouldn't have to. The damage was ongoing with these girls; Colin's damage had been quick, and only momentarily painful.

The boy awoke and mumbled to her. She turned on the bedside lamp and bent beside him. "Do you need something, Colin?" She took a plastic cup from the bedside table. "Water? Do you want water?" She touched her throat. "Are you thirsty?"

He nodded, then took a long drink and dribbled onto the collar of his pajamas. He lay his head back on the pillow and looked into Lea's eyes.

"Mom," said Lea. "I am Mom." She touched his chest. "You are Colin, I am Mom."

He nodded again, very quickly and with closed eyes, almost as if he were insulted. "Yes. Yes. Mom and Colin." It was still his voice, froggy from disuse but with the same tone and pitch.

"Are you okay?" she said.

He didn't respond, and she played with the remote on the bed until it sat him nearly upright, and he nodded. "Music?" she asked, and again he nodded.

They had learned in the hospital that he liked soft music. Television gave him headaches, so much so that he responded in a Pavlovian flinch whenever he saw one. It had taken Lea a long time to learn how to work Colin's stereo, which they had bought him for his seventeenth birthday; the five-disc CD changer had been filled with rap music. The stereo was now stocked with Billy Joel, James Taylor, John Denver, Carole King. As with so many other things, this seemed to Lea almost like a cruel joke she played on the boy she had known. Colin had always insisted that Lea and Geoffrey turn off their crap music in the living room when his friends were coming over, and now he loved it. She used the stereo's remote control to turn on "Rocky Mountain High." He moved his toes to keep awkward time, and he smiled at her. Lea sang to him, and he smiled more, he giggled.

"Music," said Colin.

"That's right, baby boy. Music."

# | thirteen |

*Jenny was enrolled* in something called the Student Work Consortium, which meant that she got to leave school at noon and still earn high school credit, as long as she proved that she worked at least thirty hours a week. It meant that she had been able to work several lunch shifts a week at the restaurant. In the listing of the courses at Breed's Township High, the Consortium was described as a kind of internship program, a chance for seniors to earn credit while gaining real-world experience. In practice, no Consortium students ever really went to work after school as bank clerks or legal interns; everyone just packed in more hours at the Baskin Robbins or the Texaco or the O'Ruddy's. As a condition of enrollment in the program, students had to provide a copy of their parents' tax returns. The Consortium kids didn't work because they wanted to learn the mutual funds business or so they could finance their spring-break trip to Cabo San Lucas. Being in the Consortium program meant that you were poor.

It also meant that Casey might be able to find Jenny in the early afternoon, so after the interview with Jake he drove to East Breed's. He remembered the way to her house, and he drove slowly, taking the route that swung him past his mother's old house and then past the downed electric pole, still ensnared in the fibrous arms of the elm tree.

He parked on the street and marched across the frozen snow of Jenny's yard. The house looked even smaller than he remembered it, even more set back from the street, as if hiding itself in shame from passing cars. The light was on in a room that abutted the screened porch. Against the gray sky and the dirty white lawns, the light looked meager, a hopelessly artificial way of staving off the bleakness that surrounded Jenny's room.

Jenny answered the door wearing a red fake-leather coat that came down to her knees. A large clip held the mass of her ruffled hair together, and she had painted her lips and her eyelids a shade of orange. She grinned at Casey when she registered his face and waited for him to speak. He wished he could see her sometime without the distraction of her quirky makeup and hairstyles. Even with them she was beautiful, and he wondered if she suppressed her attractiveness on purpose. It would have been like her to consider her beauty a sign of weakness, or at least of predictability. He knew he had looked at her for too long, because the smile quickly turned into something else, a stare of curiosity.

"What's up?"

"Jenny. Hello. I'm glad I caught you. I didn't know if you'd be working."

"I started at the damn China Pagoda last Saturday."

The China Pagoda was in East Breed's. Casey had never noticed anyone working there who was not Chinese, but it did not surprise him that she had wangled the job.

"So O'Ruddy's is done."

"Yep. Just as well. Mitch watched over things for the last week. It was pretty bad."

"Hmm," said Casey, nodding. Mitch was a pathologically humorless assistant shift manager. "Yeah. Mitch can be kind of difficult."

"Difficult?" she said. "Mitch is Hitler." She began to do an impression of Mitch that was remarkably accurate. " 'Miss Gales,' " she said in Mitch's robotic baritone, " 'I cannot tell you how it upsets me the way you roll your silverware. One would think that you had learned to roll silverware in a place where people don't use silverware.' I swear to God he said that to me once."

She stared at the doorjamb, lost in the remembrance of her torturous week.

"Jenny, I was talking to someone earlier today about that Friday night."

She zipped up her coat and straightened herself. He didn't know if she just didn't want him to stay or if she was ashamed to show him her house. "It's kind of weird to talk about that now, Mr. Fielder. I already talked to the cops, and then the newspaper kept bugging me. It's all anyone talked about at school for a long time. Everyone wants to know if I know who did it. There were a lot of rumors."

"Well, I'm sorry to be like everyone else, Jenny, but I do have a vested interest. I mean, if you know who was involved . . ."

"Shit, Mr. Fielder, no." She said *no* forcefully, as if scolding a puppy. "You saw them. How could I tell who it was?"

"But you knew the boy. You said you knew him. But I've been thinking about that, Jenny. I wonder if there was something more to it. You and the wounded boy. I think there was something between you. In fact, I feel pretty sure about it."

She didn't say anything, so he tried again. "When you came outside, after the fight . . . the way you were carrying on. It seemed to me that you must have known him. Cared about him."

"I didn't care for him very much, Mr. Fielder. But I knew him."

"And you were, um . . . You were lovers."

She laughed at the word, and even Casey recognized the archaic sound of it, and he grinned at himself, ducked his head. "I mean, you guys had a relationship."

"We fucked. That's what we did. I don't think I've ever heard you say that word. Go ahead and try it out. Ask me if we fucked." Her words were not acrimonious, but playful. She scrunched up her nose and teased him again. "Just say it, Mr. Fielder, say the word. 'Hey, Jenny, you and that kid—did you two fuck each other?' "

"Jenny, I think I should know this. I think I deserve that. I lost my job."

"So did I. Anyway, you didn't lose your job because the kid and I fucked. You lost your job because you didn't call the police."

"You said the phone was out!" The words came in an automatic screech, as if she had elicited them by pushing a button.

She looked away, embarrassed for him. He let a silence pass to cleanse the air of his strange outburst, the irrefutable evidence that there was nothing genuine about the measured tones he had tried to adopt. "You said the phone was out and I believed you," he said. "That's why I lost my job."

Casey didn't ask her; for some reason he found that he was not able to, but she answered the unspoken question anyway.

"The phone *was* out. The line was dead. What were we supposed to do?" The question was not rhetorical. She meant it, she was curious. What were they supposed to do?

"I don't know. Something other than what we did, apparently." Another silence passed. "How long had you been fucking the guy?"

She grinned and then shrugged. "Two months? Something like that."

He had a thousand questions for her but knew he would be allowed only a few more. He spoke slowly. "But he wasn't your boyfriend. You just had sex?"

"Mr. Fielder, this is way, way outside of what you can understand. You have no idea. No offense, but you're too old. You just don't know what it's like to be my age here. What my friends and me do on weekends, what we do for fun—it wouldn't make sense to you. But it does to me. So yeah, we just had sex a few times. He was a really good-looking kid, and I hadn't ever done it with a rich guy before."

"But the fight, it was just a coincidence that he was there?"

"What do you mean by that?"

"Did he know you worked there?"

She bit her thumbnail and shook her head. "I don't think so. He might have. He wasn't there to see me, though, if that's what you mean. He didn't think about me much."

Jenny looked embarrassed, or so it seemed to Casey. He had never seen her abashed before, so he wasn't sure what to think. He was sure, though, that he was running out of time, that she wanted him to leave. "But the way you acted when you saw him—you were so upset. It seemed like it was someone you cared about, that's what it seemed like to me."

Again she shrugged, and now she reached for the side of the door, a movement that would precede its closing. "I just felt bad for him. We weren't in love or anything. God, no. Colin Chase couldn't be in love. That guy wasn't interested in anything about me except getting in my pants. I've heard he was like that. He's had everyone in town, pretty much, and he's the kind of guy that can still get laid even with that reputation." She absently swung the door gently back and forth. "It's kind of impressive, if you think about it. Maybe that's what impressed me. Anyway, I'd slept with him. A few times. And I saw his brains or whatever spilling out of his head, so yeah, I was a little upset. I had the right."

He made an overture to leave so she wouldn't have to kick him off her lawn. She nodded her goodbye, and, as if remembering suddenly, she wished him good luck; in regards to what, she did not say.

"I'm sorry to pry like this, Jenny. It just seems that there are some things I don't know, that I'd like to know. I still don't understand why it all happened. I'm still a little fuzzy on a few things."

"Yeah, I can see that," she said, and then smiled broadly. "Mr. Fielder, you're fuzzy on a lot of things." She waved, stepped back, and shut the door. Through the thin wood he heard her respond to the comment with a belated giggle.

# fourteen

*He sat* on one of the living room couches, waiting for Rachel to come downstairs. The presence of her dead parents was especially palpable in the living room, and he felt vaguely guilty for having spoken to Jenny that afternoon. He worried that Rachel would smell Jenny's strong perfume on him; he had stood at least a yard away from the girl, but she wore a lot of it. Eventually Rachel came down and sat beside him with the yearbook he had requested. She laid it on her lap and began to leaf through the pages gently, narrating some of the scenes to him, giving commentaries on certain of her colleagues and students. Casey began to feel as though they were looking at a book of mug shots.

She had showed him two or three pages of last year's junior class photos before he stopped her. "I don't think this is working, Rachel. I don't remember faces too well. I might remember a face, but not if it's just a face. I need to see bodies."

Rachel nodded slowly, careful to exhibit patience. She shut the book and turned toward him. Her hair was pulled back in a ponytail, and she wore a thick knitted sweater that minimized her large chest. She knew that Casey should not be distracted tonight; he had come over with a mission, and it had nothing to do with her breasts, which sometimes seemed to be his favorite thing about her. When he had arrived at her house, she had kissed him quickly, and she had taken his hands in hers when he began to reach for her backside.

"Let's start again," she said now, still with conspicuous patience, and she opened the yearbook to the first page, the page that, if she had been a student, would have been filled with obscene jokes and reminders to have a kick-ass summer.

She took the job seriously, allotting more than a minute to each page. Even on the pages that were clearly not propitious for their task—the page dedicated to the cheerleading squad, the montage chronicling the debate team's season—she lingered, tracing her finger over each face and body. She never once asked him if he recognized any of them, understanding that if he did, he would probably tell her. Instead she would look up from the yearbook, stare at Casey for two or three intense seconds, then look back at the pictures. She was unabashed, clinical. It made Casey feel as if she were an eye doctor, watching his expression not to gauge intent or emotion but simply to see how the organs worked.

He did not recognize any kids, and the more he looked at them, the more he doubted that he ever would. The race of teenagers began to seem uniform to him. But he did not admit this to Rachel, because he enjoyed looking at the pictures. She had never shown him the yearbook before, though he was now realizing, in spite of her blank expression, that these children and this place constituted a huge portion of her life.

In the still photos, absent the noise and menace that Casey associated with teenagers, the students looked exuberant and joyful. He saw sinewy girls sweating through a basketball practice, a gang of lean, shirtless boys hurling mud at each other in some charity volleyball game, the principal handing an award to a stunted young man with an enormous head, a group of male teachers dressed in drag during the school's talent show. It was Breed's Township High the way he had never known it, the way no one had ever known it. In truth it was a stark, enormous school, homogeneous in a sense (white, poor) yet still divided into the usual cliques and sets. The teachers lasted a long time because of the favorable state benefits and a strong union. The sports teams could generally be counted on to give the township something to talk about, and Penn State recruiters sometimes visited. Thanks in part to the property taxes from the parents who sent children to St. Brendan's, the school did not want for funds. But the sense of shared purpose, of what might once have been called school spirit, the sense of affection among people at Township (apart from the lovers who necked in the parking lot, the dozen or so couples every year who produced offspring) was a fabrication of the yearbook. Still, he liked seeing it. He liked the pictures, the magic lie the photos and the enthusiastic copy and the bright fonts could conjure. He liked to imagine, for this small stretch of moments, that when Jenny and Rachel left for school, this was where they went.

Rachel spoiled this for him as they gazed at the page dedicated to the marching band. She touched the face of the band instructor, a fit man in middle age with white hair, and then the face of a flutist whose head was turned away from the camera. "This guy, Mr. Rudolph, he got this girl pregnant." Casey nodded solemnly as she watched his reaction to this, and then she turned the page.

The final twenty or so pages were dedicated to student advertisements, photos and messages that the students could design themselves and include for a fee. Most of the captions involved encrypted references to parties and sex, the photos taken during their bacchanalian weekends. Several pages from the end, Casey saw a boy posing with four others. His back was up against the back of a friend, and he was slouched, with his arms crossed tightly across his chest, in the pose of a rap star. The hair was cropped, the face indistinct, but the enormous teal Starter jacket, bearing the logo of the San Jose Sharks, gave the boy away.

"Okay," said Casey, sounding strangely disappointed, and in fact this was how he felt. Not relieved or intrigued, but disappointed — that he had not remembered this exact detail, and, he confessed to himself, that he now knew what his next step had to be. "The San Jose Sharks. Are they popular around school?"

"I don't think so. Why?"

"This kid. I don't know about the face, but it could be him. I remember the coat. Unless lots of kids have those coats, then I'm pretty sure I saw this kid out there."

She nodded at the picture, then looked up at Casey.

"He wasn't one of *them*," Casey said. "He left earlier. I remember him and his coat diving into a car before most of the others. But he was there. He was fighting. What about it? Is he that type of kid?"

She looked back at the picture and traced the form. "Brady Benson. Oh, yeah. That's your guy." Abruptly she shut the book and retreated into the corner of the couch. "He's trouble."

"You've taught him?"

"Yeah. He's the kind of kid who uses swear words when he writes reports. He has a tattoo on his neck."

Casey nodded, as if this settled something.

"Apparently they won't do that in Pennsylvania," Rachel said. "Tatoo your neck. So if you want it done, you have to drive to New Hampshire. He's definitely the kind of kid who would drive four hours to get a neck tattoo, although he wouldn't spend thirty minutes reading about the Ottoman Empire so that he'd pass history."

Rachel nudged Casey's thigh with her foot to claim his attention, which seemed to have wavered. "Now what?"

"What do you mean?" he said.

"I mean what are you going to do about this? Now that you know Brady was in on it."

"I don't know. I thought maybe you'd have some advice."

She looked at him with a face that was entirely, intentionally inexpressive, the kind of look a novice card player might confuse with a poker face. It meant, of course, that something significant was happening in the inaccessible confines of his girlfriend's head. She was defining him in some way; her mind was scribbling a judgment and filing it away where it would become her inalienable opinion of him.

"What do you think you should do?" she finally asked.

"Find him, I guess."

"What would you ask him?"

"I just want to know what they were doing there. I realize there's nothing I can do now. There's no way to really make things right. But I want to know why they chose O'Ruddy's. I want to know why they did it."

She nodded. "That's reasonable. But is it reasonable to expect him to tell you? And is it reasonable to think he could answer you if he wanted? You think they chose that place for any good reason? You think they hated each other for any good reason?"

"Maybe."

"Yeah, maybe. But more likely, no. They're seventeen-year-old kids. I know them. Not just their type, I know those kids personally. Whoever they were, I'm sure I've taught some of them. They very, very rarely have a reason for doing whatever it is they do, outside of personal gratification and peer pressure. Whatever you're looking for Brady to give you, whatever theory you're cooking up about class warfare or the honor of a lady, he's not going to let you have it. He wouldn't be able to articulate it. They fought each other just because they did. They thought they were supposed to, for some twisted reason. I just don't want you to be disappointed. I know you think you'll find some kind of exoneration here."

Casey was gratified by her little speech, because it reversed their normal roles somewhat. It was now Casey who knew something Rachel didn't, it was now Rachel who was on the receiving end of a blank look that masked a profound sense of superiority.

Rachel was wrong. He knew this more surely than anything in his tenuous world. There was a reason for the fight, something beyond Rachel's simplistic interpretation of peer pressure and vague teenage angst. The spectacle had been predetermined; there had been a goal, an arrangement. He didn't know how he knew this, but he believed it entirely. Brady Benson and his ilk had been there to maim, possibly to kill. Rachel had a point that this boy might not be forthcoming about the motives behind the fight, but at least it was certain that he knew the truth. Brady Benson, the boy with the neck tattoo. Casey knew where to go now, there was a path to follow. Rachel had said the word mockingly, or as if it were an imaginary concept, but to Casey it was a synonym for hope. Exoneration. It was out there somewhere.

# fifteen

*There had been* a smoking lounge when Casey had gone to Breed's Township High. Nestled between the home economics room and the biology lab, both of which made the hall smell bad anyway, the smokers' lounge was a kind of egalitarian community, a place where teachers and students, janitors and vice principals, caf workers and department heads were united in the bonds of addiction.

Now smoking was forbidden on school property, and so the student smokers gathered at the edge of the sophomore parking lot (parking in the main lot being restricted to upperclassmen) where a line of demarcation had been identified. There was no natural barrier, but someone had ascertained that the school property ended exactly halfway across the sophomore lot. Though no administrators ever wandered so far from the building, the smokers stayed beyond the line, mindlessly believing in its ability to make their actions licit.

This is where Brady Benson could be found, Casey learned. On

Friday morning he went to the school. He asked the secretary where he might find the boy, implying that he was a relative. The secretary did not play along, and so he wandered the halls for a time. Nothing, not the tiles, not the teenage stink, not even the tenor of the pep club posters on the walls, had changed since his own adolescence, but he did not feel comfortable in this place. When the bell rang, hundreds of bodies rushed into the corridors, and he was soon awash in youth. Although he meant to ask one of them where Brady might be found, he discovered that he could not approach them. He felt like a tourist in a foreign bazaar, unable to communicate with the teeming mass around him. Soon the bell rang again, pulling the drain on the flood of students and leaving him alone and slightly stunned.

The classrooms were grouped by department, and glancing at the wall decor of the rooms he passed, he could get a sense of where he was. After meandering through the science and language wings, he began to notice maps, timelines, portraits of the presidents, which told him he was in social studies. Finally he came to Rachel's room.

He could see her well enough through the glass strips that bordered the door. She stood in front of her desk, setting some of her weight on the edge of it, but she was quick to get up and take a few steps back to the chalkboard or over to a map. She was talking about Magellan in a conversational way, not as if she were repeating a lecture she had given a dozen times but as if someone had asked her a particular question. He thought (with something that might have been pride, with a different girlfriend) that she was a teacher the students would be glad to have. She spoke with earnestness; she looked starkly attractive in her crisp blouse and black skirt; every once in a while she said something that made them laugh. Eventually the bell rang and he waded through the outpouring students to get to her.

"I'm sorry," he said immediately. "I need your help. I'll leave right away, I just need to know how to find this kid. Brady."

"Did you ask any students?"

He shook his head firmly.

"So this is your plan? Huh. Well, I don't know where he is. I don't even teach him anymore. And I can't ask a student—that would look fishy, especially with you around."

He waited for her to speak again, and as the vanguard of the next class began to filter in, she did, in a firm whisper. "Try the sophomore lot. Where the smokers go. It may be awhile, but he'll be there eventually." He thanked her and turned to leave, and she reminded him in a whisper not to come back.

It hadn't taken long for Brady to appear. Casey staked out the sophomore lot for the next thirty minutes, then spotted the teal coat that the boy wore like a pelt. Casey got out of the car and approached the pack of smokers.

Brady was speaking to two other boys, both of them with visible tattoos as well, although not on the neck. Brady spoke to Casey first. "What the fuck? We're allowed to smoke over here, this isn't school property."

"Okay," said Casey, who had been caught by surprise.

"So get the fuck out."

"I'm not here for that."

Brady took a thoughtful drag, nodding as he did so. "That is the ugliest fucking hat I've ever seen," he said.

"Can I talk to you? Over here?" Casey gestured to his car.

"You a fag?"

Brady's friends laughed, so Casey didn't answer, loath to open himself up to more ridicule. In a surprising move, Brady stepped on his cigarette and walked away from his friends. It had been too easy to get him alone, Casey thought. He wondered if the boy thought he had come for a drug deal.

Casey shuffled ahead of Brady, and paused at his car. Brady leaned against the trunk. "Okay, go. What is it?"

"I need to ask you some questions that might be uncomfortable. For us both. In regards to Friday night."

"Something going on Friday night I should know about?"

"No, I mean that Friday night a few weeks ago. At O'Ruddy's. I know you were there. Because I was there too, and I saw you."

"Trust me, you don't know shit."

"Well, be that as it may, I recognize you. I'm not saying you were one of the kids who did the serious damage. In fact, I can vouch for the fact that you didn't. I remember you running off pretty early, actually."

Casey hadn't meant to offend him, but he could hardly have been more insulting. Brady straightened from his slouch and faced Casey. "You remember me running off?"

There didn't seem to be a way out of this. Casey had to prove to the boy that he had been there, and in what had become one of his clearest memories of that evening, he remembered that the boy in the teal jacket had been one of the first to flee, after being manhandled by a teenager in a St. Brendan's letter jacket. "I'm not making any judgments," said Casey. "I'm just saying I was there. I'm not here to get anyone in trouble, and I'm not here to talk about how you behaved during the fight. I really don't care about that much. But I have some questions."

"So what?"

Casey knew he had no way of compelling this boy to tell him anything, though he'd been able to deny this fact until now. Rachel had told him that some of the boys had already been identified, or suspected, because they had come to school on Monday, January 21, with various cuts and bruises. It seemed likely that Brady had already been hauled into the principal's office for questioning, and it seemed equally likely that he had not said anything there. Brady's question was very appropriate. Why should he care what Casey wanted to know?

Unexpectedly, Brady was the one to break the silence. "Wait a minute. You were there? What does that mean?"

"I used to be the manager of O'Ruddy's. I could see the fight happening through the window."

Brady's eyebrows raised, and his mouth slid open. "Oh shit, you're *that* guy. Okay. I get it."

"What do you mean, I'm *that* guy?" Brady didn't answer, consumed in the process of lighting a new cigarette. "You know who I am?" Casey's voice was rising toward the frantic. "What do you mean, you get it? What the hell is going on?"

"Relax. Jesus, just relax." It was windy, and he burned through several matches before looking up at Casey again. "I meant what I said. You're *that* guy, the restaurant manager. You didn't call the cops on us. Hey, thanks, man, you really saved our asses."

Casey was not certain enough of his irony to grow indignant. "I wasn't trying to save your asses," he said, in a nasal monotone that sounded so whiny he was certain Brady would imitate it later to his friends. "I just thought maybe you guys would get it out of your system. I thought you'd just leave."

"That's not what I heard."

Again Casey's voice rose, his face red. "What the hell does that mean? What did you hear?"

The boy shrugged. "I don't know. Forget it."

"It's not that easy. You heard what? Where did you hear it?"

Again Brady shrugged, raising the thick shoulders of his San Jose Sharks coat. Casey realized now that the boy was slight—five and a half feet tall and thin, the kind of thin that comes more from malnutrition than from exercise. "Shit dude, relax," the boy said. "I'm not saying anything. I just read the papers, you know. They said you didn't want the restaurant to get shut down."

It was an answer designed to pacify Casey, and to some extent it did, but for days afterward he would sort through every word and gesture of this part of their conversation, fretting over the implications. *That's not what I heard.* Casey would hear this in his dreams, until he was certain that what Brady had been about to say, whatever it was that Brady had heard, would explain once and for all to what extent Casey had been culpable.

"The restaurant got shut down anyway, Brady."

"How do you know my name?"

"I've heard things too." The response sounded incomparably lame. Brady acted as if he hadn't even heard it, perhaps to save them both from embarrassment.

"Well, shit. I can't tell you anything. I don't even know what you're doing here."

"I just want to know what happened. I want to know what you guys were doing there. I lost my job. I could be in a lot of trouble, I don't know yet. And everyone seems to think it was just a bunch of kids who didn't like each other and needed a place to fight, but I don't think so. That doesn't explain anything. What happened to that boy — his name is Colin — that's got to be explained somehow. What I saw that night doesn't make sense."

"What kind of answer do you want?" Brady asked this casually, as if offering an assortment of narcotics to a customer.

"What the hell happened?" Casey rasped. "Why did you guys do that? Why did you fight those other boys? And why did those friends of yours try to kill Colin Chase?"

Brady smirked wickedly. "Just get the fuck out of here. Go. Drive off, and never fucking bother me again."

"I can't do that. You need to understand that. I have to talk to you about this. I'm going to talk to you about this." He pulled his wallet from his back pocket, then turned around quickly, having decided that the boy shouldn't see how many bills he had on him. He considered it a reasonable thing to do, but his movements were awkward and he felt a shiver of embarrassment. He tucked the wallet into the inside pocket of his puffy coat, then turned back to the boy, holding out two twenty-dollar bills.

Brady took a deep breath, without the aid of his cigarette, then snatched the bills from Casey's hand. He looked toward the school, clearly thinking about his obligations there. Dismissing them along with his smoke, he patted the trunk. "Is this your car?" When Casey nodded, he went to the passenger side and said, "Get in."

Casey hadn't expected this, and was immediately concerned over what kind of aiding and abetting he might now be accused of, not just for taking Brady away from school but also for the wealth of illegal substances the boy certainly had on him. He drove silently out of the parking lot, squinting against the wet flakes on the windshield, and followed Brady's instructions. After ten minutes of weaving through East Breed's, they arrived at a strip mall near the highway, and Brady told Casey to park in front of the dry cleaners.

Brady pointed toward the neon window signs at the end of the strip. "Happy Jack's Liquors. One big bottle of the cheapest vodka they have, and two cases of Coors. They're on special." He pulled out and separated the two bills Casey had given him ten minutes earlier, then held out one of them. Casey wondered if Brady had already forgotten where the money had come from.

He said, "It's going to be a lot more than twenty bucks," and when Brady happily held out the remaining bill, Casey realized he must have given the impression that he would do this.

He shook his head and put his hands on the steering wheel. "Wait a second. No, this is just silly. I'm not going to buy you alcohol. You're, what, seventeen years old? For God's sake, no way."

Brady assumed a dramatic look of exasperation, the kind of look Jenny had given Casey whenever he denied her a scheduling favor. The look spoke for the entire tribe of teenagers, it was meant to imply the enormity of the adult world's failure to understand them. "Don't go all Mothers Against Drunk Driving on me," Brady said. "You think I haven't had booze before?"

"I'm certain that you have, Brady. I'm just saying it's not going to be me who supplies you with it."

Brady looked at him directly, his nose wrinkled. "You really don't know anything, do you?"

"What does that mean? This isn't going to work, you know. I'm not going in there."

"No, not that. I mean you really just don't know anything about the fight. I just thought maybe you were a perv or something. Someone told me that you had something with Jenny. But I think you're just fucking clueless. You really didn't call the cops 'cause you were afraid to lose your job? Oh man. That's almost funny."

Even if it had seemed more calculated, even if Brady were simply pulling out all the stops to get Casey to purchase liquor, it still would have worked. The mention of Jenny's name and the flippant reference to an affair between them hit him like a cold wind. "You've got to give me something." Casey stared down at the wet black floorboards, the melted snow dripping from the accelerator. "I don't know what you're talking about. I don't know anything about it. You need to tell me everything."

"Well, I don't know about everything, Pops. But you go buy me the goods and I'll tell you a story."

It had, of course, already been decided. In no alternate universe could Casey imagine himself refusing the boy's invitation to hear the story, regardless of the sacrifice it entailed. He looked around the parking lot. There would be no doubt here, he would be incriminating himself. The crime was straightforward enough this time, and he felt himself straining against it, all the while knowing that his guilt, his imminent regret, every instinct that told him to avoid the risk, was academic. He simply had to know, and the decision was not really even one that had to be made. It was like Alice swallowing the red pill; how could she not have? How could Casey not incriminate himself now by going into Happy Jack's? How could he simply drive back to Breed's Township High and eternally wonder what this hooligan had been willing to tell him? Inconceivable, worse than any torment that understanding might bring.

# | sixteen |

*I know this is rough.* Real rough. On both of you guys. I am very much aware of that." Phil Lucas wore a black suit and a black tie, and Lea knew it was because of them, because he was meeting with people who were in a kind of mourning. "But you made a real good decision to come in here today. With this kind of thing, the quicker you move, the better off you are."

"Well, that's the key," said Geoffrey. "We want to move on. And we want to make sure Colin gets the best treatment there is."

"Oh, absolutely on that, Geoff." Phil still pronounced his name with phonetic fidelity: Gee-Off. It had been his nickname in his fraternity days, and Phil, unlike the other pledge brothers, had not abandoned it. "There's a limited amount we can actually do right now, other than write some letters of intent. The fact is, since we don't know if Colin's going to make any progress, it's hard to know how much to ask for just yet. But I wanted to meet with you both to talk about strategy."

Phil looked at Geoffrey when he spoke, and Lea looked at Phil, almost daring him to return her gaze. She had always made him uncomfortable, and she knew it. He was the kind of man whose garrulity typically inspired the same in others, and with people like Lea, whom he could not seem to bring around to bonhomie, he became unsure of himself, feeling a judgment in their silence. This talk of settlement money at such a time would not improve his case. And yet there was a job to do.

"As I've said before," Phil continued, "we'll want to go after the headquarters. They're legally responsible in terms of accidental employee deaths, deaths from fires, and the like, and it's not too much to extrapolate that to what happens in the parking lot."

"And they've got more money," said Lea.

"Well, yes, that's a fact we can't run away from."

"What are we asking for?"

Phil cleared his throat in an effort to stall or to announce his discomfort, but he took it too far and dislodged a cluster of mucus that required more elaborate plumbing. He coughed and grunted, snorted, sniffed, and finally expelled the slimy ball into a handkerchief. Geoffrey and Lea looked at each other, close to smiling.

"Excuse me. Anyway. Money, that's a tricky matter. As I said, we can't really put a dollar figure on anything until we know the extent of the damage. Gee-off, you've told me that right now your boy is functioning at a four-year-old level. Is that still the case?"

"More or less. His cognitive function is about the same as the typical four-year-old's."

"Has been for how long now?"

"A little over a month."

"What does that mean, then? Any chance of improvement?"

Geoffrey spoke languidly, as if he were making up the prognosis as he went along, although he had recited it to Lea a dozen times. She could have given it herself. "The longer he goes without recovering, the less likely it is that he'll regain complex functions—problem-solving skills, adult social skills. His ability to learn new concepts. There's no formula, no way to break it down. There's no set amount of days after which we give up on it. I just don't know, Fluke," he said, lapsing into fraternity nomenclature. "It doesn't look too good now."

There were several moments of solemn nodding between the men. Lea looked at a framed photograph on the corner of Phil's desk, showing Phil, his wife, Kelly, and their son, Michael. Michael was thirteen now and very overweight, slack and loose of flesh like his parents. He would be starting high school in the fall. Lea wondered how her son, in his sentient days, would have treated Michael. Would the younger Lucas have received amnesty because of the friendship of the fathers, or would Michael have incurred Colin's disdain like all the other fat kids? Would Colin have shoved him into lockers, would he have shaved off his eyebrows?

Phil threw out a number. "We'll go for eight million, or there-abouts, if his condition doesn't improve. That may seem an arbitrary number, but we've run through precedents and figured out what can be accounted for in terms of lost wages, pain and suffering, and the like. Eight million's on the high end, but by no means unusual for this kind of thing. There will be some negotiations, of course, and they won't want to go to court."

"So they'll just pay us a lot of money in the end," Lea said.

"Their insurance company will."

"And that will solve everything."

Phil was clearly surprised by the rancor in Lea's tone. She had not meant to sound so cynical, so biting, but her tone had made him sit up straighter in his chair. "Oh geez," he said. "Lea, no one's saying this will solve anything. I'm just trying to make you all more comfortable. Just trying to make sure our guy has everything he needs for his therapy."

With anyone else she might have felt shamed. Phil was in fact try-ing to help them, and she knew it was not for money but rather because of the joy such men took in coming to the aid of old fraternity brothers. Still, she knew too many stories about Phil to feel sorry for him. She knew that he had initiated the fraternity's tradition of dog-fights — parties at which awards were handed out to the brother who had brought the ugliest date. She knew that at one of their functions he had slept with a girl who had been nearly comatose with drink; it had been date rape, but the term was not used back then. Phil, in his day, had not been too different from Colin, although quite a bit more jovial and less athletic.

"What I mean," said Lea, still with a voice that sounded robotic, metallic, to her, "is that I wonder if justice will be served. Is that going to prevent this kind of thing in the future? Are the people who are really responsible going to be made to pay for this?"

It was rhetorical, of course. She knew that Phil would say the restaurant chain had not properly trained its franchises in handling such problems, and indeed Geoffrey seemed quickly converted to this point of view. They would all pay, both men told her — the corporation, the franchise owners, the manager who had hesitated in summoning help. They would lose the restaurant, their jobs, their reputations. They would pay.

And so would Colin, the one who perhaps was most to blame, but this went unsaid. She arrived at this conclusion on her own, in the awkward silence of the lawyer's room. Colin had already paid for his crime, so why was she investigating it? There would be no parole, no rehabilitation. She felt a diminishing sense of vengeance regarding the one who was out there somewhere, the boy with the metal rod. She knew somehow that he had done it for a reason, that the crime had not come from boredom or curiosity or sheer, stupid meanness. The boy who damaged Colin, even if his response was out of measure, had been provoked. It was not the same as what Colin had done to the other boy's eyebrows. That had been a whole different level of cruelty, a different type of insanity.

Geoffrey drove her home, silent and unresponsive as a small punishment for the way she had dealt with his friend, and then went back to work. Megan had been watching Colin, and when Lea got home, the boy and his aunt were on the floor in the living room, tracing designs into the carpet. Colin wore a sweatsuit and a baseball hat turned backward, a fashion habit from his previous incarnation that he seemed to remember. When Lea walked in, instead of greeting her, he turned to his aunt and said somberly, carefully, "Mom is home," and his aunt agreed with exuberance.

Megan had to get home, since the outing to Phil Lucas's had lasted longer than expected. After Lea closed the door behind her sister, she sat on the couch and listened to the Paul McCartney album that was blaring from the stereo for Colin's sake. The boy remained on the carpet, tracing designs into it vacantly, as if he didn't see them but was instead thinking about something very complex, or perhaps trying to figure out a particular strain of the music. He sat on his knees, his chin slumped almost to his chest.

It had been more than a month since his last day with a seventeen-year-old mind. He was still muscular. His face was unintelligent, his lips so slack that he sometimes released a strain of drool onto his chin, but the muscles were still there, the taut tendons of his neck, the biceps straining against the sleeves of the sweatshirt, which belonged to Geoffrey. At the hospital they told her he had lost a few pounds, which was normal, given the nausea that came with the headaches. She imagined that someday in the future he would look very different. His body would soon become confused by the abrupt cessation of exercise, and by the influx of foods that appealed to him now: lots of macaroni and cheese, cream of chicken soup. The muscles would atrophy, and good riddance to them. They were malevolent things; they had taken him away from her as much as anything had, inasmuch as they had made him attractive to girls, fearful to boys. His body would soften, turn toward fat. She was supposed to take him swimming soon, the doctor had told her. That would be fun, she had told Colin, and Colin had nodded sincerely.

She went to the kitchen to pour a glass of wine, filling it almost to the brim in order to empty the bottle. She changed CDs, then returned to the couch, cradling her glass with both hands. Colin was still tracing in the carpet. She thought about the settlement that would probably make them rich, and she thought about what Colin would have done to Michael Lucas if he had been around long enough to notice him, to notice how fat and ridiculous the son of his father's friend had turned out to be. Soon she had finished her drink, and she set the glass on the end table.

"Colin, look at me."

He did, but she did not know if he understood the words. His speech had improved lately, though his words were still slurred, and what he comprehended was often difficult to tell.

"Colin, I know you're in there. I can see you."

His eyebrows raised, and his mouth spread in the beginning of a smile, a gift to her, for he still didn't know what she meant.

"Do you think this is funny? Are you trying to embarrass me?" She slid herself off the couch, resting on her knees in front of him. He had lost the smile but was still staring at her.

"Or are you just trying to hurt me? I know you love to hurt me, but even you can see that this has gone too far. Much, much too far. For God's sake, we went to the lawyer today. We're starting to sue. You've got to put an end to this."

Colin now sat down on his rear, unfolding his knees from under him, and he paid great attention to his own movements as he did so, as if he were bored with her.

"*Colin*. Give it up, for the love of Christ!"

He retreated from her now, alarmed, sliding on his rump toward the television. His movements were graceless and plodding, and he had begun slowly to cry.

"*No!*" Lea screamed at him. "Stop it right now! I can't deal with you like this." She softened now and touched him gently on the knee. He stopped retreating, but he was still wary.

"Colin, we'll forget about things. I'll forget about the stuff in your room—I'm sorry I looked. I'm sorry I invaded your privacy like that." She took a deep breath and blew it out of puffed cheeks. "I wanted to know you, Colin, because you never let me know you. I want to understand you better."

She heard him make a noise, but she didn't look up, lost in what she wanted to be a monologue. "You scared us both so much. Your father doesn't know what to do. It's time to end it, Colin. Let's surprise him tonight. He'll forgive you like I do."

She looked up now, gradually, certain of the look she would find returning hers. She could picture it before she saw him, she could picture the smirk on the handsome, hard face. Her boy had perfected the smirk. It managed to convey his disdain and exasperation without giving any hint of humor. She knew she would find it now, that after this tirade and this concession, after her humiliation, he would claim victory while the opportunity lasted. The expression on his face would tell her everything, and she didn't even have to hear him speak. He would stand up and refuse to explain his behavior except in the vaguest of terms. Perhaps he was hiding from an outraged girl or some problem with the police, faking his own demise. It would not be a joke, of course, she would have to explain to him the pain he had caused (out of habit and a sense of responsibility rather than any faith that it would matter to him), but in the end they might treat it lightly, their gratitude might be so enormous that they could laugh it off. Her boy would be returned, and he would give her notice with that cynical, knowing smirk of his, an expression that it would be impossible for a four-year-old to assume. Things would not change much. They would still wait for him to go away, still live in a kind of muted fear of their only son. For some reason this was more than satisfactory to her, this was necessary. She accepted that Colin had returned to her, and she unaccountably felt joy. Colin had not provided her with this feeling for a long time.

But when she looked up, the face was still slack, still obtuse. It was difficult for her to imagine this face assuming a look of disdain. He stared at her blankly, teardrops on his cheeks.

She traversed the space between them on her knees with a rising fury that seemed to have disconnected her from her senses. She felt nothing but anger, and she felt it so completely that she thought she might pass out from its weight and intensity. She reached her boy and channeled the momentum of her furious crawling into her right arm, which she cocked behind her and swung around with a gasp, slapping him on his right cheek, hard enough to leave a red handprint on his face and a sting in her palm. *"I know you're in there!"* she screamed before she collapsed on the floor in front of him, spewing muffled wails and mucus onto the carpet, and the nescient boy lay down beside her and did the same.

# seventeen

*Casey was thirty-three* years old and had broken the law perhaps four or five times in his life, though never as egregiously as when he bought thirty-seven dollars' worth of liquor for the seventeen-year-old Brady Benson. As a boy he had shoplifted on occasion, and later in life he had smoked pot a few times in a Penn State dormitory. During such moments the piercing sense of his wrongdoing had come to him like a kidney stone pain, though it never came disguised as guilt or conscience, only as fear.

The two minutes in the liquor store, during which Brady waited in the car (though not ducking low in the backseat, as Casey had suggested), did not seem to last longer than any normal two-minute span; it was just that Casey felt the time pass more acutely than most moments of his life. He thought about nothing but consequence. Jail time, maybe, given the menace to society (especially teenage society), that he had already proven himself to be. And the sheer embarrassment that would ensue did not bear thinking about. Yet he needed Brady's story. He had already decided that, and here he was, browsing along the bottom shelf of the vodka section to look for the cheapest brand, as Brady had requested.

He bought the booze and returned to the car and they fled the scene without incident. The teenager did not disguise his pleasure. Brady would be greeted kindly by his friends that night, Casey assumed, like a pioneer father who has thrown an enormous buck onto the family table. *Look what I have gained for you*, he would tell them. *Drink up, and don't ask questions.*

"Don't you have to go back to school?" Casey asked after Brady directed him westward, away from the high school.

Brady smirked away the question, then said, "I guess I owe you."

"I just want the truth, Brady. Just tell me what happened. I'm not here to get anyone in trouble. I just need to know for myself."

"Well, it's like this. The whole thing is complicated."

Brady wore braces, and beneath them Casey could see that his teeth were yellowed from smoking and that his canines stuck out from the gums at a strange angle. He frequently reined back loose saliva with sucking noises.

"I'm sure it is," said Casey, who felt the boy and his promise slipping away. He assumed they were near his house now. The neighborhood that Brady directed him to was the same as Jenny's, not far from Casey's own boyhood home. Brady must live somewhere in the area, in some house, he found himself thinking, where the adults allowed their children to get tattoos on their necks.

To Casey's surprise and consternation, Brady invited him into the house when they got to it. The one-story home was festooned with Christmas lights, though at this time of year the fact indicated the family's sloth more than their holiday spirit; even the most elaborate nativity scenes had been packed away by now. Inside, the place was musty but neat. The living room had once been carefully decorated, but this had been long ago. The drapes and thick carpeting and the floral pattern on the couch were all a shade of powder blue. Brady ushered him into a room on the west side of the house, a room that was plastered with posters of Motocross racers. He gestured to a folding chair, which Casey duly sat on, and Brady flopped onto his bed, lighting a cigarette as he fell.

"First of all, I'm not naming names. I'm not gonna snitch, not on my buddies, not on anybody. Not even for booze. So don't even bother with that."

Brady now sat up and moved to the edge of the bed, honestly perplexed about how to begin. "Shit, man. Like I said, this is complicated. This is just fucked up." He squeezed the side of his head in order to focus, sucked hard on the cigarette, then turned to Casey.

The story was told fitfully, in the strange vernacular of his age and his class. The telling of it freed him from the rigid sense of dignity that he had cultivated in the beginning, so that at times he pranced about the room in imitation of a character or turned his voice falsetto to speak the dialogue of a woman. He backtracked frequently, and "Oh, shit, no, wait, I forgot something" became a kind of refrain. At times he provided explicit detail, at other times he was vague and perhaps untruthful. But on the whole Casey believed him, or he believed in the overall veracity of the tale, if for no other reason than that Brady was not equipped to improvise a story that was elaborate and internally consistent.

First, the boy explained, the story was not about Friday night at all, or at least not the Friday night that Casey meant. It would have been impossible to start there. The Friday that needed to be reckoned with before he could get to the main event had occurred several weeks earlier, in December. The first fight.

Brady was obliged to introduce a character, and with it a name. A friend of his, a boy that Casey could conjure no image for because Brady described him in terms that were important only to him — he smoked filterless Pall Malls, they had been friends since second grade. For a while Brady referred to him as "this buddy of mine," until other friends were introduced into the narrative and this phrase became unwieldy. For the purposes of the story they would call him Rick, Brady decided, after some deliberation.

That Friday in December, Rick had found a plan for the evening. There was a house, he said, a girl he knew was house-sitting, and she said he could bring a few friends over. Not too many, and they couldn't smoke anything inside. Rick would get there early, since he and the girl had a relationship of sorts, and Brady was to arrive with his group sometime after nine.

Brady eventually showed up with a handful of friends. Something seemed wrong from the beginning, he said. The house was in Leawood, not their area at all, barely in the Township district, in fact, though anyone who lived in this house would have gone to St. Brendan's or St. Theresa's. Brady did not know whether or not it could rightfully be called a mansion, but it was clearly larger, or at least more expensively furnished, than any home he had ever visited. Though he did not express this, Casey could tell that the home's elegance had engendered a small sense of shame in him, or perhaps anger at being so overwhelmed by the sight of things that he did not have. There was a jacuzzi, which no one could figure out how to operate. A walk-in freezer, in addition to an industrial refrigerator. A pool table with purple felt, a stereo that was literally built into the wall, a sectional couch that, laid end to end, would have stretched the length of Brady's house. "The bathroom even had one of those French ass-showers," he said.

The girl who was house-sitting must have stood in the stead of the home's owners, Casey thought, to remind Brady of his poverty. She wouldn't let them use the pool table, and she made them take off their shoes in the entryway. It was almost not worth it, Brady said at one point, for all the shit they weren't allowed to touch. *This is the other world*, the girl was saying to him, *and you are a stranger here.*

The drinking commenced. After a while Rick sneaked off to a back room, only to return a minute later with a large grin and a brown bag. "Surprise," he said to them, and with an exaggerated gesture he pulled a small tray from the bag, on which rested a sandwich bag that contained fine white powder. Brady had never seen cocaine except in the movies, and the presence of it, and its connotations of expense, wild sex, rock stars, and drug lords, enticed him more than anything else in the extravagant house.

Brady had never done it before, and he suspected that none of his friends had either, despite some pretensions of familiarity. They separated the cocaine into lines with an ATM card, erring, for once in their lives, on the side of moderation, since no one knew how much was standard. This was a trying time for them, as they were beyond the boundaries of their known transgressions. Brady and his friends were perfectly happy smoking pot, drinking to excess, even taking the occasional tab of acid, but the uncharted waters of cocaine created a kind of hesitant bitterness, much as the house had done.

Brady's tone of apprehension left him as soon as he started telling about the cocaine high, just as their apprehension must have left them that Friday night when the white powder finally shimmied its way up their noses. He now spoke about the drug as if it were some old lover that he knew he could never have again. He didn't try to describe the experience to Casey, understanding his own inadequate articulation — he'd had a hard enough time trying to explain the bidet — but he made it clear that it was a profound time for him and his friends. "We just had no idea," he said more than once. "I mean, you hear stories, but shit, you don't even know . . ."

The coke-addled teenagers soon began to chafe in the confines of the sterile house in Leawood, and they decided to go out to eat. Rick drove one car, an anonymous friend drove another, and they set out into the frigid night, faces aglow, hearts hammering. The friend's car, in which Brady occupied the passenger seat, followed Rick's, and Brady became vaguely aware, without minding too much, that they had driven away from the direction of the Taco Bell they'd agreed on. Instead they went down Arthur Avenue, toward their own neighborhood and high school, past the listless center of Breed's Township, where everything was frozen and black.

They passed by O'Ruddy's without incident, or so Brady thought until his cell phone went off. At this point in the narrative, Brady felt it necessary to pause and ransack his tiny room in search of this phone, so that he could play the ringer for Casey. He finally found it, clicked a button, and Casey listened intently, wondering what kind of expression this boy might accept as one of polite interest. The cell-phone ringer played "Back in Black" as Brady nodded along, and Casey nodded too, with great sincerity, and said, "Yeah, that's a pretty good one," which seemed to satisfy the boy.

"So there I am, high as a motherfucking kite, and it takes me a while to figure out what the hell is going on, until Gr—I mean, shit, until my buddy in the backseat says, 'It's your phone, dumbass.'"

The call was from Rick, who was perturbed. For narrative purposes, Brady dropped his voice as low as he could manage to impersonate his friend. Rick asked Brady if he had seen that. *Seen what?* Brady replied. Seen the fucker in the parking lot. *What fucker?* Brady asked, *and what parking lot?*

*Colin fucking Chase, that's who. That fuck.*

It was not the first time Brady had heard his name. The boy went to St. Brendan's, Brady said, but he was pretty well known around Township. He dated a few girls at school.

By this point Casey had the idea that Colin knew a lot of girls from Township, and dating wasn't exactly the word to describe his dealings with them, and he found this small prevarication telling. Brady was almost comically protective of his nascent manhood; his references to his own virility and suavity were at times so outrageous that Casey thought he might be kidding. He would not have liked the fact that this preppy boy came to poach the women of his school, of his people.

Yet Brady did not recognize the mere presence of Colin as a proper motive for taking any sort of action. He responded with a "So what?" to Rick's information, and Rick replied with an exasperated "What? Oh, shit, I didn't tell you about this?"

Tell him what?

Colin Chase had puked on his car, Rick said. At Hennigan's party last month, a party that Brady had missed for some reason. The bastard got wasted at Hennigan's and he ralphed on the Chevy Impala, a possession that meant much, much more to Rick than the woman who currently sat next to him.

"He got all goofed up on 151," Brady said, continuing his impersonation of his friend. "He was playing sink-the-Bismarck with rum and Coke." The clear implication was that he shouldn't have been there at all, being from St. Brendan's. Then Colin Chase had gone out and vomited on the Impala, and had been escorted away by some level-headed friends before Rick got word of it. But he knew it was him. Everyone said so.

Rick related this into the cell phone as he turned onto a side road, executed a three-point turn, then redirected the convoy south on Arthur Avenue. Brady's car followed.

Brady had been doubtful. This was clear in spite of the stress he placed on his own belligerence. Twice he reminded Casey that he had not been at Hennigan's party, thereby exonerating himself from any blame that might come from an unjust cause.

There were only five or six of them, Brady said, all St. Brendan's guys. The narrative Casey heard began to blend in his mind with the one Chad Richardson had told him. The boys who had been there first, the St. Brendan's kids, had milled about in the parking lot for twenty minutes before their antagonists arrived, until the cold forced them back into their big boxy cars, which were parked in a row. Chad Richardson had watched them from the moment they arrived, at one point grabbing a bag of trash from the kitchen so that he would have an excuse to go out to the dumpster and yell at them to leave. Yes, clearly they were waiting for someone. These boys had no intention of eating at O'Ruddy's, and there had been a sense of anticipation about them.

Brady's narrative was direct and colorless, and Chad Richardson's hadn't been much better, so Casey half closed his eyes and began to see it for himself, began to tell himself the story. He tried to hear the

stentorian voice of whatever rap singer the kids would have been listening to, he tried to smell the smoke of their cigarettes, to feel the almost palpable emission of energy and idiocy. He imagined Colin
Chase lounging against a huge front-wheel-drive automobile. He pictured the boys squinting against the sharp wind, their shoulders
hunched in defense, their teeth chattering so violently from the cold
that they could pretend it had nothing to do with their fear.

When the Township boys got to the lot, they parked beside each
other and away from the SUVs, near the cars that were there for le-
gitimate purposes. Colin and his friends moved as a group toward the
Impala and the Dodge.

Brady adopted a mock-husky voice to serve as Colin's. "What the
fuck—you get lost?" He seemed so invested in his performance, in
fact, that Casey thought he must have missed the significance of the
words themselves, and so he spoke.

"What does that mean?" Casey asked. "That's what Colin Chase
said? 'Did you get lost?' "

The significance had not been lost on Brady after all. He pulled on
his cigarette, which made Casey wince, since it had already been
smoked down to the end and the boy must have been inhaling nothing but burned filter. Then he said, "Yeah, I never figured that out.
Rick seemed kind of embarrassed. Right away he started shouting at
the dude, almost like he wanted to change the subject."

"But 'What the fuck, you get lost?'—that implies Rick was late.
That means that there was an arrangement. That you guys were supposed to meet there. That's pretty clear."

The boy shrugged. "You can look at it that way. I don't know."

"But you're sure he said that. You're sure those were his words."

"Yeah, man. I'm sure of it, okay? Fuck. Yeah, we were meeting
those guys there. Rick didn't even really try to sell it that hard. It was
like he was just . . . What's the word for when you're just doing something 'cause you're supposed to?"

"Going through the motions."

"Yeah. Yeah, that's what it was like. The whole story about the kid puking on his car. Fuck that, I would have heard about that. Rick wanted to fight that kid for some reason, and he wanted us there. He shouldn't have lied to us about it, but whatever. I don't care. Nothing much happened that night, and Rick scored us some fucking cocaine." He pronounced the word obnoxiously, still reveling in the memory of it. *Ko-kane*, he said.

"You never figured out why you fought."

Brady ignored this, and he might honestly have not heard, since he had leaned across the bed to flip on a lamp, and because Casey had said it softly.

The boy continued with the story, but Casey had grown impatient. Brady continued to talk about the fight simplistically, mostly describing his own valiant deeds against a boy he had previously scuffled with at a field party in the summer. The actual fighting had been instigated by the diatribe that Rick had begun (Casey now understood) in an effort to get Colin to shut up, and it had not lasted long. Chad Richardson had called the police almost as a nervous reflex, a cruiser had been dispatched, and the policeman inside it had scattered the group of boys summarily, clearly displeased with his mission and the weather.

Brady moved back onto his bed, his back up against the bottom of a Motocross poster, and stared at Casey with his brow furrowed, as if wondering at Casey's presence.

"And?" Casey said.

"What?"

"You've told me up to the Friday night in December. That doesn't really tell me anything. I need to know about the other one, the one where the boy got hurt. Remember?"

Brady probably did not remember this, and was not happy to be reminded of it. "Man, I've been talking for like forty minutes. I got shit to do. My mom'll be home soon. I can't get into all that shit now. Like I told you, it's complicated."

"When can you get into it?"

Brady sighed, making his stringy bangs levitate. "Shit. No. You can't just grill me like this forever." Casey almost protested that his questions had been limited in scope and frequency. It had seemed that Brady loved telling the story. But the boy continued his protest, laying it on thick. "I mean, that was a painful fucking night for me. Really, it may not seem like it, but what happened still bothers the shit out of me. My friends and me don't talk about it at all. It really fucking dis*turbed* us."

"I understand that. But we made a deal."

"I told you a story, man. I told you a fucking long-ass story."

Casey didn't respond, starting to understand what was coming next.

Brady finally said, "Okay, here's the thing. There is more. I got more to tell, but it can't happen now. We'll meet up later on and I'll give you some more."

"And when is that?"

"Next Friday," he said, but he phrased it as a question.

"I see. I guess that means there's another trip to Happy Jack's involved."

The boy grinned. "You catch on fast."

"Just say it, then," Casey said, feeling a rare spurt of righteous indignation. "You'll tell me the rest if I buy you more booze."

"Okay, yeah. I'll tell you the rest if you buy me more booze." He was still grinning, and in the new light from the lamp his face seemed shiny and sinister. "What's wrong with that? Everyone gets what they want."

Casey shrugged. "But who's to say the next story won't end this way? I have a feeling it will. You're a goddamn high school Scheherazade."

Brady didn't even look confused. The comment had gone so completely over his head that his face remained placid.

"Scheherazade was a woman who told stories to her husband, but she would never finish the stories. The husband wanted to kill her, but he couldn't, because there was always a story he hadn't heard the end of. So she always had something he needed."

Now Brady looked confused. "Shit, man, I'm not going to do anything to you."

"That's not what I mean. I just mean that she had the advantage over him because he needed to hear the ending."

Brady lit up another cigarette. He didn't even bother to say, "Whatever." He picked up a magazine from a bedstand and started looking at pictures of cars. "Take it or leave it," he mumbled.

"Right. I think you probably know the answer." Casey got up to leave. His legs tingled from the immobility of the past forty-five minutes. "Next Friday. Do I just come to the same place?"

Brady looked up, grinning. "No, I don't have the same schedule every Friday. Meet me at Happy Jack's, but wait till after school, like about two-thirty. I don't think my mom works next week, so we'll have to find somewhere else to go." He got off the bed and walked Casey to the front door, reiterating the meeting time with undisguised glee in his voice.

Casey drove away from Brady's house through the bleak grid of the neighborhood. He thought about Brady's story, but he thought mostly about what he himself had said at the end—how it, like many things that had been coming from his mouth lately, seemed true in retrospect. The reference to Scheherazade had surprised him, but when he had spoken the woman's name, it had felt accurate, prescient. He didn't remember many details of that ancient story, which he must have come across in his freshman lit class at Penn State, but he knew what he associated with it. The power of those who told the stories, the weakness of those who listened.

# eighteen

*They had gone* out for ice cream, not remarking on the absurdity of doing this in such weather. Megan had insisted that they take a night out; they needed to spend some time together as a couple and talk about something other than Colin, she said. First Lea and Geoffrey went to the Italian place in the township center, but they had finished their dinners by nine, and they decided on ice cream at Harrow's so they wouldn't disappoint Megan by returning too early.

At the restaurant Lea had realized just how misguided her sister's good intentions had been. The one subject she and Geoffrey had largely avoided during the past few weeks was the boy himself and everything related to his damage—the ongoing search for the malefactors, the legal wranglings being tended to by Phil Lucas. They dealt with the mechanics of his damage and the lawsuit when necessary, but they had hardly dwelled on the subject as much as Megan assumed. Just as they had avoided making Colin the sole topic of their discussions throughout their marriage, they continued to keep him on the periphery, in part because it would have been so easy to make him the focus.

So the night out now had the opposite effect of what Megan had hoped: they began speaking about him as they had not at home. At Harrow's, seated at a small round table, Geoffrey broached the matter in a muted voice.

"He's happy. It may be a sin to say it, but by God, Lea"—here he tapped the table with his palm for emphasis—"that boy is happy, and it's the first time in years I've seen him that way."

Of course, this was something that had occurred to her often, but she had instinctively shrunk from the comfort the notion might hold. Yes, she thought, the boy was playful, joyful, brimming with love. But so were golden retrievers.

"Uh-huh," she said. "I suppose he does look happy. I mean, I'm sure he does. But it's small comfort, isn't it? Shouldn't it be?"

"In times like this, I don't think there's any such thing as a small comfort."

She was sure that he said this before, probably to some couple whose child was on life support. It was his way of being wise, to find something that sounded like this and then use it again and again. He had probably read it in the goddamn *Reader's Digest*, she thought.

"What I mean," she said, "is that . . . well, of course he looks happy. He's brain-damaged. He's retarded. Retarded kids always look happy, don't they? That doesn't seem like anything to be thrilled about."

"That's a hell of a thing to say. A hell of a thing."

"Yeah, it is. I'm sorry for that, but it's a hell of a thing to say because it's true. He was hurt. Geoffrey. He didn't go on some program that took the meanness out of him. He didn't have a change of heart about how to treat people. He just got hurt."

Geoffrey snatched at her hands, grasping so hard she clenched her shoulders. "But can't we pretend that's not what happened? Can't we just pretend this is him?" He was begging, earnest and desperate. The fact that he was now saying to her exactly what he felt—no less, no more—made her understand how seldom this had happened in their years together. "Can't this be our boy, and not the one that came before? I don't know what we did, Lea. I don't know when it got all screwed up."

"I don't either, Geoffrey. I imagine it got screwed up when we weren't noticing."

Geoffrey wasn't listening to her, and now he wasn't looking at her. "But I don't know how he got that way. When it got hard to love him like we used to, I became proud of him." Geoffrey's face was slack and tired; he looked like he had just woken from a miserable sleep. "When he got chosen defensive player of the week last year, that was a good time for us. I think he might have been happy that we were so proud. I'm telling you, he was a hell of a football player. Really."

Geoffrey's face had broken into the kind of smile that is offered up at such times to indicate emotional exhaustion, the bereaved man's way of throwing in the towel. She now understood that he had never been as ingenuous as he'd seemed about Colin, just willfully ignorant. Being a man, he might even have caught on to the boy's wickedness earlier than she had. And his coping mechanism had been much more reasonable, she granted him this. How much better it would have been for her if, instead of obstinately trying to love the boy, she had been happy with the fact that he made a pretty good linebacker.

She scooted closer to the table and rested her elbows. "Geoffrey. Tell me something."

He nodded, curious.

"How did he get that scar on his side?"

She thought that in normal circumstances he would not have told her. But he was still worn out, still a man who had just revealed himself to his wife for the first time in a long while. He too scooted up to the table, and he did not seem reluctant to tell her.

"It happened a few months ago. It was sometime in October. I woke up for my run and he was sitting on the couch, still dressed from the night before. He was pale, and he was sitting in a funny position.

He told me he had a problem and needed my help, so we went into the kitchen and he took off his shirt." Geoffrey closed his eyes and corrected his posture, like a yogi about to begin a mantra. "It was glass—a big shard had been pushed into him. I could tell that right away, even before I cleaned up the blood. I didn't ask any questions at first. I got my bag and cleaned him up as best I could right there. I was just terrified, honey. Terrified. He needed to get to the hospital, but he pretty flatly refused, as you would expect. So I pulled out the big piece and a bunch of slivers right there. I kept reminding him that it would go a lot easier if he could get a local while I was doing it. But he just cursed."

She almost laughed. Of course it would have been like this—her pedantic husband prattling on in his self-satisfied way about bacterial infection while her son simply grimaced and called him vulgar names. The fact that he was forced to put up with his father would have been as painful to Colin as the long tweezers.

"You know how he was." Lea couldn't help but notice how naturally Geoffrey used this past tense. "He just refused to go in. So I left him there and drove down to the office, got some supplies, and came back and sewed him up."

"Jesus. In our kitchen?"

"It was simple, really." He shook his head at the tabletop. "He was pretty amazing, when you think about it. I mean, that kid must have been in some pain. I told him we could go to a clinic where no one would know about it, in case that was bothering him."

"Did he ever tell you why he wouldn't go?"

Geoffrey began tearing up a napkin, and his face looked pained, as if he were standing in a cold wind. She knew that he was trying to indicate an inner struggle, that he was debating the wisdom of telling her something he didn't want to tell her. In the end, she knew, he would come clean, after his ritual of vacillation was complete.

"He was afraid of the cops. He knew that the doctors would have to report any kind of physical assault."

He reached out and touched her on the cheek, his expression gentle. "I don't mean to scare you, Lea. I knew I had to tell you, and I'm sorry I didn't at the time. He was okay, of course, he turned out fine. He was back at practice in a week."

She considered the irony, or perhaps the simple stupidity, of what he'd said. As far as she could tell, Geoffrey was comforting her with the fact that five months ago her son had recovered well from a stab wound, while at the moment the parietal lobe of his brain functioned on the same level as a rabbit's.

"There's more. If you want to hear it," he said, and she nodded. "He said not to worry, because he hadn't been in a fight. I said that I was relieved it wasn't a fight, but that he was extremely unfortunate to have been attacked by a window." Geoffrey kept a still face, but Lea knew he must have considered this remark extremely clever. "I told him I was going to worry regardless of what he said, but that I'd very much like to hear the truth. In any case, he told me, or at least I believe he told me. Again, you know how he was. It was one of his strengths, I suppose—he didn't tell us much, but then again, he didn't lie to us much either."

"He didn't lie to us because he didn't care what we thought and he wasn't afraid of what we'd do," she said.

Lea said it softly enough that Geoffrey could pretend he hadn't heard. He stared at his ice cream cup for a quiet moment and continued. "It had been a girl, Colin said. I don't know her name. He wouldn't tell me that. And he wouldn't tell me why she did it. He'd been at a party, and a girl he'd had a relationship with asked if she could talk to him in private. Then she stabbed him. I imagine she'd been drinking."

Lea raised her eyebrows and opened her mouth, but she quickly understood that this was pretense. How could she have rightfully been surprised by this news? It had been the same when she'd found the detention slips, when she'd read of his sexual exploits and his heartless treatment of Jess. The specifics of his behavior startled her, but she had no right to be surprised.

There was not much left to tell, except the part that made Geoffrey the most nervous. "I didn't want to upset you, honey. I guess it was easy for me to deal with because I knew how relatively well it turned out. She'd missed all major arteries and nerves, so I just thanked God that he didn't turn out like all the other kids I see in the hospital . . ." Again he seemed to miss the irony of his words, given Colin's present situation. "And I did what I could. I would have told you, Lea, I would have, if I'd thought it would do any good. But I couldn't see it. It killed me to have to hide it from you, but it seemed right to let it go."

She finally whispered, "Okay," a response that seemed to relieve him beyond measure, and after a few beats of ponderous silence, Geoffrey stood up, saying, "Shall we?" and Lea followed suit. It took them a while to arrange scarves and hats and overcoats, and while they were preparing them, he said, almost cheerfully, "Another thing was, I was a bit touched by how adamant he was not to tell you. He really didn't want you to worry. It's something to remember, Lea. Whatever he did, he didn't want it to upset you. And he waited on the couch for me all night so that he wouldn't have to come in and wake you up. Poor kid," Geoffrey said, "it's like he wanted to protect you from himself."

She gave him an obligatory smile, and he opened the door for her. She walked out into the frigid night, recognizing, as she often did these days, a gulf between her and Geoffrey that was intensified by the fact that he didn't see it. What he didn't know in this case, and what Lea had understood immediately, was that Colin did not want to tell his mother about the assault because he knew she would have called the police. His mother, Colin knew, would have needed to figure out what kind of cruelty must be inflicted on a teenage girl before she'll try to kill a boy with a shard of glass.

# | nineteen |

*He could picture himself* working at this place. It
had the same general layout as O'Ruddy's, with a big open nonsmoking section bordered by a windowed wall and a raised smoking area
closer to the kitchen. The theme of the Ketchikan Kitchen was Pacific
Northwest. The servers wore thick plaid button-down shirts with a
totem pole emblem on the pocket. The wall decor, which certainly
came from the same kind of factory that produced O'Ruddy's weath-
ered maps and hurling sticks, alluded obsessively to moose and
salmon. As Casey waited at a booth in the smoking section, he studied the objects on the wall: a lacquered bamboo fly rod, a MOOSE
CROSSING sign, some sort of faux Eskimo talisman, a pair of archaic
ice skates. The idea, Casey thought, was to give the feel of a north
woods fishing lodge. He hoped he would read about it soon enough in
the employee handbook.

    He tried to concentrate on the task before him, which was to steer the interview to the things that mattered. He ached to explain to someone that he was perfect for this job, that he understood the small things that worked toward the success of a place like this. He hoped to be asked about the necessity of uniform enforcement, about the importance of getting servers to push the premium liquors. But the Friday night incident would have to come up, of course, and Casey still had not readied himself to answer the question. He did not know how to present this to an interviewer the way it appeared to him—no longer a question of incrimination or culpability but merely one of circumstance and injustice. The phone cut off, the kids for some reason determined to fight somewhere. Vague orders from the owners not to harm the restaurant. The handbook had been useless, the normal protocols inapplicable. How could he convey this without whining, without raging at the injustice thrown at him by the police, by his bosses, by the solipsistic herd of seventeen-year-old boys?

The manager was of no specific type that Casey could recognize, although he might have been considered the near opposite of the hearty manager. His name was Bert Player. When he sat down he shot a compressed smile at Casey and fidgeted until his posture was sufficiently rigid. The manager's presence made Casey so uncomfortable that he could not believe anyone in this man's life—his mother, his childhood pets—had ever felt at ease around him. However, Casey noticed that he wore a wedding ring and asked him, during the brief moments of small talk that the manager seemed to have scripted, what his wife did for a living, just to have some sort of clue. A state trooper, the man answered.

"It's as cold as a well-digger's rear end out there," Bert said then. He said it with such precision that it sounded practiced, as if he had been waiting for an opportunity to say it. Bert must have read in the manager's handbook that a joke, or whatever that had been, was a good way to put the interviewee at ease.

Casey grinned and nodded, then widened his grin and barked a short laugh, as if it had taken him a while to get it. Bert curled his lips and scowled down at a napkin set. The joke had been a painful thing, something he needed to recover from. He squinted at Casey's résumé.

"I went to Penn State myself," said Bert. "Class of '88." Casey had not listed a year of graduation, since he had not graduated. The résumé read "Pennsylvania State University, matriculated 1988." There had been no degree, and some employers noticed this and some didn't. It usually didn't matter in the restaurant business, and Casey was not embarrassed.

"I left before I got the degree," he explained. "I worked at a Red Lobster, and in my sophomore year the g.m. never came back from maternity leave. They promoted the night manager and asked me to take his spot full-time." He was proud of this story, and he thought it did him more credit than people usually gave.

Casey didn't expect that Bert Player had lived the kind of life at Penn State that would have made him appreciate this sacrifice. He seemed to be one of those people for whom college had been very much like a full-time job. Penn State was probably, Casey thought, where Bert had met his state trooper wife. He could imagine them huddled together in one of the terrible married housing units, Bert the kind of student who always showed up in an ironed shirt, who asked questions that made the class run five minutes late.

They discussed Casey's work experience, beginning with his high school tenure at LuLu's Ice Cream House. Casey explained to Bert that LuLu (who had actually been a man; the nickname was short for Luther Llewellyn) taught him how to work the fryer and paid him under the table. At Penn State, he started at the Red Lobster a week after freshman orientation. His hardship grant paid only for tuition, and besides, it just would have seemed wrong not to work. After he settled himself into the dorm, a job was one of the first things he'd looked for, the way other freshmen went looking for the closest laundromats or bars that took fake IDs.

Bert was interested in this part of Casey's life, because he had worked at a Red Lobster himself, over in Harrisburg. This serendip-

itous fact gave rise to a few moments of unrestrained, easy conversation between them, as they recalled together the uniform require-
ments handed down by the chain's formidable headquarters, the
ghastly smell of seafood bits in the aprons, the ill-fated "Crabby Monday" campaign of '92. They spoke like veterans who had served in different theaters of the same war, and Casey hoped the man was
warming to him. Bert's posture remained flawless, his voice as tone-
less and blank as his face.

Bert now cut the conversation short, perhaps wary of establishing
too much rapport—it probably did not happen often—and skipped to
the middle of the résumé. "O'Ruddy's. Server, bartender, assistant
manager, general manager. Well, it's all very good, very much what
we're looking for."

"I'm glad to hear that."

"Yes. I wonder about something, however. Your reason for leaving O'Ruddy's. It seems as though things went well enough for you
there."

Casey thought Bert might be testing him. He couldn't imagine the
man wouldn't actually know. Everyone in Breed's Township knew
about the fight, even if they couldn't have placed Casey's name with
it. And this man was in the business.

Casey raised an eyebrow, hoping Bert would reveal something.
Bert did not, so Casey said, "Mr. Player, have you not heard about
what happened at O'Ruddy's?"

Bert said "Hmmm?" in a light way, curious and innocent.

He realized at once that he might now spin this, that there was
much he did not have to say. This was a large opportunity, not just to
get the job, but also to tell the story to an objective listener. Rachel
had heard it from her friend Kim, Jake at the Tacqueria de Paco had
heard about it from his franchise owners, his mother had gotten the
story at first from an old neighbor she kept in touch with. Bert didn't
know, he really didn't. Casey could be the storyteller now. Finally he
could assume that enormous power.

"It's closed, Mr. Player. There was some trouble there, in the parking lot, with some local youths. A few weeks ago one of them got hurt, and the headquarters feels that it's not worth the insurance problems. The franchise owners will sell out to headquarters, and headquarters will invoke a clause with the insurance company that will compensate them." There. The story, all that needed to be said. Culpability was nowhere in it.

"I don't understand. What kind of trouble with kids could close the restaurant?"

"I'm actually a bit surprised you haven't heard about the incident. It was in the news for a while."

He expected Bert to make some excuse for his large ignorance, but he did not. "So it was an incident? You say a young person got hurt—what do you mean by that?"

Casey had not told him enough in the beginning. He had not effectively mastered the telling yet. Now that Bert was asking questions, the tale was slipping away from him, its power shifting toward the listener. "The boy has brain damage now. He was hit in the head with a metal rod."

Bert made a strange noise, something like a bark. His voice rose an octave. "Brain damage? My gosh. A metal rod?"

"Yes."

"Why did they hit him with a metal rod?"

"I don't know."

"Why did they fight in your parking lot?"

"I don't know that either."

These answers were terrifically unsatisfactory for Bert, and he shook his head and pursed his lips, as if addressing a child who had disappointed him. Casey realized that Bert was unprepared to hear the story, because too much of it was inexplicable. This fact had flummoxed Casey as well, on that Friday night, and it continued to do so, even as he learned more about it. There had been too much that could not be explained, and these two men could not deal well with this because they lived in a world that was entirely explicable. Bert had gone into the business for this reason, just as Casey had, he was sure of it.

There was order here, and predictability, routine, systems, protocol. But what do you do when the problem doesn't have to do with napkins or schedules or the preparation of a Monte Cristo sandwich? What do you do when the problem is violent and when you are afraid? Casey half expected to see steam escape from Bert's ears, for a robotic voice to come out of his lips announcing a system malfunction.

Casey said, "I know it's strange. It doesn't make sense. Those kids just happened to fight, and one of them just happened to hit another kid with a metal rod, and the phone just happened to be out. That's the story. I can't really explain it."

He said this in response to Bert's bewilderment, but it wasn't entirely true. He had a lifelong aversion to the notion that things could just *happen*, without cause or motive. The boys did not just happen to fight there. He knew that now, he had bought alcohol for a seventeen-year-old boy in order to know it.

"Perhaps you should start from the beginning."

Casey told the story to Bert. It was almost mechanical now; he had memorized many of the more effective details and phrases, like an Anglo-Saxon bard. Eventually he began to take some sadistic delight in it, and he emphasized the chaos of that night, the way it had been entirely out of his hands. It was satisfying to horrify Bert with the violent details, to let him know that the world of Bert and Casey was pregnable, disordered. He felt like Marley's ghost. *It happened to me, Bert Player. You're not as safe as you think you are.*

He did not add much about what he had learned since that night. He reported it to Bert as he had to the police, to his mother, to Rachel. The new information was too fresh and as yet revealed nothing that might exonerate him. The exception was the phone. He quoted Jenny exactly, and went into detail about the line problems, the tangled tree on Ridge Street. He made it sound as though he would have called the police the moment he had seen the boys if it hadn't been for the dead line. This evidence at least was indisputable, Casey thought.

At times Bert interrupted, always cautious and apologetic. "What time exactly would you say this was happening?" he first asked. Then, "When you say the other servers were doing side work, what kind of side work was this?" The questions invariably dealt with the interior, with the restaurant itself. Casey knew that Bert was trying to ground himself, to make the situation more real to him, or perhaps to create distance, to assure himself that such a thing could not happen at the Ketchikan Kitchen. He was looking, in his investigation of the workings of O'Ruddy's, for something that might explain how Casey and his staff had brought this trouble on themselves.

Bert's questions provided a valuable perspective. Casey, the spectator, had not paid nearly as much attention to what had gone on inside O'Ruddy's that night as Bert was now commanding him to. It had all happened outside. To Casey, that night meant nothing but boys and blood, metal rod and churning tires, thundering insults and the frozen vapor of breath and bodies.

"Had all the tables been cleared?" said Bert.

"Yes. Except for sixteen. In the smoking section."

"What was happening at table sixteen in the smoking section?"

"There was a couple there. Eating pie, I think."

"This was the couple that called the police in the end. They used a cell phone, you said?"

"Yes, that couple. They were the only ones on the floor besides Jenny and me. They were quiet, sitting way in back. I'd mostly forgotten all about them, to tell you the truth."

Since that night he had thought about that couple only once, when the newspaper account credited them with calling the ambulance. He remembered now that they had been one of those middle-aged couples that has grown to look like each other. Black curly hair on both heads, the woman's only slightly bushier than the man's. They leaned across the table as a gesture to the privacy of their conversation, though no one was around who could have heard them. They drank coffee and shared some kind of pie.

The woman had been seated with her back toward the entrance, and so Casey had seen her more clearly. She had worn a scarf over her head when she came in, which Casey had previously seen only very old ladies do, but he put both of their ages at around fifty. They were dressed somewhat formally, as if they had returned from the theater or the symphony in Scranton, but they also seemed like the kind of people who might be dressed up all the time.

"I suppose it happened quickly," Bert said.

"What's that?"

"The fight. It must have happened fast."

"Not really. Not very fast. They screamed at each other for a while. And even when they started, it didn't seem very serious. Lots of rolling around on the ground. Lots of missed punches. It was very cold that night."

"Hmm."

"Did I tell you about the owners?"

"I don't think so. What about them?"

"Ambrose and Naomi Howard. They've owned the place for twelve years. I've worked for them for eight years. Never been to their house, never met anyone in their family. The whole time I've worked for them they've looked exactly the same. Same clothes, same white hair, same wrinkles."

"I don't understand what you're getting at in the least."

"When you asked about the couple drinking coffee, it reminded me of them. I mean, *they* reminded me of them. The couple, they seemed just like the Howards must have seemed thirty years ago. Kind of small, hunched over. The woman especially. She looked just like them. She even had the same hairdo as Mrs. Howard, it seemed like."

He had lost his listener, so thoroughly that Bert had assumed his previous look of despairing incomprehension, the expression that made Casey think his circuits might be overloaded. "I'm sorry," Casey said in a hurry. "Just rambling now. You're making me look at this from a different angle, I guess."

What did Bert care, after all, about what Casey was discovering?

He was the kind of man who would not be interested in the investigation, in the gradual compiling of explanations and justifications. He
would want it all at once. When the incident, from top to bottom,
could be explained, that would be the time to call Bert Player, and
maybe he would be grateful for it. Casey himself had been like this,
and in fact he still was. He didn't like solving riddles either, but he
didn't have much choice.

It must have been the daughter, the Howard daughter, to whom
they made frequent reference but whom Casey had never seen, not
even in a photograph. He knew she was married and lived in Leawood, supported by the Howard family's considerable investments
and by whatever bean-counting work the husband did. The resem-
blance was so strong in his memory that he wondered if he was exaggerating it. At first, in summoning the memory, he saw the Howards
themselves seated at the table, arguing in low tones over the cold coffee. In spite of this, he felt confident in this realization. The Howard
daughter.

Bert continued to pester him, and so he could not dwell on the significance of the revelation, except to recognize that he could not see
any meaning to it right away. Maybe the couple had just wanted
coffee.

Casey finished with the frantic sprint through the snow, the arrival
of the paramedics. He did not tell Bert that Jenny had been with the
boy. He sensed that Bert had reached his fill. Then the cops, the
Howards, the firing.

Bert began nodding quickly and rhythmically, with his eyes
closed, like an autistic person. He suddenly stopped and looked at
Casey. "Okay, then. I guess we're finished here. I take it you won't be
surprised if I don't offer to shake your hand."

Casey felt his face turning red. "I'm sorry, what?"

Bert had stood up and was looming over Casey like a bouncer,
with his fists touching his hips. "I've got to know—what made you
think that I would hire you after a story like that?"

Casey squinted, trapped, and tried to raise his hackles. "I don't understand what you mean. A story like what? A story about how I lost my job because of some violent children?"

"That's not the story I heard, sir. I heard the story of a man who didn't do anything to stop it."

Casey stood and squared up to Bert. Though his expression and his sharp voice might have been contrived, borrowed from some TV cop show, he truly was outraged, and he was thrilled that it was in him to do this, that he actually felt the vehemence of his conviction. "Just what the fuck was I supposed to do, you goddamn robot? What the fuck do you know about it?"

Bert winced at the swear words, as if they were jabs to the ribs. Casey began counting on his fingers. "For one thing, I knew beforehand that if the cops came one more time, I was out of a job. For another thing, when I tried to call the cops, the motherfucking phone line was out. For another thing, there's something else that's going on that I just don't even . . ." He couldn't express it. Most of it he hadn't even told Bert, so his rant would be sure to lose cohesion. It came to him all at once, in a great shower of outrage, but he couldn't put it into words. He could barely put it into thought. Jenny had slept with Colin Chase. Brady and his gang had been set up, manipulated into fighting the St. Brendan's kids. Somewhere behind that was a big house in Leawood and money for cocaine. The only two customers in the restaurant at the time happened to be the daughter and son-in-law of the franchise owners. And this was only the third point on his list of mitigating factors. Why couldn't this buffoon see that? What exactly did he think Casey should have done? Where was the culpability? He couldn't express any of this, so he cut off his rant with a shrill *"Fuck you"* and stomped out of the restaurant.

# twenty

*You never swear,"* said Rachel.

"I know, I know. I never do anything like that. I hate confrontation."

"I wonder why that is. Why it is you don't swear, I mean."

He shrugged. "My mother always said it was low-class."

"Did you believe her? I mean, is that why you still don't do it? Afraid of identifying yourself with your lower-class roots?"

He tried to give her a look that told her to cut it out. He was not in the mood for her amateur analysis. It would be a milestone in their relationship, he thought, when she could tell by his face that enough was enough.

"What?" she said. "You don't think that's a possibility?"

"I think it's kind of missing the point. I was telling you about the interview and how I lost it at the end."

"But you didn't tell me why you lost it."

Casey and Rachel were lying on their backs in the room that her parents had called the den. It still had shag carpeting and brown and orange furniture, so it looked like a Smithsonian exhibit of how the suburban middle class spent the late seventies. Casey and Rachel had just finished having sex. This was one of her favorite rooms for it, at least in the daytime. She refused to spend any daylight hours in bed, since it could lead to falling asleep, and she didn't believe in naps.

The sex had been abrupt; both of them had gone about it as if it were a chore, like a couple trying to conceive. The couch was itchy and rigid, and so they had done it on the shag rug, Casey on top. They had kept most of their clothes on, and as they lay there afterward, the only evidence of their coitus (for they weren't holding hands, weren't even touching) was his open fly, her gathered skirt, and her underwear on the floor beside him.

"I'm not trying to pry," she said, and whether or not she believed it, Casey thought that these words would always sound untrue coming from Rachel. "It's just that you're so worked up. Frankly, I didn't even want to do it, but when you came in I could tell you needed a release."

He hadn't really wanted to do it either. When he had walked into her house, she had stood a few feet in front of him, hands on hips, and appraised him. He hadn't said anything, but there had apparently been enough in his face and his stance for her to sense failure, something pitiable that would earn him sex. Before either of them had spoken, she had kissed him deeply and rubbed his leg and led him into the den. He'd thought about the interview the whole time.

"Why would you tell me that? Why can't you just do something and not explain to me why you're doing it?"

"There's that temper. Do you want to swear at me now? Do you want to call me a whore?"

"For God's sake, Rachel, don't do this to me. Don't be that way now." He buttoned and zipped his pants.

She shrugged. "Finish your story."

He waited until she had put on her underwear and smoothed

down her skirt, because the task seemed to take most of her attention. "We started talking about Friday night, of course. He asked me a lot of questions, and I told him the full story. Then he said something about how I should have stopped it."

"And this threw you into a rage."

He paused before answering. Clearly this was accurate, but he knew what kind of evidence she would see in this: it would mean that Bert Player had touched a nerve. She would draw the conclusion — without telling him, of course, but probably writing it down in a journal somewhere — that Casey unconsciously acknowledged his own culpability in the matter of the fight and simply could not deal with it. It was pop psychology, easy and trite, and he suddenly disliked her enormously for accepting it, even though she hadn't really said anything.

He didn't know what he could say to make her believe otherwise. The truth was that he recognized this possibility; he was not so blind to his own situation as to not understand that many people might see it as Bert Player had. The problem, in fact, was that he was less blind than everyone else. He knew about all the mitigating factors. He alone could see the development of a tableau that seemed to promise exoneration.

"Yes," he said. "I got mad at him when he implied it was my fault. And before you go jumping to any conclusions, Rachel, keep in mind that this is exactly the same reaction that anyone would have, whether they felt bad about what they had done or whether they felt good about it."

She didn't say anything, and he thought for a moment that he had stumped her.

"So let's drop it," he finally said.

Neither of them spoke, and soon the silence became uncomfortable. Casey wondered if they simply didn't have anything else to talk about. They had seen each other dozens of times since the fight and had spoken about little else but that Friday night and its myriad repercussions. Or at least he couldn't remember it if they had. Perhaps there was simply nothing else in his life now. He tried to think about conversations they'd had before January, and in trying to answer this, he realized he couldn't remember much of anything that had happened before the incident. He tried to picture one meal he had eaten in the month of December, one movie he had seen. He failed. To know this would have been, perhaps, to know what it was like to go to bed without a wrench in the stomach and to wake up without the instant thought that the day would bring him shame and regret. This might be irrecoverable by now. Each day exoneration was less likely, because with each day people stopped caring, and soon people would be loath to revise any opinion of Casey, or Colin Chase, or what had happened at O'Ruddy's, no matter what the truth was.

Rachel suggested that he cook something for her, and he agreed. He wanted to do something for her now that she could not do for herself, and cooking fell in that category. She followed him into the kitchen and perched on a stool while he shuffled around the linoleum, plucking his materials from her dusty cupboards. He decided on baked ziti, because it would take a long time and he liked the way she sat and watched him work.

Once the pasta was boiling, she began to read a women's magazine. She kept them stacked on the dining room table and usually read from them as she ate her takeout dinners. Casey rolled up his sleeves and took off his tie—now he felt somewhat silly for not having done so before sex—and eventually she looked up at him.

"Let's take the quiz," she said. "The *Cosmo* quiz."

Casey raised an eyebrow. "Is Your Man Mr. Right or Mr. Wrong?—one of those things?"

"It's called What Sort of Thing Is Your Guy? Multiple choice."

He nodded and stirred. "I think I can handle that."

"If you were a type of car, what type of car would you be?" She read the four offerings, and Casey answered.

"Jeep Wrangler."

"If you were a city, what city would you be? San Francisco; Paris; Eden Prairie, Minnesota; or Bangkok."

He paused, so she said, "It says you're supposed to answer quickly, without thinking about your answer."

"San Francisco."

She wrinkled her nose. "I don't see that at all. Why San Francisco?"

"I don't know. Am I taking the test wrong?"

"Next. If you were a religion, which one would you be?" Again she read the options.

"Confucianism."

"A historical period."

"I bet everyone says the Renaissance. Okay then . . . the Age of Reason."

"Cereal. Raisin Bran, Mueslix, Cream of Wheat, Count Chocula."

"Count Chocula."

She stopped and stood up, but only to resettle herself on a different stool. She put the magazine back on the table.

"Something wrong?" he said, and she shrugged.

"Are those the only questions?" he said. "How'd I score?"

"It doesn't matter."

"Why not?"

"Because you got it all wrong anyway. You were way off. You're not San Francisco, Casey. You're Eden Prairie. You're definitely not a Jeep Wrangler. You're the Buick Park Avenue, one of the older ones, from the eighties. I don't even know what to make of Count Chocula."

He stirred the pasta sauce in slow, wide circles. "What about religion?"

"Casey, you're not Confucianism. You're the Church of England. You may have been close with the Age of Reason, but I have my doubts sometimes."

He stared down into the pot of bubbling sauce instead of looking at her, and he felt very cold. He also felt stupid, more so with every word that passed his lips. He wondered if the sex had been obviously bad. "All right. How about I give you the quiz now?"

"Nope," she said.

"Well, that doesn't seem very fair."

She had no response.

"Wait. Just wait. What kind of authority are you invoking here, Rachel? How is it that you know so much? How do you know what kind of motherfucking car I'd be? What kind of cereal I am?"

"I'm surprised at you. You never swear, Casey."

"How the fuck do you know what kind of goddamn city I'd fucking be?"

She exhaled loudly, as if she were breathing out cigarette smoke, and from the tone of her voice he could tell she was smiling. "Well, Casey, you sure as hell don't know, so I guess somebody has to."

# twenty-one

*Another night out,* this time by herself.

Lea had begun to discern the pattern that their new life would follow. The new Colin woke up early, sometimes before six, and brushed his teeth by himself. He sometimes got himself dressed—he had taken to wearing ski pants and sweatshirts—but sometimes he forgot. Then he crept into her room and sat in a wicker chair by the window, waiting for her to stir. Geoffrey was always out running at this hour, so it was left to Lea to rise alone to the startling presence of the boy, to jolt out of unconsciousness and begin the wearying day.

Geoffrey would get home as they were eating breakfast. Until they began this routine, Lea had rarely been awake to see him return from his runs. She was surprised by how he looked when he came back: gaunt and wide-eyed and smelly, like a shipwreck survivor. He would quickly shower and dress and join them at the breakfast table, where they ate bland foods that would not make too much of a mess: cereal, dry toast, Pop-Tarts. Geoffrey would drive the conversation, since Lea did not function well in the morning. He performed tricks for Colin, taking some advantage, Lea thought, of the boy's credulity. He tousled Colin's hair, and sometimes they played with their oatmeal together until Geoffrey said they should stop or they'd get in trouble with Mom. Lea sat and watched these breakfasts in almost total silence, born of her sleepiness and the fact that Geoffrey seemed to be a one-man show in the mornings.

She remembered what he had asked her at Harrow's: "Can't we just pretend this is him?" She vaguely recalled that she hadn't responded, not really, and it now seemed that he had taken this as a kind of acquiescence. It certainly seemed that he was playing the role he had begged her to give him: the sensitive father of the retarded boy, delighting in the innocence of the grown child, refusing to dwell on what was lost. They did not mention the scar underneath Colin's arm again.

Geoffrey would head into the office by eight o'clock, and Colin and Lea would begin the day by going on some kind of errand, whether she needed anything or not. After the grogginess of his medication had worn off, and after they had carefully reintroduced him to the world, Colin had proved himself familiar with the fundamentals of the house, the car, the general workings of things, although the television and garbage disposal still frightened him. His vocabulary came back to him in spurts, so that on some days he would string together lucid sentences about how he wanted his cereal served to him, while on others he could only articulate through gestures and grunts that his shoelaces were too tight. He took many naps, and he was often hungry. He was not as troublesome as he'd been when he was physically four years old, in part because he liked to be close to Lea, and also because he did not have much energy. He was still as easily distracted as he had been as a toddler, but now this tendency was joined with patience, or lassitude. He could stare at things—clouds, the mailman, the stereo, Lea herself—for so long she occasionally wondered if he had fallen asleep with his eyes open.

They would sometimes eat lunch in a diner by the highway that made grilled cheese sandwiches better than she did, and sometimes they ate at home. They walked through the township center or the park when it wasn't too cold, and she talked to him as much as she could. They went to therapy sessions at the hospital three times a week, working with a short, energetic woman named Denise, whom Lea liked because she did not talk to Colin as if he were a child but who was always in danger of losing this goodwill because she pushed him so much in muscle exercises that he cried once in a while. They went to the doctor's so often that Colin came to learn and remember the name of the receptionist.

He listened to music in the afternoons, resting on the couch and staring with great intensity at the stereo, as if he could see words coming out of it. Both of them, Lea thought, embraced the afternoon as a necessary recess. These days were as exhausting as any Lea had ever passed, though by the time Geoffrey came home in the early evening and asked for her daily report, it always seemed to her that they hadn't done much.

After the music she would try to read to him. The doctors said he could get this skill back, perhaps, if they read together often enough. At first she swallowed this logic entirely and went through the attic to round up an appropriate collection — books from when he was four — and spent a couple days reading *Clifford the Big Red Dog* and *The Giving Tree*. It occurred to her one day that recovering the ability to read would be a relatively small achievement, given that his brain would not advance much past books of this kind. She wondered how many times, if this activity became another element of their routine, she would end up reading about the Star-Belly Sneetches.

One day, though, he didn't let her read. The cessation of the music sometimes made him grumpy, and on Tuesday he began to pout by pacing around the living room, walking in large figure eights around the couches. He did this, she was amazed to see, from three in the afternoon until five-thirty.

Colin stopped pacing when he heard the garage door rising for his father's car, which happened earlier than usual. He simply ceased his march and looked at his mother, who had settled on a loveseat with a magazine and a glass of chianti, and said, "That's Dad."

"That's right," Lea said without looking up, pouting in her own way, accepting it as her due. "Dad's home."

Geoffrey had no explanation for Colin's behavior but promised to ask the neurologist at the hospital. Lea wondered if Colin was beginning to show his disdain for her, if the horrible memory of the previous week, when she had slapped him for refusing to shed his idiot self, was manifesting itself in this strange behavior. Or maybe he was simply tired of her. He didn't seem to fear her, after all, and on that day she had apologized so profusely for hitting him that he had actually ended up comforting her, patting her on the head once his fit of bawling had finished (hers had just begun) and singing a Billy Joel song to her. The thought of this, sudden and piercing, made her momentarily want to begin pacing around the living room couches herself.

She told Geoffrey that she needed a night off. He had work to get done that evening, he said, and she knew that he was genuinely sorry he couldn't give this to her. "How about tomorrow?" she said. "I've been thinking about it. I could go to the basketball game."

He slapped his hands together. "Perfect. We'll have a guys' night." He grinned at his son. "Just you and me, bucko, doing guy stuff." Lea wanted to smile, but instead she softly said, "Thank you," in the voice she might use to thank someone who had just saved her life.

St. Brendan's was playing Xaverian, a school from Wilkes-Barre. Geoffrey and Lea had gone to several games this season as a kind of civil and parental obligation, but this time it was not really about supporting the team. In the beginning it was about getting out of the house, away from the boy who looked at her with that inscrutable expression, away from the newly expansive husband. But she realized on Wednesday afternoon, as she began to anticipate leaving the house with an excitement that startled her, that there was a purpose in naming the basketball game as her specific activity, rather than a quiet movie alone or a trip to her sister's. She had a reason to surround herself with the community of Jesuits and the parents of boys her son had known, befriended, ridiculed, abused. Why would she go back there, after all, without her husband, weeks after the fight, if not to learn something? The fact was that Lea had remembered who Dashner was, and now her investigation, so far confined to Colin's bedroom, was ready to extend into the outside world.

She purposely arrived after tip-off, so that she wouldn't have to sit with anyone she knew. She paid five dollars to a thin young man who was still dressed in his school uniform and waited by the large entrance until a time-out. She snaked up the first set of stairs on the bleachers and seated herself close to the back row, in the realm of the unsettled members of the community: substitute teachers, cafeteria workers, townies with nothing else to do. The opposite bleachers were traditionally reserved for teenagers—students from St. Theresa's and the public school were welcome—and the permanent faculty of the school, nearly half of them Jesuits. The priests sat in two neat rows in the front, as if their godly presence actually served to dam up the manic student body, which otherwise might spill onto the floor.

Lea spent the first half examining this mixed crowd. There were as many girls as boys, it seemed, perhaps more, given that the Brendanians drew on both St. Theresa's and Breed's Township High for their companions. Some of the girls were attached to particular boys, but more often Lea noticed parcels of them huddled together, flinching against the claxon roar of male adolescents, trying in moments of calm to whisper to each other. It must have been in places such as this that the girls had slipped Colin their notes or handed them off to a neutral intermediary. There was something egregiously childish about them, she thought, about the way they so naturally segregated themselves from the males, the way they sat and stared at the court as if condemned to this activity by a tradition that they could not question. Later tonight, Lea could not help but think, who among them would be seduced by these boys?

At halftime the noise of the gym transformed itself from squeaks and whistles, shouts and groans, into the din of a thousand conversations. After a perfunctory routine by the St. Theresa's cheerleading squad, a pair of janitors loped onto the court and settled themselves at opposite ends of one of the baselines. Each was armed with a thick push-broom, and they began to sweep the floor.

The march of the janitors was a kind of ritual, a gesture to the seriousness of the game. It never seemed that the sweeping was necessary, but they got more floor time than the cheerleaders did. One of the janitors was about thirty, with shaggy hair, two earrings, and an expression designed to imply how eager he was to leave this place and get drunk at a strip club in Scranton. He began the sweeping march at the corner of the court near the student section. The students, Lea noticed, generally left him alone, and even offered him a measure of respect, a courtesy they didn't extend to the other man.

This other janitor had more than twenty years' service with the school, but this fact earned him no clemency from the boys of St. Brendan's. Entirely bald, tubular of body, and olive-skinned, he had been nicknamed Turd by the students. His manner was slow and purposeful, his round eyes continually directed toward the floor. He leaned his weight forward onto the handle, which he gripped with both hands, concentrating on the job, his dignity lost to the accumulated humiliation of twenty years spent cleaning up the sweat of wealthy boys, sprinkling pink dust on their vomit in the hallways.

The janitors had each swept two long stripes of court and were beginning to march down the floor a third time when someone from high up in the bleachers launched something onto the floor. The object bounced twice and skidded to a rest near center court, resting on the tail of a feral-looking animal that had been painted there in the mid-seventies (the St. Brendan's mascot was the wolverine). The thing was oblong, brown, banana-shaped. It was a plastic turd, the kind children buy at toy stores with allowance money.

A chant began. *Turd, turd, turd.* Then, when this incantation lost its meaning after umpteen repetitions, it became *Sweep the turd, Sweep the turd, Sweep the turd*.

Brother Carl got on the announcer's microphone. He would not accept this kind of display, he said. The school would forfeit the game if the students didn't behave like gentlemen. He meant it, he said. *Don't test me on this*.

A race had begun, a countdown. The janitors had inexorably continued their ritualistic march. The young janitor stared at Turd, whose imperturbability had reinforced for Lea the idea that he might be deaf and given rise to the notion that he might also be partially blind. The man simply kept on sweeping, oblivious. The younger man kept going too, though his smirk had intensified, had become an almost pathetic display of his fear of humiliation.

Lea noticed that the younger janitor had slowed his pace to avoid having to deal with the plastic feces. Normally he was the hurried one; she could tell from his wide sweeps and twitchy pacing that he wanted out of there. Now he cut tight corners, and on his next trip downcourt he overlapped half of the stripe he'd just swept. He stayed a step or two behind Turd, watching him furtively, and in the end his tactics worked. Turd had not changed his pace or the range of his broom one jot, and he swept up the turd as if it weren't there at all, or as if it were simply another of the microscopic particles that fell off players during the course of a basketball game. The younger janitor escorted him down the length of the court, cringing from the wild cheers, the subtler and less concerted shouting of the other janitor's nickname.

When they finished, the two men loped over to the side of the visitors' bleachers. The younger man went down on one knee, holding a dustpan so Turd could push the dirt into it. Lea, from her position twenty feet above them, heard Turd tell him to keep it steady, and in doing this she heard the younger man's name. She felt a shiver run through her legs. She took the slip of paper she'd found in Colin's room from her pocket, then typed the number into her cell phone. After a short moment a muffled ringing came from the pocket of the young janitor's coveralls, giving him the chance to spring out of his crouch, away from the distasteful duty.

His weary colleague slowly kneeled to finish the sweeping himself while the younger man dealt with the absent caller. "Christ Almighty, Dashner," Lea heard Turd say right after she'd clapped her phone shut. "It ain't a real piece of shit, you know."

## twenty-two

*Lea followed* Dashner and Turd at a distance. They retreated to a janitors' room, secreted off a forgotten hallway, a short corridor lined with abandoned lockers. Only a few of the fluorescent bulbs along the ceiling worked, and many of these flickered, as if executions were being performed behind the thick metal doors.

She was surprised by the fearlessness with which she gave a quick rap on the plaque reading CUSTODIANS, then stepped into the room without waiting. They would have been expecting her anyway, given the sound of her clogs on the tiles. And they were in fact both looking at her dumbly, expectantly. Dashner was slumped in the middle of a short couch. Turd straddled the sill of a boxy window, a window small enough to make him have to duck his head at a certainly uncomfortable angle. He looked very much like a cat burglar who had been caught in the act, and it took Lea a moment to realize that he sat like this because he was smoking a cigarette; he not only had to hold the thing outside, he had to swerve his head into the night and blow upward whenever it was time to exhale.

"Oh Christ, Mirl, it's the smoking police," Dashner said to Turd, whose Christian name, Lea thought, didn't seem very different from his adopted one. "They've come to get you, you damn scofflaw. You've had it now." He said this with his head turned to his colleague, and he now turned it back slowly, showing a satisfied grin. "That old bastard's worked here twenty years and spent every one of those years scared that someone's gonna catch him smoking inside. Practically lives half his life with his rump on that window ledge."

Scratchy noise sputtered from a television set in the corner, a television that was surely meant to show PBS specials to students but that apparently had been coopted by the janitors. The brazen display of contraband (there was also a radio and an industrial-size percolator) made it clear that no one ever came in here but them.

"Can we help you?" Dashner asked.

"I think you can. My name is Lea Chase. My son went here." There was no response from the men, although Mirl had to swing his head outside for a moment to exhale. "For school," she added. "Here at St. Brendan's. His name is Colin Chase."

"Okay," said Dashner. He scooted to the side, patted a cushion (releasing a puff of dust that he could not ignore, that he actually had to swat out of the air), and said, "Have a seat here, why don't you."

She did as he suggested, not wanting to insult him. She wedged herself against the hard left side of the couch, a section of wooden frame that scratchy plaid fabric had been stapled to. Dashner kept his position but leaned forward to rest his elbows on his knees and let his blond bangs dangle, in a way he must have thought was seductive, over his suddenly leering grin.

"You got shit in your ears?" Mirl said through an elaborate grunt caused by the contortions required to pull his body back into the room. He had finished his cigarette. "Colin Chase, Dashner. Boy that got whacked on the head at O'Ruddy's. That's the reason we had that service a few weeks ago."

She had not thought about the service for some time. She now remembered that Brother Carl had sent her a note shortly afterward, thanking her for allowing the community to gain some sense of closure. He had ended the note with a quote: *We can complain because rose bushes have thorns, or rejoice because thorn bushes have roses.* She had read it three times. *Who's complaining?* she had thought at the time. And then she had thought, *Fuck off, Brother Carl. Just fuck off.*

"Oh, right, I'm sorry. Right, I knew Colin. I'm real sorry about what happened to him," said Dashner, and leaned himself back against the couch.

"Thank you," she said, and then, over her shoulder, she said, "Thanks," to the lurking body of Mirl, though he hadn't offered condolence.

Neither of them spoke for several moments, and the silence was laid over with the hum of Mirl's labored breathing. Dashner continued to express his sympathy with a bobbing head and pursed lips.

"So, ma'am. You need something from us?" he asked.

"That's right, Mr. Dashner. I need something from you in particular."

"Fire away, ma'am."

"It might be best to talk alone."

"Without Mirl, you mean?"

"Yes."

Dashner turned around to face Mirl, who had planted himself beside the television and was now manipulating a tangle of colorful wires that grew out of the set. The naked chest of a young woman came onto the screen before he quickly changed channels; the janitors were pirating cable.

Mirl didn't look up, but it was clear that he was talking to Lea when he spoke. "Anything you got to say to Dashner you can say in front of me."

"Mirl, that's not true. Not even close to true. I can think of a whole load of things I wouldn't want people to say in front of you."

Mirl looked up now, his face as placid as it had been when he'd swept up the plastic turd. "Why don't you two take a walk, then?"

Without argument, Lea and Dashner left the janitors' office. They both recognized in Mirl's obstinacy the reclamation of the dignity he had lost in the gymnasium. He could assert himself in the office, smoke cigarettes there, watch free porn. The will of this woman, the mother of a boy who must have taunted him as eagerly as anyone at St. Brendan's, counted for nothing.

Dashner was more deferential, almost puppylike. He suggested they go downstairs to the industrial education wing of the school, where he had to pick up some things. They walked away from the gymnasium and its crowds, heels clicking on the tile floor. They walked past butcher-paper posters ("Go Wolverines! Destroy Bishop Andrucci!"). They passed through a series of padlocked doors, so that Dashner repeatedly had to rifle through the enormous ring of keys clipped to his belt. They crossed the social studies wing, where poorly drawn images of Rosa Parks and Benjamin Banneker and W.E.B. Du Bois were tacked on the walls in recognition of Black History Month. Through the math and science wing, which smelled like boredom and dead animals.

They came to a stairwell that was dark and musty. She knew, since she had gone to Back-to-School Night for three years, that this led to the Kenneth Ebbitt Industrial Arts Wing. It was belowground, sharing the basement level with the boiler and storage rooms. The irony of the existence of such a place in St. Brendan's—for Lea honestly believed that Brother Carl would defrock himself if he learned one of his charges had become a plumber—had not, in her years of association with the school, ever been acknowledged by anyone but herself.

It would be a very good place for a rape, Lea thought as she followed Dashner down the stairs into the darkness. He had been ogling her, in his way, back in the office. What else would he be taking her down here for, if not to make some sort of hamfisted pass, if not to scour the industrial arts room for some sort of cushiony surface, maybe some soft lighting? Somehow, she was not afraid.

Perhaps she should have been more cautious, more frightened, she would tell herself later, but at the moment she trusted her instincts. Dashner was a drug dealer, a tobacco-dipper, disheveled, uncouth, a product of a part of Breed's Township that she would not drive her car through, but at the moment none of this disgusted or frightened her. The fact was that she needed whatever he could give her, and though she had not thought specifically about what the price for knowledge might be, she could not imagine that there was a limit.

He unlocked a door to the main facility, a large, cold room with high ceilings and ventilation shafts, like a small airplane hangar. And indeed there was a couch there, set in a corner of the room and thus creating, along with a refrigerator and a coffee table, some sort of lounge area. He led her toward it, and she shivered from the cold and from a tightening in her stomach and loins.

He stopped and turned back. "You, uh . . . you got to tell me what you need."

"Pardon me?"

"The stuff. How much. And the money. I got to see all this before I get it out."

She hadn't expected this, but she knew now that she should have. The man was a drug dealer. She had asked to speak with him in private. In Dashner's mind, not many alternative scenarios would have presented themselves.

"Let's sit down first," she said, and now he looked confused. She sat down, but he did not.

"What I want," she said, "is something else."

"The stock is pretty specific, ma'am."

"I mean, not drugs but something else. What I want is this: I want to know what you sold to my son, Colin Chase. I don't want you to worry about getting in trouble. I just want to know what kind of things he bought from you. And how much, and how often, and what he was like, basically. You must have known him. Or at least you must have known the side of him that I don't seem to have known at all. I just want you to tell me about him."

He plopped himself on the couch and stared away from her, holding a toothpick up against his mouth and tapping his teeth with it. "Shit. *Shit*. Lady, I'm not stupid. You think I don't know what just happened?" He leaned over and spit the toothpick on the floor. "*Fuck*. You didn't know about me. I just gave myself away."

"What? Oh, Mr. Dashner, don't worry about that. I am *not* going to tell on you. And I did know about your dealing, by the way. But I didn't come here to buy. You're just going to have to trust me."

He looked at her now, scanning her legs and her feet and her face. Lea found herself reading his thoughts fluently, or at least assuming that she did. *She didn't see me take the drugs out of the hiding place*, Dashner was thinking, *so it would just be my word against hers. Maybe we can work this out. Hell*, he thought as he cast another look at her legs, *maybe she wants a piece of me. Lonely housewife and all that*.

"What do you mean?" he asked.

"As I said, I want you to tell me about Colin. I suppose I'm interested in the sort of things he bought from you, and how often. You tell me what you know about him, and then I go home and pretend that I never even met you."

He nodded, and squinted, and stood up and got a Sprite can out of the refrigerator.

"Look, ma'am, you're making me uncomfortable. I understand you're concerned about this, but maybe this should stay between you and your kid. Maybe you could just leave me out of it."

"Colin has brain damage. He can't talk about this now. He probably wouldn't even remember you if he saw you."

Dashner whistled. "From that fight? Oooh, man, I didn't know they fucked him up *that* bad. I thought he just got worked over a bit."

"They fucked him up very bad, Mr. Dashner. Brain damage. His brain functions on the same level as a four-year-old's. He'll probably stay that way forever."

Dashner was quick to process and come to terms with this news. "So why do you care what kind of drugs he bought?"

She didn't answer at first. She tried to, then closed her mouth to reconsider.

"Yep, that's what I thought," Dashner said. "You want something for yourself. Don't be embarrassed. That must really be a shitty thing to deal with, having your kid get bashed up like that. Good-looking kid, too. Really sucks." Dashner observed a moment of silence, then continued. "So you just tell me what you want. No reason to be embarrassed about this, especially not around me. Maybe I can offer some suggestions. Wouldn't be the first time I've sold to a lady like yourself."

Lea hoped to God this was true, if only because she liked imagining certain women of her social circle—Kelly Lucas, Margot Miller— huddling with Dashner on the couch in their cashmere coats, doing their best to hold their noses without actually holding their noses.

"Really, Mr. Dashner, you've got this wrong. I'm sorry. I should have been more clear. I don't want any drugs from you. I want to know what you sold my boy. I don't know if I can explain to you why. I just feel that it's very, very important that I understand what his life was like before all this happened."

He nodded dumbly, perhaps unconvinced of her truthfulness but at least understanding that she needed to pretend this was her motive. "It would probably be best just to let this go. Like you said, Chase is pretty much out of it. I don't see why we should talk about something that he doesn't even remember."

She set six twenty-dollar bills on the coffee table. "You're not getting any more than this—it's all I have on me. What then? Marijuana, I assume? A lot? Other stuff?"

Dashner became quickly resigned, puffing out a sigh of exasperation, taking a long pull on his Sprite. He picked up the bills, an act Lea knew would have been impossible for him not to perform in spite of his dramatic moment of prevarication. "Yeah, of course. Lots of pot. Some hash when it wasn't football season. Um . . ." He tilted his head up, trying to remember. "I got a lot of customers, you know. Hard to keep some of the orders straight."

"But Colin was a good customer, wasn't he?"

"Always paid, if that's what you mean. I don't want to say anything against the kid, since he's all fucked up now, and since you're his mom. But he could be pushy sometimes. You may know that. Sometimes he acted like I was his damn butler."

She nodded.

"Oh, hey!" Dashner sat up quickly. "He bought some acid and some poppers a while back. Toward the end of school last year. He said he was going to a bunch of concerts in the summer. Kids around here don't usually want that kind of stuff. All their moms pop pills, they don't want to do drugs their parents do. But I know a guy in Philly who can get pills, and it all worked out."

"Just once, though? He did that just once?"

"Yep. At least, that's the only time he got it from me."

She didn't know what to do with any of this. Dashner hadn't really told her anything she needed. If he had been a mechanic or a shop owner, she would have asked for some of her money back. It was time to go, but she sat stiffly for a few more moments, dreading the front hallway of St. Brendan's, the muted screams coming from inside the gym, the black night that she would have to drive through, the bedtime conversation with Geoffrey. A part of her wanted to stay right where she was, on the couch in the industrial arts room, with this jerky, reeking custodian, who somehow made her feel more comfortable than anything had in a long time. Maybe it was the promise of drugs about him, the promise of release and escape. Maybe it was the way he talked about Colin, calling him "Chase," confronting the boy's character flaws with harsh honesty. She liked talking to someone about the way Colin had been, even if the terms were not flattering. Everyone else she knew had so easily adjusted to the new boy. When Geoffrey and Megan and Lea's small handful of friends talked about Colin, she knew they meant the new one, the one who was eternally four years old. Dashner meant the other Colin, the one Lea had lived with for seventeen years, not the one who was still a stranger in her house. She closed her eyes, allowing herself a few seconds to brace herself for leaving. Then Dashner's voice came again.

"There was one other special order. Now that I'm thinking about special orders. He placed it sometime in September, I think. It was almost the first thing he asked me when he saw me at school. Not 'How was your summer, Dash?' Nothing like that. He just came up to me, on like the first week of classes, and said, 'I need some rare shit.' I didn't even know what the stuff was, and I told him so. He told me to get him some anyway. He named a price, a big one. Plus he had met a guy over the summer in East Breed's who sold, and he said he'd tell everybody to go through that guy if I didn't cooperate. He was that kind of kid. You may know that."

"The order was for what? What kind of drug?"

"He wrote down the technical name for it. About a billion letters long. It turned out to be eproxyn, which I still hadn't heard of. My man in Philly hooked me up. Really a pain in the ass. I had to drive to Philly twice, just to get a hold of a small bottle of this stuff. Didn't make any money on it. But I have to keep my customers at the school. Shit, you must think I'm such a slimeball. Lady—Mrs. Chase—I know I shouldn't be selling to them. I know that." With both hands he gripped the hair at the sides of his head, a gesture of self-hatred that he must have believed excused him from justifying himself any further.

Now that he had said it, Lea supposed she did consider him a slimeball. He was smelly, obsequious, amoral, slow on the uptake. But she didn't care, not now.

"Eproxyn. What does it do? Tell me what it does." She had to say it twice, because Dashner stayed lost in his reverie of shame, dwelling on the poor choice he'd made in establishing himself as a drug dealer to children.

"They'd get the drugs anyway, you know. They'd go over to East Breed's. These kids don't belong in East Breed's. And I do almost entirely pot. A little bit of marijuana for the kids, and I make some money, and they can spare it. I know I'm a piece of shit, I know what you must think of me." His eyes got buggy and he turned to her abruptly. "You don't think I had anything to do with what happened to Chase, do you? I mean, I don't think those kids were on anything when they fought. I really don't."

"That's not what I think, Mr. Dashner. Just forget about what I think of you. It really would be best that way. Just tell me how eproxyn affects someone."

"That's the thing," he said, quickly abandoning his solipsistic remorse. "I have no idea what it does. Never thought about it, really, not until I gave it to him. Then I asked him what it was for, and he just told me to fuck off. He was that kind of kid sometimes."

"Yes, Mr. Dashner. I know that."

# | twenty-three |

*Thursday,* inconvenient though it was, happened to be Casey's thirty-four birthday. If he had not told Rachel this fact several days into their relationship—and if she had not been the kind of person who tracked such information, checking her Palm Pilot early every morning for reminders of these dates—it would have gone unnoticed, and he would not have minded. When he thought about birthdays, a vague annoyance tugged at him. He associated the occasion with the birthday celebrations at O'Ruddy's, when servers would gather around the table of the celebrant, proffering a complimentary cupcake and launching into a jazzy a cappella rendition of "O'Ruddy's says O'Happy O'Birthday." As manager, he didn't have to participate in this indignity, although his enforcement of the participation of others was draconian. The handbook declared that the O'Happy O'Birthday song should never be sung by fewer than four servers, for the sake of harmony.

Rachel called him in the morning, which meant she had broken away from one of her prep periods at school. He was surprised to note how little this kind and unnecessary gesture moved him, and he took this as a measure of the self-involvement his situation had created in him. He couldn't even think about her long enough to absorb one of her moments of thoughtfulness. They didn't come along that often. He thanked her.

"This is your one day," she said, pushing her words through a background of clomping teenage footsteps, the metallic shivering of locker doors. "For this day you get to put all the shit out of your mind. I know you didn't get yourself anything else for your birthday, so give yourself that. Just forget about it. Think about anything else, but not that."

He nodded mechanically, then realized she couldn't see him. "Okay. Yep. And you should get back to school. I'll see you tonight."

As if it were a present, he thought. As if he could wrap up a day in which he didn't think about his unemployment, his imminent destitution, his incrimination, the vitriolic accusation of Bert Player. As if respite from this were a gift he could just hand over to himself. A switch that he could turn off. *Christ*, he said into the phone after she had hung up, *if it were that easy, I would have done it a long time ago.*

She had said that she knew he hadn't gotten anything for himself, and this was true. In normal times he might have committed a small indulgence, bought a new CD or renewed a subscription to *Newsweek*. Today it was out of the question. The Monday after the fight he had estimated that his savings would last him for two months, but he now recognized that he had been optimistic. And at new jobs they never paid right away, and there were always new clothes and shoes to buy. The week before he had hinted to his mother that if she was thinking of acknowledging his birthday this year, cash might be a welcome surprise, but she had said that Oklahoma was more expensive than she'd expected.

A short man with a boxy head showed up at his doorstep a little after four.

The man was, it seemed, surprised to see the door open in front of him. He shuffled some of the papers he had clamped in his hand. "This one . . . no, this one . . . Yeah. This one is for you." He held out a triple-folded letter, which Casey took with the hand that was not smeared with microwave popcorn grease.

"Summons," said the man with the boxy head.

"Ah. Right." Casey read the heading and the opening paragraph. It was the kind of writing that he didn't think he'd ever been able to get through, the kind of writing that he'd seen in a business law class at Penn State, which had made his decision to drop out even easier. Before he had made it through three lines, Casey said, "You have any idea what it's about?"

"No. You just have to take it. That's all I know. Okay, then." And the man marched off down the walkway.

He took the summons to his tiny kitchen, flattened it on the counter, and made himself focus. He was able to discern, after some effort, that he was required to appear at a pretrial interview regarding a case that was being heard between the family of Colin Chase and Markham Corporation, the headquarters. He needed to attend a meeting at Lucas and Toole, a firm in Weston, at two o'clock on Thursday, March 21.

Another telling, then. Another hashing out of the night that, he was starting to understand, had been of utmost significance to his life. It was no longer something to try to forget about, no longer something that would go away. A night that defined him at the same time it destroyed him.

He tried to find relief in the document in front of him. It was a testament to the thing's utter tediousness that in spite of the hope that it might rescue him, he still could not manage to read more than a paragraph without stopping. Eventually he finished, then tried it again. It was indeed headquarters that would be sued. His logic followed directly to the notion that this might mean he himself was free from civil complaint, and perhaps from a criminal one as well. Would the civil case proceed before the criminal one? He thought he remembered, from following trials in the news, that some mechanism kept families of victims waiting in the wings until the cops and prosecutors had their day. If this was the case, then maybe Janda and the prosecutors had let the moment pass, had left it to the tort people to assign culpability. And they would go where the money was. *And the money,* Casey thought, *certainly is not here.*

It was possible, of course, that he would know the truth by March 21. He might have the advantage in the meeting, he might be able to stun the smarmy attorneys, and the parents of Colin Chase, with the full story of January 18. Maybe he would let them show their cards first. He would take their abuse, he would welcome it. The father would brandish rage like a clenched fist, the mother would dab at her eyes. Casey would be conscious of his posture, careful not to sit like a guilty man, like a man unsure of himself. He would have to do his best, on that day, to look like Bert Player.

The father would explode at him, a vein throbbing somewhere in a crimson head—on his neck or on his forehead, Casey couldn't decide which—and the lawyer would calm his client, then begin his own, quieter assault. Accusations couched in jargon, then simplified in their naked ugliness, a tone of contempt. Isn't it true, Mr. Fielder, that you never called the police? That you did not do a thing for nearly a half an hour? *Go fuck yourself,* he said to the lawyer in his mind (he swore even in his thoughts now). *None of you know. I know. Now let me tell you.*

And he would reveal the full story. He would lay out the details that could not be contradicted, that spoke to an understanding of the damaged Colin Chase that even the boy's parents didn't have access to. He would rehearse it ahead of time, rehearse it again in his mind as the parents and the lawyers barraged him. He would speak softly, so that the father would have to quiet his enraged breathing, but firmly, as someone whom you would not think to contradict. A tone of something else. A tone of innocence and understanding, a tone of enlightenment.

He would lay it in front of them. *This is the story,* he would say. *Be-*

*fore you go any further and say something you regret, this is what really hap-*
*pened.*

But what would it be? He would learn it on Friday night. He would purchase the alcohol and then get the rest from Brady Benson. He would ingest it stoically, chew it over, digest the important bits, spit out the chaff. He would take it to the law offices of Lucas and Toole on that Thursday in March, and it would be so profound that the animus would be swallowed by the father, and the tears of the mother would spring from a different source of hatred.

Casey understood the risk of thinking this way, and he disregarded it. He had to mine the depths to deal with this season of his life. Certainly he might be offering himself false hope. Brady might have no more to say, or he might have found another way to buy alcohol. Or the real story might not explain all that Casey hoped it would. But he shoved these thoughts aside and imagined more of that silent boardroom in the law firm, expressions of regret and shock. The Chases' lawyer would have to devise a new strategy that included nothing about the culpability of the restaurant manager, a man who had also been damaged.

Casey would find out on Friday afternoon, at the liquor store.

# twenty-four

*Geoffrey kept* a neatly organized library of medical texts in his home office, a small square room on the second floor. Like Colin's room, this was off-limits to Lea, or at least she had considered it as such for the years they'd lived in the house. It was the kind of room in which a snooping wife might find evidence of an infidelity, and so her presence there made her feel furtive, dishonest. She was fairly certain that Geoffrey had never cheated. If, during a search of his mahogany desk in pursuit of paper clips, she found something he'd been keeping from her, it was likely to be a discovery that would cause guilt — a bankbook from an account he'd set up to buy her an anniversary ring, or secret plans for a trip to Maui.

The difficulties came in the books. *Basic Clinical Pharmacology* sounded promising, but the drugs were classified into categories that she didn't understand, and she gave up on it quickly. *The General Handbook of Medicine* also failed her because of its complexity. In an enormous, alphabetical catalogue of all prescription drugs she found two listings for eproxyn, but the only information offered seemed to deal with the drug's chemical compounds. Another manual described the chemical elements, and under "Indication" it read: "Indicated for the relief of the pruritic manifestations of corticosteroid responsivity." She used a medical dictionary to decipher the meaning of this sentence, and then another to look up words she didn't know from those separate definitions, and finally she leaned back in the chair and sighed toward the ceiling, her investigation having apparently hit a wall after twenty-five minutes.

It didn't occur to her until later in the afternoon that she could simply ask Geoffrey, and as she and Colin sat in front of the stereo in the living room, listening to several repetitions of "The Wreck of the Edmund Fitzgerald," she fought through the surprisingly powerful instinct not to tell Geoffrey anything. She didn't know why it seemed so natural to keep it from him—whether it had to do with the shady world of jilted lovers and drug dealers that she had penetrated, or whether she needed to shield him from too much knowledge of Colin. More likely, she finally understood, it was that she would have to tell him everything, beginning with her excavation of Colin's room. She would have to describe the notes from the girls, the detention slips, the meeting with the drug dealer. And she knew what Geoffrey himself probably didn't know, something that would surprise him when it happened: she knew that he would be terribly, desperately, unapologetically angry with her for having done it.

Two weeks earlier Lea had unearthed an Xbox game set from the recesses of Colin's closet, under a pile of winter clothes. The old Colin had given up on the game over a year ago, another exorbitant Christmas gift thrown by the wayside. After her failed investigation of Geoffrey's library, she suddenly remembered the thing and decided that she would set it up, hoping that it might give some sense of accomplishment to her day. They still didn't watch television much, but Colin had overcome his fear of it, as long as the volume and screen brightness were set low. Colin looked quizzically at the machine when she brought it out to him, and as she spent three quarters of an hour negotiating the wires and plugs behind the television in the living room. Yet once she'd gotten it running and set the control in his hands, he remembered all the maneuvers, and the noise and luminescence of the television didn't bother him when he controlled it.

When Geoffrey came home at six, they began playing Xbox as a new family activity, a welcome substitute for the endless repetitions of easy-listening CDs. Lea and Geoffrey both held the control as if it were something very foreign, perhaps radioactive, while Colin manipulated the thing as if it grew out of his palm. He hammered his thumbs to navigate through the corridors on a game called Halo. He knew to slice his drive slightly on the fourth hole of video golf. All night they praised his dexterity, the remembrance of these skills.

Later on, both of them in bed but awake from the adrenaline rush of the video stimuli, Geoffrey leaned on his side and began to rub her stomach. He watched his hand rather than her face as he spoke.

"I know what you're thinking," he said.

"No, I don't think you do."

He shifted himself on the bedding, removing his hand from her body. "Stop playing around, Lea. You're hoping. You think this means he might be getting better, don't you?"

It was nowhere near what she had been thinking, not even close, and the cruelty of this fact made her forgiving and quick to please him. Later that night she would gratify him with her mouth and body, and it all came back to this moment, to this sad, mistaken expression of confidence in his knowledge of his wife.

"Okay, so I'm hoping, Geoffrey," she said. "Tell me more about what I'm thinking."

"The body remembers. The mind remembers but it doesn't remember, if you catch my meaning. He knows how to play the games because he's done it so often in the past. I admit I may have felt some hope myself tonight, but just for a second. That game with the guns, you know which one I mean?"

"Halo."

"Okay. During that game he seemed to know a secret. He climbed the ladder to get that extra weapon. That doesn't necessarily have to do with the body. He would have had to remember that, it's a function of the mind, not hand-eye coordination. And in the golf game, he knew how to calibrate his shots against the wind. But it doesn't really mean anything, except that he remembers how to do some things, which we already knew. A four-year-old mind can retain the things it knew in the past. It's strange, and misleading. Like I said, even I had some hope there for a second, but I believe it's false. You know that, right? The hope goes away a little more every day, and it's been more than six weeks now, and I don't have much of it left."

*Go ahead and cry, Geoffrey*, she thought, *because I'm not going to*. She had to come to terms with the fact at some point: she no longer wanted Colin to get better. Perhaps it had to do with the story Geoffrey had told her about the stabbing, which she had immediately connected with the notes from the girl named Jess. Or perhaps she had been too affected by Dashner's characterization of the boy, who was disliked even by his drug dealer, or by the accumulation of the evidence in his room. The fact was, she had not only come to accept the loss of Colin, she had come to know that she was glad to be rid of him. All the acts that had come before in the guise of hope—her constant ministrations to his body, the vigils she kept to see if anything remained of the Colin she had known, the thorough, daily examining ("Colin, do you remember what position you played on the football team?" "Colin, do you know your middle name?")—all these tests and observations, the questions to the doctors, the head hung in worry and contemplation, she now saw as functions of fear, not hope. She worried that he might improve, that Colin Chase might barge in through the corridors of the four-year-old mind and reclaim the body that was rightfully his. She constantly listened for his footsteps, her heart drumming.

Geoffrey had missed so wildly that in spite of her pity for him, she felt it safe to use him to some extent, once she had assuaged the guilt by performing something she'd seen on late-night cable.

She let several minutes pass, until his breathing slowed and he kissed her, as always after sex, on each eyelid.

"What's eproxyn?" she asked.

If he answered now, that would be it. No lies told, no smoke-screen. Alas . . .

"What kind of question is that? Eproxyn, for God's sake. Where did you get that question?"

"Something on TV. God, Geoffrey, I'm a mess. All I do now is watch TV. I never liked it before, especially not the daytime stuff, but now that Colin's around all the time, and now that he can't stand it when the TV's on, I find myself yearning for it. During his naps I go upstairs and watch soap operas. Can you believe it? It's like I'm a heroin addict or something. I'm really disappointed in myself. It's so childish. Just because I know I can't have something, now I want it all the time."

He chuckled, and her head, resting on him, shook with his chest. "Well, I'm not sure that television and heroin are quite analogous. But where'd you hear about eproxyn?"

"Why, what is it?"

"Not something you'd hear about on a soap opera."

She wondered whether he was purposefully withholding it or sim-ply being obtuse. Like anyone who had borrowed fifty thousand dol-lars for his education, he liked to exercise the power of his knowledge, and she had stepped into this constantly attended trap blatantly enough. Still, she couldn't help but feel annoyed. She could still taste his semen in her mouth, after all.

"It was on some documentary. For once I was watching something worthwhile. Something about hospitals, and it was pretty interesting, but then the phone rang. I caught a few words, and for some reason eproxyn stuck. They were talking about it a lot, but with the phone call I didn't catch why it was such a big deal, so I told myself to re-member to ask you later. Now it's later. That's all."

"A documentary on hospitals mentioned eproxyn? Huh."

He didn't speak again, and now she was nearly furious.

"So are you going to tell me," she said, "or should I start prepping for the MCAT?"

He stared up at the ceiling. He spoke with the froggy peace of orgasm still in his voice.

"Well, it doesn't come up much. I've never prescribed it. It can be used to treat certain skin infections, I think, but there are better drugs for that. I would imagine it's mostly used by free clinics and Third World relief agencies."

"Huh. That's kind of disappointing. I thought it was a new club drug or something." She took her head off his chest and turned to the side, exhausted. It was one in the morning. Geoffrey still woke at five-thirty every day to run. Colin would wake at six, demanding Fruity Pebbles. Tomorrow would be a long day, the same as today, although there would be times when she would count this blessing, the newborn son, as an enormous one. But her ignorance about eproxyn would nag at her, and she nearly cried at this. She would think about it tomorrow when she saw him, as she had done today. She would look into his eyes and think about the mysterious pill and wonder. *Why did you put that in your body, Colin? What were you after?*

"No, no," said Geoffrey after he had resettled himself on his side as well. "Hardly a club drug. More like an after-club drug in some cases."

"What does that mean?"

"Well, that's the only reason I've heard of it. A couple years ago when I was doing that pro bono stuff, I had to treat a girl who had taken a lot of it. One of the illegal uses of eproxyn is . . . Well, it's kind of sinister." His voice shifted at once from chatty to clinical. "Ingestion of a large dose of eproxyn will cause a miscarriage in pregnant women. A poor girl's abortion."

"Oh," said Lea, in a voice she had never heard come out of her before. "That's interesting."

## | twenty-five |

*Brady was waiting* for him in front of the liquor store. He stood rigid against the cold wind, gripping the collar of his jacket with one hand and holding it against his face.

Casey pulled into a spot in front of a nail salon, out of view of the liquor store clerk. He frantically waved the boy over to the car. Brady waddled toward him, tilting himself into the wind, and slid into the passenger seat.

"Brady, do you think it's wise for a teenage boy to loiter in front of a liquor store like that? Isn't that a bit obvious?"

"That's the beauty of it," Brady said. "A kid standing in front of a Chinese restaurant or a fingernail place that happens to be right next to a booze place? That's obvious. A kid standing in front of a liquor store, looking like he don't give a fuck? That kid's got nothing to hide."

Casey knew that this kind of reasoning would land Brady in an

enormous amount of trouble someday, probably before he even graduated from high school. He could not predict any kind of future for
this young man, other than one that involved impregnating women
and getting more tattoos and in general continuing the gratification of
his appetites. Brady might go to prison eventually, or he might just get
in the kind of trouble that precluded his leaving the state, working
anywhere but Jiffy Lube. He had already limited his options severely
by tattooing his neck. Casey didn't think any of this bothered the boy,
so long as he got his cache of liquor for the evening. As Brady un-
zipped his jacket and began to thaw, Casey looked at the tattoo: a car-
toonish green-and-black cobra's head, winking and wearing a top hat.

"How much do you want tonight?" Casey said.

"Two cases of Pabst and three bottles of Boone's Farm."

"Of course. Special occasion?"

Brady scowled. "What's that mean? You got it? Two cases and
three bottles. The wine should be different kinds, none of it grape.
There's a kind called Sangria—if they have that, get two bottles of
that. If not, just mix it up. But no grape, like I said. Strawberry or
wild berry's fine."

Casey took a neatly folded stack of bills from Brady and bought
the liquor from an elderly clerk. The clerk bagged each bottle of
three-dollar wine in brown paper and took so long that Casey thought
he might be stalling, waiting for the police to arrive after pressing
some secret button. During the interminable bagging process his neck
became ringed with sweat, which froze as soon as he darted out of the
store, encumbered by cheap alcohol.

"Where to?" he asked Brady.

He shrugged. "My mom's home today, can't take you there. You
sure as shit don't want me in your house, that's obvious."

Casey didn't know how he had made this obvious, but it was certainly true. Still, he reacted to Brady's self-pity and felt it necessary to
mumble that he wouldn't mind having him there but that he was having the house fumigated. Brady scoffed but didn't seem offended. He

rifled through the large brown liquor store bag and pulled out one of the bottles of Boone's Farm. He unscrewed the cap. "Kick ass—you got Sangria," he said, then took a long drink.

"The wine is for you?"

Brady squinted toward Casey with as much malevolence as he could muster. "Shut up. Fucker. Yeah, the wine's for me. So what?"

Casey shook his head, widening his eyes to imply that it didn't matter to him.

"Beer gives me gas. Yeah, big fucking joke, I drink wine." As if to confirm this, and to prove that it was a manlier habit than one might think, he took a long swig. When he set the bottle back on his knee, Casey noticed that the level of the red booze had sunk below the top of the label.

"So we'll just drive around, then," said Casey.

"Sounds like a plan. I got no other ideas. Wouldn't want to get my lungs all fumigated at your house." The reference to his lungs reminded him of something. He cracked the window and reached into his pockets. "You got to let me smoke in here, though."

Casey nodded assent. He drove away from East Breed's, away from town entirely. Highway 4 wove through the bordering woods, eventually meeting up with the interstate. Because of the winding and the rise and fall of the landscape, visibility on 4 was limited to a few dozen yards at a stretch, and so it was littered with animal carcasses. In general it was not a popular byway, and Casey felt confident about the small odds of a state trooper seeing Brady pull on his bottle of wine. They would drive to the interstate, then turn back. It would take about a half hour. A half hour could make for a substantial story.

"So?" said Casey after passing the last of the clapboard houses that could claim the postal code of Breed's Township. "What do you have for me?"

Brady had hunched low in the seat. He kept the resting cigarette close to the opening in the window, and he had zipped up his Sharks jacket all the way to his chin. He looked out the window. "Right. You want to know the story."

"Yes. The story of Friday night. The real one, the important one, not the Friday that came before. I need to find out what happened when Colin Chase got hurt."

"I got to tell you, like I did last time, I wasn't there when that kid got bashed. And no matter what, I'm not telling you who did that. Even if I knew who did it. I'm not saying I do. But if I did, I still wouldn't tell you."

"I already know who did it, Brady. Jesus. That's not what I'm looking for."

Brady stared at Casey until, in spite of the challenges of the roadway, Casey had to turn and stare back. Brady's face was ugly this afternoon, pale and shadowy. A runaway splotch of acne upon which he had tried to perform some kind of surgery overwhelmed the left side of his chin.

"Rick, Brady. Your friend Rick, from the last story. I'm not saying I'm right, or that you ratted on your friend. It's just a hunch. Forget I said anything. Just continue."

But Brady hadn't even begun, and this confused him for a moment. He got out another cigarette, but after cracking the window decided it was too cold.

"Tell me about Friday, January eighteenth," Casey prompted. "How did you guys happen to be at the parking lot of O'Ruddy's?"

Brady suddenly gained a sort of self-possession, which he signified by shifting himself in the seat, turning toward Casey and leaning his back against the passenger door. "That was gonna be a crazy night. Just had the feel, you know. We'd just got done with finals, so we were starting off the last semester of high school. Man, I'm so psyched to get out of that fucking place."

Casey concentrated on the roadway, its twists and turns, its downed animals. He had to be measured in his response to the road-kill; if he swerved too much to dodge a carcass, he might bash into the side rail or plunge into the depths of the sugar maple forest.

Over his intense focus, his attention to the wheel and the road, was laid Brady's stream-of-consciousness. The digressions of that evening, the monologues regarding Brady's concerns and dislikes and appetites. The kids wanted out of school; they were ready to begin the end. Brady and his friends had scored two bottles of vodka, probably enough for the five of them, depending on whether they eventually talked some girls into hanging out with them. It was always a struggle—you wanted to find women and you wanted them liquored up, but you didn't want to have to share too much of your booze. Brady described this conundrum to Casey with Zen-like sincerity.

But first, before they could think about women or about getting properly wasted, there was the fight. Yes, it was planned. It had been orchestrated as carefully by their tier of the Breed's Township High social ladder as the semiformal dances were by the student council kids. A fight at O'Ruddy's, where they had gotten into it last time. Another round with the St. Brendan's Academy bastards, this time with real numbers, with game plans and commitment. Brady wasn't entirely sure what the conflict was meant to resolve, he said, but they were all excited about it, or at least professed to be.

Casey wasn't sure that he believed this, or that he understood it. "How could you not know what it was about? There were at least a dozen kids there from your school. Are you telling me that all those kids showed up to fight on a subzero night for no reason?"

Brady offered a deep, sustained, significant shrug. He was not blowing off the question as much as he was indicating the complexity of the answer. "It's just . . . I don't know how many people really knew. I don't know if I really get it. I think I don't. Those St. Brendan's kids are just such fucking dicks."

Casey had to let him go at this point, not press him too much. The bottle of Boone's Farm now held nothing but backwash. Brady looked out the window with a frustrated smirk. "Fucking dicks," he said again.

"So it was kind of an old feud."

Brady looked at him suddenly. *"Yeah.* That's right. *From ancient grudge break to new mutiny, where civil blood makes civil hands unclean."*

Casey very nearly steered the car into the barrier fence when he heard this, but instead he sheared the corpse of a skunk with his left tire. "What?"

"That's from Shakespeare. Miss Lawrence made us memorize it last year. *From ancient grudge break to new mutiny.* I still remember that shit, the whole speech. It's about a fight."

"Oh."

"You think I'm an idiot, right? Miss Lawrence did too. I got a zero on the memorization quiz, 'cause me and the bitch next to me both spelled *piteous* wrong, and Miss Lawrence said that meant I copied from her. But the bitch copied off me, I fucking swear. When they think you're an idiot already, you get screwed on things like that."

Casey nodded. Brady said, "So how about it?"

"How about what?"

"Do you think I'm an idiot?"

The driving took too much focus; Casey couldn't think. He had chosen poorly in going down Highway 4. He needed a straight road, a road where he could calculate and dissemble, not this obstacle course of sharp turns and dead animals.

"Frankly, Brady, yes, I think you're a little slow. Or maybe I just think you do some idiotic things."

"I'll accept that," the boy said. Casey was glad he hadn't lied.

Brady put the empty wine bottle back in the sack. He got out another—wild berry–flavored—and screwed off the cap. His first long swig turned his lips purple. "I don't know if you can say we were feuding or anything. Maybe not so much like that ancient grudge and new mutiny stuff. But I hated those kids, most people did. Not 'cause they're mostly rich, either. I don't think all of them are rich. I went to middle school with a kid who's there now, and his mom don't have any money. He don't even play sports, but they must give him tuition for free or something. They probably make him clean the toilets."

"So why'd you hate them?"

"Shit, I don't know. Those fucking haircuts and jackets and shit.

They're just punks. I been to a couple parties with St. Brendan's kids. Some of them might not be too bad when they're high, maybe, but mostly they don't want much to do with us. I mean, that kid that got all bashed in, it's not that I think that shit should happen to them. I'm just saying it wasn't too hard to be pissed off. When I heard there'd be a rumble, I didn't have to think about it too long. Fucking St. Brendan's, you know?"

Again, Casey didn't. For all his ignorance, Brady seemed to have a way of making Casey feel that he was missing something. In his own high school days, the disparity between Breed's Township High and St. Brendan's had been the same as the current one, although no one Casey had known ever managed to get a scholarship there. But the disparity, back then, hadn't seemed to create animosity. They never thought to rumble with those kids, never thought to go to parties with them. They existed in an entirely different universe, one that had to do not just with money, as Brady said, but with the strange practice of wearing a blazer to school every day, of praying with classmates right before a geometry test. It had to do with the fact that those odd beings in plaid ties took girls to things called cotillions, traveled to Europe for spring break, could try out for a varsity squash team. A different world entirely. It wouldn't have occurred to Casey or his classmates to deal with them, except in rumors. He wondered if it were some kind of social progress he now witnessed, an East Breed's boy discussing the St. Brendan's boys as if it were acceptable for him to feel as strong an emotion as hate about them.

"So what was it, then? You said you don't quite understand, but you must have some idea why people went to fight. What was the excuse that was being passed around?"

"There was something about a girl. Some girl at Township had been really fucked over by a guy at St. Brendan's. All right, you want to know the truth, it was the kid that eventually got hurt. Colin Chase."

"So it wasn't just Rick that wanted to fight Colin Chase? Everyone knew about him?"

"Yeah, he's pretty well known. Fact is, he's kind of a player. The kind of guy that everybody knows about. And he knew how to score everything."

"I'm not sure I get it."

"He had a connection, a drug guy. We still don't have a real good one. I have to buy my pot from my mom's boyfriend. Chase knew somebody, always had some shit. People could call him if they got desperate, but he wasn't really a dealer. He charged way too much, for one thing, and he was just a big dick. He'd sell you a dime bag for thirty bucks, then make you feel like he had just rescued your family from a tornado or something. He never remembered your name, it didn't matter if he'd seen you a thousand times. People had to be pretty desperate to go to him, but he always had something."

The car was climbing an incline now, the V-4 engine maxing out at thirty and making noises about it. *A drug thing,* Casey mumbled to himself. This changed everything. He didn't have the stomach for this, nor the patience, nor the interest. A teenage drug matter—would there really be an explanation, once the depths had been plumbed? The boy was a dealer of sorts, and not a very pleasant one. No exoneration for Casey in that, except to note that his culpability was simply a matter of circumstance. They were going to fight somewhere. They were going to hurt Colin Chase, that was the plan. He could take this news to the deposition, but he was not sanguine about what it might do for him. He also knew that nothing he'd learned from Brady Benson would help him land another job. But there was something else, a word of Brady's he'd ignored.

"Brady, you said something about a girl. That this might have been about a girl."

"Yeah, that's what I was saying. Colin Chase screwed over this girl we know."

"What do you mean, screwed over?"

"I don't know, really. There were some rumors. He'd raped her maybe, or maybe club-drugged her. I don't know about that. I know the girl, and she'd fucked him before, at some party, I'm pretty sure. She seemed to like him a lot. Wrote his name on her notebook, that kind of shit. But that was mostly the rumor, that he'd raped her in some way. I guess it could have happened. It was enough, anyway, with all the other stuff thrown in."

"The drug stuff?"

Yes, the drug stuff, but Brady conceded this mildly, as if disappointed in Casey's interest in that aspect of things. What he meant, he went on to explain, was the girls. She hadn't been the first Township girl to be with Colin. In fact, it seemed to be a hobby of his. Last year a boy transferred from St. Brendan's when a tuition check bounced, and this boy had stories to tell from inside the citadel. Colin Chase, it was reported, kept a list in his locker of the Township girls he'd had. He bragged that the best head he'd ever gotten had been from the poorest of the bunch, a girl on welfare (everyone knew who they were). After they studied correlations in math class, Colin had made a chart and a formula that indicated the relationship between the estimated income of a girl's family and the amount of time it took him to get her into bed. He had passed his chart around the school, Brady said, and he'd used real names.

"It sounds territorial, Brady. Was that it? You guys didn't like the fact that he took your women?"

Again Brady shrugged, an honest shrug, as if he clearly hadn't thought of the matter in these terms before. "I guess, now that you put it that way—that's pretty whack. There's enough rich girls to go around. St. Theresa's girls, stick to them, you know? I never even met a St. Theresa's girl, so it's not like they're sharing them with us. But that prick Chase gets to be with any Township chick he wants? He's fucked more girls from my school that I have, and I ain't ashamed to admit that, 'cause, you know, I've had my share. But that shit ain't right. I can respect a guy who knows how to get himself some, but damn . . ."

"At a certain point . . ." Casey prodded.

"Yeah, at a certain point it's too much. Not even just fucking 'em, but treating 'em pretty bad too. He wasn't very cool to his girls."

"You've heard other stuff? About other girls?"

"I don't mean he did anything specific. Not like rape or roofies or anything. Really, the guy didn't have to. I ain't a fag, but he really was a good-looking guy, even I can admit that. I guess he still is, but you know what I mean."

"So what did he do to the girls?"

Another shrug, and then another long drink from the bottle, which was emptying even faster than the first one had. "Just did 'em. Said whatever he had to to get a girl to put out. We've all been there, right? But there was something about his way of doing it. He'd talk about them a lot, pretty mean shit. One time he told me that Kim Beach had the smelliest box he'd ever been around. I didn't even know the guy much, but one time I bought a bag from him and we got to kind of talking, and that was like the first thing he said. Asked if I went to Township, asked if I knew Kim, and when I said yeah he said, 'She's got the smelliest kooter on earth.' "

"Back to the fight. That's what this was about—he took your women? So this is more Helen of Troy than Shakespeare."

Brady cast a glance downward and moved his lips slightly, repeating Casey's question to himself. "You lost me there, man. I paid attention during the Shakespeare shit because it was before Miss Lawrence got fat. Once she started bulking up, I didn't get much out of that class."

"I mean it was a matter of honor, in a way. You guys got tired of him raping and pillaging, so to speak. I mean, the women were yours, like you said. He should have stuck to the St. Theresa's girls."

"I guess I mean, if you think about it a lot, I guess that's there. But really, I don't know. We were out on a Friday night. We were drinking. We'd all heard about a rumble, and we'd fought with them before but didn't get to finish. It's not like we needed a reason to go with the St. Brendan's guys. Been giving us shit all our lives, pretty much.

They'll be giving us shit for the rest of our lives too, I bet. And then this rumor came out about the girl, that she'd been fucked over even worse than normal by Chase. Lots of factors, I guess."

"That explains the fight, but it doesn't explain what happened to him, does it?"

"What kind of explanation you looking for?"

"They bashed in his brains because he slept with a girl from your school and then didn't return her calls? Or what, got her pregnant? What could he have done to her that would have made three guys try to kill him?"

"It's not that, man. It's the two grand."

"The what?" Casey tried to keep his voice smooth and unruffled, but Brady had already noticed the significance of his own words. He stared at Casey with confused, tipsy eyes, suddenly realizing that he hadn't mentioned this before, or suddenly remembering that he wasn't talking to a friend.

Brady now began to laugh, falsely and dramatically, more a gesture of embarrassment than mirth. "Yep, two thousand. And that's all she wrote for me." He laughed again. "Slipped out, I guess. God-damned Booooooone's Farm. Beer gives me gas, I think I told you that."

"Yes, you did." Casey had been a bar manager for two years, and he knew that the less you prodded a drinker, the more he would talk.

"Seriously, I'm not saying any more than that. I fucked up, so I'll finish, but you got to turn this car around."

Casey listened, waiting for the information, when Brady suddenly shouted at him, making him jump in his seat.

"Turn the fucking car around!"

"Jesus, okay," Casey said, but it was thirty seconds before Highway 4 offered room to do so.

"Take me back to my house, I got to meet some people. Shit, I'm already pretty buzzed," Brady said, looking at the wine label. "I should hold off. Okay, here it is. There was two thousand bucks in it for whoever messed that kid up. Had to be big-time, serious damage, not just a bloody nose. No one said anything about killing him, not when I was around anyway, but I guess that's what the three guys took from it."

"Brady, what is 'it'? Who offered that money? How did they get paid?"

"Nah, that's it. I can't finish everything. I don't know much anyway. Really. Seriously. I don't get it, man. What the fuck do you care, anyway? You're not a cop. Are you writing a book or something? Leave it, man. Seriously. It doesn't matter to anybody."

"Two thousand dollars for anyone who would mess up Colin Chase. That's what you're telling me, right? There was a kind of bounty on Colin Chase. And three guys ended up claiming it?"

"I already told you what you're going to hear. I'm turning up the radio, I'm taking a nap to sleep off this shit. You better be grateful to me, by the way. I gave you a goddamn bonus today," Brady said, tilting his head against the glass and closing his eyes. "Even if I didn't mean to. Wake me up when we get to my house. You remember how to get there?" But he didn't expect an answer, and Casey didn't give him one.

| twenty-six |

*Back to the bedroom,* then. She was surprised to realize how distracted she had become from her excavations of the room, how the list had sent her to the janitor, how the janitor had sent her to the medical books. And how between these investigations she had spent the hours investigating her husband as well, and staring at her son, wanting to ask him questions and speculating, with a mind as dreamy and ungrounded as his own might be, rather than trusting the unearthed evidence in his bedroom.

But now she returned, weary of learning from others. She didn't want to share her discovery process with Geoffrey, with Dashner, even if they didn't know what they were giving her. She wanted to nestle in the old smell of him, among Colin's laundry and the detritus of his sins.

She hadn't gotten very far the first time, having sorted her way through the bulk of his clothing and the top shelves of his closet, and this meant she hadn't learned much about him, not really. So he got detentions for inexplicable behavior, so he got drugs from Dashner. And so he once placed a special order for pills that would abort a fetus he had not intended to create, thus causing a girl to stab him (unless that had been done by the vitriolic Jess; it didn't seem to matter much). Were any of these behaviors beyond the pale of what she might have expected of him, back when he was himself? Last night, after the initial jolt of Geoffrey's words, she had felt a chill descend, spreading from the center of her body like the radiating pain of a heart attack. She immediately knew she would not sleep. Instead she spent the hours staring at shapes behind her closed eyes, and in the end the coldness left her and the power seeped from the words. *Ingestion of eproxyn will cause* ... She repeated it to herself, or rather, she played Geoffrey's words, spoken in his nonchalant voice, in the stereo of her head, and finally the words seemed impotent, as insignificant as most of what he had said that night. The phrase, in fact, seemed inevitable in retrospect. Of course the purpose of the drug would be sinister, outside the realm of recreation. Of course the special order Colin had placed with Dashner would be of use to him, a tool with which to exert his fierce will. How was it that the malice of this boy still managed to startle her?

On the floor of the closet she found simple, unenlightening filth: dust and food wrappers, damaged socks, old magazines (none of them pornographic, she was surprised to see), the dirty strips of athletic tape and mouthguards and clumps of grass that were the sloughs of football practice. Like a child, the teenage Colin Chase had cleaned his room (not that it was often requested of him) by shoving everything into the closet.

She also came across a tall, almost obsessively organized stack of *Sports Illustrated* magazines, dating back to August of his freshman year in high school and current up to the Thursday before his wounding. She found an album in which he kept clippings of articles about the St. Brendan's Wolverines; she found a pile of board games still wrapped in plastic; she found a duffel bag from last summer's trip to

New York that he still hadn't unpacked. In the dresser drawers she found clothes, papers, food wrappers, bottles, hair products, CDs — all of it numbing, mundane, useless.

And so she passed her morning, and then her afternoon. She rifled through his objects, his clothes, his garbage, his schoolbooks. Every half hour she went to the living room, where Colin was keeping himself occupied. He worked on a puzzle in the morning, and then she settled him into the couch, where he took his nap. She went back to his room, inspected his dresser drawers and his bedside table, and took down his posters. She went back to him, woke him up, and fed him microwaved pizza. They listened to music and then she read to him, with his body leaning against her side, eventually causing her arm and leg to fall asleep.

Afterward they did his exercises, a series of calisthenics and stretches that they performed along with a videotape from the hospital. They were conscientious about the performance of the exercises. Though Colin disliked them, he understood them to be of some importance, since he and his mother changed into different clothes before putting on the tape. When they finished the video he went to take a bath, which he could now do himself, as long as he left the door open, and she went back to his bedroom to go through the bookshelves.

As a sort of excuse for this massive violation of Colin's privacy, Lea worked under the pretext that she was packing things up. The therapist at the hospital, after all, had recommended a change in environs, and so it seemed only right to sort through his things, something she might do even if she weren't trying to excavate his past. After she had looked through the pockets of his shirts, she folded and stacked them into piles. She threw away all evidence of football except for his letter jacket, which she hung in the basement. She didn't know what to do with the *Sports Illustrated*s, so she left them in the closet. Now she came to his bookshelves, which she would have to think about. They seemed to mock the new Colin somehow, with the absurd idea that he might someday be able to read these works. The previous Colin had not been a reader, but his shelves still held books, mostly given as presents, which were now orders of magnitude beyond his ken.

She began to box them up meticulously, stacking the hardbacks according to size. On the third shelf she came across a book that had a worn feel, and she noticed it only because the others were crisp and firm and cold, like new textbooks. This one was Gibran's *The Prophet*, a book that for her was always associated with the mild embarrassment of the 1970s, when she and Geoffrey had dabbled, like everyone else, in turtlenecks and Carole King and bad poetry. She remembered Geoffrey, then a medical student, reading to her from this book in their old apartment in Philadelphia, her head resting on his stomach. They didn't smoke pot, but their apartment was decorated as if they did, with macramé and faux tapestries and dozens of fat candles, and she remembered that Geoffrey wore a beard that made him look like an Afghan tribesman. Though she had never been more in love with him than she was back then, and though she remembered those days as idyllic, the emotion that came to her now, thumbing through the book's pages, was shame. She was embarrassed by the sentimentality of Gibran, their inability to recognize it, and the sordid fact that they had gone on to live their lives in blatant contradiction of the philosophy he espoused. It was now difficult to believe that they had once been so easily fooled by earnest words, and she was suddenly mortified by the memory of the carpeting, and by the Jethro Tull that had played on the stereo, and by Geoffrey's beard and his tight pants. But mostly she was embarrassed that she hadn't recognized the silliness of it all.

She read through some of the pages with a crooked smile. How wrong all of this was, how terribly inaccurate it was in describing her life, or any life that she could imagine. She read the chapter on children and almost threw the thing away ("For their souls dwell in the house of tomorrow, which you/Cannot visit, not even in your dreams"). Then she flipped backward and came to the chapter "On Love," opening to its first page because a marker, a photograph, was holding its place.

The picture showed a girl, by herself. It was not a school photograph, and in fact did not seem to be staged at all. The girl was aware of the camera but seemed to have been made aware of it just before the click. She faced straight ahead but had not yet assumed a smile. Lea realized with delight that she might finally be attaching a face to one of the names looped in feminine handwriting on the notes in the shoebox. This might be the one who loved him, she thought, or the one who merely slept with him, or the one who hated him so much she didn't even know how to express it in writing. Or maybe the one who stabbed him. This was one of Colin's girls, though, this much was sure.

In part her beauty made Lea proud, though of course her son had been handsome, athletic, and insensitive, and thus it stood to reason that his women would be beautiful. But Lea was also proud that he had looked for the beauty in this one, because it was not an obvious kind, not like the blond exquisiteness of the St. Theresa's set, whose bronze skin was purchased from tanning booths in Scranton, whose leanness seemed mandatory somehow and would be acquired on the tennis courts or in the bathroom stalls if it didn't come naturally. The girl in the photo was not fat, but neither was she muscled or thin. She had the kind of body girls would have if they didn't care too much about boys. She wore a tight navy polo shirt, clearly proud to show her body, and her eyes were darkened by whatever shadows surrounded her. Her hair was black, mussed as if she had just gotten out of a convertible. Darkness and dishevelment, in fact, were her defining attributes, besides the exquisite face. There was a sloppiness to her dress, as if the rest of the world were of little concern to her, and as Lea looked closer she saw that the eyes would have been dark even without the shadows—black irises, and dark eye shadow, which made her look like a beautiful gypsy, or like someone who came from the past.

Her lips were bright red, and stuck out in a sort of pout, but this also was not staged. These were her lips at rest, and boys would want to kiss them almost instinctively; they would be attracted to her without understanding why at first. She thought that this was what might have initially appealed to Colin about her, unless it was simply her full chest. Lea marked her for someone outside Colin's social group by her dark features and mussed hair, and by the air of want that came across in the photo (not just the thin fabric of the polo shirt or the twenty-dollar hairstyle, but also the mirthless face—this girl did not have the hair-trigger false grin of the wealthy). Lea turned the photograph over with surging hope, but the only thing written there was "December."

Passages from the pages from which the girl had fallen were underlined: "When love beckons to you follow him,/Though his ways are hard and steep"; "For even as love crowns you so shall he crucify you. Even as he is for your growth so is he for your pruning." And then, circled twice in red pen,

> But if in your fear you would seek only love's peace and love's pleasure,
> Then it is better for you that you cover your nakedness and pass out of
>    love's threshing-floor.

Beside "threshing-floor" was written, in Colin's even cursive, "Means some sort of place where they make wheat."

This was his only contribution, but it made it impossible to explain away the find. The book, she had come to understand, was the very one she and Geoffrey had read in that apartment in Philadelphia— Geoffrey had marked it with an *ex libris* stamp. Colin must have taken it from the living room bookshelf. How on earth he had discovered it, or decided to read it, or, having been moved by love and poetry, had decided to underline certain passages and look up words from them, was anyone's guess. But the handwriting meant he had done it. The markings were his own, not some decades-old whim of Geoffrey's.

What it meant—no way around it, really, no way that she could think of—was that Colin had fallen in love with this girl in the photograph. It was a large discovery, possibly larger than the name of his dealer.

Behind her a gentle voice spoke two words, and Lea reacted as if a tornado siren had gone off. The book seemed to jump out of her hands, clattering into the box, and her legs spasmed, erupting her out of the Indian-style position and into an undignified sprawl.

Colin was unperturbed. "No wipes," he said again, with a bit more emphasis this time. Lea stayed still for a moment, so as not to further agitate her heart.

*Towels* was one of the words he'd been slow to remaster, even though he took a lot of baths. For whatever reason, his memory stuttered on the word, and they had lately resigned themselves to the substitute word *wipes*.

They were out of clean towels, then. Still recovering from the explosive breaking of the silence, she registered this fact more from Colin's nakedness than from his words. He stood in the doorway entirely nude and entirely wet, still soaped up along his chest and arms.

Colin's naked body had presented itself often enough in the past weeks, though never at this specific angle. She had given him sponge baths and real baths, she had changed his clothes and cleaned him up when he'd wet the bed. But this was a new juxtaposition—she sitting on the ground, he standing up ten feet before her, completely shameless, his nakedness not mitigated by a bed frame or towels or darkness. Here was a boy who did not know he wasn't supposed to be naked in front of his mother.

She averted her eyes, but it was difficult to do for long, since she couldn't give him a satisfactory answer. She stared at the box of books, busied herself with finding the Gibran and putting the girl's picture back into place. "Colin, run back to the bathroom and I'll come in with towels, with wipes, in just a second." But he didn't move. "Honey, you're dripping water all over the place." Again he stayed put and stayed silent, although a reasonable response might have been that she couldn't have known he was dripping water, since she was still looking away, investigating a peeling strip of wallpaper.

He spoke again. "No wipes in the closet. I looked."

"I'll get some out of the laundry room. Just run on back to the bathroom."

"No wipes in there. I looked there." He sounded as if he might cry—a desperate matter, since it would require her to hug him, as she always did. To stay seated and ignore his sadness would have been detrimental.

She turned to him as if she had a stiff neck. She stretched her eyes toward the light in the middle of the ceiling, tilting her face, reflexively exhausting every resource her body offered so as not to see what was directly in front of her. She knew that she shouldn't be so squeamish about this. It was a body she had given birth to, which had gone through natural changes, and to any objective observer it might even be considered a thing of beauty, in spite of the ten pounds the new Colin had grafted onto the sculpted figure of the old one. And she might be doing harm, since it would be impossible for him not to notice, in his instinctive, four-year-old way, that his mother found something terrible and disgusting about him right now. But she almost wanted him to know this, because it was the truth, and she wanted him never to put her in this position again.

He didn't cry. He just stood there, puzzled and dripping and watching her. She finally settled her gaze upon his face, and with a Clint Eastwood squint she was able to limit her peripheral vision. They looked at each other in this manner for a long while, longer certainly than either of them had intended, so long that by the time the silence was broken, Colin no longer needed a towel, and Lea was no longer so concerned about avoiding the sight of his penis. Finally, a calm settling over her, she stood, with the Gibran book in her hand, and walked over to him. She stood beside him, shoulder to shoulder, and opened the pages, and he touched them with a smile. "Book," he said. Although Colin could string together coherent sentences, he still did this, still touched things and announced their names when he was presented with them, as if it were some kind of trick.

Lea turned the pages to let him see the pen-and-ink drawings, the languid, naked figures twisting around like snakes. He touched these pages too. Finally she flipped in the book until she came to the chapter "On Love." She held the picture out to him. He knew about pictures. For a long time they had gone through the family photo albums, because of Lea's original idea that his brain damage was like some kind of severe amnesia. He knew to hold pictures carefully, to avoid smudging them, and he did this now and looked at the girl in the photo, the girl he had once loved, whose body he had certainly known again and again.

"What do you think, Colin? Do you remember her?" Lea said. "She's such a pretty girl. Such a beautiful girl."

"Pretty girl," Colin said, but he didn't sound convinced. He didn't really know what *pretty* meant anymore. He often used the word to describe his macaroni and cheese, his favorite track on Elton John's *Greatest Hits* CD, his father's "got-your-nose" trick.

"Yes. She really is. You were lucky once, Colin. Do you know that?" She turned to face him now, instinctively keeping a distance.

He was still looking at the picture, not as if trying to remember the face but as if it transfixed him. "Jenny," he said.

She blinked her eyes to stave off new tears, and she had to take a mighty sniff before she could talk. "Jenny, Colin? That's Jenny?"

He nodded, still looking at the girl. His voice gave away nothing. It was the same tone he'd used to say *No wipes*. "Jenny."

"Your friend? Was Jenny your friend?"

Again he nodded, but she knew that he didn't understand why; he wasn't really answering her question. The bangs of his wet hair were plastered against his forehead, and his eyes were bright with the urge to please. He looked excessively moronic, like a bad actor trying to play a moron. She knew that she would never get anything more out of him regarding this picture, this girl.

"Look at her, Colin," she said as they both turned back to the picture. "Just look at her."

And they did, together. Finally he handed the picture to her, smiling vaguely, and pattered back to the bathroom. Because Lea had let her guard down, and because the thing was conspicuous by nature, she saw as he turned that the object of her desperate fear—her son's sex organ—had, in response to the stimulus of the photograph, inflated itself majestically.

# twenty-seven

*By the time* Casey dropped off Brady, he did not see how he could last the day without learning the rest of the truth. There was something else there, Brady had practically admitted as much. "That's all you're getting" implied that there was something else to be got, and he felt sure that that something was his own exoneration. He had never felt so desperate, so furiously aggrieved by ignorance.

But how to extract the rest of the story from Brady? Threats, violence? It didn't seem likely that he could match Brady in this regard. Promises, more alcohol? In the end, he decided it needed to be a straight bribe. The idea of assault had scared Brady away from the two-thousand-dollar bounty on that Friday night, and the loss must still pain him. Casey had seen the boy's living conditions, the sad fact of the threadbare Sharks jacket. Casey had grown up in a house like Brady's, and he had once worn clothes from the Half-Price Store. Casey had been driven to work, while Brady had taken to alcohol and mindlessness, but they had both been marked by poverty, and so some of his assumptions about Brady had to be correct.

Also like Brady, Casey remembered learning Shakespeare at Breed's Township High. The phrase that had stuck with him was not about fighting but bribery: "I pay thy poverty, and not thy will." He remembered going home after class and thinking about this phrase as he put on the uniform he had to wear at LuLu's, and as he mopped the back room and changed the garbage bags and refilled the fryer. He had been startled by the truth of the phrase, how easily poverty could claim the prerogative over will, how the promise of money could deaden the intensity of one's desires.

From Brady's house he drove to the bank, expecting to return shortly, while the boy was still tipsy. A slip of paper—an ATM receipt—comprehensively rearranged his priorities. There were some sad moments of denial during which he went to another bank (surely, he thought, the printout machine had malfunctioned), until he finally sat in his car, doodled some figures on an envelope, and conceded that it was possible, as the bank suggested, that he had one hundred and eighteen dollars and fifty-eight cents to his name.

The receipt indicated that he was as poor as he had been since he was fifteen years old. Until this point, his unemployment had been an almost existential concern, representing nothing more than the large injustice he had been trying to reckon with. But now not having a job had suddenly become a very tangible problem. When the one hundred and eighteen dollars were gone, there would be nowhere to turn. The idea, not yet an hour old, that he would pay Brady for the rest of the story was now inconceivable. It was almost inconceivable that he would have enough to pay the gas bill. At what point, he wondered, would his exoneration become a luxury?

The desperate measure that followed upon his crisis was to call a man named Michael Grautz, who managed a Chik'n Shak in Wilkes-Barre. The day before his interview at Ketchikan Kitchen, Mr. Grautz had called in response to a résumé Casey had sent. The résumé had been mailed in another time of crisis, although that moment had not been as abject as the present one (Casey remembered that week, when he had been disgraced but still financially secure, with a kind of nostalgia). In the flurry of job-hunting with which he had responded to the Friday night incident, Casey had mailed his CV to virtually every chain restaurant in the tricounty region, even the ones in Wilkes-Barre, which would have meant an hour commute. He had mailed Grautz a résumé mostly as a gesture, a self-pitying nod to the direness of his situation. When Grautz had called to schedule an interview, however, Casey learned that the "atmospheric family restaurant" mentioned in the newspaper ad was in fact a Chik'n Shak: fast food. He had not at that point sunk so low as to consider a job in such a place, and certainly not one in Wilkes-Barre.

That he had indeed sunk so low now was obvious to him when he felt his throat constrict and his muscles clinch upon hearing the line ring on Grautz's end. Casey found himself barely able to speak at first, struggling with the tugging forces of his humiliation and his desperate wish that Grautz had not yet filled the position. As it happened, he had not, which Casey took as proof that even to interview for such a job would be to lower himself in the ranks of his profession to an extent he had never before considered. *A Chik'n Shak, for the love of God.*

Rachel had once asked him, in her typically clinical style, where he planned to be when he was forty. He had approached the question modestly, carefully, laying out a variety of possibilities, though in truth he assumed he would still be at O'Ruddy's, padding his savings account, making sure everything in his world ran smoothly. None of the scenarios he had presented to Rachel involved working in a fast food restaurant, wearing a paper hat, washing down plastic trays, fixing heat lamps, haggling with suppliers over mass quantities of Grade D poultry . . .

It took a little less than fifty minutes to get there the next morning. Michael Grautz turned out to be an easy man to talk to, since he was terrifically ugly—tall but with bad posture, acne-scarred, his eyes sunken so much as to almost look like a birth defect—and the man was clearly aware of this. He frequently twitched his face to the side, cast his eyes downward to avoid contact. He tugged at his shirtfront and squirmed in his chair, as if he were the one being interviewed, or as if he were a teenager called in front of the principal.

Michael Grautz, as it happened, was aware of the O'Ruddy's incident and had connected Casey's name with it. That this hadn't scared him off spoke volumes about his desperation. The job, he quickly explained, was for the night shift. To appeal to drunken students at Wilkes-Barre University, the Chik'n Shak had recently extended its hours to 4 A.M.

"So you see, Mr. Fielder, I'm aware of that situation over at O'Ruddy's. But you've got a heck of a résumé, of course, and I'm willing to assume I don't know the full story. I'm not a man to trust the newspapers all the time."

"That's wise, I think, Mr. Grautz. They tend to get a lot of stuff wrong, you can believe me."

"I can imagine you would know. Yes, sir. Now, it's a concern, I need to tell you that. It is. Because we get lots of . . . let's call them situations. Lots of college kids mostly, as I explained. College kids who've had a few, and who like to get crazy. So it's a concern. We certainly need someone who can handle these delicate situations with the public. But I can only guess that you've learned a lot from your experience. I'm a believer in giving a fella a second chance."

Casey didn't speak at first, just cleared his throat several times. Then: "Mr. Grautz, you admitted before that you weren't sure what had gone on at the restaurant. Maybe you'd like me to help you understand."

He found his tone so cold, and Grautz's reaction so instant—a straightened posture, a small glance upward—that he suspected he had lost his chance for the job. He had spoken as he would to a child, to a retarded man. It had been absolutely, purposefully insulting. Nevertheless, Grautz urged him to continue.

"I've done some investigating, you see," said Casey. "I've found some pretty interesting things. You may be interested to know, for one thing, that there were other people who were in on it, I mean besides the kids who beat up that boy. One of the servers, Jenny—she told me the phone was out, so that I couldn't call the cops. And the daughter of the owners was there too. The daughter of the Howards, with her husband. They were sitting in one of the back booths, to make sure everything went according to plan, I guess. Frankly, I haven't figured it out yet, but it can't be a coincidence, can it? Can it, Mr. Grautz? You're damn right. That's no coincidence. My guess is that the Howards instructed her to sit there and make sure it went the way it was supposed to. That's my guess. Because if you think about it, Mr. Grautz, who stands to gain from this? You wouldn't think it would be the Howards, but you may be wrong. The lawsuit from the kid's parents is targeting the headquarters, not them. And the Howards are cashing in on the insurance, I'm sure of it. Mr. Howard told me that once, he told me they'd be protected if the place were closed down. We lost money all winter. All summer too, frankly. We rearranged some of the books so it didn't look that bad, and the fall was good, but . . . To be honest with you, Mr. Grautz, the restaurant was a loser. No matter how efficiently I ran that place, it just didn't work. Not enough lunch business. Not enough Saturday business. You can't get by on good Friday nights."

Mr. Grautz looked pained.

"What?" said Casey. "What are you thinking? You have questions, right?"

"Well, sure, Mr. Fielder, I suppose. I mean, that's quite a story."

"What are your questions? I know it sounds unbelievable, so go ahead, fire away." Casey was tapping his fingers on the table, leaning forward. The man's self-consciousness and silence had made Casey aggressive.

"Well, I mean . . . You seem to be saying that your owners organized the boys to fight, then? That seems a bit strange. And you say you have proof of this?"

"Motive. They needed that place closed down. Not just to declare bankruptcy, that wouldn't have done any good. They needed something that invoked the insurance clause, something like a fire or an earthquake or an executive decision from headquarters. That last one was the easiest to put together. They had the kids fight the first night, back in December. No big deal, just a few kids high on cocaine, but there was a police report. That made headquarters wary, they said it couldn't happen again. Then the Howards made it happen again. They got Jenny in on it somehow. If I didn't call the cops, there was more chance for the fight to get out of hand, for someone to get hurt. Maybe they sent their daughter in to make sure things went the way they needed. They sure as hell couldn't have been there themselves."

Mr. Grautz shook his head. "This isn't a conversation I particularly want to have, Mr. Fielder, I have to tell you that."

"Proof, then. Proof, you asked for. A kid named Brady Benson, a senior at Township. He was at both fights. He's the one who told me about the first one, how it had clearly been orchestrated by someone. Those idiots didn't even know why they were fighting. And the second one . . . there was a price tag. Brady said that someone had offered two thousand dollars if one kid in particular was taken out."

Mr. Grautz raised his hands in the air and shook his head, as if impersonating Nixon. "I've heard enough, Mr. Fielder, enough." He smiled, but it was an embarrassed smile, and touched with fear. "I can't have this conversation. I need a manager, for God's sake. I don't have time for this. I'm sorry for whatever has . . . I'm just sorry, Mr. Fielder. But please. Please."

*Please leave,* he meant, and Casey had enough sense and enough mercy left in him to nod with sincerity and march out of the restaurant.

He shut off the radio on the drive back to Breed's Township. He understood that Grautz had thought him paranoid, possibly even dangerous, and he understood that something had snapped in him, that the rambling theory he'd spouted to the poor ugly man must have sounded like raving. If Grautz had let him stay, perhaps he would have admitted this. But he also would have liked to point out that sometimes paranoid people are right, of course. And it's not as though it was all speculation. He had evidence, didn't he? He began to day-

dream about himself as a lawyer, presenting the case to a jury. He
would lay out the facts as he had tonight, but he would be more cautious, more authoritative. He would not push the truth on them, the
way he had with Grautz; he would reveal it artfully, like a burlesque
dancer disrobing. And the evidence itself? Testimony, mostly. First
Jenny, then some technician from the phone company. Then he
would present the elusive "Rick," then Brady, then the Howards and
their insidious offspring. And finally Casey himself.

What would the verdict be? Who was the guilty party? It couldn't
have been him. Anyone could see that now, anyone who accepted the
facts he had gathered. All of them—Jenny, "Rick," Brady, the
Howards—all were more culpable than Casey. It wasn't a subjective
opinion now; he no longer protested this fact with the vehemence of
the guilty. There were people behind that sad act. The boy's damaged
brain could no longer be laid at his feet. That was the verdict, that was
what the world had to accept, if the matter was looked at honestly.

Rachel had just come back from the gym, where she spent one
hour every other day perched on a stationary bike. Casey suspected
she liked the people-watching element of it more than the exercise, for
she always returned in a garrulous state, eager to offer him opinions
about the various personality types one found at Township Fitness.
She began telling him about an event she'd witnessed that morning,
about a woman who had broken one of the club's treadmills, but she
stopped abruptly.

"You're dressed up," she observed. "Any reason, or am I being
wooed?"

"I had an interview."

"Oh, good. I mean, good?"

"Not quite."

"Like the last ones?"

"Probably worse."

"Wow. That's saying something. I guess I won't ask about it anymore."

"Okay."

"What kind of job was it?"

"The Chik'n Shak. Night-shift manager."

"That's fast food." She looked startled. "You're looking at fast food places?"

He wondered if this was the end, if this would cross a line in her great experiment. It was one thing to date someone from the hometown, someone who had gone to Breed's Township High, someone who hadn't graduated from college. But the Chik'n Shak? And he hadn't even gotten the job. The expression on her face began to soften from incredulity to pity. She ran her hands through her hair.

"I'm kind of at the end of my rope," he said.

He took her by the hand and led her into the living room, to her parents' puffy couch. They sat on the edges of the cushions, both of them leaning forward, Casey staring at the carpet.

"I need something from you, Rachel. I need to borrow a thousand dollars."

"Oh crap. Casey . . . crap. You're broke? I mean, you're completely broke?"

"It's not that. Well, I mean, yes, I am broke, but that's not what the money's for."

Now he told her about Brady. He somehow felt that this was her due, as if she'd already given him the money. He talked about both trips to the liquor store, and he summed up both of Brady's narratives in a flat voice that reflected nothing of the boy's original telling except for the bare facts. "I believe him, Rachel. He wasn't lying to me. I can't tell you how, but I just know this. That boy knows something I need to know. He knows why that other boy got hurt, why I lost my job."

Rachel stood up, and for the first time in their relationship, she yelled at him. "No, Casey! No! We know why you lost your job!" She stomped into the kitchen. He could hear her run the filter tap and drink down a glass of water, then she stomped back into the living room. "You lost your job because you didn't do what you were supposed to! Those boys were beating each other silly, and you sat there and watched. I'm not going to pretend like that's up in the air any-more, like there's some sort of ambiguity to all this."

"Christ, Rachel, you never pretended that. You've been saying that since the beginning, from day one, that it was my fault. But now you've got to listen. There's more to it. Weren't you listening to me? That whole story, the cocaine, the two grand? There's more to it, god-dammit! I need to find out the rest. I've got to get that boy to tell me, and how else am I supposed to do it?"

She sat back down next to him but kept her voice stern, impassive. "I'm going to believe you, Casey. I'm going to believe that you think there's a big conspiracy out there. I'm going to accept that you may even have reason to think that, even if it's just because you want to be-lieve in it. But this is what I'm going to say, Casey, one last time, this is the only conclusion I have to offer you: You lost your job because you just sat there. Sat there and watched."

# PART THREE

# march

Every sin is the result of a collaboration.

—STEPHEN CRANE, "THE BLUE HOTEL"

# twenty-eight

*The third day* of March was the last day snow fell on the township that season, but the cold had barely eased, and the accumulation wouldn't melt until April. The snow on the lawns and heaped at the curbs was old and thick; its underlayer was the snow that had fallen the week after the December ice storm, and it could support the weight of a man. The city crews had finished clearing the wreckage of that storm, and on the fourth of March Casey saw that the mass of trees at the corner of Newbury and Ridge, the tangle of limbs and wires that had knocked out service to O'Ruddy's, had finally been cleared and a new pole had been raised.

He drove through the neighborhood without purpose, slowing as he went past the homes of Jenny and Brady, past the house he had lived in with his mother, past the house of some childhood friends. He did not stop at any point. It was early in the afternoon, and the sun was so bright he turned down the heat in his car and unwrapped his scarf. He didn't know what he was doing there, other than killing a patch of the huge stretch of empty time that lay before him. He drove by Breed's Township High from two directions, then past the sophomore lot, where he failed to identify Brady in the mass of teenage smokers cowering beneath the gray air.

He drove down Arthur Avenue, and he pulled into the parking lot of O'Ruddy's. The building itself had not changed in any sense, and he realized that this surprised him, that he had expected something to be different. Perhaps he doubted that it could exist without him, or that its foundation could have remained after the devastation of the Friday night. But it was still there, a square brick building in the middle of a concrete patch, maintaining a solemn equidistance from both the forest and the shoddy houses to the southeast. *O'Ruddy's* was spelled out in a jaunty font on the green front awning, and the potted conifers standing sentry by the door were still there, encrusted with gray snow.

The recent layer of snow on the parking lot had not been disturbed, and the front doors were locked. Casey walked around the building and was everywhere confronted with marks of abandonment that only he might have noticed. The dumpsters were gone, as was the assorted filth that usually surrounded them and fed the raccoons. The open space beneath the roof ledge and beside the back door, where the dishwashers and cooks took their smoke breaks, was missing its typical pile of butts. During his time at O'Ruddy's, the soft lights above section four had always been left on, even during closing hours. But now the lights were out, and though he generally felt unsentimental about his return to the restaurant, this fact made him instantly sad. He supposed he had seen the lights in section four as a sort of eternal flame, and the darkness was the ultimate proof, as if he needed any more, that O'Ruddy's was finished.

Someone had meticulously lowered all the blinds to the very sill of each window, so he walked to the other side of the restaurant and stood outside the picture window by table ten, where he knew one of the slats in the blinds was missing. He pressed his head against the cold glass and cupped his hands around his eyes, and he saw that the interior did not look much different than it always had, except that the salt-and-pepper caddies were gone from the tables and the chairs had been stacked by the front door. The place would be dismantled in earnest soon enough, he thought. The fake paraphernalia on the walls—the dented tubas, the rusted street signs, the tam o'shanters and English saddles and beer steins—would be removed in strips and shipped off to be hung at an O'Ruddy's in a new city, in the same order, above the same fake mahogany tables. They would try to sell the ovens at a discount to one of the places at the Scranton mall. The booze bottles remained behind the bar and could likely be returned to the distributors. Much of the food would have gone in the final week, when they had had their "O'Ruddy's says toodle-oo" promotion.

It was a bright day, and he became aware of the suspicious figure he cut as he peered through the window, so as soon as he had seen the one thing he had needed to find there, he walked around the restaurant. A thick gray door faced the parking lot and opened into the storage room. Most employees came through the large back service entrance, and so this door was seldom used or thought about. Casey hadn't even known it worked until he'd become a manager and they'd given him a key for it. He now found that the key still worked, as did the door, and he simply opened it once, fought the temptation to go inside the restaurant, locked the door again, and went to his car.

He refused to open himself up for further mockery in the sophomore lot, so the next morning he waited in front of Brady's house. At seven the boy spurted out the front door, the San Jose Sharks jacket open at the neck now. He stopped instantly upon seeing Casey's Honda, which clearly puzzled him. He approached the car warily, ducked down to see who was inside, and Casey could hear a muffled swear word. The passenger door opened, and Brady, without getting in, said, "What the fuck, man—you come to my house?"

"Just get in and listen to me. I'll take you to school and talk to you on the way. I'm making you an offer, and it won't take any longer than the trip to school. Obviously you don't have to take the offer if you don't want. All you have to do is listen. And you get a ride to school."

Brady got in, not as hesitant as Casey thought he might be. "Man, I knew you were a fag," he said, but it came out almost gently, as if he were resigned to something.

They drove in the direction of the high school, and Casey noted for the first time how long the walk must be for Brady, and thus how long it must have been for himself, back in high school. He didn't remember it at all, though he supposed he too had taken a right onto St. Mark's Street, out of the subdivision, then a left onto Arthur, past the forested lot that would someday house O'Ruddy's, and then right on School Street. Casey had walked because he had needed to get to school earlier than the bus; the late nights at LuLu's meant he had had to show up early and do his homework in the student lounge every morning. He assumed that Brady walked because there was a stigma attached to the bus riders. He was captivated by the fact that he and Brady Benson had walked the same route to school every morning, a testament to their collective fortitude, to the fact that they were people who did things that were difficult and received very little credit for it. He supposed he now felt a small kind of respect for the boy.

Brady had acquiesced to the plan by the time Casey turned off Arthur Avenue. Casey hadn't needed to press him at all. The boy had tried in various ways to sniff out some sort of catch, but ultimately he understood that Casey was simply a desperate man and he could exploit him. Brady had the story, and he must have been starting to understand its value.

It would be this Friday, three days away, Brady said. He gave Casey his cell-phone number, emphasizing that until Friday it was to be used only in a dire emergency, the type of instance so rare that he couldn't even think of an example. And then on Friday Casey would call once, to say things were ready.

"Friday, then," Brady said as he scooted out of the car. Casey watched him walk into the school, hunched and purposeful, with his eyes on the ground.

Casey found himself nodding in agreement with Brady's words. Friday, then, he thought, and then, to make it real, he said it out loud. "Friday, then. One more Friday night."

| twenty-nine |

*The evidence,* of course, was tenuous. The boy might have been cold or nervous or just aroused by the picture of a busty young woman. He was seventeen years old, after all, brain-damaged or not. The evidence was surely not something she could take to Geoffrey. It would not hold up anywhere except in her own heart, where she did not doubt for one second that she had stumbled onto something significant, that Colin's involuntary response to the picture of the girl was a signal. A part of his brain remembered her and remembered what they had done together. And another part of his brain had remembered her name.

The next day, the second of the new month, she found two more bits of evidence. In one of the drawers of his bedstand she found a small wooden box that held a disposable lighter, a cloth necklace, and various tickets stubs from Eagles and Phillies games. It was in this box that he must have kept his bags of marijuana (it smelled the way

Colin did when he came home from concerts), though none were in there now. She assumed he'd had his stash on him at the time of his wounding, and she wondered if the police had gotten rid of it when they'd bagged up his wallet and keys for her.

Among the sports tickets, which she looked through in the spirit of intense thoroughness that now defined her search, she found two stubs for *Aïda*, which had come to the Scranton Public Theatre late in the fall. He had paid a total of a hundred and twenty dollars for the tickets, according to the list price, and had somehow managed to sit through three hours of Verdi for the sake of his date. "It must have been love," she murmured. It was what she would have said to Geoffrey, if he had been a party to her search, and he would have guffawed in agreement. But she was serious now. Perhaps it was paltry evidence as well, but in the light of what she already knew, it had to be considered. Colin would not have done that—ordered tickets over the phone, ironed his suit himself, driven into Scranton, and sat through three hours of opera—just for sex. She wouldn't have thought, before this day, that he would have done it for anything. But he'd taken this girl, whoever she was, and he'd kept the ticket stubs in this special place of honor, in the same box where he kept his pot and the memories of the 1993 NLCS game at Veterans Stadium. *She must be some girl*, Lea thought.

There was also tangential evidence of the girl in the absences in Colin's room, but Lea did not realize this until later that night, after Geoffrey got home and they played some games on the Xbox, then ate tacos together in the kitchen. Colin was speaking, in a way. He narrated the events of the dinner as he performed them, in the slow speech that reminded Lea of the voice of a deaf person.

"Taco," he said. "I eeeat it. Put it in my mouth. Whoops, I get it on my shirt." Geoffrey laughed at this and went to get paper towels. Colin stayed still, shifting only his eyes, so as not to disturb the mess on his chin and collar until his father came to wipe it off.

She thought about the great simplification that could thus take place in a life, even one as seemingly complicated as Colin's had been.

He had been driven by many desires and had recognized the necessity of feeding them, and this had led, she had come to learn, to a life
that was in many respects fuller and more complex than her own life
had ever been. She'd had Geoffrey, and he'd had work, and together
they'd had their boy, and their house in Weston once the mortgage
rates hit 4.5. She did not remember much of her own adolescence, and
she often assumed this was because she hadn't made much out of it. A
nice public high school outside Scranton. A few volleyball practices,
a couple of homecoming dances, a few classes that stood out and then
a mass of others that blended together in her memory like melted
caramels. A smooth path to Penn State, where everyone, including
herself, predicted that she would quickly meet a husband, because
there would not have been many options otherwise. It had not been a
difficult life to organize. In retrospect, she did not see any messiness
to it, and she credited this to a lack of desire. She had not wanted anything but stability, the kind her parents and Megan had given her, the
kind Geoffrey gave her. She had not wanted sex except for a few
times, she had not wanted drugs or booze except to get some pushy
host off her back, she had not wanted to hurt or damage or make any
kind of authoritative mark, not the way Colin did. Her boy had had
desires, severe ones, and they had made his life cluttered, dangerous,
and intensely interesting. She now wondered if she had admired him
for it.

Geoffrey wiped off the boy's chin, and he smiled with all his teeth,
an obnoxious, almost mocking smile. Geoffrey swatted his head with
the cloth. "Goofy guy."

"No. Good guy."

"Yeah, okay. I suppose you're right. You're a good guy."

"Yep. Good guy. You too, Dad. Mom too. Good guys."

It seemed extraordinary that it could all end so suddenly for him,
that anything short of death could put to rest so many complications.
The money owed to some drug dealer, explanations and apologies due
to some girl, spring-break plans with the football buddies, extra credit
to hand in so that he might still graduate—all of it had vanished too

suddenly. A life made simple. There was not enough residue, she thought, in spite of what she had uncovered in her searches.

In particular, she had not found what she might have most expected to find—evidence of his libido. The last notes had been written just after the St. Viator's game, late in November, and in them the girls had made vitriolic reference to Jenny, their replacement. Lea had not found any condoms anywhere in his room or in his clothes. There were no phone numbers scrawled on the scraps in his pockets; no girls had called in December to ask him to the St. Theresa's winter semiformal. There were no other pictures, no other names. All the evidence was dated, all of it at least three months old. It must have been the girl that cleared his life of this mess. He had met the Township girl sometime in the late fall, and the sexual predation, the unwanted pregnancies, the jilted lovers with shards of glass, the lies and promises and broken teenage hearts, had stopped.

"I love your tacos," said Geoffrey. "Really fantastic, Lea, really." Geoffrey took a bite, turned to Colin, and said, *"Fantastic"* with his mouth open wide, showing him a mess of masticated food, which made the boy giggle.

"Geoffrey. Keep your mouth closed—no one needs to see that," Lea said, because it was what she was supposed to say. Geoffrey looked dramatically guilty, said "Sorry" in the same comic tone he'd used for "Fantastic," and Colin, who could not understand irony, suppressed his next giggle.

On Wednesday afternoon Lea took Colin to his therapy session at the hospital. She usually stayed and watched, but today she made a quick excuse and left him in the enthusiastic hands of Denise.

She drove to Breed's Township High. Though she hadn't been sure about this, the timing had been just right; a flood of students coursed out of the double doors no more than ten minutes after she'd parked in the circular front drive, just behind the last in a caravan of yellow buses. The students were expelled from the school in a flurry of noise and motion, and she tried to track them with her eyes. She held the photograph in her lap, glancing at the picture, then back at the students. But there were too many of them, and they moved too frenetically, twitching their heads as they gossiped and laughed, complained and conversed. Hair in their eyes, hats pulled low over their brows, faces turned away in an eternal search for someone to latch on to—Lea could see barely half their faces clearly. She waited a half hour. The first flow of students lasted for some minutes, and then came a steady trickle, and then the doors closed, opening every few seconds to expel the stragglers. But the girl named Jenny was not among them. It had been a long shot, Lea knew. There were other exits to the school, and besides, Jenny could very well have passed unnoticed among the initial throng. Lea didn't know what she would have done if she had seen her. Certainly she couldn't have spoken to the girl; certainly there was nothing Lea could have said to Jenny, the love of her absent son's life. She was almost relieved. She drove back to the hospital in time to participate in the last ten minutes of Colin's therapy by joining along as her son and Denise jumped rope.

That night she arranged for Megan to watch Colin the next morning, early. She didn't need to make excuses to Megan anymore, didn't offer them. Lea assumed it was Megan's position that her sister deserved whatever time she could get to herself.

Watching them trudge toward the building was different. They came from a thousand angles, from cars and bikes and walking routes and buses. As she expected, they walked with less haste than they had yesterday. Lea parked this time and stood inside the front doors, the ones that seemed to be favored as an entrance. There was a solemnity to this part of the school; the doors were situated at the base of an enormous brick rectangle that was topped by a spire. The architecture lent a sort of formality to the somber arrival process, and the students had the tragic aspect of immigrants arriving at Ellis Island.

They ignored her as they passed. Though she felt wildly out of place, the students seemed to think she was an algebra teacher they'd never had, or maybe one of the office secretaries who worked in the back. She was free to examine them as they passed her, and no one looked back for more than a few seconds. No one asked her what she wanted. She realized that many of these children, coming from East Breed's, would be used to having a suspicious eye cast over them.

They didn't all look poor, the way she'd expected them to. She had been to East Breed's enough times, to eat at O'Ruddy's or the Chinese restaurant or to shop at the big hardware store, but she had never seen the school and never really interacted with people from this neighborhood, except when they were serving her food, helping her find the right light bulbs. Geoffrey had stopped truly being one of them, she knew, long before she'd met him.

And so she had expected certain things of them. Silly assumptions, she now knew, since poor children know how to hide their poverty. And they were not all poor. Some of the ones that passed her now would be from Leawood or even Weston, and perhaps had parents who believed in public education or were anti-Catholic. And although many of the others would be on welfare and food stamps, this didn't manifest itself obviously in the way they looked. The poor kids didn't show up with smudged faces, patches on their jackets, missing teeth. But she could spot them, or so she thought, the way she had noticed something in Jenny that marked her as a Township girl. Something about her stare, the total absence of security or comfort, the vague dissatisfaction with the way things are. She spotted the same look in some of the adolescents before her now.

She wandered the halls with them, feeling more determined to find the girl than she'd thought she was. When she finally caught sight of Jenny, she saw her from behind. She didn't know what she recognized about her, as the picture showed her in one dimension, from the stomach to the head, but Lea knew it was she. Jenny stood before an open locker, her hands on her hips, staring at a mass of clutter. She was speaking to another girl, who leaned against the adjacent locker and looked at Jenny as she spoke.

Lea approached from the side, playing the role of teacher and poking her head into a nearby classroom, then lingering to eavesdrop.

"Consortium day," Jenny said. "I got the one-to-nine shift."

Her friend made an unintelligible noise of sympathy. "Why don't you quit that place already?"

"Money money money."

"I told you Gary would hire you. Come *on*. Work with me—it'd be a fucking blast."

"Jesus, girl. I told you about this. I need thirty hours a week for Consortium. Besides, I can walk to the China Pagoda. Can't walk to Leawood."

"*Ugh*. I can't believe you work at that place. It's sooo gross. Don't they, like, cook cats and shit?"

"Yeah, Beth. They cook cats. That's mostly what they serve. Cats."

It was impossible not to stare, and so Lea was detected quickly. Jenny closed her locker with a brusque slap, then turned to face Lea, squinting to make her own stare more purposeful. "Can I help you with something?"

Lea had heard the words of the conversation, more or less, and she heard the words that were spoken to her now, but in looking at Jenny some part of her was overwhelmed with memories of Colin. She saw him now, in flashes, as a baby, as a boy, on his first day in the blazer and khakis. She knew that this girl ten feet in front of her had been able to capture some of what he had been; she had brought out love in him. Lea had thought that his capacity for love had been gone for a long time, that it belonged to his past as much as his Go Bots and Richard Scarry books, but Jenny had found it in him and brought it out, so that he had spent his time looking up and annotating sentimental poetry, had spent his money buying tickets to *Aida*. Here she was, the girl who knew Lea's boy the way no one else had. Lea didn't blame herself for staring, or for being so slow to respond.

"No," she said finally, "I'm sorry. I'm a little out of it today."

Jenny nodded with what seemed to be genuine sympathy. Lea continued to stare. There were no surprises about her appearance. She looked very much like she did in the picture. Her black hair was disordered and thick, and she wore a white buttoned blouse that strained against her large chest. Her skin was smooth, her eyes round and darkened with purple mascara. She stared back at Lea, unabashed by the scrutiny.

"Okay," said Jenny, and walked away rigidly, still aware, it seemed to Lea, that she was being watched.

| thirty |

*Rachel suggested* that they have dinner in Scranton that
night. *But it's a Friday,* he almost said. On Fridays everyone stayed in
Breed's Township. It was on Saturdays that people drove to the city—
that's why the Fridays had been special at O'Ruddy's. It was a fact he
had counted on for a long time.

It actually didn't much matter to him, since every day was the
same now. He only knew it was a Friday because it was *that* Friday,
the first day that would matter, that would be of signal importance to
his life, since the Friday in January. In any case, he knew he had to
make an excuse to Rachel, but he couldn't think of one; she knew very
well that he had literally nothing in the world but free time. He simply said, "Not tonight."

She sighed on the phone. "Casey. Come on. Let's do this. Let's get
out of the house and eat something nice and talk. It'll be like a real
date. I'll pay."

It was not as coarse a suggestion as it might have sounded, since Rachel had literally never, in his memory, offered to pay for anything, and she would see this as a large gesture, a reaching out, especially given the fact that a few days earlier she'd turned down his request for the thousand-dollar loan. He was touched by the offer, he said, and he was not lying. But he still couldn't go. She gave up quickly and said she'd call him later.

He got to O'Ruddy's at nine o'clock and parked in the back, where the dumpsters used to be. He stayed in the driver's seat and counted the number of cars that drove past on Arthur Avenue. Traffic was sparse, but it would take only one person to notice that something was not right. Another thing that was out of his hands, that perhaps he should have thought about before now. But that wasn't the issue; it wasn't a lack of forethought. He *had* thought about it ahead of time. He had even assumed the worst, and he had decided that it would be worth it, no matter what happened. Knowing was the most important thing in the world.

At ten the first car pulled up, a dark green Chevy sedan. He didn't remember whether he'd seen it at the fight, but it looked like the kind of car that had been there: modified hubcaps and fenders but otherwise a cheap, ugly thing. Before Brady Benson emerged from the passenger side, the car sat idling for a few moments, basking in the tremendous bass that emanated from the self-installed speakers. Casey got out to meet Brady.

"All set?" asked Brady, who looked alert and sober. Casey wondered if it was the only time he'd been around the boy when he wasn't stoned.

"Everything's in there." He nodded to the restaurant. "Is this everybody?"

"No, no. I told you, man, I got a lot of friends."

"How many more? This can't get out of hand."

Brady shrugged. "Whoever comes, comes. I got five in the car right now. There may be ten, fifteen others by the end of the night. Fuck if I know."

"Make sure you get that guy to park right beside my car. And you've got to make sure your friends listen to me in there. It can't get out of hand."

Brady left him without speaking and slid back into the green sedan. The car reparked, still fuming bass notes, next to Casey's Accord. From the car came a small pack of boys and one girl, who was chewing gum loudly and clutching a tall, pale boy.

"Shit. O'Ruddy's. This is weird," the driver of the green sedan said, after clicking the alarm on his car. "My grandparents bring me to eat here on my birthdays."

"Not anymore they don't," said Casey. He walked to the back entrance and heard them follow. He opened the storage door and led them through the maze of the back rooms, then out onto the floor. He turned on the lights behind the bar, and they sat themselves on the leather stools.

"A few ground rules," he said. He had their attention, even Brady's. They were silent, somehow cowed by this experience. "This is the only light that can come on. Take what you want, but don't break anything. And keep it down. For God's sake, keep it down."

As if to mock Casey's burgeoning sense of authority, a fist thundered against the wood paneling of the front double doors, and a booming voice followed. *"Hey, B? You in there?"*

Brady looked at Casey almost apologetically, which made Casey swallow the curse he was about to throw at the latecomer. Brady hustled over to the door and leaned up against it. "Chuckie, man, I told you. You got to go around back. There's a back door. Make sure you park your car close to Sprott's."

Chuckie obeyed wordlessly, and a minute later Brady retrieved the new arrivals from the back. Seven of them had somehow crammed themselves into one car, and they greeted their friends with the casual salutations that indicated they'd not only seen each other recently but were used to seeing each other every day, all day. The seven teenagers — four boys, three girls — did not seem as disconcerted by the environment as the others had. They did not need to be told where to sit, and they did not wait for anyone to explain the rules to them. They threw off their coats in a pile by the kitchen, sat at table three, and began asking immediately about drinks. Casey gave way as Brady shuffled behind the bar. The boy did not even look at him, and he seemed tense, as if he could not believe the plan was actually happening, as if he couldn't look at Casey for fear of reminding him that this favor was too extreme. Casey wondered, for a terrible moment, if perhaps the story would not be worth it after all.

Another knock, this time on the back door, brought three new boys, who merged with the group. The others had already begun drinking.

As Casey had noted on Monday, the liquor bottles were still behind the bar, though the refrigerators had been turned off and the kegs returned to the distributors. The wine bottles had been boxed up, but not the liquor or the mixers. The bar looked very much the same as it had when he'd left. The bounty was too much for the children at first. None of them could have told the difference between the premium liquors and the well drinks that cost the restaurant four dollars a liter. Some of them even asked if there was any beer left. *No*, said Casey, from his lonely perch at the end of the bar. *I'm afraid you'll have to drink Maker's Mark.*

They quickly became accustomed to the wealth of strange booze before them. Brady found a bartending book, and they experimented with the more rakish-sounding drinks, after a few rounds of straight tequila shots. Casey could tell, after a half hour, that the boy was getting frustrated behind the bar. He had probably not realized how much work it was to provide pleasure for others. He had stripped down to a sweaty T-shirt, the cobra on his neck revealed in its full glory, and he wore a constant grimace and began swearing with little provocation. Every so often he would drink his own shot, which didn't seem to help matters.

Another group arrived, a car packed with four girls and one strangely fortunate boy, and Casey began to worry in earnest.

"There's twenty kids here, Brady. That's a lot. I wasn't thinking in terms of those numbers."

Brady shrugged. "What the fuck? Am I supposed to tell them to leave? They're my friends. Besides, they wouldn't go anyway."

"I'm just saying . . . Geez. Twenty kids. How many kids do you know?"

"I told you. I got a lot of friends," he said, but this didn't sound like the brag it might have been. Scowling toward a feathery-haired girl who had demanded a Buttery Nipple shot from him, Brady looked as if having a lot of friends could be a large pain in his ass.

"Soon, Brady," Casey said to him.

The frazzled boy looked up at him quickly, at first confused, then annoyed. "What do you mean soon, motherfucker? Soon my ass. I haven't even sat down yet. It's not even ten-thirty. I told you, man, I'll tell you when it's time. It's not time."

That quickly, that definitively, Casey lost whatever control he had. He stood up from the bar and made his way to the smoking section, where he sat in a booth. He watched Brady and his friends plow through the free liquor.

They sat in a great cluster around tables two and three, which they had shoved together, as the police had done in January. They did not seem so different from the groups that assembled at O'Ruddy's for birthday dinners or retirement parties. They had the natural air of festivity that emanates from any large group of drinkers, not just the noise but the animated faces, the preening and touching and hyperbolic smiles. They almost looked like they belonged there, as if this were a Friday night ritual of theirs, which Casey supposed it was. What seemed conspicuous to him, or at least surprising, was that they were happy. He didn't know what he had expected; a night of free drunken revelry could hardly have made them otherwise. But their happiness warmed him to them, so that at times he felt pangs that were not caused by his awkwardness, by the strange glances some of them cast, but that might have been a form of jealousy. Casey did not have friends like this; he suspected not many adults did. The boisterous Fridays in the fall now seemed like an illusion, a trick of memory.

It seemed to him now that Breed's Township was a joyless place, full of people who were perpetually lonely, in spite of girlfriends or wives or families. The only people in Breed's Township who were truly comfortable with their fellow men and women, he thought, were these teenagers.

In time they became rowdier. They played a variety of drinking games. Some of them had brought cards and and lucky shot glasses for the occasion. Some of the girls, getting drunk fast, began to whoop and shriek in response to the games, and Casey found himself unable to hush them, although he tried scowling at Brady every once in a while. None of the teenagers talked to Casey or asked questions, and no one seemed worried about the transgression they were undertaking. They must have understood that the booze had not been paid for, and that their entrance had been illegal. None of them, not even the girls, seemed to care very much. They laughed and drank and flirted and sometimes kissed and groped, and they became oblivious of everything but themselves. It seemed appropriate, then, to leave them alone. Casey told Brady that he would be in the back, and then he went into his office, which was bare and cold.

At eleven he heard Brady stomp through the kitchen, past his office, to let in more of his friends. This happened again at eleven-twenty. Casey sat still at his old desk, staring ahead of him. There had been twenty kids when he had left them, perhaps there were thirty now. He had already incriminated himself tonight, and there was no going back, there would be no justification or exoneration for these crimes. He told himself that he had already come to terms with this, already accepted the consequences, and so he tried to quell the intensifying clench in his stomach by staring into space, thinking of nothing but the air in front of him.

By twelve-thirty he could do this no longer, especially since the noise from the floor had become, in the past fifteen minutes, constant and frightening. It was the sound of chaos, a few breaking glasses or bottles, a few wild screeches, terrifying to him because of his ignorance. He had been waiting for Brady, counting down seconds and minutes and then hours, certain that the boy would finally burst in, tipsy and happy, and say to him, finally, "Okay, you've earned it."

But Brady did not come. It had been long enough; the boy could not deny it. So Casey rushed out onto the floor, then took a moment to adjust to the scene before him. He couldn't at first accept what he saw because it was his old place, it was O'Ruddy's, and he was used to seeing it in a variety of guises—packed to the brim on a Friday night, sparse and sad on a Sunday afternoon, empty and dark once the last server had left—but never like this. A couple was making out, horizontally, in the booth in the smoking section where the Howards' daughter had watched the fight. A small crew of boys had lined up empty bottles in the front entrance for a makeshift game of bowling. Behind the bar a girl was vomiting in the sink, her hair held from behind by a friend. The friend looked accusingly at Casey and said, "Your bathrooms are locked."

At various booths, teenagers could be seen slumped in attitudes of severe drunkenness, so much so that Casey's first instinct was to do a round to make sure everyone was breathing. In looking at these figures, he finally spotted the lean body of Brady, using his Sharks jacket as a blanket. His feet touched the ground, but he was laid flat in the booth, his head slumped up against the wall, a few inches below the window through which Casey had watched him fight seven weeks ago.

Casey slapped his face, but the only effect was to loosen some drool, which slid down his chin. Casey whispered his name fiercely, touching him on the chest and shaking him. The boy did not respond, except to moan and grumble and assume a look of intense despair. Casey slapped him one more time, and Brady waved a weak hand in the air and mumbled, "Leevmeethfuckalone." He smelled like the floor mat of the bar, back when Casey had had to hose it down after every shift.

"He's pretty out of it," said a girl's voice behind him. Casey knew it was Jenny, and so he did not turn to look.

"That's very helpful," he said, and kept staring at the boy. He decided to leave it up to her for the moment, to explain herself without any help from him.

"Mr. Fielder?"

Now he had to turn. He didn't fake surprise. "Yeah, Jenny."

"Brady's done for the night, I think."

"How's he getting home?"

She shrugged. "How are any of us getting home?" And now, as startling to Casey as anything he'd seen that night, Jenny smiled. Her smile was enormous and pure, her teeth impossibly white and straight for someone from East Breed's, her cheeks exuberant and dimpled.

"But that's okay," she said. She moved suddenly to sit in the booth behind Brady's, table nine. Casey followed and sat opposite her. "I kind of miss it here, in a weird way. It hasn't been that long, I guess. But do you know what I mean? I never liked working, but I miss it."

"I know what you mean. I thought I missed it too. But now I'm not so sure. Maybe it's just like any other place."

She nodded slowly, not understanding. He realized he had never been vague with her before, nor had he ever told her what he was feeling.

"Why is it okay, then, Jenny? You said it was okay."

She nodded again, this time with confidence and vigor. "It's okay, Mr. Fielder. He couldn't have given you what you wanted anyway."

"You know about me and Brady, I guess. Our conversations."

"Brady and me are friends. We grew up together."

"That makes sense." Their houses were no more than fifty yards apart, though Casey only now realized it. They lived on different streets, in different small houses in that stark neighborhood. It was difficult to imagine the interaction between the homes at this time of year. In the past months, whenever he'd driven down the streets, they had been beyond empty, void of everything that might have united people.

"So he told me about you showing up and asking him all those questions. I guess I can understand that, Mr. Fielder. But this?" She ducked her head and looked at him with smug disapproval. "A party at the restaurant? Shit, that's a bit extreme, isn't it?"

"I suppose. I'm kind of at the end of my rope," he said. "I kind of need to know."

"Have you figured anything out?"

"I was supposed to find out tonight. Brady was going to give me the rest. You know that, I imagine."

Jenny jerked in her seat as a bottle crashed somewhere, followed by convulsive laughter ending in a hacking cough. Casey thought that she seemed alert, almost edgy, and it was clear that she hadn't been drinking, though she must have arrived with the last group, at eleven-twenty. What had she been doing? he wondered now. Waiting for him?

"Pretty out of hand," she said, in reference to her friends.

"I guess so."

"Maybe you should get them out of here. Before you get in trouble."

He gave her a vacant, meaningless nod. "Maybe." It might have appeared, he realized, that he too was drunk. He felt somehow desensitized, slow.

After a moment he sat up straight and coughed out a laugh. "You're full of good advice, Jenny. You always seem to know the right thing to do. It's an impressive quality." She looked down at her fingers, registering his sarcasm and looking ashamed. He took his chance. "What did you do to me, Jenny? Why did you do that to me?"

She shook her head, avoiding his eyes. "Fuck. What did I do to you? You weren't going to call the cops, Mr. Fielder. I depended on that from day one. You weren't going to put your ass on the line like that." She rummaged in her purse, found and lit a cigarette. He knew now that his only job was to listen, that Jenny had come as Brady's proxy, that her quick words of comfort—*but that's okay*—were very true. It was okay. He didn't need Brady to learn the truth, he needed Jenny.

"I don't know why I said the phone was out. I guess I got

spooked . . . I thought for a minute that you really were going to call the cops. But you weren't going to, I know that now. Just had to make sure, I guess."

"So the phone wasn't out. I've known that all along, I think, but just so we're clear. The phone wasn't out?"

"Nope. It was a risk. I had a feeling you wouldn't check on it your-self if I told you it was broke. I remembered it hadn't worked much that week. But like I said, it didn't matter. You weren't gonna call."

He nodded, gravely satisfied. There was more to learn, but this confirmation went a long way toward removing his doubts about tonight. That information alone might be worth it. And there was more, though he didn't quite know how to mine it from her. She spoke again.

"So I lied about the phone. Didn't want you to call the cops. I guess I could say I didn't want to lose my job either. I guess maybe I was as selfish as you were."

"But that's not really it."

"How do you know that?"

"Because you're not like me."

She nodded emphatically. "Yep. That's right, Mr. Fielder. Any other situation like that, I would have called the cops. I would have made you call them. I wouldn't have let you stand there like that, looking at those kids like they were animals in a zoo."

He felt the dig keenly; he had thought himself immune to the pains of judgment by now, but he had not taken it from her before. "So what was it that made these circumstances so different?"

She stared at him, her face immobile. He wondered if she was try-ing to decide whether or not to tell him, and he felt the injustice come upon him in a wave. He squealed out his response. "I've already paid, goddammit, Jenny. You're not doing me a favor. I paid Brady for this, I get to know this." He was clenching his teeth, gripping the table as if getting ready to pull it from its moorings.

Again she shrugged, as if it didn't matter, as if she wouldn't deny him such a small thing. "I know what Brady told you. It sounds like he told you a lot. And here I am, the one who lied about the phone. The one who would have called the cops if I hadn't wanted it to happen. So what else do you need to know?"

"You wanted the fight to happen. But Brady was telling me the truth—he didn't even know why they were fighting. He knew there was something in it for him. Cocaine at first, then maybe two thousand dollars."

"Uh-huh."

"You put up the two grand? How on earth could you have done that?"

"Shit, Mr. Fielder, think about it. With help."

"The Howards. The lady sitting at table sixteen that night, that was their daughter." He almost laughed. "I knew that, I really did!" His satisfaction was intense. It quite literally felt like a dream—one he'd had many times lately—come true. "I actually told someone that, but he thought I was crazy. I can't believe this." He had not smiled like this in months.

"Good work. Not too hard to miss, though, was it? She looks just like the old bag."

"But she called the cops, that's what the paper said. The Howards' daughter ended up calling them."

"Yeah, that's right. About ten seconds after Colin got his head smacked in."

The smile drifted off his face now. It had seemed like a game for a few moments. All night, in fact, he had not thought about Colin Chase. And now Jenny had summoned him and thus made their words weighty again.

"Which you apparently wanted to happen. You wanted that to happen to the boy. You put out the two-thousand-dollar bounty on Colin Chase. The boy you'd been sleeping with. Or maybe you made that up."

"No, no. I was fucking him. For two months. And it was more than that, I guess. I was his girlfriend, in a sense. Actually . . ."

Casey raised his eyebrows; her pause lasted almost a minute.

"It's complicated. But I was his girlfriend. Leave it at that."

"And you wanted him dead."

"Not dead. Not really."

She looked different tonight, he now noticed. Her hair had been tended to, strapped into a long ponytail. She wore a heavy red sweater, and she had not painted her face with her typical zest. The overall effect was to make her seem subdued, earnest.

"The Howards, though, they wanted him dead? Or just injured, I guess. It probably wouldn't have mattered, right? So long as something happened. As long as a police report got filed."

She nodded firmly. "Pretty much."

He was frustrated now, because he couldn't fill in any of the rest; he wanted her to tell him. Like Bert Player, he had never liked riddles. He had always just wanted to be told the answer, and did not rate highly the satisfaction that came from figuring it out for himself. "Why did they want Colin Chase hurt, though?" he said, though he knew the question was misguided.

"Mr. Fielder. Please." She was slightly exasperated. "They didn't know who he was—it didn't matter to them. It just had to be someone."

"You're the one who decided on Colin. I get it." Casey wasn't sure if he wanted to know the rest. Or rather, he wasn't sure how to go about asking. The fact that he wanted to know was a given. He thought about what Brady had told him, that the fight had been for the honor of a Township girl. But he didn't know how to ask it. *What did that boy do to you to make you want him dead?*

Instead he retreated into more formalities, into questions he could have answered himself. "The cocaine party? That was just a warmup? A trial run?"

"The Howards figured one fight wouldn't be enough. They weren't going to lay out much money for the first one, but they said it had to happen. They gave me some money. I found some coke, told some lies, got someone to pick a fight with Colin. You should have seen Chad Richardson that night. He may have been stoned, I think.

He was pretty freaked out. And you filed the report. So that worked out pretty well."

"So it did. When Brady told the story, I pictured you there, but I didn't really think much about it. The house in Leawood—the Howards' daughter's house, yes?"

She raised her eyebrows, an evasion that was the same as a nod.

"You and Rick. You must have been sleeping with him too, I guess."

"Brady told you his name?"

"His real name is Rick? I thought Brady was giving me a fake one. But yeah, he said it was Rick."

She leaned up and raised her head to peer over Casey's shoulder at the snoring body of Brady. "Fucking idiot." She sat back down. "I mean, it doesn't matter, but Jesus. Can't even think up a fake name."

"I guess I don't see how you got the St. Brendan's kids to fight."

"They did what Colin said. I told Colin certain stories, just like I did with Rick. It's not difficult. Guys don't need that much of a reason."

"From what Brady told me, Colin Chase didn't seem like the kind of kid who would fight for the honor of a lady."

She smiled at him without showing teeth. "You've caught on to a lot, Mr. Fielder. I guess you've been thinking about this for a while."

"You could say that."

She gave a brief laugh at the obvious understatement, and at the tone of despair that even he could acknowledge as tragically funny. "I guess you feel sorry for yourself. Maybe you think I should feel sorry for you too."

"I just want to know what happened."

"And now you do. Everything that matters, anyway. The fight was a setup. No one had any reason to be there, except that I wanted them to be, and so did the Howards. They gave me some money to make it happen, and they sent their damn daughter to make sure everything went right. If you really had called the cops that night, she would have called Rick on his cell and told them to get out of there."

"Jesus. Was the insurance really that much?"

"You'd know more about that than I would."

She was right, though he knew little enough. He had no idea how much the Howards would be compensated for the revocation of the franchise owing to circumstances that were out of their hands. But of course the settlement didn't matter as much to them as winning at this, at getting rid of a loser restaurant, making the headquarters and the insurance companies eat the cost of the closing. It was neater and safer than an insurance fire. He almost admired their acumen, for they were in fact coming out ahead. The lawsuit from the Chase family was aimed squarely at the headquarters, the deeper pockets.

"You didn't tell me everything, though. Like I said, Colin Chase . . ." He trailed off, because she was no longer paying attention. She had turned to the window, resting her head on her palm, her elbow on the table. The restaurant was dim, but the outside world was black, and so she saw only her reflection in the window. Still, she stared intently, as if watching the fight all over again.

"Colin Chase," Casey said again, hoping this would be enough.

"Yeah, you were right, he wasn't the kind of guy who would fight for the honor of a lady. Except he did in my case. It was weird. He fell in love with me."

Casey raised his eyebrows, and though she couldn't have seen this, she broke from her lazy stare and glared at him as if direly offended. "Yes, he was a big fucking prick who didn't care about anything in the world except football. And sex. And pot and beer. But for some reason he loved me. I met him at a party in November, and that was it. I don't know what it was. I'm not going to sit here and flatter myself. But I'm telling you the truth. He loved me, and when I asked him to fight those guys, he did it, and he brought his friends. Twice."

"And in return you orchestrated his brain damage."

"There's a lot of things you don't know, Mr. Fielder."

"What did he do to you? Just tell me that." She didn't say anything, and didn't look as if she planned to. "Jenny. Look around you. Look at what I've done. This is how badly I need to know."

"It wasn't to me, Mr. Fielder. He was wonderful to me."

"Well, then?"

"My friends. Even girls who weren't my friends. All the Township girls, ever since we started school. All of us. Meredith, April, Kim, Beth. Seriously, the shit he did to them, and the shit he said about them. He loved to do it to the poor kids."

"So you became his girlfriend and then took him out as a public service."

"You can't be like that, Mr. Fielder, you can't make fun of this. There's too much you don't know. The terrible things he did." Her face remained hard and still, but her voice quavered. "The thing he did to Beth."

Before he knew he was doing it, Casey turned to look around the restaurant. A small pack of teenagers continued to drink and giggle at table five. Others had broken away in pairs to kiss and fondle. Still others had gone off alone, like dying animals, to pass out. Meredith, April, Beth. The girls were probably all around him. He hadn't thought about their names. Jenny had invoked them with ferocity, as if they were the names of battlegrounds, or martyrs.

"Like Scheherazade," he said. Jenny sat up straight, wide-eyed.

"Exactly." She said it with great tenderness, as if she were grateful to him for understanding. "Yes. Like Scheherazade. Someone had to put a stop to it, that's all. It was the right thing to do, Mr. Fielder. It may sound fucked up, but I did the right thing."

"What did he do to Beth, Jenny?" It was his last question.

Suddenly the dark world outside the restaurant became illuminated. The strobe of revolving red lights traced through the darkness. Two police cruisers skidded to a stop in the parking lot, and dark-uniformed bodies scurried out of them. The front doors thundered, until Casey walked over and undid the lock.

# thirty-one

*The case* was settled with surprising haste. Or at least it surprised Lea, until she realized upon reflection that it did not just appear out of the blue, that Phil Lucas must have been taking some
liberties in speaking on their behalf, or that Geoffrey had decided to
make some decisions without her. If this was the case, she did not
mind so much; she had ceded this authority to him weeks before.

Geoffrey explained it to her over the phone, from his office. He
couldn't hide the fact that many of the mechanics of the deal had been
worked out over the past few weeks, though she didn't really understand this until she had hung up the phone. Instead she noticed all
that Geoffrey was hiding, that which he glossed over and which had
likely been glossed over when Lucas explained it to him.

The boy's past, of course, had damaged their case. It had been
light work for the restaurant headquarters in Dallas, and presumably
their insurance carriers, to determine what set of circumstances miti-

gated their guilt in the matter. The lawyers and investigators had pe-
rused the police reports, spoken with Brother Carl, talked informally
with some of Colin's friends and enemies. Geoffrey dispensed with
their investigations and conclusions in a few vague sentences. "They
learned about his behavior problems. Apparently . . . well, Phil thinks
they could paint a pretty dark picture of him."

It occurred to Lea that her own investigations of her boy would
have helped them enormously. *They don't know the half of it,* she thought.
Her close access had allowed her to unearth details that even the insurance company's investigators couldn't have learned. Colin owed
money to a drug dealer. He had gotten a girl pregnant and slipped her
a pill so that he wouldn't have to bother to convince her to get an
abortion. He had been stabbed by a jilted lover. A pretty dark picture
indeed, she thought, as Geoffrey continued to justify the deal he'd accepted.

In spite of Colin's violent background, the headquarters offered
$300,000. Phil Lucas had aggressively countered their accusations,
relying on the restaurant manager's negligence, which the headquarters did not try to explain away. Geoffrey's pride in his friend Phil's
tactics was obvious. The old fraternity brother would take his large
cut, of course, but Geoffrey nearly begged Lea to understand the service he'd done for them, how it had become personal at the offices of
Lucas and Toole, how Phil had taped a copy of Colin's team photograph on every file they opened for the case. Lea maintained a respectful silence, let him praise his friend, and agreed that the sum was
large, given the challenges.

The issue of what to do with the money was not one that she
would cede to Geoffrey's better judgment, though he had many ideas,
which he told her about over a late Friday night dinner. They ate at
the dining room table, which was becoming as rare as eating in the
kitchen had once been. It seemed, she thought, that some kind of difference in their routine was called for today. Neither of them would
have said that a celebration was in order, but Geoffrey seemed

pleased, and not entirely surprised, that Lea had decided on a kind of formality. Colin was generally unaffected by the change, though he wriggled and shifted in the hard, high-backed chair of the dining room and was made suspicious by the complex and serious conversation of his parents.

Geoffrey presented his ideas in the same cautious manner in which he'd told her about the lawsuit and, in another life, the tone he had used to convince her to let Colin matriculate at St. Brendan's. He sought something very specific with his tone, it seemed to her. He wanted her to feel included, he wanted her to understand that he was taking the point on these matters not because she couldn't, or shouldn't, but because he wanted to protect her from such vulgarities. She wondered what would happen if she called him on this, but of course she didn't. It would have been a violation of their rules.

He had spoken with bankers and had gotten referrals from Phil Lucas. She became cynical about his tone, and realized it was likely that he didn't mean to protect her at all, that in fact he believed she didn't know enough to deal with such things. She acknowledged privately that she didn't, but felt a huge resentment that he might think so. Suddenly, staring at a pile of brown chicken and sauce and listening to him drone, she realized that she didn't care what his motives were. She simply didn't care whether Geoffrey was as earnest as he seemed, or whether he was in fact a manipulator who got his way because of the guise of sincerity. Either one seemed unappealing to her, as unappealing as the congealing mass on her plate.

"Who gives a shit?" she said, and she may have been responding to a number of things running through her head, though she was startled to hear herself say this out loud.

"Pardon me?"

"I mean this talk about interest rates and CDs and growth stocks. Where to put the money. Who gives a shit?"

He sat up straight and tossed his napkin on the table. It was now impossible for Lea to see in his actions anything but choreography, deliberation. "I give a shit. And I assume our son cares about how he's going to be supported. Look, Lea, if you don't want a part of this, I understand, but I think . . ." She didn't see any reason to keep listening.

Colin's care was in fact not much of an issue yet. The surgery and hospital stay had been largely covered by insurance, and the few out-of-pocket expenses had been within their budget. Geoffrey had been speaking in the long term, about funds they might set up for the future. It was all very disturbing for her to imagine. The image of the years ahead, the years of Colin's young adulthood spent in their constant company. The image of her as an elderly woman, living in the same house and playing the same music for him on the stereo, wiping his chin after a meal of SpaghettiOs and drying his hair after a bath. Long after his body had lost the firm muscles, after the crisp yellow hair had fallen away, after the sharp Nordic face had melted into jowls. The image of him attending the funerals of his parents. The vacant look as he gaped at the lowering caskets. *He'll always be four,* she thought, now slipping even further from Geoffrey's world of practicalities.

"I want to do something with the money," she said.

"I'm all ears," he said, though he wasn't looking at her.

"We should set up some kind of fund. A scholarship or something."

"Hmm. A nice thought. But Lea, there's problems with that sort of thinking."

"Such as?"

He leaned forward, glancing to his right. Geoffrey was squeamish about saying certain things in front of Colin, as if he didn't really believe the assurances he'd given her about the boy's comprehension level. He spoke in a low voice, the absurdity—Colin was closer to him than Lea was—apparently lost on him.

"That's the sort of thing you do as a memorial. It wouldn't be appropriate here."

She took a long pause, followed by a long drink of wine. She reached out her hand to rest it on Colin's. He smiled, but he did not look up from his plate; he was poking the remains of his sandwich with a butter knife.

"I've thought about this, Geoff. It *would* be appropriate. That boy"—she found herself whispering now as well—"is very much gone. Very much dead. The name and the body have stayed, but everything else is gone. Let's commemorate that."

She knew that Geoffrey was affected by the argument, because he didn't say anything and his expression didn't change. But neither did he agree to her proposal—not that it had been a proposal in any specific sense—and they spoke to Colin for the rest of the meal, out of guilt, and she stayed with the boy in the living room as Geoffrey tended to the cleanup.

In bed that night, he asked her what sort of memorial she had in mind. A scholarship, she suggested. Not at St. Brendan's, though. Lea still partly blamed St. Brendan's for the boy Colin had become. She remembered Brother Carl once telling her, in his somber, euphemistic way, that it did not seem as if Colin was becoming the sort of man they expected to produce at St. Brendan's. She had wanted to tell him that he was wrong, that much about Colin—the athleticism, the physical courage, the graceful confidence—was in line with the St. Brendan's model, and that this had led directly to the temper, the violence, the cruelty. But she had not told him this, in part because his tone had been so definitive. He had said it the way an electrician might have explained that her wiring was corroded. He had said it as if the depravity of her son was the will, or perhaps the fiat, of God.

She did not explain this to her husband, but simply said that she'd like to set something up at the public school. Geoffrey did not protest. She wondered if it was cowardice or calculation. In giving in on the small things, Geoffrey often managed to hoard her goodwill for later use. Again, this was something she was only just realizing.

But in the end they decided on nothing, or rather decided to sleep on it, and by morning she knew that it wouldn't happen the way she wanted. They could set up a scholarship for a worthy student at Breed's Township High, and maybe in the end it would go toward making up for the havoc Colin had wreaked on the girls there, maybe the younger sibling of one of his concubines would eventually benefit from the insurance settlement. But Lea knew she couldn't steer the funds directly to Jenny, or to whichever girl had miscarried because of the eproxyn, and this was what she wanted.

It would just be easier to give Jenny the cash, perhaps, but she didn't see how she could make that happen either. She needed to know more about her, and in the morning she found herself bracing for this task, feeling the same determination and purpose she had when she'd first decided to plumb the depths of Colin's previous life. She could bribe a guidance counselor, talk to Jenny's friends, maybe begin to frequent the China Pagoda and establish a relationship with the girl herself. She would find out where she planned to go to college, where she lived, what she wanted to be. She could engage in the sort of relationship with Jenny that she might eventually have had if, in an imaginary future, Colin had finally decided to let his parents in on his life. After all, this girl might have become, in the fullness of time, her daughter. She didn't feel silly for taking these logical leaps. The adolescent Colin had never loved anyone, as far as she knew, but this girl. Before Jenny he had enraged a girl to the brink of homicide, he had drugged a young woman to avoid the obligations of paternity. And this one had driven him to opera, poetry. It must have been love, and for love to grow in such unlikely ground as Colin's heart . . . well, she knew that they would have been married, knew it in her soul. Jenny would have become her daughter.

The stab of pain that came with this certainty deflated her entirely, so that after Geoffrey left for work and when Colin was scribbling pictures in the living room, Lea shut herself in the bathroom and vomited. She had never felt such loss. The sadness of that Friday night gushed inside her in a way that it never had before. She sank onto the tile, too weak to give much energy to her crying. She made low, guttural noises. The loss she felt was especially keen because it was so unexpected. She had dealt with the loss of Colin, she had mourned in her way, had investigated him so that she could feel comfort in the presence of his new self. That had been done. She had learned his secrets and had put him to rest. But she hadn't expected to learn anything about Colin that would give new dimensions to the tragedy of his brain damage. She hadn't expected to discover that there had been hope for him. She had not just lost the son that she had been unable to love; she had lost one that might have become better.

When she walked out of the bathroom, she knew that she wouldn't investigate Jenny the way she had planned. She didn't want to know anymore, she didn't see what good it would do. The girl would go on and live her life now, oblivious of the discoveries Lea had made. Jenny would mourn in her own way; she must already have done so.

Besides, Lea couldn't just hand a stack of cash to the girl. Geoffrey wouldn't let her, for one thing, not without knowing the story, which Lea would never tell him. And she couldn't imagine the scene—what would she do, walk into the China Pagoda, or into the high school, and pass her an envelope stuffed with hundreds? The girl would have to get by on her own, then, without help from the woman who might have been her mother-in-law.

She would let Geoffrey play with his mutual funds and portfolios. They had money, they always would. It didn't concern her much where it was or how often it reproduced. Plus they had the college fund, which they could now liquidate.

She cleaned herself up and went to see Colin in the living room. He lay on his back on the carpet, pleased by the feel of it on his skin, and lolled his head to the side, singing along with the Eagles. He smiled when she stood over him. "Myoo-sic," he said.

"That's right, baby boy. Music."

## thirty-two

*Rachel wouldn't* have paid his bail, he didn't think, if the Howards had pressed charges for breaking and entering, theft, and destruction of property. As it happened, they did not, and so he was left with several counts of a single charge—corrupting a minor—for which the bail was reasonable, though she told him that he needed to pay her back. It was the first thing she said, in fact, when she met him in the lobby of the county courthouse.

She'd left him there overnight, but he couldn't blame her for that. He had called her from the jail at three in the morning, and she had made it clear that she did not consider it an emergency. She had not, in fact, seemed the least bit surprised, though he hadn't let her in on the plan, hadn't even hinted about it. She posted his bail a little after ten Saturday morning, and when he got in her car, he noticed from the wrappers on the floor that she'd stopped off to get herself breakfast.

Casey's stay in prison had been unremarkable except for the tingling, awesome fear that was as intense an emotion as any he'd ever felt. He had been by himself all night and had slept on a bench in the holding cell, and so loneliness and discomfort conspired with this fear to give him repeated nightmares that were not so different from his spells of wakefulness. He didn't know at the time that the Howards would not press charges, but even if he had, it wouldn't have given him comfort. He did not think in terms of charges, jail time, lawyer's fees; this was not why he was afraid. The terror came from the eyes. He could feel the naked stares, the thousand judgments. There was no doubt about it now; he had done the wrong thing. He had acted foolishly, dangerously, contemptibly. Anyone who saw him now would recognize this. There could be no exoneration of this act, no shifting of the blame. Guilty as charged.

When morning came, however, he felt better. He acknowledged that there was a kind of freedom in such a blatant case as his. Yes, he had sneaked a group of kids into O'Ruddy's, yes, he had given them free rein with what remained of the bar. Yes, he was culpable. It was that easy, and it felt almost refreshing to admit this. It was what Jenny must have felt, he realized. *Yes, I got someone to bash in his head*, she could say to herself, *and I knew I was doing it*. She would spend no time trying to talk herself into believing that she had not done it or that other factors were involved. She took the great weight upon herself, and welcomed the load. It felt good, Casey realized with some surprise, to know exactly what you've done.

It also helped that the cell was not the bleak iron box of movies and television but instead a large rectangle furnished with two padded benches. It was painted taupe, somehow free of graffiti, and in general more like a spartan hospital waiting room than a jail cell. And of course it helped that he now knew the truth. He had gotten what he'd gone for, more or less, though he never learned what had happened to Jenny's friend Beth. That was the one that really mattered, he knew, that was the one that had driven her to violence. The boy had done something to Beth, something beyond the parameters of his typical recklessness, and this had been the impetus for Jenny's righteous machinations. He thought about Jenny in the jail cell as soon as he woke up. How blissful it must be, he thought, to be so certain of righteousness, to disregard the judgment of the eyes. On the bus when the boys teased the retarded man, at the restaurant when he'd asked if she'd studied the menu, that Friday night when her friend needed vengeance and Jenny had told whatever lie or committed whatever sin necessary to carry out the plan. Jenny did not need guidance in anything. She was the only adviser, and the only judge, that she required. How wonderful that must be, Casey thought.

When the deputy came to set him free, he almost wondered if it was Jenny who had bailed him out. He continued to think of her for most of the car ride home, and in the end decided it must have been she who convinced the Howards, somehow, not to press charges against him. He couldn't imagine how she might have talked them into that, until he suddenly realized that it was in their interest to be good to him, that the information he'd obtained at the price of a Class A misdemeanor was actually quite valuable. Jenny might have simply warned them that the information was out, that Casey now knew that others were culpable, that the Howards had incriminated themselves. Perhaps he could blackmail the Howards, he thought, and then, thinking again of Jenny, he felt ashamed.

"So, just whenever you get the money, I guess. I know you don't have it now, but you know how these things go. The longer you wait, the easier it is to forget about it, and I don't think it'd be good for either of us if you forgot about it."

He didn't know how long Rachel had been talking, though it must have been a while, because they were well out of East Breed's now. He looked at her with a grave, tired face. "Can we deal with this later? I'm kind of tired. And hungry." He stared down at the empty Dunkin Donuts bag.

"Later?"

"Just not right now?"

She didn't speak again until they got to his house, where she stopped the car against the curb, threw it into park, switched off the radio, and turned to him with her seatbelt still on.

"So I guess you know what this means," she said.

"We're finished."

She looked quizzical, and for a moment he wondered if maybe he'd assumed wrong and had accidentally given her what she considered to be a hell of an idea. She began to nod. "So we're on the same page with that?"

"I don't know if that's true. I know that we're finished. What else do you want to hear?"

"Do you know why we're finished?"

"There seem to be a few possible reasons."

She laughed in one brief, surprised spurt. "That's for sure."

He breathed deeply. He didn't want to go down this road with her again. The tiresome banter, the way their conversations seemed a series of hesitations and blurtings. He had never been able to speak to her honestly without undergoing a thrilling fear, the cocktail of freedom and terror that a schoolboy gets when he finally tells the teacher she's a bitch. Indeed, he had often thought his fear of her might have come from the fact that she was a teacher. The creased dark skirts, the severe reading glasses, the crisp blouses and pantyhose and sharp-toed pumps. He had never lost the notion of her absolute authority, though now he knew that she did not intimidate him because of his schoolboy memories but because she had the sternest, most judgmental eyes of them all, and because she was always watching him.

"So the experiment's over," he said.

"I'm not sure I get what you mean."

"You gave me money. You can't give money to your subject. It's unethical."

She nodded, but he could see that she didn't understand. He thought she too must have been weary of their conversations.

"It's been interesting, Casey. You're not like anyone I've ever dated before," she said, and then, as if understanding the insulting obviousness of this statement—it was, of course, the reason she'd gone out with him in the first place—she said, "You're not like anyone I've ever *met* before."

"Same here."

There was a long pause. Rachel took a drink of her coffee, and Casey could only imagine she meant to remind him that she hadn't bought him anything at the Dunkin Donuts.

"That's it, then? Anything you want to say?" she said.

"You mean reasons? You want me to run down the reasons you're breaking up with me, just so I'll know?"

"In a way, yes. I want to make sure you know what went wrong. I'm not leaving you because times are tough. Or because of the money. I'm doing this because . . . well, you tell me. Go ahead, tell me why this is over." Again, exactly as a schoolteacher would have done, she had brought herself to the verge of answering her own question, then retreated, to make sure her pupil got the answer himself.

He waited awhile before speaking. He began to wonder if he really did know the answer. He had been waiting for Rachel to break up with him for several weeks now, simply because it was her prerogative to do so. He was unhandsome. His career had been middling, embarrassing to her even in the good times. He was from East Breed's. And he had been in the papers for being apathetic, amoral, unheroic, in a time of crisis. The only question was, why hadn't she done it sooner?

"Because, because, because. I don't fucking know, Rachel. You just are. I'm me, you're you, this was kind of screwy from the beginning. It's done. I'd rather not go through an autopsy right now."

"Because you failed me. You might not see it that way, but you did fail me. I had some faith in you. Maybe not much, but I did have my expectations, and you didn't live up to them. Even after that Friday night. That was a terrible thing you did, but I thought in the end you would own up to it. You still haven't. I don't think you ever will. For God's sake, you bribed a bunch of teenagers—a bunch of my students!—with liquor so that they'd tell you what happened in your little conspiracy. That's how far gone you are. Can you see that? Can you see how crazy this is?"

"But they *did* tell me, goddammit! There *was* a conspiracy!"

"So what?"

He puffed air into his cheeks and held it there, then let it out in a long wheeze. She didn't let him respond.

"You still don't think you're guilty. That's a joke, Casey. That's what I'm talking about. I don't care if there was a conspiracy—nobody does. That's not the point. You very well may have been caught up in things beyond your control. I don't really doubt that. I've heard rumors at school, everyone has . . ."

He began to stammer and his eyes got wide; hers rolled up and to the left in unutterable exasperation. She said, "Just listen to me, don't interrupt. There have been whisperings, but nobody knows anything. And like I said, I don't think that matters. I don't think anyone will ever know anything. The point is that you could have stopped it, that all this could have been stopped. And then, after you didn't, you could have acknowledged that. It's what I've been waiting for. Every day. All your talk about Brady Benson, and the Howards and their stupid insurance, and the damn tangled phone line. Through all that, I've been waiting for you just to stop for a fucking second and say, 'You know, none of this means that I didn't screw up.' You failed me there, though. And last night pretty much proves that you're never going to snap out of this. Right?"

She had been watching him this entire time. She had been watching, waiting for him to do something specific and prescribed, and she was now disappointed in her rat for failing to get out of the maze. But he hadn't even known that he'd been undergoing a test—how could he have performed well? He thought about the torrent of injustice that the world had tried to drown him with, and now he just felt tired.

He decided not to defend himself. He did not stay in the car long enough, or look at her fully enough, to see any expression of pity on her face, if she ever adopted one. He didn't think she would, no matter how long he stayed in the car. She would continue looking at him forever with that same face: curious, serious, gorgeous, cruel. He mumbled that he would send her a check, then lumbered out of the car gracelessly, stumbling on a vestige of ice.

Inside his house, Casey dropped onto his bed facedown, without taking off his shoes or coat, without even shutting the door completely. He stared into the white fabric of the sheet and counted how many seconds passed before he had to blink. It kept him from thinking, and so he did it again. Then he counted how long he could hold his breath. He felt the cold wind seeping into his room from the unlatched front door. He listened to the hum of the music from the upstairs neighbors. The bass put a slight tremor in the walls. He counted his heartbeats, which were terrifically audible.

It was not a surprise that Rachel had given up on him, but it pained him nevertheless, and he wasn't sure why. He had never felt anything for her that approached love, or even friendship. Lust, certainly, and pride at having obtained her, but the pain did not seem consistent with that. His feelings were hurt, there was an ache in his chest that made him wince. Again he counted the seconds, then blinked, then breathed.

That he had disappointed her, and that she had told him so in such frank terms, embarrassed him. He had been shamed, it was that simple, which implied neither that he accepted her judgment nor that he considered it appropriate for her to offer it; it just meant that she had humiliated him, that she had turned the weapon of his trust and his weaknesses against him. She had been fascinated by him as a species, so much so that she had to get close, like Jane Goodall among the chimps, and then he had disappointed her by acting according to his nature. That was it, he thought, the balm of this shame, the comfort he could take: he had done nothing that was not in his nature. If she was disappointed in him, then she didn't know him.

He did not, in the two hours he spent planted facedown on the bed, admit to himself that his nature needed to be apologized for. He was almost defiant on this point. He had never held himself up as a righteous man. He was honest about his dependence on systems, order, handbooks; he was even proud of it. It seemed very simple to Casey. The instinct to judge a moment and to respond to it—immediately, at any cost—was not in him, he just did not have the reflex. He had envied it in Jenny, and he realized that he still did, in spite of the terrible act she'd confessed to. Hers had been a crime of commission, the only moral kind of crime. You have to know what you're doing, he now knew, if you expect any exoneration. If she hadn't conspired in the damaging of Colin Chase, if it had just been a random schoolboy fight, she would have run out there in an instant, weather and gender and fear be damned. Casey had sat idly by because it was in his nature to do so. He knew that this was a flaw that could not be repaired, but this idea came to him obliquely, it shuffled through his head like the red spots that flash in the darkness when one shuts one's eyes tight. He did not admit it outright, he did not give the notion haven in his blank, stupefied brain.

Instead he lay for two hours, contented to do nothing but be still. Eventually the wind blew the front door fully open, and so he got up and shut it and then made tea and looked for something to eat. It was one o'clock in the afternoon. He boiled water for instant oatmeal, and as he ate it he thought in practical terms.

Paying Rachel back would have to wait, though he did write it down as an element of a list he was preparing on the back of a phone bill. At the top of the list he wrote "The Howards." Blackmail had occurred to him earlier, followed by a weltering shame when he thought of Jenny, but he reconsidered. How could he feel shame now? How debased does one have to be before it no longer matters what one does?

He didn't think, in the end, that he could go through with anything like extortion. He wouldn't get money out of them, most likely, since money was the one thing they would do anything to protect. Perhaps freedom, then. They could still press charges—the county officer had made this clear to him—and perhaps they would hold this over his head. It would be mutually beneficial, in any case. Maybe they would make him pay for the booze, but no real harm had been done, and if they knew he had the story, maybe they would be scared. Casey liked the idea that he had become a concern, something they would worry about the way they used to concern themselves with distributors, dependents, the headquarters. They would have to add him to their list of troubles, and to make it easy on themselves in their old age they would promise to drop the charges, maybe even sign some sort of agreement. Maybe even help him find a new job.

That was second on the list. He did not want to put it there. He wanted to write *"Breed's Township Beacon"* or "Sergeant Janda" or even "Bert Player." He wanted to take the knowledge to someone it would matter to, someone who could clean up the mess, expose the truth, clear his name. He had the story, though he also knew he had no proof. And besides, Jenny was at the heart of the crime. He still didn't know how he felt about what she'd done, largely because he still didn't know what Colin Chase had done to her friend Beth, but he was certain he didn't want her in trouble. It was a dead end. There could be no exoneration without incriminating her.

A job came second, then. After dealing with the Howards, making the arrangement that would save him from prison, he would find work. He had put it on a similar list as soon as he'd lost O'Ruddy's, and the task had proved daunting. He did not know how that would change today, but he knew that it had to.

# EPILOGUE

## january

# casey

*This winter* had been gentler than the last, though it did not necessarily seem that way to those who were stuck in it. There had been no ice storm, no power outages or canceled school days, but again Breed's Township was frozen and dark and the roads to Wilkes-Barre were pebbled with salt and sand.

The drive to Wilkes-Barre had become routine, and necessitated other routines. The Honda made a wheezing noise when it revved too hot, and so Casey had begun to change the oil himself every two thousand miles. On Tuesday mornings he visited the public library to check out the two or three books on tape that would see him through the week and to return the ones from the week before. Every day but Thursday, his day off, he would count out one dollar and eighty cents and set it in the coin tray, knowing that he would stop at the Hess station at exit 19 for a medium coffee. If his throat was sore from the weather, he would set out one dollar and sixty cents, because on those days he bought tea.

The commute itself did not conform to routines the way he would have liked, because of the vicissitudes of traffic. Sometimes the trip took only forty-five minutes, sometimes up to an hour and a half. Casey had a genuine phobia of tardiness, and so he always left early, and thus another routine emerged: he would usually get to work with time to spare, park the Honda in a neighboring lot (where he could not be seen by his coworkers) with a newspaper and the remnants of his coffee, and do the crossword puzzle. Three minutes before the shift, regardless of his progress on the puzzle, he would drive the thirty feet into the employee parking section, lock up his car, and walk through the back entrance of the Chik'n Shak to report for duty.

He was familiar with routine in general, of course, and throughout his life had actively sought it out. O'Ruddy's had been nothing but routine, honed and shaped over eight years, under the aegis of the handbook. Routines naturally and tenaciously associate themselves with the senses, and at O'Ruddy's these associations had provided comfort to him: the awkward squeak of someone's bottom on the fake leather booth seats, the sharp fumes of the cleaning solutions, the wall of wet heat that smacked him when he walked into the kitchen. They had been sensory delights for him, had brought out Pavlovian jolts of contentment, so that even now whenever he caught the smell of the same brand of cleaner, or when he heard the harsh squeak of Nau-gahyde, he still felt a brief thrill. And now he had a new routine, ex-actly what he had been looking for during the dark winter a year in the past. He had order, protocols, a paycheck (meager though it was), a place in the world. Yet ten months at the Chik'n Shak had taught him that patterns can also work against you, that the smells and im-ages and sounds of a routine can cause dread just as easily as they cause comfort.

Every day, when he opened the thick employees' door in the back, he was met by a very particular smell made up of chicken fat, plastic, sweat, and salt. The clicking noise of the time clock signaled the beginning of an eight-hour block of cold, mundane, unsatisfying work (the word had never before seemed ugly to Casey, but now when he said it, it sounded like a curse). The sounds and sights and smells and tastes that marked the routine of the Chik'n Shak signified only misery and fatigue. Even the crossword puzzle had begun to annoy him.

It was what had to be done, however. There had been no recourse, back in March. The credit cards were maxed out quickly, and his mountain bike and stereo had been pawned for less than five hundred dollars. Appeals to his mother ended awkwardly—she couldn't loan him anything, but she suggested he come out to Oklahoma to stay with her until he got back on his feet. He had declined in vague but appreciative terms, unable to tell her that under the conditions of his probation he was not allowed to leave the state.

Casey's punishment remained something of an afterthought. The year's probation meant little in practical terms; there had not been a time in the past ten months when he'd thought about crossing the state line. He was still paying off the fine that had been settled on in early April, during a chaotic meeting with the public defender and a Napoleonic prosecutor. And, of course, there was still the bail money he owed to Rachel. But these debts seemed almost theoretical, given the size of his Chik'n Shak paychecks. The payments to the township were garnished from his wages, the forty-dollar monthly checks to Rachel he mailed to her house. It would take several years to be rid of the two debts, and so they were easy for Casey to accept as part of the order of things—just another annoyance, like the gas bill or the red warning light on the Honda.

It was because of these debts, however, that Casey had taken the offer from the Chik'n Shak. Or rather, it was why he had gone to Mr. Grautz and more or less begged for mercy. The ugly fast-food manager, who was so discomfited by Casey's second appearance at the restaurant that he actually held up his hands in defense, had finally succumbed to the pleas, though of course the night manager job was off the table. There was an opening he could have, Mr. Grautz said, but he was probably overqualified.

About three more months of probation, Casey thought today, although that was not the true significance of the date, that was not why he was thinking about the fact that today was January 18. He was not counting down to the end of his probation. It was unlikely that he would get into any kind of trouble in the next ninety days that would bring down the wrath of the state. The sins he had committed belonged to his past. He was too tired to harp on those old happenings, or to cope with the Howards anymore.

The deal with them had been made a mere three days after his arrest and release. He had put away thoughts of extortion, though at times, when the forty-dollar check to Rachel seemed ruinous, he wished he had tried it. Because they pitied him, they would not press charges, Mr. Howard had said over the phone, and whatever Casey thought he knew—not that there was an ounce of truth to his entire crazy story—he would keep to himself. There had been no room for bargaining, and even in his destitution Casey had to admit to himself that it was worth it never to see the Howards again and not to worry about a statute of limitations on the breaking-and-entering charge, for which, Janda had assured him, he would go to prison. It had come as a relief, then, to learn that the Chases had settled with headquarters and that he would not be tempted to lay out the story before them at the deposition.

He had finished the crossword and now read the *Beacon*'s "This Day in History" column on the next page. It is just another day, he reminded himself, like his birthday, like Christmas. It wasn't even a Friday—January 18 fell on a Sunday this year. Still he could not help but read the column, look for significance in it. Captain Cook discovered Hawaii in 1778. Birthday of Cary Grant. Robert Scott got to the South Pole in 1912. He certainly hadn't expected to see anything about the fight at O'Ruddy's, though he had scoured the regional section to see if the paper acknowledged the anniversary.

The history column set him onto a rumination about the consequences of days. He considered how one specific day, with its limited scope of hours, could be more devastating, more enormous than any he had ever thought to encounter, with the likely exception of the one that would someday end his life. And no one heeded it. It mattered to him and to the Chases and to Jenny and to the Howards, and possibly to Rachel, and there the list ended. He had once taken comfort in this fact, in the knowledge that the radius of the damage had been small. Today this notion was piercing. In a few minutes he would walk into the Chik'n Shak and perform his menial duties, and he would stop at the Savin' Maven on the way home to spend the seventy dollars he budgeted for his monthly groceries (always on the third Sunday of the month), and no one he encountered in this small range of activity would know that this day—or one of its facsimiles, removed only by a digit in the year—had ruined his life. The thought did not quite make him suicidal, but it made him understand, with an empathy he had never before experienced, what is going through the minds of those who do kill themselves. And when these thoughts were exhausted, he looked at the electric clock on the dash and saw that it was time to go to work.

Throughout his shift, Casey was supervised by Wallace, a young man who was considered something of an up-and-comer in the Chik'n Shak community. At twenty-three, he had already been a shift manager for a year and a half, and he was quick to talk about his degree in hotel and restaurant management (the degree was from someplace called International Technical University, a detail Wallace was not so eager to offer). Used to dealing with the raging and identifiable incompetence of his teenage underlings, Wallace did not seem to know what to do with Casey, and he watched him with almost paranoid attention.

Casey was confident under his observation; he felt that he had learned everything there was to know about the Chik'n Shak in the first two weeks on the job. Today he entered the stream of work fluidly, taking over the chicken fryer for Darrell, an extravagantly tattooed senior citizen. The customer lines were four and five deep when he got there, but after two hours of frantic frying, grilling, spreading, order-taking, register-punching, and food-wrapping, the crowd dissipated and Casey took a moment to empty the trash while his colleagues argued about who would get the first smoke break.

After tossing the bags into the dumpster, Casey went to the supply closet for straws and cup lids. When he came out, Mr. Grautz called to him from inside the office. Casey had known Grautz was in there; throughout the shift he made forays onto the floor, overtly watching the crew. Casey had thus been onstage during the lunch shift, fixing Maria's register errors because he could sense Grautz's eyes, smiling at the customers because he knew Wallace looked for this. It was the job of managers, after all, to observe, especially in a place like this, where the employees, like second-graders, cannot possibly be expected to behave well unless they know that someone is constantly supervising. The eyes were on Casey all the time now, and it had become the only comfort in his new life; he didn't fear the eyes anymore, because they did not ask as much of him. They expected him to fry chicken and potatoes, to ring up orders, to wrap sandwiches, to mop the floor. These things he could do perfectly, and anyone who watched him, even Wallace, could not find fault.

Mr. Grautz was polite today, almost jovial. He still had difficulty looking Casey in the eyes, and in fact he seemed even more loath to do so than he had ten months earlier. Casey had come to learn very little about Mr. Grautz. He didn't know if he was married, where he lived, how long he'd been at the Chik'n Shak. The employees gossiped in the break room, of course, but there was nothing of substance, and most of Casey's colleagues, being teenagers, did not care to look beyond the man's homeliness or his insistence that they remove all piercings before a shift.

As he spoke, Mr. Grautz looked exclusively at a paper clip that he twisted and untwisted with his fingers. "Casey, it's time for your review, you know."

"I forgot about that, Mr. Grautz. But yeah, I guess it's been three months."

"Yep. Just like last time, a form I fill out, a form you fill out, and then we have to sign both."

"Right."

"I've done it already—filled out my form," Mr. Grautz said, but he didn't stop twisting the paper clip, or staring at it.

"I'm eager to see it."

"Yeah, well, it's just like the last one. You know that. Casey, there's nothing wrong with the way you work, of course. I don't really know what to say in those reports. Wallace said he'd like it if you smiled more, but I'd feel silly writing that in there. Kind of seems like nit-picking."

"Okay."

"What I'm getting at, Casey, is this." He stopped twisting the paper clip and leaned forward, with his elbows on his desk. He focused on Casey's shirtfront, as close as he could come, apparently, to looking into his eyes. "There's a shift manager spot opening up soon. Probably by the end of the month. Now, I know I had my reservations last time, Casey. I don't want to get into that. But a guy like you, working the fryer and the register and nothing else? It seems a little silly to me. Last month you had to help Georgia with the books—I heard about it, don't ask me how. But what I mean is, it seems like your talents are being wasted. I think maybe it's time you moved up."

Casey wondered if Mr. Grautz knew what day it was, if this were some sort of reward for making it through the year without committing some further act of self-destruction. It couldn't be a coincidence, he thought at first, but then he remembered sitting in the car, enumerating the people January 18 actually mattered to, and he realized that of course it was just chance. Mr. Grautz didn't know and didn't care when Casey had allowed Colin Chase to meet his fate in the O'Ruddy's parking lot, just as he had never cared about the myriad forces involved in deciding that fate. He simply wanted the restaurant to run smoothly, and he wanted people to stop staring at his misshapen face.

Mr. Grautz continued to speak, but Casey could think only about time, about the convulsive year that had passed since that Friday night, a year of fallout from an even smaller measurement, a day, an hour, twenty minutes, according to Sergeant Janda. But really all stemming from a moment, a decision. It had all come from this, like the expansive radiation that explodes from a single split atom. But perhaps the fallout was over, perhaps now life stirred among the wreckage. An opportunity, an indication that things moved forward, that the watchers could be favorable. The eyes could reward as well as punish.

He almost said no. Just like that, an instantaneous reaction—his instincts, he knew, were flawed, but this felt right to him in that moment. He liked the way he was watched now. The new life that Mr. Grautz held out to him entailed scrutiny on a different level. He could handle the details, he could give his faith over to a new handbook; the yearning for this had not gone away. But the recalibration of the watchers scared him. The standards would be different now. He would be judged on his decisions, on his instincts, on his humanity, on his righteousness. Perhaps he exaggerated it to himself, but this is what had happened the last time. They had not faulted him for his failure to keep an accurate inventory or to schedule the appropriate shift workers. They had judged him as a moral being, and he had been found wanting. It could happen again, perhaps, but only if he allowed them to watch him in a different capacity.

Practical considerations, in the end, might have won out. They were difficult to ignore. A salary, benefits. His mother would no longer worry so much (he refused, after so many months, to sugar-coat the experience for her anymore). He could increase the payments to Rachel and sever that cord sooner than expected. There were other advantages, a thousand of them. Managers didn't have to wear the paper hats. Managers didn't have to punch the time clock.

But it was more than that, in the end, that led him to accept the offer, and this made him proud, a feeling that he savored on the way home. He had not been proud of himself in a very long time. He had accepted the position, in the end, in spite of the fear that nagged at him, and that he knew would nag at him for as long as he worked at the Chik'n Shak. There would never be a shift when he did not fear the chaos of life. He would order his world minutely, and his tri-monthly reports would glow with as much luster as the ones at O'Ruddy's had. He knew how to do this job, and it would feel good to be so competent at something that seemed significant again. But he accepted the job knowing that there were things he would not control, that would not be acknowledged by the Chik'n Shak handbook (he had thumbed through it a couple of times and judged it to be some-what cursory). The chaos might not invade the order of his life as mightily as it had done twelve months ago, but chaos would certainly come, and Casey would not be any more ready for it than he had been the first time. And he took the job anyway. With a thrilling blend of confidence and fear he grasped the ugly Mr. Grautz's hand and told him he would not disappoint him. He might be trampled again, he thought on the way home, and it might be even worse. But it did not matter all that much, he thought, or at least it did not matter as much as the fact that he had not laid down and died.

He drove home differently this time. He stopped at a different exit, went to a different gas station, bought a cranberry juice and a cookie. The old routine would change as soon as he had finished a week of management training in Pittsburgh, and he would start a new one. The sensory associations of the Chik'n Shak routine might be-come as pleasant as the ones at O'Ruddy's had been, and a year would pass, and then another, and at some point in the vast future a Janu-ary 18 would arrive and he would simply be reminded of his failure on that day, instead of overwhelmed by it. And he might say, as he had not yet done, *I am sorry, I am so very, very sorry.*

| lea |

*It was a birthday* of sorts. It had been a year; the new son was one year old. And yet she had already acknowledged the contradiction inherent in his prognosis. He was four years old in a practical sense, and would always be so. It had been a full year since the damaging, a full year since he had become four, and yet he was not five. Nor was he eighteen, as his body insisted. He was still four years old, and on the next January 18 the new son would be two, with the body of a nineteen-year-old, but he would still be four. He would be, as she had previously thought of it, nowhere, yet he was everywhere he would ever be.

The idea of having a celebration, some sort of anti-birthday party, was a sick notion, of course, and she was almost ashamed of herself for thinking of it. Yet it made a kind of sense upon reflection that they should do something in commemoration, or at least something that broke the routine they had fallen into. The therapist had said that routines would be important to Colin, and she had been so thoroughly correct in this prediction that Lea now thought it had been malpractice for the therapist not to warn her how stultifying these routines might be.

The year had brought its joys, however. For one thing, the Chase house now brimmed with affection. The boy loved her for providing his routine comforts, for tucking him in and reading him stories (they were still on Dr. Seuss) and serving him grilled cheese. Their Christmas had been made pleasant simply by the absence of the old Colin, who had always been especially surly on holidays. Geoffrey showed his tenderness almost as adamantly as Colin did; he acted very much as he had in the early days, when Colin was a baby and love had gushed from him in uncontrollable torrents. Now he bought her flowers, gave her long foot massages, e-mailed her poems, planned elaborate vacations in her honor. Lea was showered with love these days, and this too had become routine.

Most nights they ate at the dining room table, having fallen back into formality as a matter of course. Colin did not like noise or crowds, and so they had not visited a restaurant since Thanksgiving (they had never been a family of traditions, and Megan and Shane usually went to Ft. Lauderdale to see his parents). On the afternoon of the anti-birthday, however, as she spoke to Geoffrey on the phone, she suggested that they go out that night. She pushed past his passive objections and realized that, befitting an anti-birthday celebration, she had given herself a gift, in the form of the restaurant she had chosen.

The girl still worked there. When Lea ate out, it was generally during lunch dates with old friends, with the St. Brendan's mothers who had been sufficiently conscientious to pull her back into their circle. Sometimes she left Colin at his therapy sessions so that she could go eat lunch with these people, and she always suggested the China Pagoda, and they rarely demurred.

She'd been six times, maybe seven, in the past ten months, ever since she heard the girl utter the name of the restaurant in the hallways of Breed's Township High. It was remarkable, Lea thought, that the girl still worked there. No sign of college, of a change in lifestyle, though she seemed to have graduated from high school. Sometimes the women were seated in Jenny's section, sometimes they were not. It did not matter so much to Lea. Though she loved to hear the girl's voice and note the breeziness she gave to her words, and to see up close the smile that was as vigorous and natural as a waterfall, it was often enough for Lea just to look at her from far away.

That night Colin would see her again. Lea didn't expect anything; she was well past believing—or fearing—that he would snap out of his handicap. He had remembered Jenny's name when he looked at the picture, and his body had apparently remembered what they used to do together, but that had been a long time ago. It was impossible to see Colin, even in her fantasies, as anything but what he was now.

She supposed she just wanted to see them together. This was the gift she gave herself. And who would it hurt? she wondered, battling a vague sense of guilt as she dried her hair. Geoffrey was helping Colin straighten his sweater in the hallway, and it sounded like it was not going well.

Geoffrey did not know anything about Jenny, of course. It had not surprised Lea that she had been able to keep literally everything she'd learned from her husband. Nothing about Colin ever slipped out; she never broke down and spilled the details of the aborted baby, the notes, the drugs, the investigation. She knew that she never would, and it was pleasing how absolute her conviction was on this matter.

The China Pagoda was quiet, recovering from the flurry of the Sunday luncheon buffet. Lea did not have to steer them into Jenny's section, because Jenny was the only waitress on duty. She wore a high-necked Asian-style blouse, and her hair was held together with neatly arranged chopsticks. Her eye shadow was laid on thickly and her cheeks were rouged; it was as if she were trying to look like one of the dancing women in *The Mikado*. She didn't look Asian, however, not even close, and Lea wondered if it was just a joke, a nod to the strange fact that she was the only Caucasian who had ever worked at the China Pagoda.

Lea closely watched her approach their table. The girl did not check when she saw her old lover. She didn't slow her approach to the table at all, though she quickly looked away from his face, toward Lea, whom she had seen before.

"Hi there," she said with an exaggerated brightness. She recognized Lea from the restaurant, not from the day when Lea had staked her out at the high school.

"Hello again. It's Jenny, isn't it?"

"That's right."

Jenny continued to look alternately at Lea and Geoffrey and not at Colin, and soon it became evident that Lea had made a large mistake. At first the girl seemed composed, but the more she spoke, describing the dinner specials to Geoffrey, who had recited a list of his allergies, the more a shakiness crept into her voice and into her body. Her skin grew pale, and there was sweat on her forehead. Her voice cracked twice. Once she stopped to clear her throat and close her eyes, and she paused for so long that Geoffrey asked her if everything was okay, and then he told her he was a doctor.

"I'm fine. I have the hiccups." She turned from Geoffrey and strode toward the hostess stand.

He raised his eyebrows at Lea and said sardonically, "O-kaaay," then looked back at the menu. Colin stared at the reflected shapes in his water glass. His parents would order for him.

Jenny returned much faster than Lea had expected. She walked back to the table using the same measured stride she had left it with. "I'm sorry about that." She looked at the center of the table and began biting her thumbnail. "I don't really have the hiccups. I know your son. I knew him, I guess. Colin and I were friends, but I guess he doesn't recognize me."

"Is that right?" said Geoffrey. "You were friends with Colin?"

She nodded vigorously, still biting her thumb.

"Do you go to St. Theresa's?"

"I went to Township. I just kind of knew him from . . . We had some friends in common, that sort of thing."

In the past year, Lea had not yet run into anyone who had admitted knowing Colin. She had taken him to the mall, to the main street, to the diner by the highway, and she was certain she had passed kids who had known him, probably those who had been his friends. Some of the teenagers they had passed had looked away conspicuously, or tried to stare with peripheral vision, or begun whispering. But none of them had introduced themselves or checked to see whether Colin remembered them. Lea felt bitter toward these adolescents, although she also knew that if a boy they passed had identified himself as a friend of the old Colin's, she would have been suspicious of his character.

This was also Geoffrey's first experience with one of the boy's old friends, and he was simply, eagerly glad. He did not, however, know what to say. He only seemed to know that it made him happy that the girl admitted to her knowledge, and it was clear that he didn't want her to be made uncomfortable by Colin's presence.

"You're right, Jenny," Geoffrey said. "He probably doesn't remember, but he's still a good guy. You can still talk to him."

She fidgeted, and flashed a pained smile at both the father and the son. "Hi, Colin," she said. "It's good to see you again."

Colin continued looking at his water glass as he spoke. "Yep. Hi there. Hello there." He started coughing, and when he finished he said again, in a much quieter voice, "Hi there."

Lea sat still through all of this, chilled and guilt-racked. She should not have done this. Jenny continued to squint out a smile in Colin's direction, and Lea saw the full burden of the weight she had put on the girl. She honestly didn't know what she'd been thinking, only that she had wanted to see them together. As if that would make anything okay, as if that would do anything but destroy this girl, remind her what she had lost. She wondered if what the girl was feeling now was what Lea had felt that day in March when she'd thrown herself on the bathroom floor and vomited into the toilet, literally sick with grief. Lea could not believe she had done this, and her brain whirred to think of an excuse to get them out of there.

But it was too late. Jenny had crossed her arms tightly across her chest, and the smile had gone, and now her face looked numb and depleted. The mascara had already begun to smear, and she closed her eyes and then erupted into a fit of weeping that thundered through her body, from her legs to her middle, through her quivering shoulders and her contorted face. She kept her arms tight against her chest, as if she could physically hold the terrible sound of her crying inside. Her head drooped, and Geoffrey stood, holding his napkin to her with one hand and lightly touching her back with the other. "Jenny," he said. "Please don't be sad for him."

Lea couldn't watch. She turned to Colin, who was suddenly interested in this girl. He had stood up when his father had, but Lea got him back into his seat and told him everything was okay. She told him that they were going home and they needed to get his coat on, and for some reason this produced another spurt of noise from the debilitated waitress.

Geoffrey held out a chair for Jenny, and she sank into it. Lea and Colin busied themselves with his coat, his gloves, his scarf and hat. Geoffrey continued to pat the girl's shoulder, and handed her another napkin. He leaned down and whispered something to her. All of this calmed her somewhat, so that she no longer cried so loudly, but her face was still crimson and sodden, and she breathed as if she'd just done sprints.

Geoffrey leaned across the table toward Lea. "Darling, why don't you two go on out to the car? I want to make sure she's not hyperventilating." He sifted through his pockets and handed her the keys. "Go ahead and start it up, I'll be out in a second." He gave her a grin of sad fortitude. *It's something that we just have to deal with now*, his expression conveyed. *People just have a hard time seeing him this way.*

She would feel bad for him later, for his obliviousness. It wasn't his fault, it was hers. She wished that she too could write off Jenny as a hysterical old girlfriend who was simply shocked to see Colin in his new form. Geoffrey would never know how much more there was to it. He would never know what this girl had been to Colin, or what he had been to her. She envied him his ignorance, because learning about Jenny, learning about Colin's capacity for love, had been the most difficult discovery.

She put her arm around Colin and guided him away from the table. He looked back as he walked, nothing more or less than confused. Lea turned back just once and saw Jenny from behind, her head still drooping and her shoulders still shuddering. She wished she could comfort her, but it was out of the question now, here, in front of her husband. Lea wanted her to understand that the loss was reconcilable. She wanted to tell her the awful and damnable and irrefutable truth: *It's good that it happened, Jenny. Colin is better this way.*